畫個圓

學得快・記得牢・用得好

關鍵英單
EASY K

Boost Your Vocabulary with One Circle

近義字速記同心圓，關鍵英單一次KO！

KO ① 英文記憶拓展圓
Try it!

KO ② 動詞的N種學習方法
Got it!

KO ③ 黃金練習題
Give it a shot!

KO ④ 字辭聯想記憶
Level up!

使用說明

用對動詞，讓你從英文loser翻身英文Master！

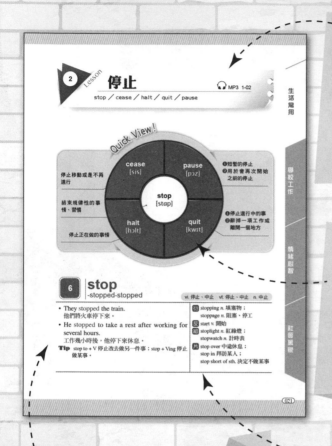

方法1 語音即時聽

專業外師錄製MP3，跟著英語人士學道地的單字發音，用聽的方式加深學習印象，掃描右頁下方QR code讓你隨時隨地都能學英文！

方法2 速記同心圓

以必備字義為核心做成同心圓圖表，網羅高同義單字並加以說明，讓你瞬間明辨每個單字的精確意思，作文造句都能信手拈來不混淆！

方法4 句子構造Tip

書中例句也是值得挖掘的寶庫，除了讓你了解單字運用外，亦增設獨家Tip把句型中涉及的特殊用法或構造拉出解說，全力提升英文實力！

方法3 進階大補帖

除了收錄動詞的三態變化、衍生字、同反義字、近型字、組合字、以及片語等基礎的單字元素外，搭配中英例句更能強化你的單字力！

USER'S GUIDE

方法5 聯想學習Plus

提供趣味聯想、諧音聯想、同義集合、相關延伸、情境串聯等記憶方式，讓你不小心記住更多單字！

方法6 小試身手UP

特別設計單元演練，學習後馬上檢驗，刻劃學習成效，讓你甩開金魚腦7秒記憶力，打造全新金頭腦！

語音線上聽QR code

手機掃描下方二維碼，即刻進入本書網頁，點擊要播放的曲目編號，也能將音檔打包下載至個人電腦裝置上，線上播放隨播隨聽，沒有網路的人，也能線下收聽，省去帶光碟片的麻煩！

https://goo.gl/bMoZ19

方法7 隨手練習本

撇開傳統的選擇題作答模式，採用填寫式作答，擺脫僥倖猜題的心態，讓你動手寫答案，手腦並用記住單字正確拼法！

拋開多頭馬車學習方式，
群組式記憶法讓你舉一能反十！

　　有很多同學背單字的習慣是遇到一個字背一個字，一段時間沒用，如臨新對手一般又從頭背起，如此往復循環下來，仍無法掙脫背不熟、記不牢、學不快的死胡同。同學往往就知道死背，而無法將單字的意義、用法、同義反義字、詞類變化等串連起來，導致雖然背了大量單字，但其實每個字都是各自獨立，缺乏一套系統將之結合，費時費力所記下的單字最終記得七七八八、零零落落。

　　坊間教人學單字的書層出不窮，每一本都有一套記單字的法寶，也是每位作者嘔心瀝血的經驗結晶，吸引無數為英文苦惱的迷途羔羊們為之瘋狂，每當有創新的記憶新法時，往往都能掀起一股學習熱潮，有利用諧音幫助記憶的、有利用音韻解構單字的、有利用圖像進行連結的、也有利用字首字根字尾簡化單字複雜度的，各有道理，各有值得令人激賞的優點。然而，這種令人眼花撩亂的記單字方式也是一種雙面刃，病急亂投醫的人可能會囫圇吞棗，看到什麼學什麼，不去深究哪種方法才是最適合自己的，反而造成多頭馬車並行，成效仍一無所獲的境地。

　　筆者常年觀察英文成績好的同學，發現他們背單字時，大多不是依照A到Z的順序逐個背誦，而是按照特定的邏輯將單字歸納整理後再記下來。當單字彼此產生關聯時，我們的大腦就可以啟動推理、聯想的

功能喚起相關記憶連結，如此不但比逐個強記來得更快，也更不容易忘記，達到長期記憶的效果！

為了讓更多學子更有效率的收穫單字，筆者特別幫同學整理出一套完整的自學與複習方式。本書中將重要常考的單字分成四大主題，共131組同字義的字群LESSON，以此為主架構，進一步延伸出詞性變化、同反義字、衍生字、組合字詞、慣用語與片語、動詞三態變化，時不時提點常見用法，還有特製獨門法寶，用趣味聯想的方式串聯字群單字，搭配每單元末尾的隨堂演練，讓讀者可以馬上檢測自己的學習成效！

一次就要背一群，把相關的字通通記起來，如看到success（成功）這個字，就能立刻聯想到還有win（成功、勝利）、triumph（勝利）、conquer（征服）、lose（失敗）等單字，這就是字群的效應，舉一反三信手拈來！

書中收錄的單字涵蓋了學測、指考、英檢中級、中高級到公職的考試範圍，單字、片語、中英例句、句型，面面俱備，因此不論面臨升學考試的同學，或是需要準備英文檢定的社會人士，皆可按照本書歸納的系統，以期在短時間內大幅提升字彙量，有效達成目標！背單字最忌埋頭苦背，唯有巧妙運用正確方法，才能避免背過即忘的窘境，瞬間累積高手級實力！

目錄

【使用說明】

【前　　言】拋開多頭馬車學習方式，群組式記憶法讓你舉一
能反十！

PART 1 生活常用 Daily Life

CONTENTS

目錄

CONTENTS

PART 2　學校工作 School & Work

目錄

CONTENTS

PART 3 情緒心智 Emotions & Mind

目錄

CONTENTS

目錄

PART 4 社會萬象 Social Phenomenon

CONTENTS

目錄

PART 1

生活常用
Daily Life

衍 衍生字　　同 同義字　　反 反義字　　近 近型字　　組 組合字　　片 片語

發現

🎧 MP3 1-01

find / discover / search / unearth / seek

Quick View !

find
[faɪnd]

discover
[dɪsˋkʌvɚ]
❶指在別人之前發現
❷時常透過某些工具協助

seek
[sik]
❶試圖去尋找
❷多數是尋找抽象的事物

有價值的發現、強調找到的結果

透過（地下）挖掘而發現

search
[sɝtʃ]
為了尋找而仔細的搜索檢查

unearth
[ʌnˋɝθ]

---

find
-found-found

vi. 發現　vt. 找到、發現　n. 發現

- Did you find out what time the movie starts?
  你知道電影幾點開始嗎？
- Scientists are trying to find out a remedy for AIDS.
  科學家正設法找治療愛滋病的藥。

Tip find 的過去式 found 也是另一動詞，為「建立、建設」之意。

衍 findable *adj.* 可發現的；
finder *n.* 相機取景器；
finding *n.* 發現的結果
組 found and lost *n.* 失物招領處
片 find out 找出、查明；
find oneself 找到自己的特質

discover
-discovered-discovered

vt. 發現、發覺

- He discovered oil on his property.
  他在他的土地上發現了石油。
- It was a surprise to discover the scandal about the movie star's past.
  發現那個電影明星的過往醜聞是個意外。

衍 discovery n. 發現的事物；
discoverer n . 發現者；
discoverable adj. 洩漏的

同 detect vt. 發現、察覺

組 Discovery Day 又稱 Columbus Day，是美國紀念哥倫布發現新大陸的紀念日

---

search
-searched-searched

vi. 搜尋 vt. 搜查 n. 搜查

- I searched everywhere in my room for the missing earring.
  我為了找不見的耳環搜遍了房間各處。
- Foreign workers move from one city to another in search of jobs.
  外籍工人為了尋找工作從一個城市移動到另一個城市。

衍 searchable adj. 透過搜查能找到的；searching adj. 透徹的

組 search and rescue 搜救；
search engine 搜尋引擎；
search warrant 搜索令；
search for 搜尋

---

unearth
-unearthed-unearthed

vt. 挖掘、發現

- The archaeologist helped unearth an ancient city.
  考古學家幫助挖掘一座古城。
- The police spent five years unearthing organized crime.
  警方耗費五年揭發一樁有組織性的犯罪。

衍 unearthed adj. 考古出土的；
unearthly adj. 超自然的；
unearthliness n. 神祕、異常

同 excavate v. 挖掘；
uncover v. 揭開覆蓋物

生活常用

學校工作

情緒心智

社會萬象

5 | **seek**
-sought-sought

vi. 尋找　vt. 尋找

• The dog was seeking the bone that he had left in the yard. 這隻狗正在找留在院子裡的骨頭。 • Five people who had sought refuge in the English Embassy returned to their country safely. 五位曾向英國大使館尋求庇護的人安全地返國了。	衍 seeker *n.* 尋找者 同 hunt for *v.* 尋找 片 seek out 尋找事物、人； 　seek one's fortune 尋找發達的機會； 　far to seek 差得遠

聯想學習Plus

• unearth 是指挖掘土地進而發現事物，過程中首先會碰到 rock（大石塊）或是 stone（小石頭）。
• find 是發現，過去式為 found，因此最先創立的人叫 founder（創立者），co-founder 則是指共同發起人，當組成 company（公司）後，就會需要 member（成員）加入來 run the business（經營公司）。

小試身手UP

(　) 1. The police are _____ the thief who stole the paintings from the museum.
　　(A) discovering in　(B) finding on　(C) unearthing　(D) searching
(　) 2. In order to complete a thorough investigation of the crime, the police required a _____ warrant.
　　(A) search　(B) seek　(C) find　(D) finding

Ans　1. (D)　警方正在搜索偷走博物館油畫的竊賊。
　　　2. (A)　為了對這起犯罪進行徹底的調查，警方需要搜索令。

Lesson 2 停止

🎧 MP3 1-02

stop / cease / halt / quit / pause

Quick View !

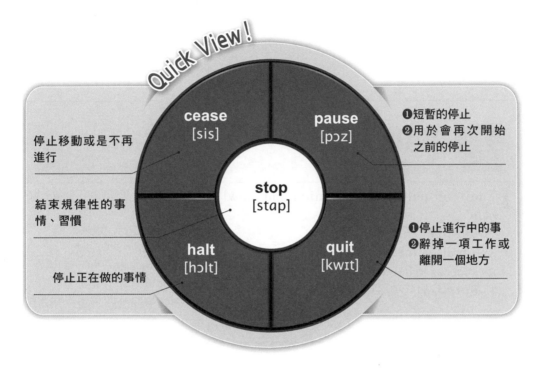

cease [sis]

停止移動或是不再進行

結束規律性的事情、習慣

停止正在做的事情

halt [hɔlt]

stop [stɑp]

pause [pɔz]

❶短暫的停止
❷用於會再次開始之前的停止

quit [kwɪt]

❶停止進行中的事
❷辭掉一項工作或離開一個地方

---

6 | **stop**
-stopped-stopped

vi. 停止、中止　vt. 停止、中止　n. 中止

- They stopped the train.
  他們將火車停下來。
- He stopped to take a rest after working for several hours.
  工作幾小時後,他停下來休息。

Tip stop to + V 停止改去做另一件事;stop + Ving 停止做某事。

衍 stopping n. 填塞物;
　stoppage n. 阻塞、停工
反 start v. 開始
組 stoplight n. 紅綠燈;
　stopwatch n. 計時錶
片 stop over 中途休息;
　stop in 拜訪某人;
　stop short of sth. 決定不做某事

7 | cease
-ceased-ceased

vi. 停止、終止　vt. 停止、結束　n. 停息

- The enemy ceased fire and surrendered.
  敵人停火投降了。
- The two countries decided to cease fire after fighting for many years.
  經年打仗後，兩國決定停火。

衍 ceaseless *adj.* 不停的；
ceaselessly *adv.* 持續地
反 continue *v.* 繼續、持續
組 cease fire 停火；Wonders never cease! 奇蹟總是會發生！（挖苦之意）；without cease 不停的

8 | halt
-halted-halted

vi. 停止、終止　vt. 使停止行進　n. 中止

- The train pulled in the station and slowly halted.
  火車進站後，慢慢停下。
- She praised the new government because of its success to halt economic decline.
  她讚揚新政府成功遏止經濟下滑。

衍 halter *n.*（馬等的）籠頭、韁繩；halting *adj.* 蹣跚的
反 march *v.* 進行、進展；
go *v.* 開始、開動
組 halter-neck（女用）三角背心
片 come to a halt 停止；
call a halt to sth. 要求某事停止

9 | quit
-quit/quitted-quit/quitted

vi. 停止　vt. 停止　adj. 了結的

- The doctor suggested that I quit drinking and smoking.
  醫生建議我戒酒戒煙。
- Sarah determined to quit her job at that moment.
  莎拉那時決心要辭職。

Tip quit + Ving 放棄、戒除……

衍 quittance *n.* 免除、收據；
quitter *n.* 輕易放棄工作的人；
quits *adj.* 互不相欠的
反 stay *v.* 停留、留下
組 quitclaim 放棄權利
片 be quit of 擺脫、脫離

10 **pause**
-paused-paused

vi. 中斷、暫停、停頓　n. 斷句

- The plan is very rough. Please pause and ponder.
  這個計畫很粗糙，請先暫停好好思考一下。
- Don't invest too much in the stock market. Why not pause and consider?
  不要在股市上投資太多。何不停下來仔細考慮呢？

衍 pauseless *adj.* 未停下來的
同 suspend *v.* 暫停、中止
組 pause and ponder 停下仔細考慮
片 give sb. pause 讓某人謹慎思考；pause upon 停下來想一下

聯想學習Plus

- cease 是指停止之意，過世的人已經停止呼吸，所以死者成為 deceased。
- 請（Please）借我一些錢，讓我生活好過些（easy），否則我就會餓死了（deceased）。

小試身手UP

( ) 1. He decided to _____ his job when the boss yelled at him.
　　(A) stop　(B) quit　(C) cease　(D) pause
( ) 2. She _____ her high-paying position because there were too many business trips involved.
　　(A) stop　(B) quit　(C) cease　(D) pause
( ) 3. He _____ the bottle with a cork.
　　(A) stopped　(B) quit　(C) ceased　(D) paused

1. (B)　當他的老闆對他大吼時，他便決定要辭職。
2. (B)　她辭掉高薪的工作，因為太常需要出公差了。
3. (A)　他用塞子塞住瓶子。

3 Lesson 要求

MP3 1-03

ask / claim / demand / need / request / require

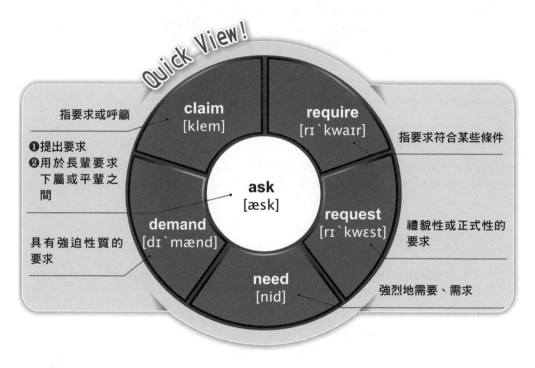

Quick View!

claim [klem]

require [rɪ`kwaɪr]

ask [æsk]

request [rɪ`kwɛst]

demand [dɪ`mænd]

need [nid]

指要求或呼籲

❶提出要求
❷用於長輩要求下屬或平輩之間

具有強迫性質的要求

指要求符合某些條件

禮貌性或正式性的要求

強烈地需要、需求

11 ask
-asked-asked

vt. 請求准許、要求　vi. 要求、請求

- The teacher asked him to close the window.
老師要求他將窗戶關上。
- He asked to see the leader of this campaign club.
他要求與這個競選社團的領袖見面。

衍 asking n. 詢問；
asker n. 請求者；
askew adv. 歪斜地
組 asking price 要價
片 ask for it 活該；
ask for 要求；
be asking for trouble 自找麻煩；
ask of 要求

12 claim
-claimed-claimed
vt. 要求、認領、索取　vi. 提出要求　n. 宣稱

- The children claimed a lot of her attention.
  這些孩子需要她很多的關注。
- Some people claimed that they had been kidnapped by aliens.
  有些人聲稱曾被外星人綁架。

 claimable *adj.* 可要求的；
claimant *n.* 主張者、要求者；
claimer *n.* 申請者、索賠者；
reclaim *v.* 要求收回

反 deny *v.* 拒絕要求

組 claim a life 奪命

片 lay claim to 宣稱某人的權利；
sb.'s claim to fame 成名的理由

---

13 demand
-demanded-demanded
vt. 要求、請求

- I demand that you sit down and listen to me.
  我要求你坐下聽我說。
- The kidnappers are demanding 3,000,000 dollars as ransom, or they will hurt the hostage cruelly.
  綁匪要求三百萬的贖金，否則就要殘忍地傷害人質。

衍 demandable *adj.* 可要求的；
demanding *adj.* 高要求的

組 demand note 即期票據；
demand deposit 銀行活期存款；demand-pull 因需求增加導致價格上升

片 in great demand 受到眾人的喜愛；on demand 按照自己的需要

---

14 need
-needed-needed
vt. 需要　vi. 需要、必需　n. 需要　aux. 需要

- You need to stay in bed until your fever is gone.
  你必須待在床上直到燒退了。
- You need to get an A level on the professional test to get the certificate.
  你必須在專業測驗中得到 A 級才能取到證書。

 needful *adj.* 需要的、必需的；
neediness *n.* 貧窮；
needy *adj.* 貧窮的；
needless *adj.* 不需要的

片 A friend in need is a friend indeed. 患難見真情。
need sth. yesterday 現在就要；
in need 有需要

15 | request
-requested-requested

vt. 要求、請求　n. 要求

- We requested a bigger table at the restaurant.
  我們要求餐廳給我們大一點的桌子。
- The valet service is available at the customer's request.
  隨侍人員服務可應客戶要求而提供。

同 beg for 請求
反 grant v. 給予、授予
組 request stop（公車等的）招呼站
片 at sb.'s request 受到某人的請求；request sb. to do sth. 請求某人做某事；request sth. from sb. 要求某人提供某事

16 | require
-required-required

vt. 要求、命令

- The hotel requires that its guests check out before noon.
  飯店要求房客在中午前退房。
- This position requires a person who is fluent in French.
  這個職位需要會講流利法文的人。

衍 requirement n. 需要、必需品；required adj. 必須的
反 refuse v. 拒絕、拒受
片 require sth. from sb. 要求某人做某事；require sth. of sb. 期待某人完成某事

小試身手UP

(　) 1. Human beings _____ water to live.
　　　(A) asked　(B) demanded　(C) need　(D) requested
(　) 2. His mother _____ him to close the window.
　　　(A) asked　(B) demanded　(C) need　(D) requested
(　) 3. "I _____ the report yesterday," yelled the boss.
　　　(A) needed　(B) demanded　(C) demand　(D) need

1. (C)　人類需要水以維生。
2. (A)　他的母親要他關上窗戶。
3. (D)　老闆吼道：「我現在就要看到報告。」

Lesson 4 關閉

🎧 MP3 1-04

close / shut / slam / turn off

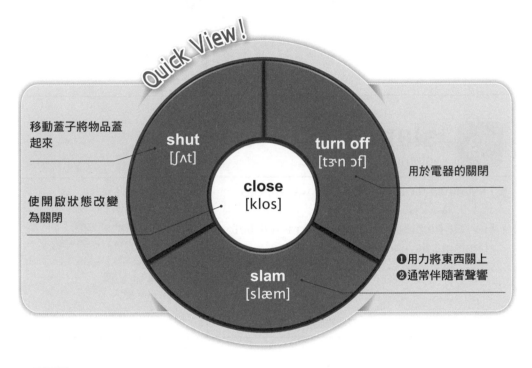

Quick View!

移動蓋子將物品蓋起來

shut
[ʃʌt]

turn off
[tɝn ɔf]

用於電器的關閉

close
[klos]

使開啟狀態改變為關閉

❶用力將東西關上
❷通常伴隨著聲響

slam
[slæm]

---

 close
-closed-closed

vi. 關閉、蓋上   vt. 關閉、闔上   n. 收盤價

- Close the door.
  把門關上。
- The police closed the street.
  警方將街道封起來。
- Please ensure that the windows are all closed before you go to bed.
  在你睡覺前,請確定窗戶全都關上了。

衍 closed *adj.* 關閉的;
closely *adv.* 謹慎地

組 close call 千鈞一髮;
close-mouthed 沉默寡言的;
close-minded 保守的

片 close in 包圍;
close off 隔離;
close with 接近

18 | shut
-shut-shut

- Please shut the window.
  請把窗戶關上。
- Misha shut the book and looked up at me.
  蜜莎將書闔上後抬頭看著我。
- Shut your mouth!
  閉上你的嘴！

衍 shutter *n.* 關閉物、百葉窗
組 shutterbug 業餘攝影迷；
shut-in 不能外出的、閉塞的
片 shut down 停工；
shut up 使某人閉嘴；
shut out 擋住、隔在外面；
shut off 關閉、隔絕、切斷

19 | slam
-slammed-slammed

- I slammed the door because I was furious.
  我太生氣了因此用力甩門。
- He felt humiliated and embarrassed before slamming the phone down.
  他感到羞辱和尷尬，於是砰一聲地掛斷電話。

衍 slammer *n.* 監獄
同 bang *v.* 發出砰的一聲
組 grand slam 滿貫全壘打、大滿貫；slam-bang 氣勢兇猛地、砰然
片 slam down 猛擊；
slam into 撞入；
slam dunk 灌籃

20 | turn off
-turned off-turned off

- Please turn off the radio when you leave the house.
  離開房子時記得關掉收音機。
- It struck me that I didn't turn off the heater when I left home.
  我突然想到我出門的時候忘記關暖氣機了。

反 turn on 打開
組 turnoff 旁道、側路
片 turn down 轉小聲、拒絕；
turn sb. off 讓人失去興趣

 聯想學習Plus

- close 是指關上的，disclose 則是指揭露，enclose 則是指裝入的意思。
- 如果你常常用力甩門（slam），有一天門被甩壞了，就會被父母罵（blame），到時你可得自己難過懊悔（lament）一陣子了。
- 將店內收拾好準備打烊（shut up shop），現在只想上樓回房間睡一覺（shut-eye），卻忘記狗兒被關在門外（shut out）了。

小試身手UP↑

( ) 1. The door is wide open. Why not _____ it?
     (A) slam   (B) close   (C) turn off   (D) shut

( ) 2. The _____ of the window awoke the sleeping baby.
     (A) slam   (B) close   (C) turn off   (D) shut

( ) 3. My mom reminded me to _____ the gas before leaving the dormitory.
     (A) slam   (B) close   (C) turn off   (D) shut

1. (B) 門大開著，為什麼不把它關上呢？
2. (A) 窗戶砰地一聲將睡著的嬰兒吵醒了。
3. (C) 我媽提醒我離開宿舍之前要關掉瓦斯。

選擇

choose / pick / screen / select

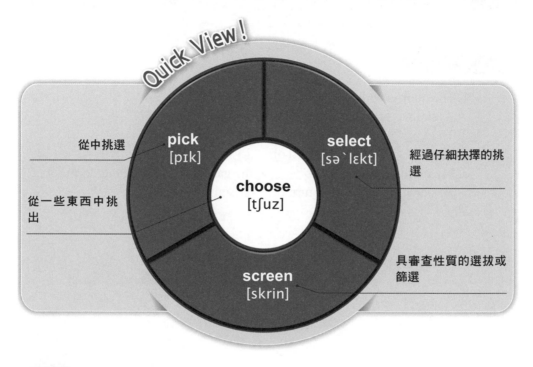

Quick View!

從中挑選 — **pick** [pɪk]

從一些東西中挑出 — **choose** [tʃuz]

select [sə`lɛkt] — 經過仔細抉擇的挑選

具審查性質的選拔或篩選

screen [skrin]

21 | choose
-chose-chosen

vi. 選擇、挑選　vt. 選擇、挑選

- Paul chose three books from the library.
  保羅從圖書館挑了三本書。
- She got the matriculations of the two colleges to choose from.
  她得到這兩間大學的入學許可，以供選擇。

衍 choosy *adj.* 難以取悅的；
chooser *n.* 選舉人

反 reject *v.* 去除、丟棄

片 choose sides 選邊站；
choose from 從中挑選；
pick and choose 仔細挑選；
cannot choose but 只得

22 | **pick**
-picked-picked

vi. 採摘　vt. 挑選、選擇　n. 選擇權

- From the five flavors of ice cream, I picked chocolate.
  這五種冰淇淋口味，我挑了巧克力。
- Don't pick at me. I'm not your employee.
  不要挑我的毛病。我不是你的員工。

Tip pick up steam 表示逐漸受到重視或注目，也可用 gather、gain、get 來替換 pick up。

衍 pickings n. 不義之財；
　 picky adj. 吹毛求疵、挑嘴的
組 ice pick 冰鑽、冰鋤；
　 pick up the bill 付錢；
　 pickpocket 扒手
片 pick up steam 漸入佳境；
　 pick sth. over 仔細觀察

---

23 | **screen**
-screened-screened

vi. 上螢幕　vt. 甄別、審查、選拔　n. 紗窗

- Will you screen my phone calls?
  你會過濾我的電話嗎？
- They will screen out some participants at the primary election.
  他們會在初選時篩選掉一些參賽者。

衍 screening n. 篩過、審查
組 screen saver 螢幕保護；
　 screenager 電視迷；
　 screen actor 演員；
　 big screen 大螢幕（電影）；
　 AIDS screen 愛滋篩檢
片 screen from 以……隔開

---

24 | **select**
-selected-selected

vi. 挑選　vt. 挑選、選拔　n. 被選出的人或物

- The teacher selected me to read the poem to the class.
  老師挑我給班上讀詩。
- There are over 40 exquisite designs to select from.
  這裡有四十多種精美的設計圖案可以選擇。

衍 selectee n. 入伍者；selection n. 被挑選出的人（或物）、精選品；selective adj. 有選擇性的；selectivity n. 選擇性
片 select A from B
　 從 B 中挑出 A

聯想學習Plus

- 比別人更快選擇（choose）一隻好的鵝（goose），不要選輸了（lose）。
- 不要對他人吹毛求疵（nit-pick），特別是要求對方來接（pick up）你下班的時候。

小試身手UP↑

（　）1. Rex ＿＿＿＿ to leave when being asked something private.
　　　(A) chose　(B) picked　(C) screened　(D) selected

（　）2. The book is a ＿＿＿＿ collection of proses from various authors.
　　　(A) choose　(B) picked　(C) screen　(D) select

（　）3. Professors always ＿＿＿＿ her to do complicated jobs.
　　　(A) choose from　(B) pick on　(C) screen　(D) have been selected

1. (A) 當雷克斯被問及隱私的時候，他選擇離開。
2. (D) 這本書是多位作者的散文精選集。
3. (B) 教授們總是找她做複雜的工作。(A) choose from 指從某範圍中挑出，基本上要多數或大量的範圍內，與題意不合；(C)篩選的對象亦要多數或大量，題旨只有「她」，不符用法；(D)「教授們」不是被挑選的對象。

6 Lesson

看見

🎧 MP3 1-06

see / look / observe / behold / view / watch / witness

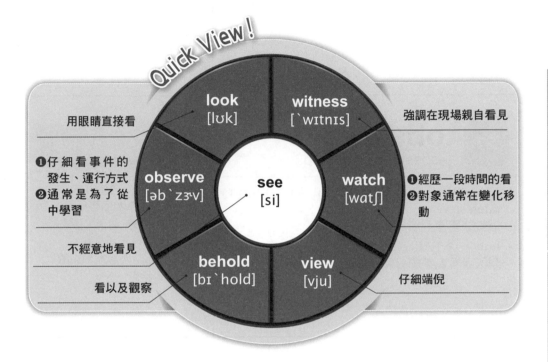

Quick View !

用眼睛直接看 —— **look** [lʊk]

witness [ˋwɪtnɪs] —— 強調在現場親自看見

❶仔細看事件的發生、運行方式 ❷通常是為了從中學習 —— **observe** [əbˋzɝv]

see [si]

watch [watʃ] —— ❶經歷一段時間的看 ❷對象通常在變化移動

不經意地看見 / 看以及觀察 —— **behold** [bɪˋhold]

view [vju] —— 仔細端倪

---

25 **see** -saw-seen

vi. 看、觀看　vt. 看見、看到　n. 主教的轄區

- Let's go and see the animals at the zoo!
  我們去動物園看動物吧！
- I suggest that you go to see the doctor right now.
  我建議你馬上去看醫生。

衍 seeing *adj.* 有視覺的

組 Holy See 教廷；
look-see 快速的觀看或檢查；
see eye to eye 看法一致；
see the light 領悟

片 see through 看穿；
see to 照料、照顧

26 | look
-looked-looked

vi. 看　vt. 調查、查明　n. 外表

- I feel happy when I look at my puppy.
  當我看著我的愛犬時，我就感到快樂。
- He looks like his father.
  他長得像他的父親。

衍 lookalike n.（尤指與名人）相像者

片 look for 尋找；
  look out 注意；
  look into 深入調查；
  look after 照顧；
  look over 仔細檢查；
  look like 看起來像……

27 | observe
-observed-observed

vi. 注意、觀察　vt. 看到、注意到

- The cat observed the bird with hungry interest.
  這隻貓相當熱切地注意著那隻鳥。
- I observed Alice meeting a stranger yesterday.
  昨天我看到愛麗絲和一個陌生人見面。

衍 observation n. 觀察；
  observable adj. 看得見的；
  observance n. 禮儀、儀式；
  observatory n. 天文台；
  observant adj. 觀察敏銳的

反 miss v. 錯過

28 | behold
-beheld-beheld

vt. 看、看見　int. 看呀（語助詞）

- We beheld the beautiful sunset.
  我們看著美麗的落日。
- The red sunset at the mountain peak was a sight to behold.
  山頂的日落紅霞是值得一看的景色。

衍 beholden adj. 蒙恩的；
  beholder n. 旁觀者

組 Lo and behold! 你瞧！（表示驚訝的感嘆詞）；marvel to behold 值得一瞧

29 **view**
-viewed-viewed

vt. 觀看、查看、察看　n. 視力、視野

- We viewed the film on the animals of Australia.
  我們看了這部介紹澳洲動物的影片。
- With a view to making more money, Becky decided to open a second store.
  為了賺更多的錢，蓓琪決定要開第二家店。

衍 viewable *adj.* 值得一看的；
viewless *adj.* 無景色的、無意見的

組 viewpoint *n.* 觀點、見解；
take a dim view of 持悲觀看法；
bird's eye view 鳥瞰、俯視

片 come into view 進入視野、出現；in view of 因為、鑒於

---

30 **watch**
-watched-watched

vi. 注視、觀看　vt. 觀看、注視、留神觀察　n. 錶

- He watched the bug crawl across the table.
  他盯著看一隻小蟲爬過桌子。
- The boy is asked to shorten the time spent in watching TV.
  男孩被要求減少看電視的時間。

衍 watchable *adj.* 悅目的；
watcher *n.* 看守人；
watchful *adj.* 警惕的；
watchman *n.* 巡夜者

反 ignore *v.* 忽視

組 night watch 守夜；
watch fire 營火；
watch list 觀察名單

---

31 **witness**
-witnessed-witnessed

vi. 作證、證明　vt. 目擊　n. 目擊者

- He witnessed the accident happen.
  他目睹了車禍的發生。
- The judge extracted some information from the witnesses of the car accident.
  法官從車禍目擊者的身上提取資訊。

衍 witnessable *adj.* 可目睹的

組 witness box 證人席；
witness stand 法庭中的證人席

片 witness against 作證指控；
bear witness to sth. 見證

 聯想學習Plus

- witness 原意是「證人」，擔任證人有時也要有 wit（智慧）。witness 這個字是從 wit 而來，在古英語中指「知識」（knowledge）的意思。
- 建築師繪製藍圖不外乎用 worm's eye view（透視法、仰視法）或是 bird's eye view（鳥瞰法）。

小試身手UP

( ) 1. _____ at the beautiful sunset!
   (A) Look   (B) See   (C) Watch   (D) Witness
( ) 2. She _____ the murder.
   (A) looked   (B) saw   (C) watched   (D) witnessed
( ) 3. I _____ the people walking down the street.
   (A) look   (B) seesaw   (C) watch   (D) witness

Ans
1. (A) 看那美麗的黃昏！
2. (D) 她目睹了凶殺案。
3. (C) 我看著人們在街上行走。

分辨

🎧 MP3 1-07

distinguish / discern / identify / label / recognize / spot / tag

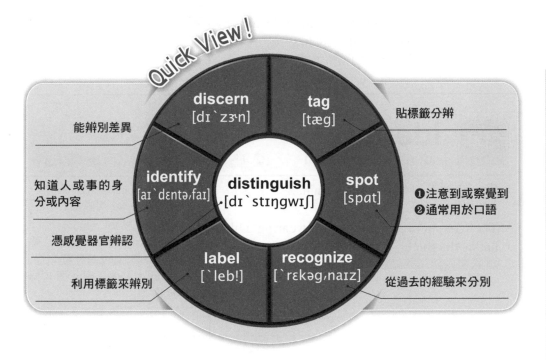

Quick View !

discern [dɪ`zɝn]
能辨別差異

tag [tæg]
貼標籤分辨

identify [aɪ`dɛntə,faɪ]
知道人或事的身分或內容

distinguish [dɪ`stɪŋgwɪʃ]

spot [spat]
❶注意到或察覺到
❷通常用於口語

憑感覺器官辨認

label [`leb!]
利用標籤來辨別

recognize [`rɛkəg,naɪz]
從過去的經驗來分別

---

32 | ## distinguish
-distinguished-distinguished

vt. 辨認出　vi. 區別、識別

- People who are colorblind cannot distinguish red from green.
  有色盲的人無法分辨紅色跟綠色。
- Their uniforms distinguish sophomores, juniors and seniors from one another.
  從他們制服可以分辨二年級、三年級和四年級生。

Tip distinguish A from B 辨別 A 與 B

衍 distinguishable adj. 可辨別的；
　distinguished adj. 卓越的；
　distinguishing adj. 有區別的；
　distinguishability n. 可區別性
同 designate v. 標出、表明

discern
-discerned-discerned

vi. 辨明、分清　vt. 分辨、察覺到

- He discerned some sympathizers in the hostile crowd.
  他在一群敵對的群眾中看到了幾位持同情立場的人。
- At dark night, I even had trouble discerning between the roads and the ditches.
  在黑夜我甚至不能辨別道路和水溝。

衍 discernible *adj.* 可識別的；
discerning *adj.* 眼光敏銳的；
discernment *n.* 識別
近 concern *v.* 關於、使關心
片 discern between 辨別……不同

identify
-identified-identified

vt. 確認、識別、鑑定、驗明　vi. 一致、感同身受

- She identified him as the criminal.
  她認出了他就是犯人。
- The woman identified the man wearing a blue hat as the thief.
  這個女人認為戴著藍色帽子的那個人是小偷。

衍 identification *n.* 認出、識別；
identifiable *adj.* 可識別的；
identity *n.* 身分
組 identity crisis 對自我的無法確定；identity card 身分證
片 identify A with B 視 A 與 B 為同一件事；
identify as 認為是……

label
-labeled/labelled-labeled/labelled

vt. 貼標籤於　n. 貼紙

- She labels each rock in her collection.
  她將收藏的每一顆石頭貼上標籤加以區別。
- All the commodities in the shop are labelled with simplified instructions.
  店內所有商品皆標有簡化的使用說明。

衍 labelmate *n.* 同屬一唱片公司的藝人
同 tag *v.* 給……加標籤、把……稱作
片 label A as B 稱 A 為 B

36 recognize
-recognized-recognized

vi. 承認、確認　vt. 認出、識別、認識

- I can easily recognize you in a group of people.
  在一大群人中我很容易就能認出你來。
- I can still recognize him even though I haven't seen him for years.
  即使好幾年沒見面，我仍然能認得出他來。

衍 recognizable adj. 可辨認的；
recognizance n. 保證金；
recognition n. 認出、承認
同 place v. 看清、想起（多用於否定或疑問句中）
片 recognize sb. as 認出某人的身分為……

37 spot
-spotted-spotted

vt. 認出、發現　vi. 探明　n. 斑點

- He spotted his sister in the crowd.
  他在人群中看到他的妹妹。
- My teacher spotted several counting mistakes in the papers.
  我的老師在報告中發現一些計算錯誤。

衍 spotless adj. 無斑點的；
spotted adj. 有斑點的；
spotty adj. 多斑點的
組 beauty spot 名勝景點；
blind spot 盲點；
hot spot 危險區域；
spot check 進行抽查
片 hit the spot 完全正確

38 tag
-tagged-tagged

vt. 給……加標籤　vi. 尾隨　n. 吊牌

- She tagged him as an egotist.
  她將他歸類為自大的人。
- According to the price tag, this costs $120 USD.
  根據價格標籤，這個價格一百二十美元。

衍 tagger n. 加標籤者
組 dog tag 狗牌、身分識別證；
name tag 胸牌；
tag sale 清倉拍賣；
price tag 價格標籤
片 tag out（棒球）刺殺出局；
tag along 尾隨跟著；
tag question【語】附加問句

生活常用

學校工作

情緒心智

社會萬象

- 養狗時除了會用到 tag（狗牌）外，還需要碗（bowl）、刷子（brush）與狗鍊（leash）。
- 警方辨識屍體身分要用 identify；如果是從一群人中認出一個人就用 recognize；若要區別兩個不同的東西，則用 distinguish from。
- 當她在舞台上的聚光燈（spotlight）下摔倒時，觀眾席（auditorium）傳來的笑聲猶如在傷口撒鹽（touch a sore spot），使她的演藝生涯頓時陷入難處（be in a tight spot / corner）。

小試身手UP

（ ）1. She _____ him as her former neighbor.（複選）
　　(A) discerned　(B) labeled　(C) recognized　(D) spotted

（ ）2. The _____ of the dead person is still unknown. No one recognizes him.
　　(A) identify　(B) identified　(C) identifying　(D) identity

1. (A)(C)　她認出了他是以前的鄰居。
2. (D)　死者的身分依舊成謎，沒有人認得他。

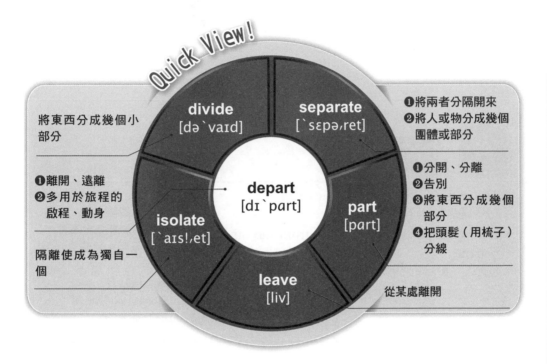

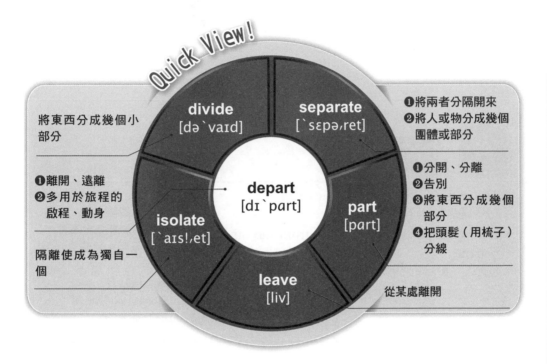

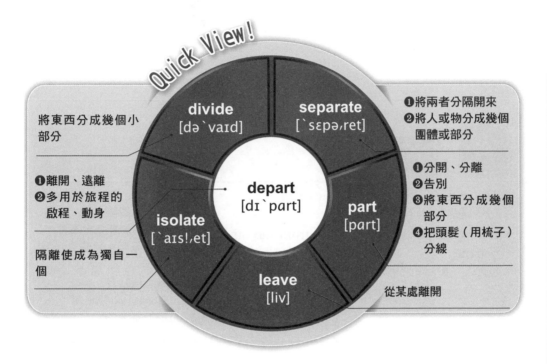

8 Lesson 分開

🎧 MP3 1-08

depart / divide / isolate / leave / part / separate

Quick View!

divide [də`vaɪd]
將東西分成幾個小部分

separate [`sɛpəˌret]
❶將兩者分隔開來
❷將人或物分成幾個團體或部分

depart [dɪ`part]

isolate [`aɪslˌet]
❶離開、遠離
❷多用於旅程的啟程、動身
隔離使成為獨自一個

part [part]
❶分開、分離
❷告別
❸將東西分成幾個部分
❹把頭髮（用梳子）分線

leave [liv]
從某處離開

---

39 depart
-departed-departed

vi. 起程、出發、離開、離去

- The bus departs every five minutes.
  公車每五分鐘發一班車。
- My grandma departed from her life when I was twenty.
  我的外婆在我二十歲時過世了。

Tip depart from this / one's life 過世、亡故

衍 departed *adj.* 過去的；
department *n.* 部門；
departure *n.* 離開

組 departure lobby *n.* 出境大廳；
departure ceremony *n.* 告別儀式；departure lounge 候機室；
departures board 班次顯示牌

片 depart for 去到某處；
depart from 從某處離開、背離

生活常用

學校工作

情緒心智

社會萬象

40 divide
-divided-divided

vi. 分開　vt. 使分開、使隔開、除以　n. 分水嶺

- Let's divide the pie among all of us.
我們自己把派分著吃吧。
- Eight divided by two equals four.
八除二等於四。

衍 dividing *adj.* 區分的；
divided *adj.* 分裂的；
divider *n.* 分配者、圓規
反 unite 使團結
組 dividing line 分界線；
digital divide 數位落差；
divide sth. fifty-fifty 五五分帳

---

41 isolate
-isolated-isolated

vi. 孤立、隔離、脫離　vt. 使孤立、使脫離

- The mother isolated the angry child.
母親讓生氣的小孩獨自一個人。
- He was immediately isolated from the other patients.
他被立刻與其他病人隔離。

衍 isolated *adj.* （被）隔離的；
isolation *n.* 脫離；
isolationist *n.* 孤立主義者
同 separate 分開、脫離、分手、分散
反 combine 使結合
組 isolation period 隔離期
片 isolate from 隔離

---

42 leave
-left-left

vi. 離去、動身　vt. 離開（某處）　n. 休假

- I'll take a French leave at the party.
舞會時我會偷偷溜走。
- Allen will leave for Chicago tomorrow.
艾倫明天將動身前往芝加哥。

衍 leaved *adj.* 有……葉的；
leaven *n.* 逐漸影響、酵母
同 quit 離開、退出
組 sick leave 病假；
shore leave 船員上岸假期
片 absent without leave 未假缺勤；
leave sb. alone 不要干擾某人；
leave behind 留下；
leave for 動身前往

43 part
-parted-parted

vi. 斷裂　**vt.** 使分開　**n.** 一部分　**adv.** 部分地　**adj.** 部分的

- I parted the dog and the cat because they were fighting.
  我把在打架的貓跟狗分開。
- A part of the movie is rather boring.
  這部電影有一部分很無聊。

衍 partial *adj.* 部分的；
parting *n.* 告別；
parted *adj.* 分開來的
反 unite 使團結
組 for the most part 通常；
part-time 兼職的
片 take part in 參加；
do one's part 盡本分；
be part of the furniture 融為一體

44 separate
-separated-separated

vi. 分開　**vt.** 使分離、使分散　**adj.** 不同的

- The teacher separated the two children who were talking in class.
  老師將兩位在上課時講話的同學分開來。
- The two villages are separated by a river.
  這兩個村莊被一條河隔開。

衍 separated *adj.* 分居的；
separates *n.* 單件衣著；
separation *n.* 分開；
separately *adv.* 個別地；
separator *n.* 區分者；
separatism *n.* 分離主義
反 mix 相混合、相溶合

小試身手UP↑

(　) 1. _____ this cake into eight pieces.
　　　 (A) Divide　(B) Separated　(C) Isolate　(D) Isolated
(　) 2. Their plane _____ Los Angeles at noon.
　　　 (A) departed　(B) left　(C) quit　(D) leaving

1. (A) 將這個蛋糕分成八等分。
2. (B) 他們的飛機中午已經離開洛杉磯。(A) depart 為不及物動詞，只能用 depart from 表示離開某地方。

生活常用

學校工作

情緒心智

社會萬象

移動

carry / migrate / move / remove

Quick View!

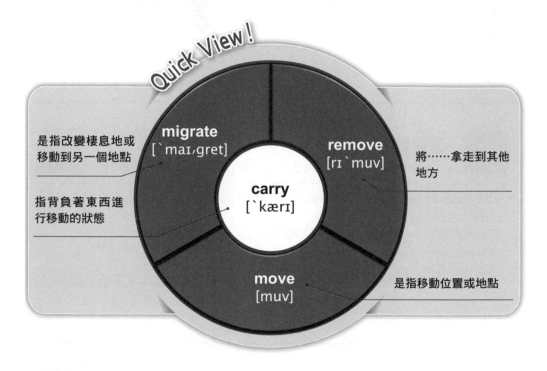

migrate
[`maɪˏgret]

是指改變棲息地或移動到另一個地點

指背負著東西進行移動的狀態

carry
[`kærɪ]

remove
[rɪ`muv]

將……拿走到其他地方

move
[muv]

是指移動位置或地點

---

45 carry
-carried-carried

vi. 被攜帶、被搬運　vt. 運送、運載、搬運　n. 射程

- She carried my suitcase up the stairs.
  她提著我的皮箱上樓。
- If you don't carry on, you'll fail.
  如果你不能堅持，你就會失敗。

衍 carrying *adj.* 運送的
同 take *v.* 帶去、帶領
反 drop 丟下、扔下、降低
組 carrying charge　利　息；carry coals to Newcastle 多此一舉
片 carry away 拿走；
carry on 繼續、進行；
carry out 完成、實行；
carry weight 有影響力

46 | **migrate**
-migrated-migrated

vi. 遷移、移居

- Their grandparents migrated from Ohio to Florida.
  他們的祖父母從俄亥俄州搬到佛羅里達州。
- Many Asian people used to migrate to the USA to chase their American dreams.
  以往有許多亞洲人移民美國去追尋美國夢。

衍 migrant *adj./n.* 移居、（尤指移出國境）的移民；
migration *n.* 遷移
同 move 移動、離開、前進
反 immigrate *v.* 遷入、遷移
組 migratory bird 候鳥
片 migrate from A to B 從 A 遷徙到 B；migrate between A and B 在 A 與 B 之間移動

47 | **move**
-moved-moved

vi. 移動、離開、前進　*vt.* 使移動、搬動、開動　*n.* 遷徙

- Let's move to better seats up front.
  讓我們移到前面好一點的位置。
- The Browns bought a new house and decided to move in the next week.
  布朗家買了新房子，打算下週搬進去。

衍 movable *adj.* 可動的、可移動的；
moveless *adj.* 不動的；
movement *n.* 運動、活動；
mover *n.* 行動者、鼓動者
組 move heaven and earth 竭盡全力
片 move to 搬到；
move over 挪用；
move on 繼續前進

48 | **remove**
-removed-removed

vi. 遷移、搬家　*vt.* 移動、搬開、調動　*n.* 距離

- He removed all the posters from the wall.
  他將牆上的海報全都撕下來。
- The mayor was removed from office because of the scandal.
  市長因為醜聞下台了。

衍 removed *adj.* 遠離的；
removal *n.* 移動、搬遷；
removable *adj.* 可移動的
反 replace 把……放回（原處）
組 remove the scales from sb.'s eyes 使某人看清真相
片 remove sb. from sth. 將某人從某處撤職、帶離

- 動物對人類的用途，除了可以 carrying（背負重物）外，也能為耕種（farming）、騎乘（riding）出力，甚至作為食物。
- 因為她被解職了（was removed from office），所以她們全家決定搬到（move to）新加坡去。

小試身手UP

( ) 1. We _____ all the old paint.
    (A) removed (B) move (C) migrated (D) carried

( ) 2. I can't see the screen. Let's _____ to the front row.
    (A) move (B) migrate (C) remove (D) carry

( ) 3. He is addicted to surfing the Net. That's why he always _____ his iPad with him all the time.
    (A) moves (B) migrates (C) removes (D) carries

1. (A) 我們將舊油漆全部去除。
2. (A) 我看不到螢幕。我們移到前排去。
3. (D) 他沉迷於上網。這也是為什麼他總是隨身攜帶他的平板電腦。

Lesson 10 集合

🎧 MP3 1-10

assemble / collect / compile / flock / gather / group

Quick View!

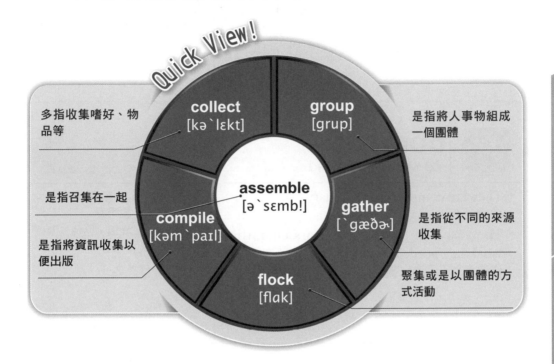

- collect [kə`lɛkt] — 多指收集嗜好、物品等
- group [grup] — 是指將人事物組成一個團體
- assemble [ə`sɛmbḷ]
- gather [`gæðɚ] — 是指從不同的來源收集
- compile [kəm`paɪl] — 是指將資訊收集以便出版
- flock [flɑk] — 聚集或是以團體的方式活動
- 是指召集在一起
- 聚集或是以團體的方式活動

---

49 | assemble
-assembled-assembled

vi. 集合、聚集、集會　vt. 集合、召集、聚集

- Mr. Perez assembled the staff for a meeting.
  皮瑞茲先生召集員工開會。
- Every bicycle is carefully assembled and inspected.
  每輛自行車都經過仔細地裝配和檢查。

衍 assembler *n.* 裝配工、裝配器；
assembly *n.* 集會、集合

同 collect 聚集、堆積

反 dismiss 解散、遣散

組 assembly line 裝配線；
assembly hall 議場；
assemblyman 議員

collect
-collected-collected

vi. 聚集、堆積　vt. 收集、使集合　adj. 受話人付費

- I collected the papers that had fallen on the floor.
  我將掉落到地上的文件撿起來收好。
- You can make a collect call if you don't have enough change.
  如果你沒有足夠的零錢，你可以打對方付費的電話。

衍 collectable *adj.* 可收集的；
collective *adj.* 共同的；
collection *n.* 收藏品

組 collect on delivery 貨到付款；
recollect 回憶；make a collect call 打由對方付費的電話

片 collect (money) for sth. 為……
募款

compile
-compiled-compiled

vt. 收集（資料等）

- They are compiling a dictionary.
  他們正在編纂一本字典。
- The research team spent years compiling what they needed for the project.
  研究團隊花了數年時間收集計畫所需的資料。

衍 compilation *n.* 編輯（物）；
compiler *n.* 編輯者

同 accumulate 堆積、累積、聚積

片 compile A from B
由 B 編寫成 A

flock
-flocked-flocked

vi. 聚集、成群地去（或來）　n. 羊群

- People flocked to the new museum on the opening day.
  新博物館開幕當天湧入大批人群。
- A flock of people are taking a walk in the city park.
  一群人正在城市花園中散步。

衍 flocky *adj.* 毛茸茸的

同 group *v.* 聚集

組 flock bed 毛絨床褥；
flock paper 毛絨壁紙

片 Birds of a feather flock together.
物以類聚。
a flock of 一群（指人、羊或鳥類）

53 | gather
-gathered-gathered

vi. 積聚、集合　vt. 收集、使聚集　n. 收穫量

- The reporter gathered information for her report.
  這位記者為了報導去收集資訊。
- I gather that someone must have stolen my money.
  我猜一定有人偷了我的錢。

衍 gathering *n.* 集會、聚集；
gatherer *n.* 採集者
同 assemble *v.* 集合、召集、聚集
反 scatter *v.* 使分散
片 gather dust 棄之未用；gather your wits 讓自己冷靜下來；gather that 猜想、判斷

54 | group
-grouped-grouped

vi. 聚集　vt. 把……聚集　n. 群、團體

- The teacher grouped the students in a circle.
  老師將學生圍成一個圓集合在一起。
- We can group English learners into three types: beginners, intermediate learners, and advanced learners.
  我們可以把英語學習者分成三種：初學者、中等程度的和進階的學習者。

衍 grouper *n.* 石斑魚；groupie *n.* 追星族；grouping *n.* 群集、編組
組 blood group 血型；ethnic group 種族團體；interest group 利益集團；peer group 同儕群體
片 group A under B 按照 B 分類 A；group into 把……分成

小試身手UP

(　) 1. The mechanic ＿＿＿＿ the car engine.
(A) assembled　(B) assembling　(C) gathers　(D) gathered
(　) 2. My dad is ＿＿＿＿ our new picnic table.
(B) compiling　(B) assembling　(C) compiled　(D) assembled

1. (A)　技工組裝汽車引擎。
2. (B)　我父親正在組裝新野餐桌。

聚積

🎧 MP3 1-11

accumulate / amass / heap / pile

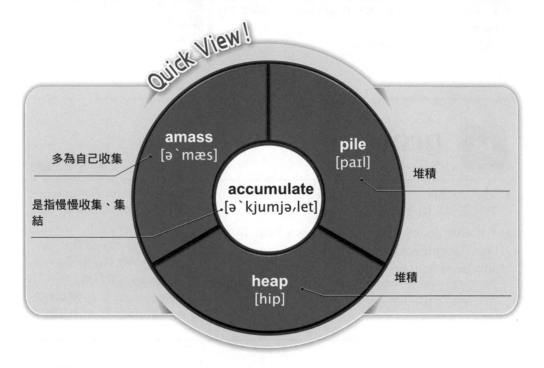

Quick View!

amass [ə`mæs]

多為自己收集

是指慢慢收集、集結

accumulate [ə`kjumjə,let]

pile [paɪl]

堆積

heap [hip]

堆積

---

55 | accumulate
-accumulated-accumulated

vi. 積成堆、聚積　*vt.* 累積、積攢

- The library accumulated many more books this year than last year.
  圖書館今年收來的藏書比去年多更多。
- Thousands of coins have been accumulated during the past few years.
  過去幾年來，累積了數千個硬幣。

衍 accumulation *n.* 積累；
　accumulative *adj.* 堆積的；
　accumulator *n.* 聚財者
反 dissipate *vt./vi.* 使消散；
　waste *vt./vi.* 消耗、使荒廢
組 accumulated value 累積結餘

56 amass
-amassed-amassed

vt. 積聚（財富）、積累

- The owner of the steel mill amassed great wealth.
鋼鐵廠的老闆為自己累積了許多財富。
- Jackson amassed evidence to prove that Johnson was the real burglar.
傑克森收集證據證明強森才是賊。

衍 amassment *n.* 積蓄、聚積；
amassable *adj.* 積蓄的、聚積的
同 collect 聚集、堆積
反 distribute 分發、分配
近 mass *n.* 團、堆、塊、群；
mess *n.* 伙食團、混亂
組 amass evidence 收集證據

57 heap
-heaped-heaped

vi. 積成堆、堆起來　vt. 堆積、積聚　n. 一堆

- He heaped all his books on the desk.
他將所有的書堆在桌上。
- The heap of socks will be sold at a cheaper price.
這堆襪子將以較便宜的價錢出售。

衍 heaped *adj.* 滿滿的
同 pile 堆積、疊、累積
組 heap coals of fire on sb.'s head 以德報怨；scrap heap 垃圾場；
knock all of a heap 使大吃一驚
片 a heap of 大量的；
the bottom of the heap 品質差的；
heap up 堆積

58 pile
-piled-piled

vi. 堆積、累積　vt. 堆積、疊、累積　n. 大量

- He piled up the wood at the corner of the house.
他將木柴堆在房子的角落。
- I saw a pile of money in the bank.
我看到銀行裡有一大堆錢。

衍 piles *n.* 痔瘡；piling *n.* 樁基；
piled *adj.* 有細毛的
近 pillar *n.* 柱子、墩
組 pile on the agony 過分渲染悲痛；atomic pile 原子爐
片 make a pile 賺大錢；
pile up 撞毀、堆積；
a pile of 一堆

- 跟工業有關的動作，除了組裝（assemble）外，還包括製造（manufacture）、處理（process）與召回（recall）。
- 一群（a flock of）鵝（geese）跑到戶外去沒回來，最後就被關在（lock）門外了。

小試身手UP

( ) 1. One of his habits is to _____ wood and make it furniture.
　　(A) accelerate　(B) accumulate　(C) altogether　(D) gathered
( ) 2. Several _____ of books laid on the hallway makes it difficult to pass through.
　　(B) masses　(B) piles　(C) pillows　(D) accumulates

1. (B) 他的嗜好之一是收集木材，做成家具。
2. (B) 玄關堆放好幾疊的書影響了出入。

12 Lesson 散布

🎧 MP3 1-12

allot / disperse / distribute / scatter / spread

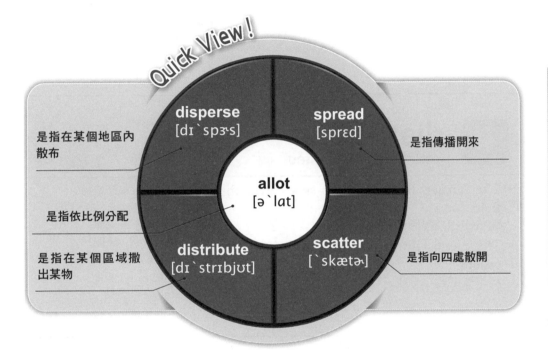

Quick View!

disperse [dɪ`spɝs] — 是指在某個地區內散布

spread [sprɛd] — 是指傳播開來

allot [ə`lɑt]

是指依比例分配

是指在某個區域撒出某物

distribute [dɪ`strɪbjʊt]

scatter [`skætɚ] — 是指向四處散開

---

59 | allot
-allotted-allotted

vt. 分配、分配給

- The government allotted the land to the farmers.
  政府將土地分配給農民。
- Each dancing group was allotted ten minutes to perform.
  每個舞蹈團體都分配到十分鐘的表演時間。

衍 allotment *n.* 分配、分派；
allotted *adj.* 指定的；
allottee *n.* 受到分配的人

同 distribute 散布、分布

近 lot *n.* 多數、全部、一批、一塊地

片 allot to 分配

60 | **disperse**
-dispersed-dispersed

vt. 驅散、解散、疏散　vi. 分散、散開

- My job was to disperse leaflets about the sale.
  我以前的工作是將促銷傳單發出去。
- We should wait till the mist disperses.
  我們應該等到霧消散為止。

衍 disperser *n.* 藥劑師；
　　dispersal *n.* 疏散、散布、傳播；
　　dispersed *adj.* 被驅散的；
　　dispersible *adj.* 可分散的
反 collect 收集；
　　withdraw 收回、取回、提領

61 | **distribute**
-distributed-distributed

vt. 散布、分布

- The farmer distributed the seeds over the field.
  農夫在田裡播撒種子。
- The scientist distributed the animals into three groups.
  科學家把動物分成三類。

衍 distribution *n.* 配給物；
　　distributable *adj.* 可分配的；
　　distributary *n.* 支流
同 spread 散開、流開
反 collect *v.* 收集
片 distribute over 分配；
　　distribute to 分給；
　　distribute into 分成

62 | **scatter**
-scattered-scattered

vi. 消散、散　vt. 撒、撒在上面、散布　n. 消散

- Strong winds scattered the clouds.
  狂風將雲吹散。
- The string was cut down so the pearls scattered over the floor.
  繩子被切斷，所以珍珠散落了一地。

衍 scattered *adj.* 散亂的；
　　scattering *n.* 散落；
　　scattershot *adj.* 廣泛的；
　　scatteration 分散
同 disperse *v.* 驅散、解散
反 collect *v.* 收集
組 scatter rug 小幅地毯

63 spread
-spread-spread

vi. 散開、傳開　vt. 撒、散布、傳播、普及　n. 伸展

- Please spread the news that there will be a meeting tonight.
  請將今晚有會議這個消息傳下去。
- Don't spread false rumors. It's not moral.
  不要散播不實謠言，這樣很不道德。

衍 spreadable *adj.* 可以塗開的；
spreader *n.* 散布者；
spreadeagled *adj.* 四肢張開的
同 disperse 驅散、解散、疏散
組 middle-age spread 中年發福
片 spread out 使（某人）離開其他人或是散開

生活常用

學校工作

情緒心智

社會萬象

聯想學習Plus

- 農夫耕種灑種子，除了撒出去（distribute）外，其餘動作還包括施肥（fertilize）與插秧（plant）。
- 他分配（allot）到很大（a lot of）面積的土地，打算蓋座停車場（parking lot）。

小試身手UP

( ) 1. A gunshot _____ the flock of geese.
　　(A) dispersed　(B) allotted　(C) spread　(D) distributed
( ) 2. The supervisor _____ safety goggles to the workers.
　　(A) distributed　(B) dispersed　(D) spread　(D) scattered
( ) 3. He _____ the map on the table.
　　(A) spread　(B) dispersed　(C) allotted　(D) distributed

Ans
1. (A) 槍聲將鵝群嚇得四散。
2. (A) 主管將護目鏡發給員工。
3. (A) 他將地圖攤開在桌上。

13 Lesson

傳遞

🎧 MP3 1-13

consign / convey / deliver / hand / pass / send / transfer

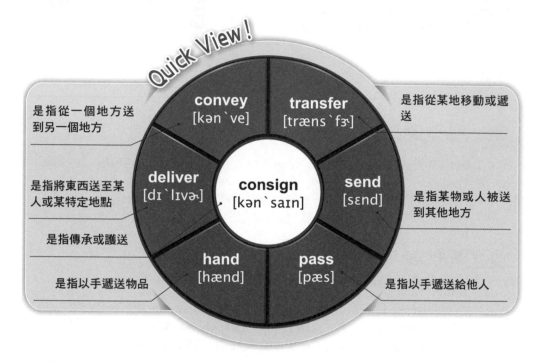

Quick View!

是指從一個地方送到另一個地方
convey [kən`ve]

transfer [træns`fɝ]
是指從某地移動或遞送

deliver [dɪ`lɪvɚ]
是指將東西送至某人或某特定地點

consign [kən`saɪn]

send [sɛnd]
是指某物或人被送到其他地方

是指傳承或護送

hand [hænd]
是指以手遞送物品

pass [pæs]
是指以手遞送給他人

---

64 consign
-consigned-consigned

vt. 發送（商品）、託運、寄存

- He consigned his property to his sister and set off on his adventures.
  他將財產過戶給他妹妹，然後展開他的冒險。

- The bike was consigned to the teacher to see who the real owner was.
  這輛腳踏車已經交給老師了，讓老師查出它真正的主人是誰。

衍 consignable *adj.* 可交付的；consignation *n.*（商品之）委託；consignment *n.* 託賣品、委託貨物；consignor *n.* 委託者、發貨人

同 transfer 搬遷、轉移

片 consign to 交託（寄貨）

65 | **convey**
-conveyed-conveyed

vt. 傳達、傳遞、表達

- Please convey this letter to the principal.
請將這封信交給校長。
- Ted decided to convey his house to his own daughter, Lucy.
泰德決定把他的房子轉讓給女兒露西。

衍 conveyance *n.* 運送、運輸；
conveyancer *n.* 運輸業者
近 convoy *n.* 護航、護送、護衛
組 conveyor belt 傳送帶、傳遞帶
片 convey to 運送至、轉讓至

66 | **deliver**
-delivered-delivered

vt. 投遞、傳送、運送　vi. 投遞、送貨、傳送

- The dairy delivers fresh milk to the supermarket every day.
乳品業者每天將新鮮牛奶送到超市。
- If you send the package by express delivery, it will cost more.
如果你用快遞寄郵包的話，收費會更高。

衍 deliverable *adj.* 可以傳送的；
deliverance *n.* 釋放、解救；
delivery *n.* 投遞、傳送
組 deliver the goods 履行諾言、不負眾望
片 deliver to 傳送；
deliver from 解救

67 | **hand**
-handed-handed

vt. 面交、給、傳遞　n. 手

- Please hand me an apple.
請遞給我一顆蘋果。
- My teacher required that I hand in the paper next Monday.
我的老師要求我下週一交論文。

衍 handed *adj.* 有手的；
handful *n.* 一把、一握；
handily *adv.* 靈巧地、熟練地
組 bite the hand that feeds one 恩將仇報；
green hand 新手
片 hand on 交給、傳遞；
hand out 發送；
hand in hand 手牽手

68 pass
-passed-passed

vt. 傳遞、通過　vi. 傳遞　n. 越過、通行證

- Please pass me a pair of scissors. I need to cut off the rope.
  請給我一把剪刀，我要把繩子剪斷。
- I failed to pass the examination. I should have studied harder.
  我考試不及格，我應該更用功的。

衍 passed *adj.* 已經過去的；
passage *n.* 通行、通過；
passbook *n.* 存摺

組 come to pass 發生、實現；
pass the buck 推卸責任

片 pass by 經過；
pass down 傳遞下去；
pass away 過世

69 send
-sent-sent

vi. 差使、派人、送信　vt. 寄送　n. 波浪的推助力

- When I settle down in Seattle, I will send you a letter.
  等我在西雅圖安頓好後，我會給你捎個信。
- Dave sent his daughter away to a Catholic school in London.
  戴夫把他的女兒送到倫敦的一所天主教學校就讀。

衍 sender *n.* 寄件人

同 dispatch *v.* 派遣、發送、快遞

反 receive *v.* 收到、接到

組 send to Coventry 放逐、疏離；
send sb. on a wild-goose chase 讓某人毫無頭緒的尋找

片 send in 呈交；send for 派人去請；send away 趕走、送走

70 transfer
-transferred-transferred

vt. 搬遷、轉移、調任　n. 遷移、移交

- Hold on a second, and I will help transfer your call to extension 333.
  請稍待片刻，我幫您將電話轉給分機 333。
- Andy wanted to transfer to another school.
  安迪想轉學到另一所學校。

衍 transferable *adj.* 可轉移的；
transferability *n.* 可移動性；
transferee *n.* 受讓人、承買人；
transference *n.* 轉移、傳遞

組 transfer agent 過戶代理人

片 transfer to 將某人調往某處

• 廚師要將雞肝（liver）運送（deliver）到另一家餐廳。

小試身手UP↑

（ ） 1. We _____ our savings from the old bank account to the new one when we decided to move to Australia.
(A) transferred (B) sent (C) consigned (D) handed

（ ） 2. The package needs _____ to the customer by 5 p.m., so you'd better call the express.
(A) transferring (B) sent (C) consigned (D) delivering

1. (A) 我們決定要舉家搬到澳洲後，就將存款從舊銀行戶頭轉到新戶頭。
2. (D) 這份包裹要在下午五點前送到客戶手上，所以你最好叫快遞公司。

問候

🎧 MP3 1-14

greet / hail / salute / welcome

Quick View !

為了吸引注意而呼喊某人

hail
[hel]

用特別的言詞或行為來歡迎某人

greet
[grit]

welcome
[ˋwɛlkəm]

用親切客氣的方式迎接某人的到來

尤指行舉手禮，向某人致敬的正式手勢

salute
[səˋlut]

---

71 | **greet**
-greeted-greeted

vt. 問候、迎接、招呼

- The Porters greeted their guests at the door.
  波特一家在門口迎接客人。
- The audience greeted her singing with a big cheer.
  聽眾們對她的歌聲報以熱烈的歡呼聲。

衍 greeting n. 祝願詞、賀詞、問候語

同 hail 招呼

組 greeting card（生日、節慶假日等場合致親友的）賀卡

片 greet with 以……問候、招呼、對……作出反應

72  hail
-hailed-hailed

vi. 招呼致意　vt. 招呼　n. 歡呼　int. 好啊、歡迎

- The crowd hailed their hero as he passed by in the parade.
  當英雄走過遊行隊伍時，群眾呼喊他為英雄。
- A hail of applause came right after Professor Yang finished his lecture.
  楊教授的演說一結束便響起了一陣掌聲。

同 welcome 歡迎
組 Hail Mary 萬福馬利亞、聖母經；hail-fellow 親熱隨便的；hailing distance 近處；give sb. Hail Columbia 嚴厲責罵某人
片 hail from 來自；
hail a cab 攔計程車；
a hail of applause 一陣掌聲

---

73 salute
-saluted-saluted

vi. 行禮、致敬　vt. 向……行禮　n. 敬禮

- The veterans saluted the flag with the hand.
  退伍軍人向國旗行舉手禮。
- Sally waved at us in salute.
  莎莉對我們揮手打招呼。

衍 salutary adj. 有益的；salutation n. 招呼、致意、行禮、問候；salutatorian n. 代表畢業生致詞之學生；salutatory adj. 歡迎的
同 greet 問候、迎接、招呼
片 take the salute 行答禮、還禮

---

74 welcome
-welcomed-welcomed

vt. 歡迎　n. 歡迎　adj. 受歡迎的　int. 歡迎光臨

- We welcomed them to our home.
  我們歡迎他們到我們家。
- You are welcome to call me at any time.
  歡迎你隨時打電話給我。

Tip welcome to ＋ 地點，是表示「歡迎光臨某地方」之意。

衍 welcoming adj. 歡迎的、款待的
同 hail 招呼、招呼致意
組 welcome mat 門墊；
welcome wagon 迎賓人員
片 I don't want to wear out my welcome. 不想叨擾他人過久。
welcome sb. with open arms 給予他人擁抱歡迎

聯想學習Plus

• 經理將從美國回來（come back），我們已經準備好要歡迎（welcome）他。

小試身手UP↑

(　　) 1. She ＿＿＿＿＿ her guests with a smile and a bow.（複選）
　　　 (A) welcomed　(B) saluted　(C) greeted　(D) hailed
(　　) 2. We ＿＿＿＿＿ the newcomer to our office.
　　　 (A) welcomed　(B) greeted　(C) hailed　(D) saluted

1. (A)(C)(D)　她用微笑鞠躬歡迎來客。
2. (A)　我們歡迎新人到辦公室報到。

Lesson 15 危害

🎧 MP3 1-15

aggress / attack / encroach / endanger / jeopardize

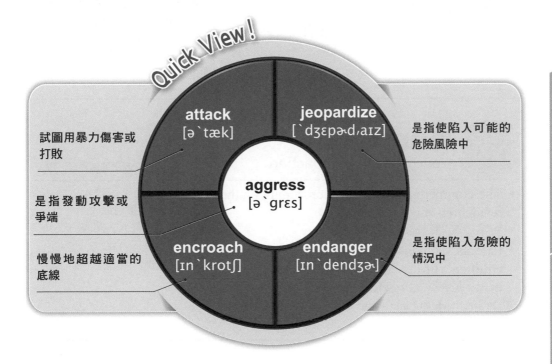

Quick View!

attack
[ə`tæk]
試圖用暴力傷害或打敗

jeopardize
[`dʒɛpəd,aız]
是指使陷入可能的危險風險中

aggress
[ə`grɛs]

是指發動攻擊或爭端

encroach
[ın`krotʃ]
慢慢地超越適當的底線

endanger
[ın`dendʒə]
是指使陷入危險的情況中

---

75 aggress
-aggressed-aggressed

vi. 侵略、挑釁、攻擊

- According to the witness, he was the guy who aggressed upon women with a knife.
  目擊者指證，他就是那個用小刀攻擊女人的傢伙。
- He claimed that he just defended himself, and it was the other guy who aggressed upon him first.
  他宣稱他只是自我防衛，是另一個男子先攻擊他的。

衍 aggressive *adj.* 侵犯的、侵略的、攻擊性的、進取的；aggressor *n.* 侵略者
同 attack *v.* 攻擊
反 defend *v.* 防守

attack
-attacked-attacked

vi. 進攻、襲擊　vt. 進攻、襲擊　n. 攻擊

- The cat attacked the mouse.
  貓捉老鼠。
- Cruel soldiers began their attack on the innocent people.
  士兵殘酷地對無辜百姓進行攻擊。

衍 attacker n. 攻擊者
同 raid v. 突然襲擊
反 defend v. 保護；guard v. 守衛
組 attack ad 攻擊性競爭廣告；
　heart attack 心臟病發作；
　ground attack 地面進攻；
　sneak attack 偷襲
片 under attack 遭受攻擊

---

encroach
-encroached-encroached

vi. 超出通常界限、侵入

- The commercial district is encroaching on the residential zone.
  商業區範圍已經跨越到住宅區了。
- Parents shouldn't encroach too much on their children's life.
  家長不應該太過干涉孩子們的生活。

Tip encroach on / into + sth. 是指「干涉、插手……」的意思。

衍 encroachment n. 侵入
同 trespass v. 擅自進入；
　intrude v. 侵入、闖入

---

endanger
-endangered-endangered

vt. 危及、使遭到危險

- She endangered all of us with her reckless driving.
  她漫不經心的開車讓我們身陷危險。
- A mother would never do anything to endanger her child's life.
  身為母親是不會做任何危及她孩子生命的事。

衍 endangered adj. 快要絕種的
同 jeopardize 使瀕於危險境地
組 endangered species 瀕臨絕種的物種

79 jeopardize
-jeopardized-jeopardized

vt. 使瀕於危險境地、冒……的危險、危及

- This scandal is jeopardizing her position in the company.
  這件醜聞波及她在公司的職位。
- My teacher always tells us that failing in exams would jeopardize our chances to get a well-paid job.
  老師總是跟我們說，考試考不好會影響以後找好工作的機會。

衍 jeopardous *adj.* 冒險的；
  jeopardy *n.* 危險、風險、危難
同 endanger 危及、使遭到危險

聯想學習Plus

- 野生動物會出現的行為，除了攻擊（attack）外，還有保護地盤（defend）、獵食（hunt）與交配（mate）。
- 隨便跟一個陌生人（stranger）聊天，是很危險的（dangerous）。

小試身手UP

（　）1. The rapid consumption of wood _____ the whole planet, people and animals included.
(A) endangers　(B) endures　(C) enforces　(D) emphasizes

（　）2. The army _____ the enemy.
(A) attacked　(B) endangered　(C) encroaching　(D) jeopardized

Ans
1. (A) 快速的消耗木材讓地球、人類與動物都陷入危機中。
2. (A) 軍隊攻擊敵人。

說話

🎧 MP3 1-16

say / speak / talk / tell

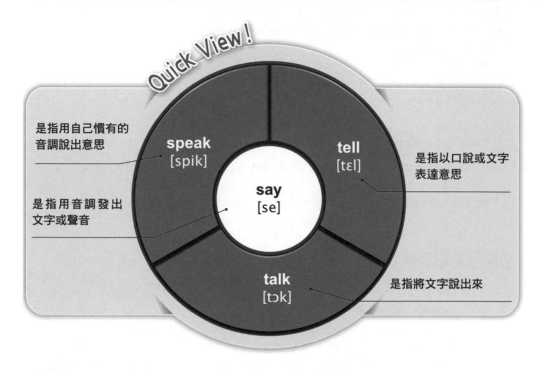

Quick View !

是指用自己慣有的
音調說出意思

speak
[spik]

tell
[tɛl]

是指以口說或文字
表達意思

是指用音調發出
文字或聲音

say
[se]

talk
[tɔk]

是指將文字說出來

---

80 **say**
-said-said

vi. 說、講、發表意見 vt. 說、講、唸 n. 發言權

- Did you say something just now?
  你剛剛有說什麼嗎？
- The manager said that we should set up a branch in Maryland.
  經理說我們應該在馬里蘭州設立一家分公司。

衍 sayable *adj.* 可說的；
saying *n.* 發表言論；
say-so *n.* 隨便說說的話
同 voice *vt.* （用言語）表達、說出
組 say grace 飯前禱告；
you don't say 真的嗎？
片 say for oneself 為自己辯解；
needless to say 不消說；
strange to say 說來奇怪

speak
-spoke-spoken

vt. 說（話）、說出　vi. 說話、講話

- Can you speak a bit louder?
  你可以說大聲點嗎？
- Seize every opportunity to practice speaking English.
  抓住每個能練習說英語的機會。

衍 speaking 談話；speaker 演說家；speakerphone 喇叭擴音器

片 speak one's mind 直接表達；speak for 代表……講話；speak ill of 詆毀；Speak of the devil. 說曹操，曹操就到。speak up 響亮地說；speak well of 稱讚

talk
-talked-talked

vi. 講話、談話、演講　vt. 講、說　n. 談話

- Can the baby talk yet?
  小嬰兒會說話了嗎？
- They are talking about their trip to Dubai.
  他們正在談論去杜拜的旅行。

衍 talkative adj. 健談的；talkatively adv. 愛說話地

組 talk turkey 講話直率；talk dirty 說下流話；small talk 閒聊

片 talk about 談論；talk around 繞圈子說；talk back 頂嘴；talk big 說大話

tell
-told-told

vi. 講述、分辨　vt. 告訴、講述、說

- You can never tell what will happen.
  誰也不知道會發生什麼事。
- Mary told me that she would move to Singapore soon.
  瑪麗告訴我她馬上就要搬去新加坡了。

衍 teller n. 講故事者；telling adj. 有力的

組 fortune-telling 算命；story-telling 說故事的；Blood will tell. 有其父必有其子（貶義）。

片 tell about 告訴；tell apart 辨別；tell by 由……知道；tell from 從……知道；tell of 講述

 聯想學習Plus

- 溝通（communication）的種類，除了說話（talk），還包括廣告（advertise）、接觸（contact）、說服（persuade）與口耳相傳（tell）。

小試身手UP

( )1. I am sorry for what I _____ just now. Would you forgive me?
　　(A) said　(B) spoke　(C) told　(D) talked

( )2. Can you _____ louder? We can hardly hear you.
　　(A) say　(B) speak　(C) talking　(D) talk

( )3. He is an decent man, and he _____ nothing but the truth.
　　(A) says　(B) speaks　(C) talks　(D) tells

1. (A) 我為剛剛說的話感到抱歉。你願意原諒我嗎？
2. (B) 你可以講大聲點嗎？我們聽不見你的話。
3. (D) 他為人正直，只說實話。

17 Lesson 發聲

🎧 MP3 1-17

articulate / pronounce / sound / utter / verbalize / voice

Quick View!

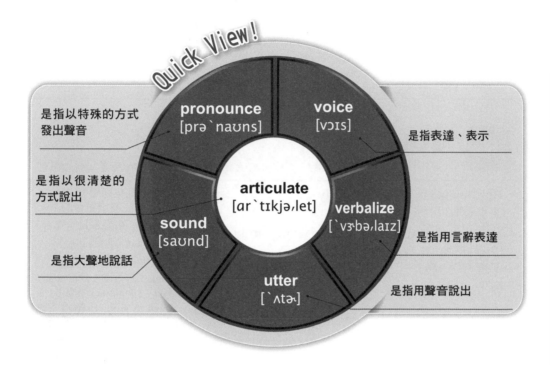

是指以特殊的方式
發出聲音 —— **pronounce** [prə`naʊns]

voice [vɔɪs] —— 是指表達、表示

articulate [ar`tɪkjə‚let]

是指以很清楚的
方式說出 —— **sound** [saʊnd]

verbalize [`vɝbə‚laɪz] —— 是指用言辭表達

是指大聲地說話 —— **utter** [`ʌtɚ]

是指用聲音說出

---

84 articulate
-articulated-articulated

vi. 清晰地發（音）　adj. 口才好的

- She articulated the words with great feeling.
  她很激動地說出這些話。
- Slow down and articulate what you want to express.
  慢慢來，把你要表達的話說清楚。

衍 articulation *n.*（清楚的）發音；
articulable *adj.* 可分音節的；
articulator *n.* 發音清楚的人或物；
articulatory *adj.* 發音清晰的

同 pronounce 發音

反 mumble 含糊地說、咕噥著說

85 pronounce
-pronounced-pronounced

vi. 發音　*vt.* 發……的音、注……的音

- The "h" of "hour" isn't pronounced.
  「hour」的「h」不發音。
- The judge pronounced a sentence of license suspension on the chauffeur.
  法官宣判吊銷駕駛的駕照。

衍 pronounceable *adj.* 可發音的；pronounced *adj.* 讀（或講）出來的；pronouncement *n.* 公告；pronunciation *n.* 讀法

片 pronounce a sentence 宣判；pronounce sb. dead / guilty 宣判某人死亡／有罪

---

86 sound
-sounded-sounded

vt. 使發聲　*vi.* 發聲、響起　*n.* 聲音　*adj.* 健康的

- He sounds his words carefully.
  他小心地說話。
- The bodyguard is alert to everything around himself, such as unnatural sounds.
  保鏢對周圍的一切都很警覺，例如不尋常的聲響。

衍 sounder *n.* 使東西鳴響者；sounding *adj.* 發出聲音的；soundings *n.* 徵集意見；soundless *adj.* 無聲的；soundly *adv.* 堅實地

組 soundman 音效師；soundproof 隔音的；soundtrack 電影配音

片 as sound as a dollar 相當安全可靠；safe and sound 安然無恙

---

87 utter
-uttered-uttered

vt. 發出（聲音等）、說、講、表達　*adj.* 完全的

- The baby uttered its first words.
  寶寶說了第一個字。
- When he heard of her running away, he uttered nothing but a slight sigh.
  當他聽說她逃家時，他只是輕嘆一聲。

衍 utterance *n.* 發聲；utterly *adv.* 十足地；uttermost *adj.* 最高的

同 say 說、講、發表意見

片 not utter a word 不發一語

88 | **verbalize**
-verbalized-verbalized

vi. 以言語表述　*vt.* 以言語表述

- It is important that you verbalize your feelings instead of holding a silent grudge.
  重要的是將感受說出來，別生悶氣。
- I found it hard to verbalize my love towards my wife.
  我覺得難以用言語表達我對我妻子的愛。

衍 verbalization *n.* 以言語表現；
verbalist *n.* 善用詞藻者；
verbalism *n.* 言語表達；
verbality *n.* 言詞表達；
verbally *adv.* 言詞上
verb *n.* 動詞

同 say 說、講、發表意見

89 | **voice**
-voiced-voiced

vt. 表達、說出　*n.* 聲音、嗓子

- Keep your voice down in a public place.
  公眾場合請小聲說話。
- Fat Amy has a wonderful voice. Joining the singing contest is her dream.
  胖艾咪有天籟歌喉。參加歌唱比賽是她的夢想。

衍 voiceless *adj.* 無言的
組 voicemail 語音信箱；
voice box 喉頭；
voice activation 聲控
片 at the top of one's voice 以最大的音量；
lower / raise one's voice 降低／提高音量

小試身手UP

(　) 1. Don't move. I heard some ＿＿＿＿ from that bush. It might be a snake.
　　 (A) sounds　 (B) pronunciation　 (C) verbs　 (D) voices
(　) 2. Professors in universities encourage students to ＿＿＿＿ viewpoints in their minds in class.（複選）
　　 (A) voice　 (B) verbalize　 (C) pronounce　 (D) sound

1. (A) 別動！草叢那邊有聲響，可能是蛇。
2. (A)(B) 大學教授鼓勵學生在課堂上發表自己的觀點。

治療

🎧 MP3 1-18

cure / heal / remedy / treat

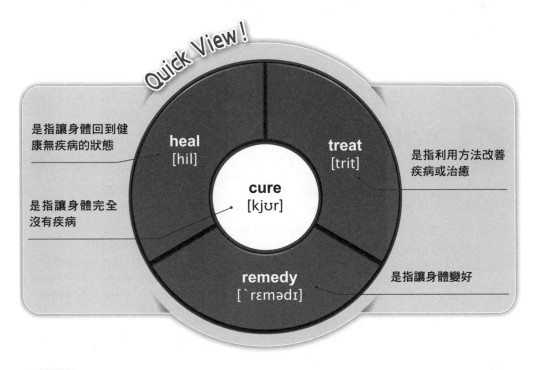

Quick View !

是指讓身體回到健康無疾病的狀態

heal [hil]

treat [trit]

是指利用方法改善疾病或治癒

cure [kjʊr]

是指讓身體完全沒有疾病

remedy [`rɛmədɪ]

是指讓身體變好

---

90 | # cure
-cured-cured

vi. 起治療作用、受治療　vt. 治癒　n. 治療

- Antibiotics cure many people who have been infected.
  抗生素治癒許多受到感染的人。
- The doctor finally cured Tom of the flu.
  醫生最終治好了湯姆的流感。

衍 cureless *adj.* 醫不好的；curer *n.* 醫療者；cureall *n.* 萬靈藥

同 heal 治癒、使恢復健康

組 faith cure 透過信仰治病；water cure 水療法

片 cure of 治癒疾病、擺脫惡習；take the cure 開始治療；kill or cure 生死攸關

91 heal
-healed-healed

vt. 治癒、使恢復健康　vi. (傷口) 癒合、痊癒

- When I got hurt, I was surprised at how quickly my body healed itself.
  當我受傷時，我身體快速自癒令我感到訝異。
- Your words healed my broken heart.
  你的話治癒了我受傷的心。

衍 healer *n.* 醫治者；
healing *adj.* 有治療功用的
反 injure *v.* 使受傷；
wound *v.* 使受傷
組 faith healing 信仰療法；
self-heal 有醫療作用的植物
片 heal of 治療疾病；
heal over 傷口治癒；
heal up 受傷部位治癒

---

92 remedy
-remedied-remedied

vt. 醫治、治療　n. 治療

- This medicine will remedy my cough.
  這種藥會治療我的咳嗽。
- The best remedy for being dumped is hard work.
  治療失戀最好的解藥就是努力工作。

衍 remediless *adj.* 醫不好的；
remediation *n.* 矯正；
remedially *adv.* 補救地
組 Desperate diseases must have desperate remedies. 重病須用猛藥。There is a remedy for everything except death. 凡事都有補救方法。
片 a remedy for... 治療某病的藥

---

93 treat
-treated-treated

vi. 請客　vt. 醫療、治療、看待、處理　n. 請客

- She treated her cold with vitamins.
  她服用維他命來治療感冒。
- The police treated what he said as a joke but finally found out it was true.
  員警把他說的話當成玩笑，但最後發現他說的是真的。

衍 treatable *adj.* 能治療的；
treatment *n.* 治療
同 cure 起治療作用、受治療
組 Dutch treat 各自付帳的聚餐或娛樂活動；illtreat 虐待；retreat 撤退；trick or treat 不給糖就搗蛋
片 treat as 當作；treat to 請客；go down a treat 相當受歡迎

- 要醫治疾病（disease），要先仔細檢查（examination）後，醫生才能確定症狀（syndrome），判斷是要開處方（prescription）、動手術（operation、surgery）或是進行治療（treatment）。
- heal 是治療，讓身體恢復成 health 的狀態。
- 藥有 pill（藥丸、藥片）、tablet（藥錠）、powder（藥粉）或 potion（藥水）的形式。drug、medicine、remedy、cure 都能指藥，drug 泛指藥品；medicine 有內服藥、藥品的意思；remedy 和 cure 都是指解藥，或是解決辦法而言。

小試身手UP

( ) 1. Her wound _____ in about a month.
　　 (A) healed　(B) cure　(C) remedied　(D) treated
( ) 2. My grandmother had a good _____ for an earache.
　　 (A) remedy　(B) healed　(C) cured　(D) treated
( ) 3. She _____ her cold with hot soup, vitamins and enough rest.
　　 (A) cure　(B) remedy　(C) healed　(D) treated

1. (A) 她的傷口差不多一個月內就癒合了。
2. (A) 我的祖母有一帖治耳朵痛的特效藥。
3. (D) 她以喝熱湯、吃維他命與充分的休息治療感冒。

19 Lesson

衰敗

🎧 MP3 1-19

decay / decease / decline / die / rot / spoil

Quick View!

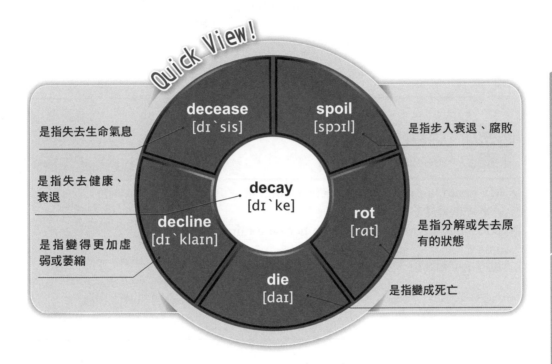

- decease [dɪˋsis] 是指失去生命氣息
- spoil [spɔɪl] 是指步入衰退、腐敗
- decay [dɪˋke]
- rot [rat] 是指分解或失去原有的狀態
- decline [dɪˋklaɪn] 是指失去健康、衰退 / 是指變得更加虛弱或萎縮
- die [daɪ] 是指變成死亡

94 | ## decay
-decayed-decayed

vt. 使腐朽、使腐爛　*vi.* 衰敗、衰退　*n.* 蛀牙

- Her health has decayed over the past years.
  過去這些年來她的健康狀況已經慢慢退化。
- Brushing your teeth often and properly can help you fight tooth decay.
  經常刷牙並配合正確的刷牙方式可以對抗蛀牙。

衍 decayed *adj.* 腐敗的
反 improve *v.* 改善
組 urban decay 城市衰敗；
　radioactive decay 放射性衰變
片 fall into decay 腐敗

decease
-deceased-deceased

vi. 亡故　n. 死亡

- After his wife deceased, he never married again.
  自從他妻子過世後，他就未曾再娶。
- The deceased left nothing to his wife and children.
  死者沒給妻兒留下任何東西。

衍 deceased *adj.* 已故的；
decedent *n.* 已故者
近 cease *v.* 停止、結束；
decrease *v.* 減少
組 the deceased 死者

decline
-declined-declined

vt. 婉拒　vi. 下降、減少、衰退　n. 下降

- My grandpa's status of health is declining.
  我爺爺的健康狀態每況愈下。
- I declined to go shopping with her on a rainy day.
  我婉拒了和她雨天去購物。

衍 declination *n.* 偏角；
declinable *adj.* 格變化的；
declinatory *adj.* 謝絕的
同 fall *v.* 下降
近 incline *v.* 傾斜、傾向
片 go into a decline 失去力量；
on the decline 在消退

die
-died-died

vt. 死於（……狀態）　vi. 死　n. 骰子

- The plant died because he never watered it.
  因為他從未替植物澆水，結果它枯死了。
- The dog was maltreated terribly and died at last.
  狗被殘酷虐待最後被虐死。

衍 dying *adj.* 垂死的、瀕死的
反 live *v.* 活著
近 dye *v.* 染色
片 die away 消退；die down 逐漸減弱；die for 為國捐軀；die of 因（疾病、寒冷等）死亡；die out 滅絕；die from 因（受傷、外力因素等）死亡

98 | rot
-rotted-rotted

vt. 使腐敗　**vi.** 腐爛、破損　**n.** 腐爛　**int.** 胡說、混蛋

- Don't water the plant too much in case its roots rot.
  別給植物澆太多水，以免根爛了。
- The meat has rotted. It gives off a bad smell.
  這塊肉已經爛掉了，散發出惡臭。

衍 rotten *adj.* 腐爛的
同 decay 使腐朽、使腐爛
組 wet rot 軟腐病；
foot rot 根腐病；
dry rot 乾腐病
片 rot away 爛掉；
rot off 因腐爛而脫落；
rot out 破損

99 | spoil
-spoiled/spoilt-spoiled/spoilt

vt. 損壞、溺愛　**vi.**（食物等）變壞、腐敗

- Meat spoils easily in hot weather.
  肉類在炎熱的氣候下容易變壞。
- There are two types of parents. One pushes their kids, and the other spoils the kids.
  父母可分為兩種類型。一種會逼迫小孩，另一種則寵壞了小孩。

衍 spoilable *adj.* 能夠被損壞的；
spoilage *n.* 損壞物；
spoiled *adj.* 被寵壞的
組 spoilsport 專事破壞他人樂趣者；rotten apple spoils the barrel 一顆老鼠屎壞了一鍋粥
片 spoil for a fight 存心尋釁；
be spoiled for choice 無從選起

 小試身手UP

（　）1. The _____ of productivity in this country can be blamed on the laziness of its citizens.
(A) addition　(B) decline　(C) increase　(D) solution
（　）2. Leaves _____ on the forest ground.
(A) died　(B) decay　(C) rot　(D) spoil

 Ans

1. (B)　這個國家生產力下降要歸咎於公民的怠惰。
2. (C)　樹葉落在森林土地上會漸漸腐爛。

保存

MP3 1-20

conserve / hold / keep / preserve / reserve / save / stock

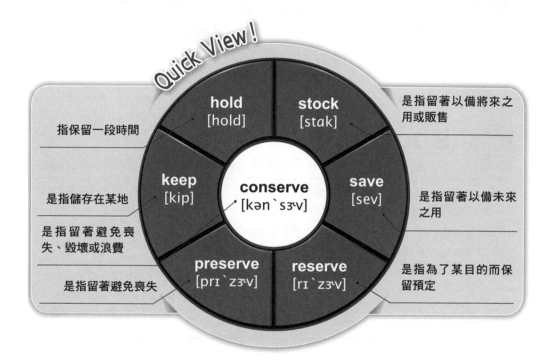

Quick View !

指保留一段時間	**hold** [hold]
	stock [stak]	是指留著以備將來之用或販售
是指儲存在某地	**keep** [kip]	**conserve** [kən`sɜv]	**save** [sev]	是指留著以備未來之用
是指留著避免喪失、毀壞或浪費	**preserve** [prɪ`zɜv]	**reserve** [rɪ`zɜv]	是指為了某目的而保留預定
是指留著避免喪失			

100 conserve

-conserved-conserved

vt. 保存、保護、節省　n. 蜜餞、果醬

- We are conserving our supply of water.
  我們正在儲水備用。
- Vegetables and fruits are usually conserved for winter.
  蔬果常被保存以過冬。

衍 conservatory *adj.* 保存性的；
conservator *n.* 保護者

同 preserve 保存、保藏、防腐

101 hold
-held-held

vt. 擁有、握有、持有　vi. 持續、保持　n. 抓住

- Hold on to the rope and don't let go.
緊緊抓住這條繩子，不要放手。
- Many people hold a belief that God does exist.
許多人相信上帝真的存在。

衍 holding *n.* 把持；holder *n.* 保持者；holdfast *n.* 鉤子、夾鉗

同 keep 保持著某一狀態

組 hold water 合情合理

片 get hold of 捉住、掌握；
hold on to 緊緊抓住；
hold on 堅持、持續；
hold up 搶劫

生活常用

102 keep
-kept-kept

vi. 保持著某一狀態　vt. 存放、保管、保存　n. 生活費

- She is in the habit of keeping a diary.
她有寫日記的習慣。
- Could you keep an eye on my house when I'm on a business trip?
我出差時你可以幫我照看房子嗎？

 keep an eye open on + N 是指「留意、注意、看好」之意。

衍 keeping *n.* 保管、保存、看守；
keeper *n.* 保管人；
keepsake *n.* 紀念品

組 finders keepers【諺】誰找到歸誰

片 keep sb. company 陪伴某人；
keep good time（時鐘）走得準；keep...(away) from 使……遠離；kccp on 繼續

學校工作

103 preserve
-preserved-preserved

vt. 保存、保藏、防腐　n. 蜜餞、果醬

- The court will preserve the right to freedom of speech.
法院將會保留言論自由的權利。
- The refrigerator can preserve the food from rotting for some time.
冰箱可以在一定時間內防止食物腐壞。

衍 preservative *adj.* 保護的、保存的、防腐的；preserver *n.* 保存人；preservation *n.* 保護、維護、維持

近 reserve *v.* 儲存、預約、保留

組 life preserver 救生用具

片 preserve against 對抗；
preserve from 保護

情緒心智

社會萬象

reserve
-reserved-reserved

vt. 預約、預訂 n. 儲備（物）

- Let's call the restaurant and reserve a table.
  我們打電話給餐廳訂位吧。
- Let's make a reservation for a room at the hotel before we start off.
  我們出發前先跟旅館預訂一個房間吧。

Tip make a reservation for + N 是指「預訂、預約」之意。

衍 reservation *n.* 保留；
reserved *adj.* 預訂的；
reservist *n.* 後備役軍人；
reservoir *n.* 蓄水庫、貯水池
同 book *v.* 預訂
片 in reserve 備用的；
without reserve 毫不保留地

save
-saved-saved

vi. 節省、節約 vt. 儲蓄、儲存 n. 救球

- They are saving money for college.
  他們為上大學存錢。
- He was awarded a medal for he saved an old man from the fire.
  他從大火中救出老人，因而被授予一面勳章。

衍 saving *adj.* 節儉的、節省的；
savior *n.* 救星、救世主；
savings *n.* 積蓄
同 store *v.* 儲存；preserve *v.* 保留
反 consume *v.* 消耗、花費、耗盡
組 save it for a rainy day 未雨綢繆；save face 保留尊嚴；save the day 扭轉頹勢
片 save up 儲蓄

stock
-stocked-stocked

vi. 辦貨 vt. 貯存 n. 貯存、股票 adj. 庫存的

- People are crazy for stocking commodities when the price goes up.
  當物價上漲時，民眾就會瘋狂囤積民生用品。
- The stockbroker persuaded me to invest more money in the stock market.
  股票經紀人說服我在股市投資更多錢。

衍 stockpile *n.* 儲備物資；
stocky *adj.* 健壯結實的；
stockish *adj.* 愚鈍的
同 keep 保有、持有
組 capital stock 股本；
a laughing stock 笑柄
片 in stock 庫存；
out of stock 無庫存；
stock up 存放

聯想學習Plus

- 去銀行除了可以存錢（save），也可以貸款（loan）、儲蓄（deposit）、兌換（exchange）與支付（pay）。
- reserve 是指餐廳預訂，serve 則是指服務生來服務（service）。Dinner is served 便是指晚餐上菜了！
- 他存了（save up）很多錢，而且都深藏（keep）在很深（deep）的土裡。

小試身手UP

( ) 1. The government urges that people take quick showers instead of baths to _____ water resources.
(A) conserve　(B) keep　(C) save　(D) hold

( ) 2. That café is quite popular, so we'd better _____ before we go.
(A) conserve　(B) preserve　(C) reserve　(D) serve

( ) 3. Grandma left me quite a few old photos, and I _____ them all.
(A) keep　(B) stock　(C) save　(D) hold

1. (C) 政府呼籲民眾以快速淋浴取代盆浴以節約水資源。
2. (C) 那家咖啡店很有人氣，我們去之前最好先訂位。
3. (A) 奶奶留給我許許多多舊照片，而我全都保留了下來。

吸引

🎧 MP3 1-21

allure / attract / entice / fascinate / infatuate / lure / tempt

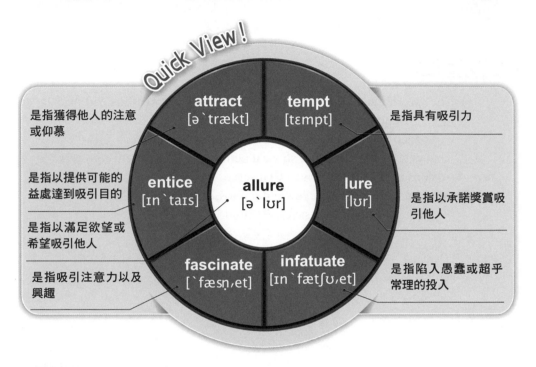

Quick View!

是指獲得他人的注意或仰慕
attract
[ə`trækt]

tempt
[tɛmpt]
是指具有吸引力

是指以提供可能的益處達到吸引目的
entice
[ɪn`taɪs]

allure
[ə`lʊr]

lure
[lʊr]
是指以承諾獎賞吸引他人

是指以滿足欲望或希望吸引他人

是指吸引注意力以及興趣
fascinate
[`fæsṇˌet]

infatuate
[ɪn`fætʃʊˌet]
是指陷入愚蠢或超乎常理的投入

107 allure
-allured-allured

vi. 誘人　vt. 引誘、誘惑、強烈地吸引　n. 誘惑力

- Investors were allured by the prospect of making a quick fortune.
  投資客被快速致富的前景所吸引。
- Some advertisements are used to allure students and their parents.
  一些廣告專門用來吸引學生及其家長。

衍 alluring *adj.* 極吸引人的；
allusion *n.* 暗示；
allurement *n.* 誘惑；
alluringly *adv.* 極吸引人地

同 attract *v.* 吸、吸引；
charm *v.* 使陶醉、吸引

108 | attract
-attracted-attracted

vt. 吸、吸引　vi. 吸引

- The unusual exhibit attracted a large crowd.
  這個另類的展覽吸引很多人前來。
- To attract attention, she cried loudly on the street.
  為了引起注意，她在街上大哭起來。

衍 attractable *adj.* 可被吸引的；
attraction *n.* 吸引力；
attractive *adj.* 有吸引力的
反 distract 分心、分散注意、轉移
組 tourist attraction 觀光勝地
片 be attracted to sb. 吸引某人

---

109 | entice
-enticed-enticed

vt. 誘使、慫恿

- Her hints of a stock split enticed me to invest.
  她暗示會有股票分割，激發我想投資的欲望。
- The thought of being able to go anywhere I want enticed me into buying the bicycle.
  因為能去任何想去的地方這個念頭，誘使我買了這輛腳踏車。

衍 enticement *n.* 引誘物；
enticing *adj.* 迷人的；
enticingly *adv.* 誘人地
同 allure 誘使；seduce 誘惑（使其犯罪或墮落）
片 entice into + Ving / N 教唆從事……

---

110 | fascinate
-fascinated-fascinated

vi. 有吸引力、迷人　vt. 使神魂顛倒、強烈地吸引

- The northern lights fascinate me.
  北極光令我著迷。
- Johnny is still fascinated with cartoons.
  強尼還是很愛看卡通。

衍 fascinating *adj.* 迷人的；
fascination *n.* 魅力；
fascinator *n.* 迷人的東西
同 attract 吸、吸引
片 be fascinated with / by 迷上、愛上

111 infatuate
-infatuated-infatuated

vt. 使沖昏頭、使糊塗

- His love for that idol infatuated him to do many crazy things.
  他對那名偶像的愛令他糊里糊塗做出許多瘋狂舉動。
- Ted is infatuated with the girl now.
  泰德現在對這個女孩很迷戀。

衍 infatuated *adj.* 入迷的；
infatuation *n.* 熱戀、著迷；
infatuatedly *adv.* 著迷地
同 captivate 使著迷、蠱惑
片 be infatuated with 迷戀、癡迷於

112 lure
-lured-lured

vt. 引誘、誘惑、以誘餌吸引　*n.* 誘惑物

- They lured the dog back to the house with a bowl of food.
  他們以一碗食物引誘小狗回到屋內。
- Life in big cities is always a lure for many young men in the country.
  大城市的生活對於鄉下年輕人永遠都充滿誘惑。

同 attract 吸、吸引
反 repel 驅除
片 lure into + Ving 引誘做……

113 tempt
-tempted-tempted

vt. 引誘、誘惑、勾引

- The idea of swimming in the sea tempts me.
  在海裡游泳的念頭令我心動。
- Hunger tempted Andy to steal money.
  飢餓誘使安迪去偷錢。

衍 tempted *adj.* 有興趣的；
temptable *adj.* 可誘惑的；
temptation *n.* 引誘物；
tempter *n.* 引誘者
近 temp *n.* 臨時雇員；temper *n.* 情緒、脾氣；attempt *v.* 試圖
片 tempt into + Ving 引誘做……；
tempt fate 冒險、魯莽

聯想學習Plus

- 釣魚時除了要準備魚鉤（hook）、網子（net）或是釣竿（fishing pole），也要有釣餌（lure）才能吸引（lure）魚上鉤。

小試身手UP

( ) 1. Lights _____ insects.
　　　(A) attract　(B) attempt　(C) enchant　(D) attach
( ) 2. Your offer sounds _____. No one can resist it.（選錯的）
　　　(A) appealing　(B) attractive　(C) tempting　(D) distractive

1. (A) 燈光會吸引昆蟲。
2. (D) 你的提議很吸引人，沒人可以抗拒。

著迷

 MP3 1-22

bewitch / captivate / charm / enchant

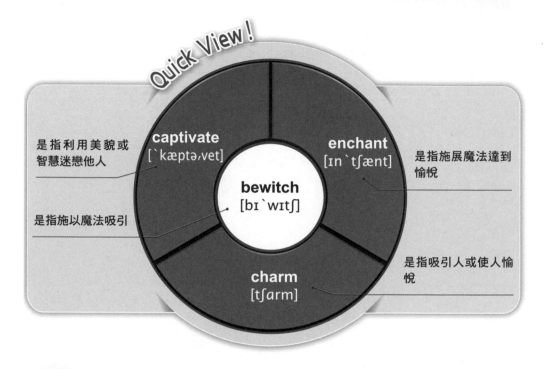

是指利用美貌或
智慧迷戀他人

captivate
[`kæptə,vet]

enchant
[ɪn`tʃænt]

是指施展魔法達到
愉悅

bewitch
[bɪ`wɪtʃ]

是指施以魔法吸引

charm
[tʃɑrm]

是指吸引人或使人愉
悅

---

114 **bewitch**
-bewitched-bewitched

vt. 施魔術於、蠱惑

- The evil fairy bewitched the princess.
  邪惡精靈蠱惑了公主。
- Joseph was bewitched by her beauty at first sight.
  喬瑟夫第一眼看到她就被她的美貌所吸引。

衍 bewitching *adj.* 迷人的；
bewitchment *n.* 誘惑

同 enchant *v.* 使著魔、對……用魔法

近 witch *n.* 巫婆

115 captivate
-captivated-captivated

vt. 使著迷、蠱惑

- She was captivated by the gracefulness of the dancers.
  她被舞者優雅的動作所吸引。
- The readers were captivated by the interesting and funny stories in the book.
  讀者沉迷於書中有趣又好玩的故事。

衍 captive *n.* 俘虜；
captivity *n.* 束縛；
captivation *n.* 迷惑；
captivating *adj.* 令人入迷的
同 charm 使陶醉、吸引
近 capitate *adj.* 頭狀的、錘型的

---

116 charm
-charmed-charmed

vt. 使陶醉　vi. 施魔法　n. 魅力、符咒

- Only when you live here for some time will you know its charm.
  只有當你住在這裡一段時間，你才會發現此地的迷人之處。
- I was charmed by her diligence.
  我被她的勤奮所吸引。

衍 charming *adj.* 迷人的；
charmless *adj.* 無吸引力的
同 bewitch 蠱惑
組 charm offensive 討好對手；
charm school 美姿學校；
Prince Charming 白馬王子
片 work like a charm 立見功效

---

117 enchant
-enchanted-enchanted

vt. 使著魔、對……用魔法

- The magician enchanted the prince and turned him into a frog.
  魔術師對王子施法，將他變成一隻青蛙。
- The audience was enchanted with Yo-yo Ma's performance.
  觀眾都被馬友友的表演給迷住了。

衍 enchanter *n.* 使人著迷者；
enchanting *adj.* 迷人的；
enchantment *n.* 迷人之處；
enchantress *n.* 迷人的女人
近 chant *v.* 歌唱、吟誦
片 be enchanted with 為……陶醉

• 女巫（witch）善於魔法（magic）、巫術（witchery），不是對人施咒（cast a spell）就是蠱惑（bewitch）他人。

小試身手UP↑

（　）1. It's said that Lorelei would _____ the seamen with her beautiful voice. （複選）

    (A) attract　(B) enchant　(C) lure　(D) amuse

（　）2. The mean fairy put a sleeping _____ on the infant princess so that she would fall into a long sleep if she gets her finger pricked by a spindle of a spinning wheel.

    (A) enchant　(B) charm　(C) lure　(D) allure

1. (A)(B)(C)　據說女妖羅蕾萊會用動人的歌聲迷惑水手。
2. (B)　壞心的仙女對小公主施下沉睡魔咒，當小公主手指被紡車的紡錘刺到，就會陷入漫長的沉睡。

Lesson 23 給予

MP3 1-23

afford / award / bestow / contribute / give / grant / present

Quick View!

是指給予獎品或榮譽 —— **award** [ə`wɔrd]

是指給予禮物或獎勵 —— **bestow** [bɪ`sto]

是指有足夠的金錢能夠支付

是指為了某目的而給予 —— **contribute** [kən`trɪbjut]

afford [ə`ford]

present [`prɛznt] —— 是指給禮物或獎勵

grant [grænt] —— 是指因要求或需要給予

give [gɪv] —— 是指給出去

---

118 | afford
-afforded-afforded

vt. 提供、給予、支付得起

- I can't afford (to buy) a new car.
  我買不起新車。
- He can't afford to rent a suite, so he lives in the dormitory.
  他租不起套房,所以他住在宿舍裡。

衍 affordable *adj.* 負擔得起的
同 supply 供給、提供;
  offer 提供
片 can't afford to 不能冒……之險、負擔不起……

119 | **award**
-awarded-awarded

vt. 授予、給予　n. 獎狀

- The college awards scholarships to students with high grades.
  這所學院給予成績優異的學生獎學金。
- Peter was awarded first prize in the science competition.
  彼得在科學競賽中獲得冠軍。

衍 award-winning *adj.* 應獲獎的、獲獎的
近 reward *n.* 報酬、獎賞；
aware *adj.* 察覺的
組 Academy Award　奧斯卡金像獎

120 | **bestow**
-bestowed-bestowed

vt. 把……贈與、把……給予

- The president bestowed an award on the famous scientist.
  總統頒獎給這位知名科學家。
- He doesn't deserve the reputation that was bestowed on him.
  他是浪得虛名。

衍 bestowal *n.* 授予；
bestowment *n.* 贈與之物
同 award 授予、給予
近 tow *v.* 拖吊
片 bestow sth. on / upon sb. 給予某人某物

121 | **contribute**
-contributed-contributed

vi. 捐獻　vt. 捐（款）、貢獻、投稿

- She contributed all her savings to the religious group.
  她把所有的積蓄都貢獻給了那個宗教團體。
- He contributed nothing to the rescue work.
  他對搜救工作一點貢獻也沒有。

衍 contribution *n.* 貢獻；
contributive *adj.* 貢獻的；
contributor *n.* 捐贈者；
contributory *adj.* 捐助的
同 donate *v.* 捐贈
近 distribute *v.* 分發、發送、分類
片 contribute to 捐給

122 give
-gave-given

vi. 捐贈　**vt.** 給、送給　**n.** 伸展性

- Is it really better to *give* than to receive?
  施比受真的更有福嗎？
- *Aesop's Fables give* children knowledge and entertainment.
  《伊索寓言》帶給孩子知識和娛樂。

衍 giving *n.* 禮物；giver *n.* 贈予者
反 take 拿
組 give and take 互諒互讓；
give a backhander 行賄；
given name 名字（不包括姓）
片 give away 分發；give birth to
生（孩子）；give in 讓步、
屈服；give up 放棄；give way
讓開

123 grant
-granted-granted

vt. 給予、授予、同意、承認　**n.** 獎學金

- The genie *granted* the girl three wishes.
  精靈給予少女三個願望。
- Parents love their children, who should not take their love for *granted*.
  父母愛他們的孩子，孩子們不該把父母的愛視為理所當然。

衍 grantee *n.* 受頒贈者；
grantor *n.* 讓與人；
granted *conj.* 假定、就算
組 grant-in-aid 資助款；
death grant 死亡撫恤金
片 take sth. for granted 認為某事
理所當然

124 present
-presented-presented

vt. 贈送、呈獻　**n.** 現在　**adj.** 在場的

- The host will *present* the special guest to the audience later.
  主持人待會將跟觀眾介紹特別嘉賓。
- After all the evidence was *presented*, Allen made a confession of his crime.
  所有的證據都呈上後，艾倫承認了自己的罪行。

衍 presentable *adj.* 可提出的；
presentation *n.* 授予、表演；
presentative *adj.* 直覺的；
presentee *n.* 受饋贈者
組 present-day 當代的；
present participle 現在分詞；
present arms 舉槍致敬
片 at present 現在；
live in the present 活在當下

- 雖然他負擔（afford）不起高額的學費（tuition），但他力爭上游，苦練網球，不但獲得了政府的補助金（grant）外，還出國比賽獲獎（award）光榮歸國，讓他的努力有了回報（reward）。

小試身手UP

(　) **1.** All of the students were _____ in class today.
(A) present　(B) contributed　(C) presents　(D) bestowed

(　) **2.** I can't _____ a fancy television. I have no money.
(A) afford　(B) give　(C) supply　(D) award

(　) **3.** My sister _____ me a jigsaw puzzle for my 13th birthday present.
(A) bestowed　(B) gave　(C) supplied　(D) granted

Ans
1. (A) 所有的學生今天都有出席上課。
2. (A) 我買不起豪華的電視，我沒有錢。
3. (B) 我姊姊送我拼圖作為我十三歲的生日禮物。

24 Lesson 到達

🎧 MP3 1-24

arrive / attain / come / land / reach

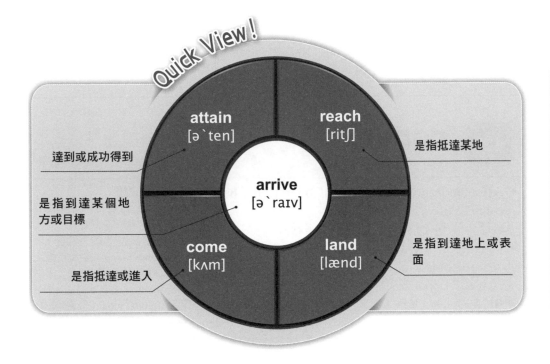

Quick View!

attain [ə`ten]
達到或成功得到

reach [ritʃ]
是指抵達某地

arrive [ə`raɪv]

是指到達某個地方或目標

come [kʌm]
是指抵達或進入

land [lænd]
是指到達地上或表面

---

125 arrive
-arrived-arrived

vi. 到達、到來

- After driving all day, we finally arrived at the beach.
  經過整日開車，我們終於抵達了海灘。
- The plane finally arrived and landed safely after meeting some turbulence.
  在遭遇亂流後，飛機終於抵達並安全降落。

衍 arrival n. 到達
同 come 來、來到
反 depart 出發；leave 離開
組 arrival lobby 入境大廳；
　arrive at an agreement with
　與……達成協議
片 arrive at / in 抵達

126 | attain
-attained-attained

vt. 達到、獲得　vi. 達到、獲得　n. 成就

- The climbers attained (to) the summit.
登山客抵達了山頂。
- My nephew has nearly attained to my height.
我外甥快跟我一樣高了。

衍 attainable *adj.* 可達到的；
attainder *n.* 被剝奪財產和公民權利；
attainment *n.* 達到
同 reach 抵達、到達、達到
片 attain to 達到、獲得

---

127 | come
-came-come

vi. 來、來到　vt. 擺出……的樣子、裝出

- After undergoing a series of operations, he came to life in the end.
經歷一連串的手術後，他終於甦醒過來。
- I made up my mind to study harder for the year to come.
我下定決心來年要更加用功。

Tip N + to come 是指「未來的……」之意。

衍 coming *n.* 到達；
comely *adj.* 合宜的、恰當的
反 go 去、走、離開
組 come a cropper 失敗、摔倒；
come home to roost 得到惡報；
come to life 甦醒過來
片 come to fame 成名；come after 緊跟；come along 一起來；
come true 實現

---

128 | land
-landed-landed

vi. 登陸、降落　vt. 使登陸、使降落　n. 陸地

- The spacecraft successfully landed on the moon.
太空船成功登陸月球。
- Peter landed up being a beggar because of his laziness.
由於懶惰，彼得最後淪為乞丐。

衍 landed *adj.* 擁有土地的；
lander *n.* 著陸器；
landing *n.* 降落、著陸、登陸
組 land use 土地利用；
Promised Land 應許之地；
landlord 地主、房東；
a never-never land 虛幻世界；
land a blow 【俚】攻擊

129 reach
-reached-reached

vt. 抵達、到達　vi. 達到、延伸　n. 可及範圍

- We reached the lake after a three-hour drive.
  開了三小時的車後，我們抵達了湖邊。
- The lazy man put everything to eat within his reach.
  這個懶惰鬼把所有可以吃的東西放在他伸手可及之處。

衍 reachable *adj.* 可達到的；
reachless *adj.* 不可及的；
reach-me-down *adj.* 現成的

同 attain 達到、獲得

片 reach out 伸出；reach to 達到；
out of reach 拿不到、超出……
的理解範圍；beyond reach 達
不到；within reach 伸手可及

 **聯想學習Plus**

- 透過身體所做的動作，除了摸到（reach）外，還包括屈身（bend）、跳（jump）、搖（shake）與彎腰（stoop）。
- 如果你能克服（overcome）困難，堅持下去，你的收入（income）就會滾滾而來（come）。

小試身手UP

（　）1. The children are hungry when they ＿＿＿＿ home after school.
　　　(A) arrive　(B) came　(C) comes　(D) reached
（　）2. I ＿＿＿＿ into the room through the window.
　　　(A) comes　(B) came　(C) reached　(D) land
（　）3. The plane couldn't ＿＿＿＿ because of the fog.
　　　(A) comes　(B) came　(C) reached　(D) land

 Ans
1. (A) 孩子放學回家後都非常餓。
2. (B) 我從窗戶爬進房間。
3. (D) 飛機因為大霧無法降落。

發生

🎧 MP3 1-25

cause / happen / occasion / occur

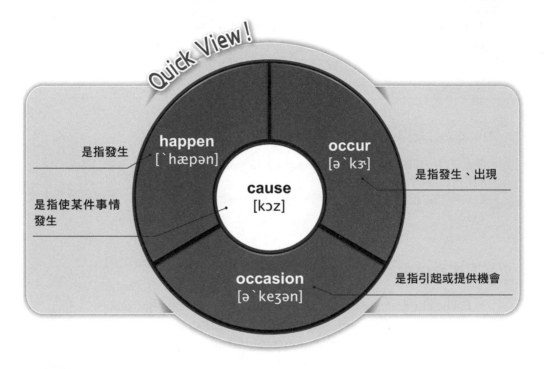

Quick View !

是指發生 — **happen** [ˋhæpən]

是指使某件事情發生 — **cause** [kɔz]

occur [əˋkɝ] — 是指發生、出現

occasion [əˋkeʒən] — 是指引起或提供機會

---

130 | cause
-caused-caused

vt. 導致、使發生、引起　n. 原因

- The heavy rain caused floods.
  豪雨引發洪水。
- He discovered the cause of flu and became famous.
  他發現流感的起因,並因此成名。

衍 causeless *adj.* 原因不明的;
causer *n.* 肇因者;
causative *adj.* 成為原因的

反 result in *v.* 導致、結果是

組 cause and effect 有因果關係的;cause celebre 有名的案例

片 cause a commotion 引起騷動;cause (some) eyebrows to raise 嚇到某人

131 happen
-happened-happened

vi.（偶然）發生

- A bank robbery happened in broad daylight.
  光天化日下竟發生了銀行搶案。
- I happened to meet one of my old friends on my way home.
  我回家途中巧遇一位老友。
- No one can predict what will happen next, so stay alert all the time.
  沒有人能預測下一秒會發生什麼事，所以隨時保持警覺吧。

衍 happening *n.* 事情、事件；
happenstance *n.* 偶然的事情

同 occur 發生；
take place 舉行、發生

片 Accidents will happen. 萬事皆有可能。happen (up)on 碰巧遇見；happen to 發生、碰巧；sit back and let sth. happen 別擔心

132 occasion
-occasioned-occasioned

vt. 引起、惹起　n. 場合

- That someone leaked information to the press occasioned his resignation.
  由於有人向媒體洩露資訊造成他辭職。
- I saw Justin having a fight with his girlfriend on an occasion.
  我有一次看見賈斯汀和他女朋友起爭執。

衍 occasional *adj.* 偶爾的；
occasionally *adv.* 偶爾

組 occasional table 臨時用的小桌子；occasion of sin 犯罪的機會

片 on occasion 有時；
keep sth. for another occasion 保留

133 occur
-occurred-occurred

vi. 發生

- It occurred to me that I'd been here before.
  我想到我以前曾來過這裡。
- No idea occurred to me.
  我想不到任何點子。

衍 occurrence *n.* 發生、出現

同 happen 偶然發生

片 occur to 在……心裡出現、想到、想起

- happen 是「發生」的意思，為不及物動詞，happen to 有兩種用法，以物當主詞時，是指「發生」，以人當主詞時，則做「碰巧、巧遇」解釋。
- 小心（caution）使用（use）這個東西，不然不好的事情會發生（cause to happen）。

小試身手UP↑

(　　) 1. The drunken driver _____ the car accident.
　　　(A) caused　(B) occurred　(C) happened　(D) took place

(　　) 2. The rain _____ the game to take a rain check.
　　　(A) occurred　(B) caused　(C) happened　(D) resulted

(　　) 3 Taiwan is located in the seismic zone. Earthquakes _____ now and then.
　　　(A) happen　(B) cause　(C) result　(D) effect

1. (A)　這名喝醉的駕駛釀成了車禍。
2. (B)　這場雨使得比賽改期了。
3. (A)　台灣位於地震帶上，時不時會發生地震。

Lesson 26

得到

🎧 MP3 1-26

acquire / gain / get / obtain

Quick View !

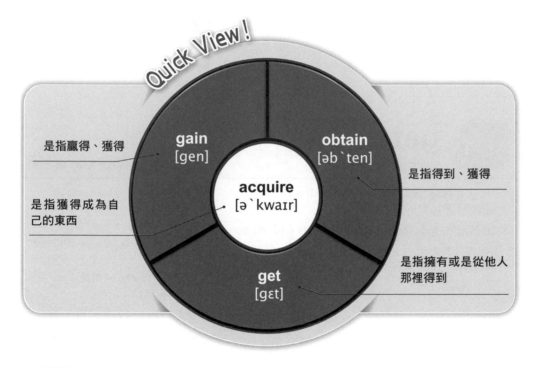

gain
[gen]

obtain
[əb`ten]

acquire
[ə`kwaɪr]

get
[gɛt]

是指贏得、獲得

是指獲得成為自己的東西

是指得到、獲得

是指擁有或是從他人那裡得到

---

134 | acquire
-acquired-acquired

vt. 取得、獲得

- He acquired some bad habits from his friends.
  他從朋友那裡學到一些壞習慣。
- If you go to college, you'll acquire a better education.
  如果你上了大學，就能獲得更好的教育。

衍 acquired *adj.* 養成的；
acquirement *n.* 學得；
acquirer *n.* 收買者

同 get 獲得、得到、贏得

近 require *v.* 需要、要求；
inquire *v.* 訊問、調查

組 Acquired Immune Deficiency Syndrome 愛滋病

135 | gain
-gained-gained

vt. 得到、獲得　vi. 獲利、賺錢、得益　n. 獲得

- He worked hard to gain respect.
  他努力工作以獲得別人的尊敬。
- Joan gained a good fortune by selling toys and dolls.
  瓊安靠賣玩具和洋娃娃賺了一大筆錢。

衍 gainer *n.* 獲得者；
gainful *adj.* 賺錢的；
gainless *adj.* 無利可圖的
反 lose 失、丟失、喪失
近 grain *n.* 穀粒
片 One man's loss is another man's gain. 一人之失即是他人之得。
gain with acceptance 受歡迎

---

136 | get
-got-gotten/got

vt. 獲得、得到、贏得　vi. 到達

- I got a new bicycle for my birthday.
  我生日禮物是一部單車。
- If you get an MBA, you'll be popular among companies.
  如果你取得企業管理碩士的學位，你將受到各家公司的歡迎。

衍 gotta【口】= have got to
同 receive 得到、收到
反 give 給；lose 失去
片 get a foot in the door 獲得機會參加；
get a glimpse of 瞥見；
get it 懂得；
get screwed 受騙上當

---

137 | obtain
-obtained-obtained

vt. 得到、獲得　vi. 得到公認、通用、流行、存在

- To obtain a driver's license, you have to pass a road test and a written test.
  為了要得到駕照，你必須通過路考與筆試。
- If you want to take one-day leave, you should obtain permission from the manager.
  如果你想請一天假，你必須得到經理的同意。

衍 obtainable *adj.* 能得到的；
obtainment *n.* 獲得、得到
同 get 獲得、得到、贏得
近 attain 達到、獲得
片 obtain acceptance with 受……歡迎；
obtain with acceptance 受歡迎

聯想學習Plus

- 透過溝通（communicate）與傳遞（convey），我們可以獲得（gain）、認識（know）及學習（learn）到知識（knowledge）。
- 有失（lose）就有得（get）。

小試身手UP

( ) 1. I always _____ some weight in winter.
　　(A) obtain　(B) get　(C) gain　(D) receive

( ) 2. I need to _____ some milk at the supermarket.
　　(A) get　(B) obtain　(C) acquire　(D) gain

( ) 3. He _____ his college degree in just three years.（複選）
　　(A) gained　(B) obtained　(C) awarded　(D) reached

1. (C) 我冬天時體重總是會增加一些。
2. (A) 我需要到超市買些牛奶。
3. (A)(B) 他只花了三年就拿到大學文憑。

繫上

🎧 MP3 1-27

affix / attach / bind / fasten / link / tie

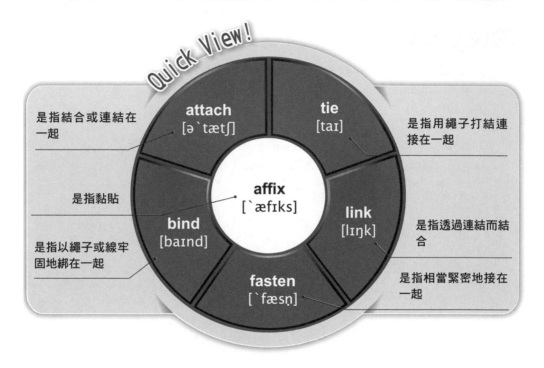

Quick View!

是指結合或連結在一起 — **attach** [ə`tætʃ]

tie [taɪ] — 是指用繩子打結連接在一起

affix [`æfɪks]

是指黏貼

bind [baɪnd]

link [lɪŋk] — 是指透過連結而結合

是指以繩子或線牢固地綁在一起

fasten [`fæsn̩] — 是指相當緊密地接在一起

---

138 affix
-affixed-affixed

vt. 貼上、把……固定　n. 添加物

- She affixed a poster to the wall.
  她將海報貼在牆壁上。
- Amy affixed her photo to the resume.
  艾咪在履歷上附上照片。

衍 affixation n. 附加法；
affixture n. 附加（物）

同 attach 裝上、貼上、繫上

反 unfasten 解開、脫開

近 prefix n. 字首；infix n. 插入詞；
suffix n. 字尾

片 affix to 附貼上；
affix one's signature to 在……
簽名

139 | attach
-attached-attached

vt. 裝上、貼上、繫上　**vi.** 附屬、附加

- He attached the telephone wire to the wall.
  他將電話線貼附在牆壁上。
- Louis is attached to Helen, one of the most beautiful girls in our class.
  路易喜歡海倫，她是我們班最漂亮的女生之一。

Tip　be attached to + sb. 是指「喜愛、愛慕某人」之意。

衍 attachable *adj.* 可附上的；
attached *adj.* 充滿愛心的；
attachment *n.* 連接、附著
同 affix *v.* 貼上、把……固定
反 detach *v.* 分開、拆卸、使分離
片 attach importance to 重視；
attach to 屬於

---

140 | bind
-bound-bound

vi. 黏結、黏合　**vt.** 捆、綁　**n.** 綑綁物

- Ladies and gentlemen, welcome aboard Taiwan High Speed Rail. This train is bound for Zuoying, stoping at Panciao, Taichung, and Tainan. We wish you a pleasant journey.
  各位旅客您好，歡迎搭乘台灣高鐵。本列車開往左營，沿途停靠板橋、台中與台南。祝您旅途愉快。

衍 binder *n.* 裝訂工、捆縛（或包紮）者；bindery *n.* 裝訂所；
binding *n.* 裝訂、封皮
同 tie 被繫住
反 untie 解開、解除；
loosen 鬆開、解開
片 in a double bind 處於進退兩難的狀態；
be bound for 前往（某地）

---

141 | fasten
-fastened-fastened

vi. 扣緊、閂住　**vt.** 紮牢、繫緊、閂住、釘牢

- The policeman fastened the badge to his uniform.
  警察將徽章別在制服上。
- Passengers should fasten their seatbelts tight during landing.
  降落期間乘客應繫緊安全帶。

衍 fastener *n.* 緊固物、扣件、鈕扣；fastening *n.* 緊固件
同 attach 裝上、貼上、繫上
反 loosen 解開、鬆開
組 fasten shoelaces 繫鞋帶；
fasten the seatbelt 繫安全帶
片 fasten down 扣住、紮緊；
fasten on 盯住不放、全神貫注於

<table>
<tr><td>

142 **link**
-linked-linked

vi. 連接起來　*vt.* 連接、結合、聯繫　*n.* 環、節

- We are linked by our love for music.
  我們因為對音樂的喜愛而有了連結。
- The broker links up the buyer and the seller.
  經紀人連接了買方和賣方。
- The little boy linked these pieces of torn paper together with glue.
  小男孩把這些撕碎的紙片用膠水拼接起來。

</td><td>

衍 linkage *n.* 連接、連合、聯合、聯繫；linked *adj.* 連接的；links *n.* 高爾夫球場
同 connect 連結
組 linkboy 火炬手；missing link 缺失的一環；weak link 弱點；linking verb 連綴動詞
片 link together 連結在一起

</td></tr>
</table>

<table>
<tr><td>

143 **tie**
-tied-tied

vi. 被繫住　*vt.* 繫、拴、捆、紮　*n.* 領帶

- The hostage was tied to the chair by the bandits.
  人質被歹徒綁在椅子上。
- The suspect kept pleading to untie him for he claimed that he was innocent.
  嫌犯不停地懇求鬆綁，因為他自稱清白。

</td><td>

衍 tied *adj.* 出租給雇工居住的；tier *n.* 包紮的人
同 bind 捆、綁
反 untie 解開、解除；unbind 鬆開；release 放鬆、鬆開
組 necktie 領帶；tie the knot【口】結婚；tongue-tie 舌頭打結
片 tie down 約束；tie in 搭配

</td></tr>
</table>

小試身手UP

（　）1. He used to _____ a Post-it to the note to remind himself of important things.（複選）
(A) attach　(B) tie　(C) link　(D) affix

（　）2. It's obligatory for the passengers in the back seat to _____ the seatbelt.
(A) tie　(B) bind　(C) affix　(D) fasten

1. (A)(D)　他習慣在筆記上貼上便條紙，好提醒自己重要的事項。
2. (D)　後座乘客也強制需要繫安全帶。

Lesson 28 開始

🎧 MP3 1-28

begin / commence / inaugurate / initiate / start

Quick View!

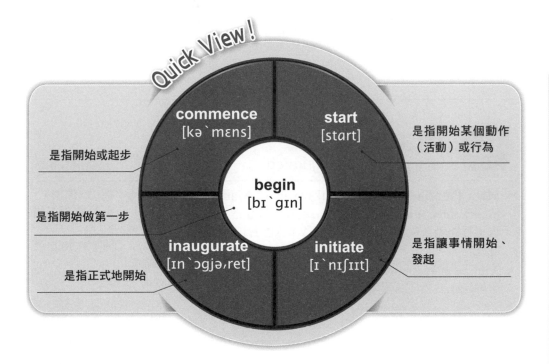

是指開始或起步 — **commence** [kə`mɛns]

是指開始某個動作（活動）或行為 — **start** [start]

begin [bɪ`ɡɪn]

是指開始做第一步 — **inaugurate** [ɪn`ɔɡjə‚ret]

是指正式地開始

是指讓事情開始、發起 — **initiate** [ɪ`nɪʃɪɪt]

---

144 begin
-began-begun

vt. 開始、著手、動手　vi. 開始、開始進行

- I'm innocent. To begin with I didn't know that guy, and secondly I stayed home all day on that day.
  我是無辜的。一來我不認識那個傢伙，二來當天我整天都待在家裡。
- I began to learn Japanese last month.
  我上個月開始學日語。

衍 beginner *n.* 生手；
beginning *n.* 開始

組 beginner's luck 新手的好運氣

片 to begin with 首先；
begin by 以做……事開始；
from beginning to end 從頭到尾

commence
-commenced-commenced

vi. 開始　vt. 開始、著手

- The press conference will commence in five minutes.
  記者會再五分鐘就要開始了。
- It commenced raining, and people on the street rushed to find shelter from rain.
  開始下起雨來了，路上行人急忙找地方躲雨。

Tip commence + Ving 表示「開始做某事一段時間了」，commence + to-V 則是「開始要做某事」。

衍 commencement n. 畢業典禮、發端、開始
反 finish v. 結束；end v. 結束
近 commerce n. 商業、貿易
片 commence with 以……開始

---

inaugurate
-inaugurated-inaugurated

vt. 開始、開展

- Mars Pathfinder's successful rover on Mars inaugurated a new era of space exploration.
  火星探路者號成功探索火星，開啟了太空探險新紀元。
- Anita was inaugurated as general manager.
  雅妮塔正式就任總經理。

衍 inauguration n. 開始、開創；inaugurator n. 舉行就職典禮者、就職者
組 Inauguration Day 1 月 20 日美國總統就職日
片 inaugurate as 擔任

---

initiate
-initiated-initiated

vt. 開始、創始　adj. 新加入的　n. 新加入者

- The teacher initiated a new policy of giving no homework on weekends.
  這位老師發起了週末不派功課的新政策。
- There are many initiates in Congress this year. People expect them to do something different to better our society.
  今年國會有許多新科議員。人民期待他們能有不一樣的作為，改善整個社會。

衍 initiation n. 開始；initiative n. 主動的行動；initiator n. 創始者；initiatory adj. 起始的；initial adj. 開始的、最初的
同 commence 開始
片 initiate an investigation 啟動調查

148 start
-started-started

vi. 開始、著手　*vt.* 使開始、開始　*n.* 出發

- Let's start with the appetizer.
  我們從開胃菜開始吃起吧。
- When someone pleads for help, the police would start off immediately.
  一有人請求幫助，員警就馬上出動。

衍 starting *n.* 開始；
   starter *n.* 起動裝置
同 begin 開始、著手、動手
反 end 結束
組 start-up 新運作的公司
片 start with 從……開始；start over 重新開始；start off 開始、出發；start up 啟動；at the very start 一開始

 聯想學習Plus

- 有的時候，我們會因為開始（start）做一件事而感到害怕（fear）。

小試身手UP

（　）1. All the participants _____ to run as soon as the whistling is heard.
　　(A) start　(B) beginning　(C) initial　(D) inauguration

（　）2. The _____ of the story is narrated in the first person, but it is changed to the third person in the end.
　　(A) beginning　(B) initiate　(C) starting　(D) commence

（　）3. Most of the fairy tales usually _____ with the sentence "Once upon a time...."
　　(A) inaugurate　(B) end up　(C) start　(D) commerce

 Ans

1. (A) 當哨音一響起，全部參賽者便開始起跑。
2. (A) 故事一開始是用第一人稱描述，但最後卻轉變成第三人稱視角了。
3. (C) 大多數的童話故事經常以「很久很久以前」這句話當開頭。

Lesson 29

養育

🎧 MP3 1-29

foster / nourish / raise / support

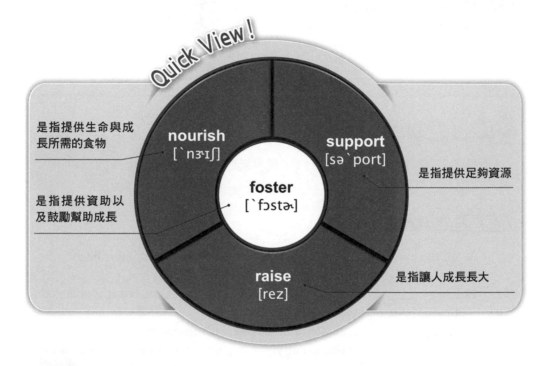

Quick View!

是指提供生命與成長所需的食物 — **nourish** [`nɝɪʃ]

support [sə`port] — 是指提供足夠資源

foster [`fɔstɚ]

是指提供資助以及鼓勵幫助成長 —

raise [rez] — 是指讓人成長長大

---

149 **foster**
-fostered-fostered

vt. 養育、領養   adj. 養育的、領養的

- They fostered trust in their family by always being honest.
  他們以誠實在家庭中培養出信任。
- The new policy allows childless couples to foster one from the orphanage.
  新政策允許膝下無子的夫妻從孤兒院領養孩子。
- Despite the fact that he is their foster child, they treat him as their own son.
  儘管他是他們領養的孩子,但他們將他視如己出。

衍 fosterage *n.* 養育;
fosterer *n.* 養父或養母;
fostress *n.* 養母

同 nourish 養育、滋養

組 foster mother 養母;
foster child 養子(女);
foster father 養父

nourish
-nourished-nourished

vt. 養育、滋養、為……提供養分

- Mammals nourish their babies with milk.
  哺乳類動物以奶水養育後代。
- Farmers nourish the soil before they sow.
  農夫會在播種前先滋養土壤。

衍 nourished *adj.* 營養……的；
nourishing *adj.* 有營養的；
nourishment *n.* 營養品

同 feed 餵養；
nurture 培養、養育；
nurse 培育、照料

片 Desires are nourished by delays.
愈難得到的愈想得到。

raise
-raised-raised

vt. 養育、種植、飼養　**n.** 加薪

- He was born and raised in a poor family, but
  he started his own business in his twenties
  and made a big fortune.
  雖然他出生於窮困家庭，但二十幾歲時他開創了
  自己的事業，並大賺一筆。
- The coming of the typhoon raised alarm.
  颱風將近引發人們的注意。

衍 raised *adj.* 升高的

片 raise the alarm 引起警覺；
raise a finger 盡舉手之勞；
raise hell 吵鬧；
raise up 提起、舉起、扶起、
豎起

support
-supported-supported

vt. 扶養、贍養　**n.** 支撐

- Parents support their families by working.
  父母親外出工作維持家庭。
- The prosecutor's accusation against the
  suspect lacked the support of evidence.
  檢方對嫌犯的指控缺少證據的支持。

衍 supportable *adj.* 能扶養的；
supporter *n.* 扶養者；
supportive *adj.* 支援的；
supportless *adj.* 無支持者的

反 neglect 忽視、忽略

組 means of support 生計來源；
emotional support 情感支持；
supporting role 配角

 聯想學習Plus

• 這個國家藉由港口（port）進行進口（import）與出口（export）貿易，以支持（support）整個國家的經濟基礎。

小試身手UP

(   ) 1. Sunlight and rain help to _____ all things on earth, including plants.
    (A) nourish   (B) supported   (C) support   (D) raise

(   ) 2. Good books _____ the mind.
    (A) fostered   (B) support   (C) raised   (D) nourish

(   ) 3. The farmers _____ beans and corn.
    (A) raise   (B) nourish   (C) rise   (D) support

1. (A) 陽光和雨水滋養包含植物在內的萬物。
2. (D) 好書可以滋養心靈。
3. (A) 農夫種植豆子與玉米。

30 Lesson 報復

repay / requite / retaliate / revenge

🎧 MP3 1-30

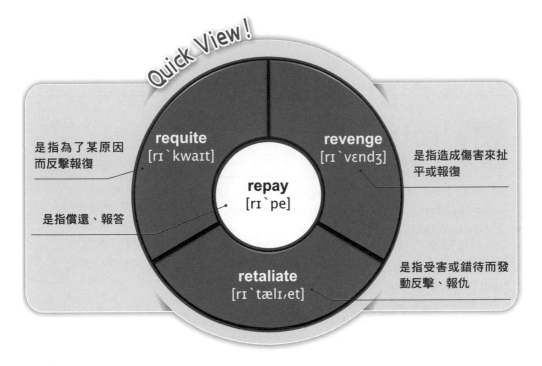

Quick View!

requite
[rɪ`kwaɪt]
是指為了某原因而反擊報復

是指償還、報答

revenge
[rɪ`vɛndʒ]
是指造成傷害來扯平或報復

repay
[rɪ`pe]

retaliate
[rɪ`tælɪ,et]
是指受害或錯待而發動反擊、報仇

---

153 | repay
-repaid-repaid

vi. 償還、報答、報復　vt. 報答、回報、報復、回敬

- How can I repay you for your kindness?
  我該如何報答你的好意？
- I treat you well, and that's how you repay me!
  我待你不薄，你卻是這樣回報我的！

衍 repayable *adj.* 可報復的；
repayment *n.* 報復、報恩
同 requite 報答、回報
片 repay by 藉……回報；
repay with 提供某物回報

154 requite
-requited-requited

vt. 報答、回報、報復

- Mother's Day is a wonderful chance for us to requite Mom for what she's done for us.
  母親節是我們回報媽媽為我們所做一切的絕佳機會。
- Requiting evil with good is a virtue.
  以德報怨是種美德。

Tip requite sb. for... 是指「報答或報復某人所做的事」之意。

衍 requital *n.* 報復、報酬；
  requitable *adj.* 可回報的
近 require 要求
片 requite evil with good 以德報怨

155 retaliate
-retaliated-retaliated

vi. 報復、回敬 *vt.* 就（傷害等）進行報復

- Her brother made a disparaging remark, so she retaliated by hitting him over the head with a cushion.
  她的哥哥說了汙衊的話，於是她便拿起墊子打他的頭。
- Johnson retaliated against the dog that bit him by throwing a stone at it.
  強森向咬他的小狗扔石頭作為報復。

衍 retaliation *n.* 報復；
  retaliative *adj.* 報復性的；
  retaliatory *adj.* 報復的
同 revenge 報復、洗雪
片 retaliate against / upon / on 報復

156 revenge
-revenged-revenged

vt. 報復、洗雪 *n.* 報仇

- The musketeer vowed to revenge the death of his brother.
  劍客誓言要替他兄弟的死報仇。
- The secretary took revenge on her boss by taking important documents away.
  祕書拿走重要的文件來報復老闆。

衍 revengeful *adj.* 報復的；
  revengefully *adv.* 燃起報復念頭地
同 get even with 報復
近 avenge *v.* 報復、報仇；
  vengeance *n.* 復仇
片 revenge oneself on ＝ take revenge on 向……報仇

- 《復仇者聯盟》（*Avengers*）雖然取名復仇者（avenger），但片中跟復仇（revenge）沒有什麼關係。

小試身手UP↑

( ) 1. He _____ the money that he had stolen.
　　(A) repaid　(B) requited　(C) repay　(D) revenged

( ) 2. You must _____ her for the loan she gave you.
　　(A) revenge　(B) repay　(C) repaid　(D) avenged

( ) 3. She cared for him but could not _____ his love.
　　(A) requite　(B) reply　(C) revenge　(D) retaliate

1. (A) 他償還曾經偷來的錢。
2. (B) 你必須償還她借你的錢。
3. (A) 她雖然喜歡他，但卻無法回報他的愛。

侵擾

🎧 MP3 1-31

intercept ／ interrupt ／ intervene ／ intrude

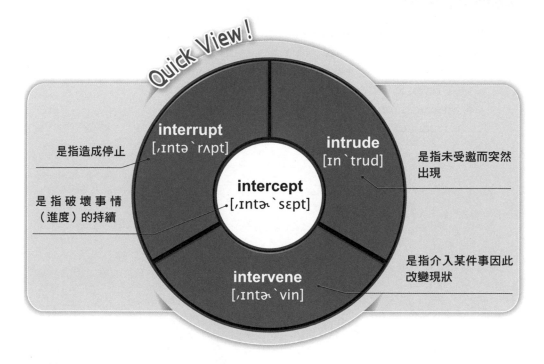

Quick View！

interrupt
[ˌɪntəˈrʌpt]

是指造成停止

是指破壞事情
（進度）的持續

intercept
[ˌɪntəˈsɛpt]

intrude
[ɪnˈtrud]

是指未受邀而突然
出現

是指介入某件事因此
改變現狀

intervene
[ˌɪntəˈvin]

---

157 | intercept
-intercepted-intercepted

vt. 攔截、截住、截擊　n. 攔截

- Luckily, they intercepted the package before it was delivered to the wrong address.
  他們幸運將包裹攔下來，才沒有寄錯地址。
- The man usually intercepts the police radio communication and takes action before the crime occurs.
  男子經常攔截警方的無線電通訊，並在犯罪發生前先一步採取行動。

衍 interceptor *n.* 攔截者；
interceptive *adj.* 遮斷的；
interception *n.* 攔截

同 interrupt *v.* 中斷、阻礙；
stop *v.* 中止

近 interpret *v.* 說明、翻譯、口譯

158 interrupt
-interrupted-interrupted

vt. 中斷、遮斷、阻礙　vi. 打斷

- His sudden showing up interrupted the conversation.
  他突然現身打斷了所有人的對話。
- Don't interrupt me when I'm talking.
  不要在我講話的時候打斷我。

衍 interrupted *adj.* 中斷的；
interrupter *n.* 打斷者；
interruptible *adj.* 可打斷的；
interruptive *adj.* 打岔的；
interruption *n.* 中止
同 cut in 打斷
近 erupt *v.* 噴發、爆發

159 intervene
-intervened-intervened

vi. 干擾、阻擾、打擾

- The teacher intervened in the children's quarrel.
  老師出來調停孩子間的爭執。
- She is the one who intervenes between you and me.
  她就是介入你我之間的第三者。

衍 intervening *adj.* 介於中間的；
intervention *n.* 干預；
interventionism *n.* 干涉主義
同 involve *v.* 涉入、關於
片 intervene between 調停；
intervene on sb.'s behalf 代表某人出面干涉

160 intrude
-intruded-intruded

vt. 把⋯⋯強加　vi. 侵擾、打擾

- The salesman intruded on their dinner with his phone call.
  那位銷售員打電話來，打斷了他們用晚餐。
- Even though you're their parent, you don't have rights to intrude on their privacy.
  即便你是他們的父母，你也沒權利侵犯他們的私生活。

衍 intruder *n.* 侵入者；
intrusion *n.* 侵入；
intrusive *adj.* 侵入的；
intrusively *adv.* 侵入地
同 intervene 干涉、干預、調停
反 extrude 逐出
片 intrude on 干擾；
intrude into 介入、干涉

• 你突然擠進來（intrude）還打斷（interrupt）我們講話，是很沒有禮貌的（rude）。

小試身手UP

（　）1. Please don't _____ me while I'm talking.
　　　(A) intrude　(B) intervened　(C) intercepted　(D) interrupt

（　）2. If the neighbor had not _____, a tragedy might have occurred.
　　　(A) intervened　(B) intrude　(C) interrupt　(D) invaded

（　）3. I'm sorry to _____, but you've got your facts wrong.
　　　(A) intruded　(B) intervened　(C) interrupt　(D) intercepted

1. (D)　我在講話時，請不要插話。
2. (A)　假使鄰居當時沒有介入的話，悲劇可能就發生了。
3. (C)　很抱歉插話，但是你的論據是錯的。

32 Lesson 避開

MP3 1-32

abstain / avoid / escape / evade / shun

Quick View !

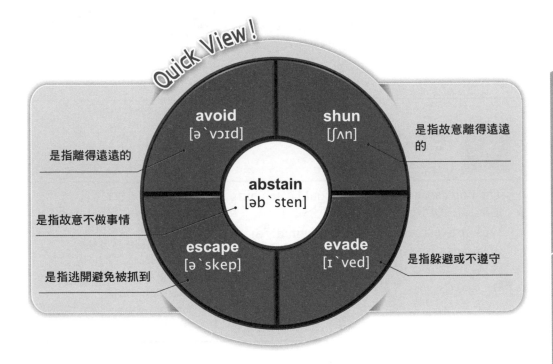

avoid
[ə`vɔɪd]
是指離得遠遠的

shun
[ʃʌn]
是指故意離得遠遠的

abstain
[əb`sten]

是指故意不做事情

escape
[ə`skep]
是指逃開避免被抓到

evade
[ɪ`ved]
是指躲避或不遵守

161 abstain
-abstained-abstained

vi. 戒、避免、避開

- He abstained from dessert because he had eaten too much already.
  因為他吃得太飽，所以沒有吃點心。
- If you don't abstain from smoking, you'll get lung cancer one day.
  如果你不戒煙，總有一天會得肺癌。

衍 abstainer *n.* 節制者；
abstemious *n.* 有節制的；
abstention *n.* 戒絕、節制

近 sustain *v.* 支撐、維持；obtain *v.* 得到；stain *n.* 汙漬

組 vote abstention 棄權票

片 abstain from 放棄；
abstain from voting 拒絕投票

162 **avoid**
-avoided-avoided

- He avoided other cars by swerving.
  他突然轉向以避開其他車輛。
- One should learn from mistakes and avoid making the same ones.
  人應從錯誤中汲取教訓，避免犯同樣的錯誤。

Tip avoid + Ving / N 是指避免「做某事或某事物」而言。

衍 avoidable *adj.* 可迴避的；
avoidance *n.* 躲避；
avoidless *adj.* 無法避免的

同 evade 躲避、逃避、迴避

片 avoid...like the plague 避之唯恐不及

163 **escape**
-escaped-escaped

- The dog escaped before we could catch him.
  這隻狗在我們幾乎抓到牠之前就逃走了。
- Jackson escaped being drowned for the lifeguard saved him right away.
  因為救生員立即出手相救，傑克森因此免於淹死。

Tip escape + Ving / N 是指免於「做某事或某事物」而言。

衍 escapee *n.* 逃脫者；
escapement *n.* 脫逃、逃路；
escapism *n.* 逃避現實

組 escape clause 例外條款；
fire escape 太平門、太平梯

片 avenue of escape 逃脫路徑；
escape from 逃離；
a narrow escape 千鈞一髮的脫險

164 **evade**
-evaded-evaded

- It is illegal to evade paying taxes.
  逃漏稅是違法的。
- Diana evaded taking the exam by taking a sick leave.
  黛安娜請病假來躲避考試。

Tip evade + Ving / N 是指逃避「做某事或某事物」而言。

衍 evasion *n.* 逃避、藉口；
evasive *adj.* 逃避的、託辭的

反 confront 迎面遇到、面臨、遭遇

組 tax evasion 逃稅

165 shun
-shunned-shunned

- He has shunned his brother for years.
  他故意閃躲他哥哥已經好幾年了。
- That man behaves in a sneaky manner. That's why he is shunned by people around him.
  那名男子舉止鬼祟，所以周遭的人都避著他。

Tip shun + Ving / N 是指避免「做某事或某事物」而言。

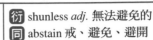

衍 shunless *adj.* 無法避免的
同 abstain 戒、避免、避開

 聯想學習Plus

- escape 是從古法語而來，是指遺落某人的披肩，很符合匆匆離去發生的結果。
- 他匆匆逃跑（escape），結果不小心把帽子（cap）丟了。

小試身手UP↑

( ) 1. She _____ from voting in the election.
  (A) escaped　(B) abstained　(C) avoid　(D) shunned
( ) 2. He always tries to _____ hard work and does the easy one.
  (A) escape to do　(B) abstain to do　(C) avoid doing　(D) shun from doing
( ) 3. The prisoner _____ from jail.
  (A) escaped　(B) abstained　(C) avoided　(D) shunned

 Ans

1. (B) 她在選舉中放棄投票。avoid 和 shun 都是及物動詞；abstain 有棄權的意思，較符合文意。
2. (C) 他總是逃避辛苦的工作，只挑輕鬆的來做。escape、avoid、shun、evade 當及物動詞時，後接 Ving 或 N 當受詞；abstain 只能當不及物動詞，須與 from 配合。
3. (A) 囚犯從監獄脫逃了。escape from jail 是逃獄之意，為慣用語。

擊打(1)

🎧 MP3 1-33

bat / bang / beat / crack / knock

Quick View !

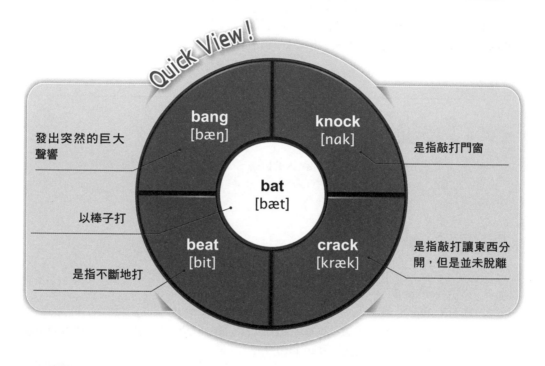

發出突然的巨大聲響

bang
[bæŋ]

knock
[nɑk]

是指敲打門窗

以棒子打

bat
[bæt]

是指不斷地打

beat
[bit]

crack
[kræk]

是指敲打讓東西分開，但是並未脫離

---

166 **bat**
-batted-batted

vi. 輪到擊球　*vt.* 用球棒（或球拍）打（球）　*n.* 球棒

- Bat the ball back to me.
  將球打給我。
- The man wandering on streets always wears peculiar clothes. He must have bats in the belfry.
  那名在街上徘徊的男子穿著怪異，他想必有點瘋癲。

衍 bats *adj.* 心情反常的；
batting *n.* 擊球

組 vampire bat 吸血蝙蝠；
batting average 打擊率

片 bat around 討論；
blind as a bat 看不清的；
right off the bat 立即；
have bats in the belfry 發瘋

167 **bang**
-banged-banged

vi. 發出砰的一聲、砰砰作響　*vt.* 砰地敲　*n.* 砰砰的聲音

- Tom banged his head against the wall.
  湯姆的頭撞到牆了。
- Father was furious and banged the door shut when leaving.
  父親盛怒，離開之際「砰」地將門甩上。
- There's a bang upstairs. Something must have fallen on the floor.
  樓上發出砰的一聲，一定是有東西掉到地上了。

同 strike 打、擊、襲擊、進攻
組 whizz-bang 笑話；
　big bang 宇宙大爆炸；
　slam bang 氣勢兇猛地
片 bang on 嘮叨不停；
　with a bang 成功地

168 **beat**
-beat-beaten

vt. 打、擊、敲　*vi.* 打、擊敲　*n.* 敲打

- He beat the drum with his new drumsticks.
  他用新的鼓棒打鼓。
- A man named William was beaten to death in the park last night.
  一個叫威廉的男人昨晚在公園裡被打死。
- He who has a mind to beat his dog will easily find a stick.
  欲加之罪，何患無辭。

衍 beating *n.* 脈動；
　beater *n.* 敲打者；
　beatable *adj.* 經打的
組 beat a retreat 拔腳溜掉；
　beat box 電子鼓；
　heart beat 心跳
片 beat about 搜尋；
　beat down 壓低；
　beat around the bush 拐彎抹角

169 **crack**
-cracked-cracked

vt. 使爆裂　*vi.* 發出爆裂聲　*n.* 裂縫、純古柯鹼

- A stone cracked the car windshield.
  一顆石頭砸裂了汽車的擋風玻璃。
- The shell of the egg has a tiny crack on it. It might be hit.
  蛋殼上有一個微小的裂縫。它可能有撞到。
- After a huge shaking, a crack appeared on the road.
  在一陣劇烈搖動後，路面上出現一道裂縫。

衍 crackable *adj.* 會裂開的；
　cracked *adj.* 碎的；
　cracking *adj.* 敏捷的；
　cracker *n.* 破碎機、餅乾
組 crackbrained 精神錯亂的
片 crack up 撞壞；
　crack down 取締；
　take a crack at... 嘗試

170 knock
-knocked-knocked

vi. 敲、擊、打　vt. 敲、擊、打　n. 爆炸聲

- Please knock before you enter the room.
  進門前請記得敲門。
- Someone knocked me to the ground and took my mobile phone away.
  有人把我擊倒在地上，拿走了我的手機。

衍 knocker *n.* 敲擊者
同 punch 用拳猛擊
組 knock into a cocked hat 擊潰；
　knockout 淘汰賽
片 knock about 毆打、虐待；
　knock down 擊倒、擊落；
　knock it off 別吵了

聯想學習Plus

- 這裡禁止（ban）敲打（beat）任何樂器。
- right off the bat 的 bat 是指球棒，是指球一被球棒擊中，便以非常快的速度彈飛出去，現在被廣泛運用在各種場合中，有立即而迅速地或是直截了當的意思。

小試身手UP

(　) 1. She slammed the door with a _____.
　　(A) knockout　(B) bang　(C) beat　(D) bat
(　) 2. She slipped and _____ her head on the counter.
　　(A) banged　(B) batted　(C) cracked　(D) knocked
(　) 3. The tree branch _____ in the storm.
　　(A) knocked　(B) cracked　(C) beated　(D) banged

1. (B) 她「砰」一聲將門甩上。beat 有跳動、打擊、擊敗的意思，而 bat 則是指用棍棒擊打，因此都跟甩門（slam the door）無關，故不選。
2. (A) 她滑倒結果頭撞到櫃台。crack 是指敲打以致裂開的意思，knock 則是指不停地敲、拍、打，並製造出聲響而言，皆不合題意，故不選。
3. (B) 樹枝在暴風雨中被折斷。

34 Lesson 擊打(2)

🎧 MP3 1-34

strike / slap / smack / punch / poke / whack

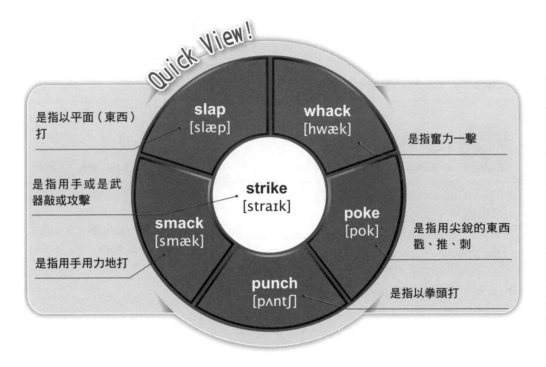

Quick View!

是指以平面（東西）打 — **slap** [slæp]

whack [hwæk] — 是指奮力一擊

是指用手或是武器敲或攻擊

strike [straɪk]

poke [pok] — 是指用尖銳的東西戳、推、刺

smack [smæk]

是指用手用力地打 —

punch [pʌntʃ] — 是指以拳頭打

---

171 strike
-struck-stricken

vi. 打、擊、進攻 *vt.* 打、擊、攻擊 *n.* 打擊、罷工

- He struck me with the back of his hand.
  他用手背打我。
- Workers are striking for better welfare.
  工人為爭取更好的福利罷工。

Tip It strikes / struck + 人 + that + 子句是指「某人突然想起某事」之意。

衍 striking *adj.* 敲擊的、打擊的；
striker *n.* 打擊者；
strikingly *adv.* 顯著地

組 strikerate 成功率；
hunger striker 絕食抗議者；
strike zone 好球區；
on strike 罷工中

片 strike up 建立；
strike for 為……罷工

172 | slap
-slapped-slapped

vt. 摑耳光、用手掌打　vi. 摑、拍擊　n. 用手掌打

- She slapped the mosquito when it landed on her arm.
  她拍掉停在手臂上的蚊子。
- Ada gave me a slap on my cheek.
  艾達給了我一巴掌。
- What a magnificent scene that waves keep slapping against the reefs!
  海浪不停拍打礁石的畫面真是壯觀啊！

衍 slapping adj. 非常快的；
slapper n. 淫婦
近 clap v. 拍手、鼓掌；
slip v. 滑動、滑跤
組 slap bang 突然；slap-up 上等的
片 a slap in the face 一記耳光；
slap down 壓制；
slap around 連續擊打

---

173 | smack
-smacked-smacked

vt. 啪的一聲甩　vi. 啪的一聲甩　n. 滋味

- He smacked the horse to make it move.
  他拍馬一下要牠起步。
- Look! The woman is walking smack-dab into the river.
  看啊！那名女子正朝著河裡走去。
- The birthday boy had a piece of pie smacked on his face.
  一塊派砸在了壽星臉上。

衍 smacker n. 發出聲音的接吻；
smacking adj. 活躍的
同 hit、strike、slap 擊、打、拍
片 smack down 擊倒；
smack-dab 不偏不倚地、恰好地；
smack of 隱約帶有

---

174 | punch
-punched-punched

vi. 用拳猛擊　vt. 用拳猛擊　n. 力量

- The challenger gave the champion a punch on the chin and ended the round.
  挑戰者給衛冕者下巴一記重拳，結束了這個回合。
- Remember to punch your card when you get off work.
  下班的時候別忘了打卡。

衍 punches n. （拳）擊；
puncher n. 打孔器
組 punch press 沖床；
key punch 打孔機；
punch card 打孔卡；
punching bag（拳擊用）沙包
片 beat sb. to the punch 先發制人；
punch the clock 打卡上下班

175 poke
-poked-poked

vi. 戳、捅、撥弄　vt. 戳、捅

- The shepherd poked the goat with a stick to make it walk up the hill.
  牧羊人用棍子趕羊上山。
- You'll poke someone in the eye if you keep waving your umbrella.
  假如你一直揮動雨傘，你會刺到別人眼睛的。
- The baby is so cute that everyone wants to poke it on the cheek.
  寶寶是如此可愛，每個人都想戳戳他的臉頰。

衍 poker *n.* 戳（或捅）的人、撲克牌
近 pork *n.* 豬肉
組 poker face 撲克臉（毫無表情的面孔）
片 poke fun at 戲弄；
　poke into 干涉；
　poke about 摸來摸去

176 whack
-whacked-whacked

vi. 用力打　vt.（用棍棒等）重打、猛擊　n. 重擊聲

- He whacked the baseball over the fence.
  他用力將棒球打飛越過圍籬。
- The furious crowd whacked the suspect for he committed a cruel crime of killing a little girl.
  犯下殺害無辜小女孩殘忍行徑的嫌犯遭到憤怒群眾的圍剿。
- The authorities announced they would whack annuity payments for seniors to balance the budget.
  當局宣布削減老人年金以平衡預算。

衍 whacked *adj.* 疲憊不堪的；
　whacking *adj.* 巨大的；
　whacker *n.* 重擊的人；
　whacky *adj.* 怪人的
片 out of whack 不正常、故障；
　whack out 謀殺；
　whack up 破壞

 小試身手UP

（　）1. He was dumped and _____ in the face by Amy because he was cheating on her.
　　(A) whacked　(B) smacked　(C) knocked　(D) poked

（　）2. He got a _____ in the belly, so he threw up all he had eaten at noon.
　　(A) poke　(B) puke　(C) slap　(D) punch

 Ans

1. (B) 他被艾咪甩了，還被甩耳光，原因在於他劈腿。
2. (D) 他腹部受到重擊，因此把中午吃進的東西全都給吐了出來。

Quick View !

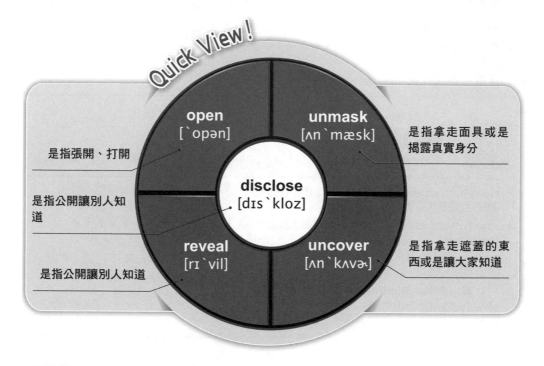

open [`opən]
是指張開、打開
是指公開讓別人知道

unmask [ʌn`mæsk]
是指拿走面具或是揭露真實身分

disclose [dɪs`kloz]

reveal [rɪ`vil]
是指公開讓別人知道

uncover [ʌn`kʌvɚ]
是指拿走遮蓋的東西或是讓大家知道

---

177 disclose
-disclosed-disclosed

vt. 揭發、透露、公開

- She doesn't want to disclose her name.
  她不願公開她的名字。
- This letter disclosed his affair with many other girls.
  這封信揭露了他與其他多名女子的風流韻事。

衍 disclosure *n.* 揭發
同 reveal *v.* 顯露出；
   uncover *v.* 揭開、發現
反 conceal *v.* 隱蔽；
   hide *v.* 隱藏、藏起來

178 open
-opened-opened

- The bird opened its wings and flew away.
  鳥張開翅膀飛走了。
- Let the door open and keep the air flowing.
  讓門敞開，保持空氣流通。
- The bank is opened until 3:30 pm, so you need to hurry if you want to do banking.
  銀行營業到下午三點半，如果你有什麼銀行業務要辦，就要趕快。

衍 opening *n.* 開頭；
opener *n.* 開啟者
組 open-air 露天的；
open-minded 心胸開放的
片 open fire 開火；
open Pandora's box 引來災難；
open to 對……抱持開放；
with open arms 熱烈地

179 reveal
-revealed-revealed

- I won't reveal your secret.
  我不會公開你的祕密。
- Andy revealed that Amy loved him very much.
  安迪透露艾咪非常愛他。
- When she lifted her veil and revealed her face, all of us were astonished.
  當她揭開面紗露出真面目時，我們全都驚呆了。

衍 revealable *adj.* 可展現的；
revealer *n.* 展示者；
revealing *adj.* 透露真情的；
revelation *n.* 顯示
同 display *v.* 展出
反 conceal *v.* 隱瞞
片 reveal one's hand 攤牌；
reveal to 顯示

180 uncover
-uncovered-uncovered

- We uncovered the pie before eating it.
  我們發現派之後就開始吃了。
- The detective uncovered the murderer's scheme and succeeded in stopping a tragedy.
  偵探識破兇手的詭計，成功阻止悲劇的發生。

衍 uncovered *adj.* 無覆蓋物的
同 expose 使暴露於、使接觸到
反 cover 覆蓋

生活常用

學校工作

情緒心智

社會萬象

181 unmask
-unmasked-unmasked

vi. 撕下假面具、揭露　vt. 撕下假面具、揭露

- The villain was unmasked by the hero at the end of the story.
在故事結尾，壞人被主角給揭穿了。
- At first, the paparazzi followed the celebrities to get some headlines, but they unmasked a scandal that a governor took a bribe by accident.
起初狗仔隊只是想跟蹤名人，打算取得獨家頭版新聞，卻無意間揭發了官員收賄的醜聞。

同 expose 使暴露於、使接觸到
近 mask 戴面具、偽裝、遮蔽

 聯想學習Plus

- can opener 是指開罐器。
- 他只用了一枝筆（pen）就把書打開了（open）。
- 字首 un- 是表示「不、非、無、相反」的意思，因此 cover 是蓋上，uncover 就是不蓋上、打開的意思；mask 是戴面具，unmask 就是拿掉面具、拿掉遮蔽物的意思。

小試身手UP

( ) 1. Can you _____ the canned food for me?
(A) disclose　(B) reveal　(C) unmask　(D) open

 1. (D) 你可以幫我打開這個罐頭食物嗎？

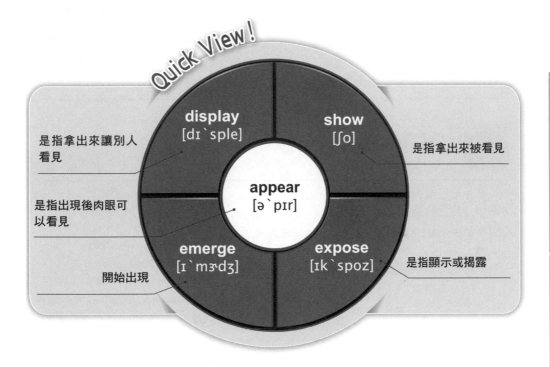

36 Lesson 顯示

🎧 MP3 1-36

appear / display / emerge / expose / show

Quick View!

- **display** [dɪ`sple] 是指拿出來讓別人看見
- **show** [ʃo] 是指拿出來被看見
- **appear** [ə`pɪr]
- 是指出現後肉眼可以看見
- **emerge** [ɪ`mɝdʒ] 開始出現
- **expose** [ɪk`spoz] 是指顯示或揭露

182 appear
-appeared-appeared

vi. 出現、顯露

- Suddenly, a figure appeared out of nowhere.
  突然間，有一個人不知道從哪裡冒出來。
- Cats differ greatly from tigers in physical appearance.
  貓和老虎的外表有很大的不同。
- It appears as if he has made up his mind.
  看來他似乎已經下定決心了。

衍 appearance *n.* 顯露；
apparent *adj.* 明顯的、表面的
反 disappear *v.* 消失
近 appeal *v.* 呼籲、懇求
組 appearance money 出場費
片 appear at the hearing 出席聆訊；
it appears as if / though 看來、
似乎

183 | display
-displayed-displayed

vt. 顯示、表現、顯露　n. 炫耀

- Artists display their paintings along the sidewalks of New York City.
  藝術家沿著紐約市人行道展示畫作。
- My paintings are on display in the museum now.
  我的畫作正在博物館展出。
- There is a firework display on Taipei 101 annually.
  每年台北 101 都會有煙火表演。

同 show 顯示、露出
組 display cabinet 展示櫃；
plasma display 電漿顯示器；
liquid crystal display LCD 液晶顯示
片 on display 展出中；
display to 展示給

184 | emerge
-emerged-emerged

vi. 發生、顯露

- A shape emerged from the mist.
  霧中浮現一個輪廓。
- Sprouts will emerge out of soil a few days later.
  新芽過幾天就會從土壤中冒出。

衍 emergence n. 露頭；
emergency n. 緊急狀況；
emergent adj. 突現的；
emerging adj. 新興的
同 appear 出現
近 merge v. 合併、融合
組 emerging technology 新興技術
片 emerge from / out of 從某處出現

185 | expose
-exposed-exposed

vt. 使暴露於、使接觸到

- We exposed our skin to the sun.
  我們讓皮膚暴露在陽光下。
- Tony was exposed as a liar.
  湯尼被指是個騙子。
- If you are exposed to UV rays too long, you'll get skin cancer easily.
  如果你接觸太久的紫外線，很容易會得皮膚癌。

衍 exposed adj. 暴露的；
exposedness n. 暴露；
exposition n. 展覽會、說明
同 open 開、張開、展開
片 exposed A to B 將 A 暴露於 B 中

186 | show
-showed-shown

vt. 顯示、露出　vi. 顯現、露面　n. 展覽

- Irene showed her report card to her parents.
  艾琳將成績單拿給父母親看。
- I suppose he'll show up in ten minutes.
  我想他十分鐘內就會出現。

衍 showing n. 展覽會、陳列；
　showiness n. 顯眼；
　shower n. 陣雨；
　shown adj. 已出現的
同 display 陳列、展出
反 hide 隱瞞
組 showgirl 廣告女郎；
　showroom 陳列室

聯想學習Plus

- 廣告的種類除了展示（display），還有宣傳（announcement）、公告（notice）及電視廣告（commercial）。
- 告訴我如何演出（perform）一場精采的表演（show）。
- 展覽品可以用 exhibit、display 或 show 展出。

小試身手UP

(　) 1. The sculptures on _____ are forbidden to touch.
　　　(A) appear　(B) shower　(C) display　(D) expose
(　) 2. Parents who _____ their children to any danger will be accused.
　　　(A) show　(B) appear　(C) expose　(D) display

1. (C) 展示中的雕刻品禁止觸碰。
2. (C) 讓小孩遭到任何危險的父母都會遭到譴責。

生活常用

學校工作

情緒心智

社會萬象

穿透

🎧 MP3 1-37

perforate / penetrate / pierce / puncture

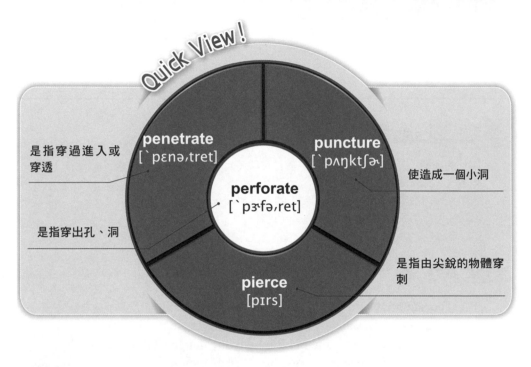

Quick View!

是指穿過進入或穿透

是指穿出孔、洞

penetrate
[`pɛnəˌtret]

puncture
[`pʌŋktʃə]

perforate
[`pɝfəˌret]

pierce
[pɪrs]

使造成一個小洞

是指由尖銳的物體穿刺

---

187 perforate
-perforated-perforated

vi. 穿孔　vt. 穿孔於、打眼於　adj. 穿孔的

- The windshield is bullet-proof, so the bullet can't perforate it.
  這片擋風玻璃是防彈的，子彈無法貫穿。
- Did you live in the age when the conductor would perforate every ticket whenever a passenger got on the bus or the train?
  你有經歷過車掌在乘客上車時替車票打孔的年代嗎？

衍 perforated *adj.* 穿孔的；
perforation *n.* 穿孔；
perforator *n.* 剪票鋏
同 pierce 刺穿、刺破

penetrate
-penetrated-penetrated

vi. 穿入、刺入、透過　*vt.* 穿過、刺入、透過

- The dart penetrated his chest.
  飛鏢穿過他的胸膛。
- It's terrifying for me to penetrate into some unknown regions in Africa.
  我對深入非洲某些未知區域感到很害怕。

衍 penetrating *adj.* 有穿透力的；
penetration *n.* 穿透；
penetrative *adj.* 動人心弦的；
penetrant *adj.* 穿透的；
penetrator *n.* 滲透物
同 pierce 刺穿、刺破
片 penetrate with 以某物穿刺；
penetrate into 刺入

pierce
-pierced-pierced

vi. 穿入、進入、透入　*vt.* 刺穿、刺破

- Pierce the potato before baking it.
  烤馬鈴薯前要先在上面刺洞。
- Many girls have their ears pierced for the sake of beauty.
  許多女生因為愛美去穿耳洞。

衍 piercer *n.* 刺穿者；
piercing *adj.* 尖厲的；
piercingly *adv.* 刺透地
同 penetrate 穿入、刺入、透過
組 piercing scream 刺耳的叫聲；
have one's ears pierced 穿耳洞
片 pierce into 突破

puncture
-punctured-punctured

vi. 被刺穿、被戳破　*vt.* 刺穿、戳破　*n.* 穿刺

- She punctured the balloon with a pin.
  她用別針刺氣球。
- A spear went through the man's ribs and punctured his lung.
  一根長茅穿過男子的肋骨刺穿了他的肺。
- My tire got a hole on it. It must have been punctured by something sharp on the road.
  我輪胎上有個洞。一定是被路上某個尖銳物品給刺破的。

衍 punctuator *n.* 加標點者；
punctual *adj.* 準時的；
punctually *adv.* 準時地；
punctuation *n.* 標點
同 pierce 刺穿、刺破
近 acupuncture *n.* 針灸
組 lumbar puncture 腰椎穿刺

聯想學習Plus

- 碼頭（pier）附近有一家幫人穿耳洞（pierce）的刺青店。
- 醫生用細針（thin needles）在皮膚表面扎針（puncture）的治療方式，中國人稱之為針灸（acupuncture）。

小試身手UP

（　　）1. The archaeological team ＿＿＿＿＿ the jungle and arrived at a primitive tribe.
　　　　(A) penetrated　(B) pierced　(C) perforated　(D) punctuated

（　　）2. You can use a puncher to ＿＿＿＿＿ these sheets of paper and make them together with a string.
　　　　(A) perforate　(B) puncture　(C) pierce　(D) penetrate

1. (A)　考古團隊越過叢林來到了一座原始部落。
2. (A)　你可以用打孔機在這些紙頁上打洞，再用繩子將它們串起。

38 Lesson 請求

MP3 1-38

apply / beg / beseech / entreat / implore / plead

Quick View!

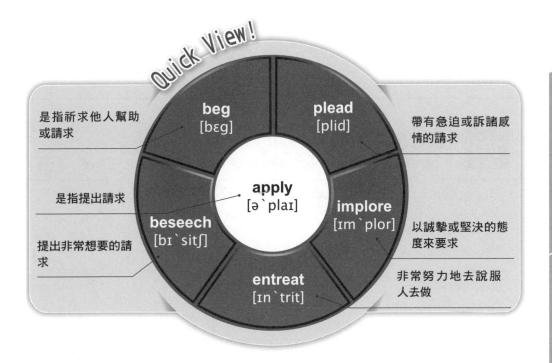

- **beg** [bɛg] — 是指祈求他人幫助或請求
- **plead** [plid] — 帶有急迫或訴諸感情的請求
- **apply** [ə`plaɪ] — 是指提出請求
- **beseech** [bɪ`sitʃ] — 提出非常想要的請求
- **implore** [ɪm`plor] — 以誠摯或堅決的態度來要求
- **entreat** [ɪn`trit] — 非常努力地去說服人去做

191 apply
-applied-applied

vi. 申請、請求　vt. 應用於

- Mr. Kane is applying for jobs across the country.
  肯恩先生在全國各處找工作。
- Apply some lip balm to the lips, or they will go dry.
  塗些護唇膏吧,不然嘴巴會乾裂的。

衍 applicant *n.* 申請人;
application *n.* 應用、申請、應用程式

近 supply *v.* 供應;reply *v.* 回覆

組 Department of Applied Foreign Languages 應用外文系

片 apply for 請求得到;
apply to 申請、適用於

192 beg
-begged-begged

vi. 請求、懇求　vt. 乞討

- The vagrant sat there and begged for some coins from passersby.
  流浪漢坐在那裡，向路過的行人乞討零錢。
- I beg your pardon. What did you just say?
  抱歉，你剛才說了什麼？

衍 beggar *n.* 乞丐
同 appeal 呼籲、懇求
組 begging letter 討錢信
片 beg off 請求免除；
beg the question 迴避問題；
beg one's pardon 請求原諒；
go begging 剩餘的、沒人要的

193 beseech
-beseeched/besought-beseeched/besought

vi. 乞求　vt. 懇求

- The queen beseeched the knight to kill the dragon.
  皇后請求騎士殺死巨龍。
- The mother besought her son not to join the army.
  那名母親哀求兒子不要去從軍。
- Do me a favor, I beseech you.
  幫幫我吧，我求你了。

衍 beseechingly *adv.* 懇求地
同 beg 請求、懇求

194 entreat
-entreated-entreated

vi. 懇求、乞求、請求　vt. 懇求、乞求、請求

- I entreated him not to tell anyone my secret.
  我拜託他不要告訴別人我的祕密。
- The killer entreated for the forgiveness of the victim's family.
  兇手乞求被害者家屬的原諒。

衍 entreatingly *adv.* 懇求地；
entreaty *n.* 懇求、乞求
同 beg 請求、懇求
近 treat *v.* 治療、款待、對待；
entrant *n.* 進入者、新學員
片 entreat for 懇求……

195 | implore
-implored-implored

vi. 懇求、乞求、請求　vt. 懇求、乞求、請求

- He implored his friend's help with the matter.
  他拜託朋友幫忙這件事。
- The man made a confession and implored for God's mercy.
  男子告解，乞求上帝垂憐。

衍 imploringly *adv.* 懇求地；
imploration *n.* 懇求
同 plead 懇求
近 explore *v.* 探險、探查

196 | plead
-pled/pleaded-pled/pleaded

vi. 懇求　vt. 辯護、作為答辯提出

- The students pleaded with the teacher to turn on the air-conditioner.
  學生們拜託老師開冷氣。
- I once heard him plead for his innocence in court.
  我曾聽過他在法庭上為自己的清白辯護。

衍 pleader *n.* 請願者；
pleading *n.* 請求、懇求；
pleadingly *adv.* 祈求地
同 beseech 懇求、哀求
組 special pleading 特別申訴
片 plead for 請求；
plead innocent / guilty 辯稱無罪／坦承有罪

小試身手UP↑

( ) 1. Some seniors begin to _____ for a job and some prepare for the institute studies.
　(A) beg　(B) plead　(C) apply　(D) implore
( ) 2. We can hear that there are some people pretending piteous to obtain public sympathy by _____.
　(A) begging　(B) applying　(C) pleading　(D) imploring

1. (C) 有些大四生會開始找工作，有些則為升上研究所而準備。
2. (A) 我們常聽到有些假裝可憐的人藉由乞討來獲得公眾的同情。

恢復

🎧 MP3 1-39

rally / recover / recuperate / regain / retrieve / revive

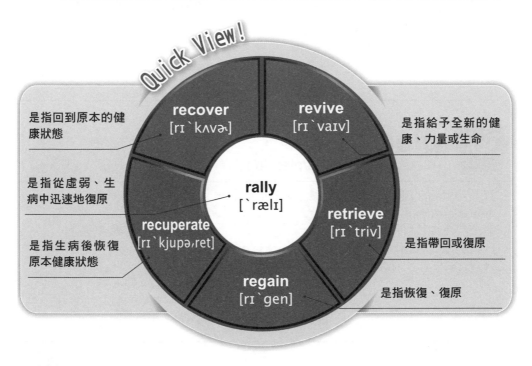

Quick View!

是指回到原本的健康狀態 — **recover** [rɪ`kʌvɚ]

revive [rɪ`vaɪv] — 是指給予全新的健康、力量或生命

是指從虛弱、生病中迅速地復原

rally [`rælɪ]

recuperate [rɪ`kjupəˌret]

retrieve [rɪ`triv] — 是指帶回或復原

是指生病後恢復原本健康狀態

regain [rɪ`gen]

是指恢復、復原

197 | rally
-rallied-rallied

vi. 恢復、復元　vt. 重新振作、恢復　n. 大會

- After a week of fever, the patient rallied and began eating.
  經過一週高燒，病患已經慢慢復原可再度進食。
- After a couple of days of meditation, he finally rallied from his failure in business.
  在經過兩天的沉思之後，他終於從事業失敗的打擊中振作起來了。

同 recover 恢復、使恢復原狀
組 pep rally 鼓舞士氣的集會；
   rallying cry 召喚
片 rally around 集結支持；
   rally to 集結支持

recover
-recovered-recovered

vi. 恢復健康、恢復原狀、恢復　vt. 恢復

- She came home from the hospital after recovering from her illness.
  病好了後她就從醫院返家。
- Lisa finally recovered from SARS and was discharged from the hospital.
  麗莎終於治好 SARS 出院了。

衍 recoverable *adj.* 可恢復的；
recovery *n.* 重獲
同 regain 取回、收回、收復、恢復
反 lose 使失去
組 recovery room 恢復室
片 recover from 自疾病或異常狀態恢復

---

recuperate
-recuperated-recuperated

vi. 恢復、挽回　vt. 恢復、挽回

- He is recuperating from the measles.
  他麻疹病情正逐漸好轉。
- To recuperate her loss, the employee sued her company for breaching the contract.
  員工為討回損失，控訴公司違反合約。

衍 recuperation *n.* 恢復、挽回；
recuperative *adj.* 具恢復力的；
recuperator *n.* 恢復者
片 recuperate from 從……恢復

---

regain
-regained-regained

vt. 取回、收回、收復、恢復

- He regained his balance on the tightrope.
  他在鋼索上重新找到平衡。
- The national government attempted to regain control of the nation from rebel forces.
  國民政府試圖從叛軍手中取回國家政權。
- Little by little he regains his health by regular exercise and a light diet.
  藉由規律的運動與清淡的飲食，他逐漸恢復健康。

同 recover 恢復、使恢復原狀
近 gain *v.* 得到；
grain *n.* 穀粒、細粒
片 regain one's nerve 重新鼓起勇氣；
regain one's balance / footing 恢復平衡／重新站穩

生活常用

學校工作

情緒心智

社會萬象

201 retrieve
-retrieved-retrieved

vi.（獵犬等）銜回獵物　vt. 使恢復　n. 恢復

- The lifeguard retrieved my glasses from the bottom of the pool.
  救生員從池底取回我的眼鏡。
- Once the hunter shot his prey, he sent all his dogs to retrieve it.
  獵戶一射中獵物，就派出全部的狗兒去拾回。

衍 retriever *n.* 找回東西者；
retrieval *n* 取回、恢復；
retrievable *adj.* 可恢復的
同 recover 恢復、使恢復原狀
組 Golden Retriever 黃金獵犬；
Labrador Retriever 拉布拉多獵犬
片 retrieve from 從⋯⋯尋回

202 revive
-revived-revived

vi. 恢復精力、復元、恢復生機　vt. 使甦醒

- The rain shower revived the crops.
  陣雨過後復甦了作物。
- A hot bath revived the cold, tired traveler.
  熱水澡讓這個又冷又累的旅人重新活了過來。

衍 reviver *n.* 興奮劑；
revivalist *n..* 信仰復興運動者；
revivify *v.* 使復活；
revival *n.* 甦醒；
revivable *adj.* 可復活的
近 vive *int.*【法】萬歲！
組 revival meeting 復興布道會

小試身手UP

（　）1. It took a few weeks for Jean to ＿＿＿＿ from her illness.
　　　(A) recover　(B) retriever　(C) regaining　(D) revival
（　）2. After their mistake, the bank worked hard to ＿＿＿＿ my trust.
　　　(A) regain　(B) uncover　(C) recover　(D) revive
（　）3. The hunter's dog was trained to ＿＿＿＿ ducks.
　　　(A) retrieve　(B) revive　(C) recover　(D) regain

1. (A) 珍從病倒到復原花了數個星期。
2. (A) 有了這次疏失，銀行盡力再次獲得我的信任。
3. (A) 獵人的狗被訓練來找回鴨子。

PART 2

學校工作
School & Work

衍 衍生字　同 同義字　反 反義字　近 近型字　組 組合字　片 片語

Lesson 1

表示

connote / describe / express / hint / imply / signal

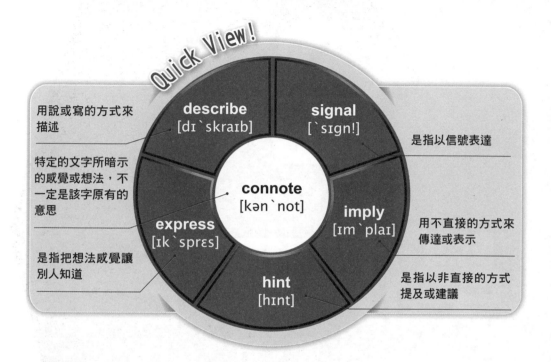

Quick View!

用說或寫的方式來描述 — **describe** [dɪ`skraɪb]

signal [`sɪgn!] — 是指以信號表達

特定的文字所暗示的感覺或想法，不一定是該字原有的意思

connote [kən`not]

imply [ɪm`plaɪ] — 用不直接的方式來傳達或表示

express [ɪk`sprɛs]

是指以非直接的方式提及或建議

是指把想法感覺讓別人知道

hint [hɪnt]

connote
-connoted-connoted

vt. 意味著、暗示

- The word "beach" often connotes happy times in warm sunshine.
  「沙灘」這個字有夏日歡樂時光的意涵。
- To me, having a smoke after meals connotes not only relaxation but also satisfaction.
  對我而言，飯後一根煙不僅意味著放鬆，還有滿足的意涵。

衍 connotative *adj.* 隱含的；
connotation *n.* 言外之意

近 intonate *v.* 語調

2 describe
-described-described

vt. 描寫、描繪、敘述

- He described the costumes shown in the movie to all of his friends.
  他將電影中出現的戲服描述給他所有的朋友聽。
- The politician described himself as the savior to our society.
  那位政治人物把自己形容成社會的救星。

衍 describable *adj.* 可描寫的；
description *n.* 描寫；
descriptive *adj.* 描寫的；
descriptor *n.* 描述符號
同 characterize 描繪……的特性
近 prescribe *v.* 開處方、規定
片 describe as 形容成；
describe to 向某人描述

生活常用

3 express
-expressed-expressed

vt. 表達、陳述、表示　*n.* 快車　*adj.* 快遞的

- Her big smile expressed her happiness and gratitude.
  看到她燦爛的笑容就知道她的高興與感激。
- If you send the parcel by express delivery, it will be faster than usual.
  如果你用快遞寄包裹的話，會比平常快一些。

衍 expresser *n.* 表達者；
expressible *adj.* 可表達的；
expression *n.* 表達、表示；
expressional *adj.* 表現的
反 suppress 壓制、隱瞞
組 express mail 快信；
express train 特快列車；
beyond expression 無法表達

學校工作

4 hint
-hinted-hinted

vi. 作暗示、示意　*vt.* 暗示、示意　*n.* 暗示

- She hinted that she wanted a new pair of shoes.
  她暗示她想要一雙新鞋。
- What are you hinting at? Why not tell me directly?
  你在暗示什麼？為什麼不直接告訴我？
- Jason's dropped some hints to his boss that he would quit if he doesn't get a raise.
  傑森暗示他老闆好幾次，若再不給他加薪他就要離職。

同 imply 暗指
片 drop a hint 稍微暗示；
hint to 暗示；
hint at 暗指；
take a hint 收到暗示

情緒心智

社會萬象

5 | imply
-implied-implied

vt. 暗指、暗示、意味著

- When she said that the floor was dirty, she was implying that I should mop it.
  當她說地板髒了時，她是在暗示我應該擦地板了。
- I noticed some implied discontent by the way she spoke.
  我注意到她說話的方式隱含著不滿。

衍 implied *adj.* 含蓄的；
impliedly *adv.* 隱含地；
implication *n.* 含意；
implicit *adj.* 含蓄的
同 hint 暗示
組 implied volatility 隱含價格波動率；
by implication 含蓄地

6 | signal
-signaled-signaled

vi. 發信號　vt. 用信號發出　n. 暗號

- The horn signaled the end of the game.
  號角響起表示比賽結束了。
- The tour guide signaled to the people walking behind that they were going the wrong way.
  導遊示意走在後面的人走錯了路。

衍 signaler *n.* 信號裝置；
signalize *v.* 發信號；
signally *adv.* 顯著地
同 alert 使注意
組 signal box 信號所；
time signal 報時信號；
signal tower 信號塔；
traffic signal 交通號誌

小試身手UP

( ) 1. According to his detailed _____, I could get a vivid picture of the place.
　　(A) implication　(B) hint　(C) connotation　(D) description
( ) 2. The president's speech _____ his ideas on education.
　　(A) signaled　(B) expressed　(C) designed　(D) intonated
( ) 3. The teacher _____ the class how to do the sand pictures.
　　(A) signaled　(B) expressed　(C) showed　(D) hinted

Ans
1. (D) 根據他鉅細靡遺的描述，我對那個地方有了清晰的畫面。
2. (B) 總統的演講裡闡述了他對教育的看法。
3. (C) 老師向學生示範了如何做沙畫。

建立

🎧 MP3 2-02

build / construct / form / found / establish / make

Quick View!

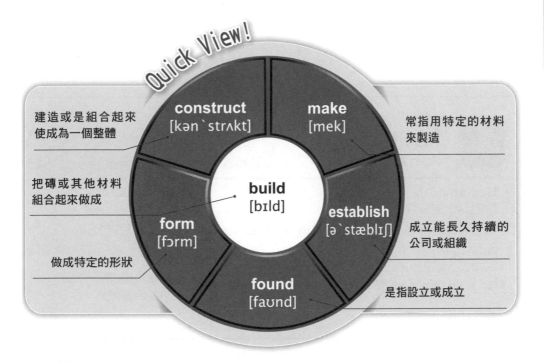

- 建造或是組合起來使成為一個整體 → **construct** [kən`strʌkt]
- **make** [mek] → 常指用特定的材料來製造
- 把磚或其他材料組合起來做成
- **build** [bɪld]
- **establish** [ə`stæblɪʃ] → 成立能長久持續的公司或組織
- **form** [fɔrm]
- 做成特定的形狀
- **found** [faʊnd] → 是指設立或成立

---

7 | build
-built-built

vt. 建造　vi. 建造、建築　n. 體型

- We're going to build a tree house.
  我們將造一間樹屋。
- People who build houses belong to the working class.
  蓋房子的人屬於工人階級。

衍 building *n.* 建築物；
builder *n.* 建築者

組 well-built 堅固的；
built-in 嵌入的；
building block 基礎材料；
jerry-builder 偷工減料的建造商；
building contractor 建築承包商

construct
-constructed-constructed

- They constructed the garage in three days.
  他們花了三天打造車庫。
- The construction of the highway is still in progress.
  公路的建設還在進行中。

衍 construable *adj.* 能解釋的；
constructer *n.* 建設者；
construction *n.* 建造；
constructional *adj.* 構造的

組 construction in progress 在建工程；under construction 建構中；
construction management 施工管理

form
-formed-formed

vi. 成形、被形成　vt. 形成、構成、塑造　n. 外形

- He formed the clay into a pot.
  他把黏土捏成罐子。
- Class, form these letters into a sentence, please.
  同學們，請把這些字母組成一個句子。

Tip in the form of + N 是指「以……的形式」的意思。

衍 formal *adj.* 正式的；
formally *adv.* 正式地；
formation *n.* 形成

同 make 製造

組 life form 生物；
re-form 再編成；
clipped form 縮寫

found
-founded-founded

vt. 建立、建造　vi. 被建立在

- In 1857, Dr. Elizabeth Blackwell founded a hospital run by women.
  1857 年，伊麗莎白·布萊克威爾博士設立第一家由女性管理的醫院。
- The library was founded in 2001.
  這間圖書館是 2001 年建立的。

衍 foundation *n.* 建立；
founded *adj.* 有基礎的；
founder *n.* 創立者；
founding *adj.* 發起的

同 establish *v.* 建立

組 well-found 設備完善的；
all found 膳宿全部供給；
lost-and-found 失物招領處

establish
-established-established

vt. 建立、設立、創辦

- He established a new club.
  他成立一家新俱樂部。
- Mom established a home rule, and every one of us had to follow it.
  媽制定了一套家規，我們每一個人都要遵守。

衍 established *adj.* 已建立的；
   establishment *n.* 建立
同 build 建築、造
反 ruin 毀滅
組 well-established 信譽卓著的

make
-made-made

vi. 正要做   *vt.* 做、製造、建造   *n.* 品牌

- Tommy made a model airplane.
  湯米做了一架模型飛機。
- It's against the rules of the company to make private calls during work hours.
  在上班時間打私人電話是違反公司規定的。

衍 making *n.* 製造；
   maker *n.* 製作者
同 build 建築、造
組 makeup 補考；
   film-maker 電影攝製者；
   trouble-maker 惹麻煩的人
片 make a living 謀生；
   make no difference 沒差別

小試身手UP

(   ) 1. The big shopping mall is under _____, and it will be done in the next year.
   (A) making   (B) formation   (C) building   (D) construction
(   ) 2. Stop _____ so much noise!
   (A) making   (B) building   (C) constructing   (D) establishing
(   ) 3. They _____ a table out of wood.
   (A) formed   (B) made   (C) constructed   (D) established

1. (D) 大型購物商場正在施工中，來年才竣工。
2. (A) 別再製造這麼多噪音！
3. (B) 他們利用木頭製作一張桌子。

戰勝

🎧 MP3 2-03

prevail / overcome / succeed / win

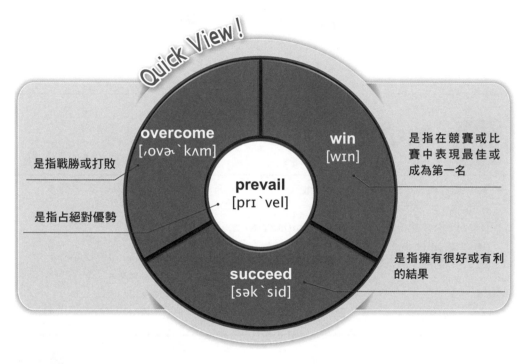

Quick View !

overcome
[ˌovɚˋkʌm]

是指戰勝或打敗

是指占絕對優勢

win
[wɪn]

是指在競賽或比賽中表現最佳或成為第一名

prevail
[prɪˋvel]

是指擁有很好或有利的結果

succeed
[səkˋsid]

---

13 | prevail
-prevailed-prevailed

vi. 勝過、戰勝、盛行

- We prevailed over hardship.
  我們戰勝了困境。
- We finally prevailed on Linda to go picnicking with us.
  我們最後說服了琳達跟我們一起去野餐。

Tip prevail on sb. to-V 是指「說服某人去做某事」之意。

衍 prevailing *adj.* 占優勢的；
  prevalence *n.* 流行；
  prevalent *adj.* 流行的
同 predominate 占主導（或支配）地位
片 prevail on 說服；
  prevail upon 勸說；
  prevail with 勸說

14 overcome
-overcame-overcome

vi. 得勝　vt. 戰勝、克服

- He overcame many obstacles.
  他克服了許多障礙。
- Don't resign yourself to fate. You should overcome it.
  不要屈服於命運，你要克服它。
- The mother was overcome with sorrow for losing her only child.
  這名母親因為失去獨子而悲不自勝。

同 defeat 戰勝
反 lose 輸去；
　 yield 讓步、屈服
近 outcome n. 結果

15 succeed
-succeeded-succeeded

vi. 成功、獲得成效　vt. 接續

- No one thought he would succeed in running a business.
  沒有人認為他能成功經營一間公司。
- Paul succeeded his father as principal of the school.
  保羅接替他父親成為校長。

衍 succeeding adj. 後繼的；
　 success n. 成功；
　 successful adj. 成功的；
　 succession n. 連續
反 fail 不及格；lose 失敗
組 success story 一個人的成名史
片 succeed in 成功；
　 succeed to 繼承

16 win
-won-won

vi. 獲勝、成功　vt. 在……中獲勝　n. 成功

- Our school team won the state basketball championship.
  我們籃球校隊贏得州際盃冠軍。
- Full of confidence, Amy determined to win the ballet contest.
  艾咪充滿自信，決心要贏得芭蕾舞比賽。

衍 winning n. 獲勝；
　 winner n. 獲勝者；
　 winnings n. 贏得的錢
反 lose 輸去
組 award-winning 獲獎的；
　 win-win 雙贏的
片 win back 重獲；
　 win the day 獲勝

生活常用

學校工作

情緒心智

社會萬象

聯想學習Plus

- win 在古英語是指奮力掙扎或努力工作之意，winner 便是指贏得比賽的人。
- 不論是中樂透（win the lottery）還是得頭彩（hit the jackpot），都是人生一大樂事。

小試身手UP↑

（　）1. _____ or lose, you are a respectable opponent to me.
　　　(A) Succeed　(B) Prevail　(C) Overcame　(D) Win

（　）2. The plague _____ over the city.
　　　(A) overcome　(B) prevailed　(C) won　(D) conquered

（　）3. People who _____ must have some characteristics for us to learn.
　　　(A) succeed　(B) win　(C) prevail　(D) overcome

1. (D) 不論輸贏，你都是我可敬的對手。
2. (B) 城市瘟疫盛行。
3. (A) 成功的人必定具備某些我們值得學習的特質。

教導

🎧 MP3 2-04

educate / instruct / teach / train

Quick View!

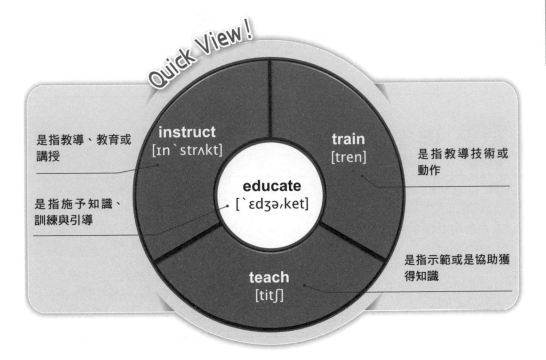

是指教導、教育或講授 —— **instruct** [ɪn`strʌkt]

是指施予知識、訓練與引導

educate [`ɛdʒə,ket]

train [tren] —— 是指教導技術或動作

是指示範或是協助獲得知識

teach [titʃ]

---

17 | educate
-educated-educated

vt. 教育

- A teacher's job is to educate students.
  老師的工作就是教育學生。
- Grace, born in Korea, was educated in Japan.
  葛瑞絲在韓國出生,在日本受教育。

衍 educated *adj.* 受過教育的; education *n.* 教育

同 teach 教、講授、訓練

組 wll-educated 接受良好教育的; re-educate 再教育; physical education 體育

18 instruct
-instructed-instructed

vt. 教授、訓練、指導

- Don't panic. Follow my instructions, and I promise all of you will be out of here safe and sound.
別驚慌,遵循我的指示,我保證你們全都能安然無恙地離開。
- The teacher instructed me in the chemistry research.
老師指導我做化學研究。

衍 instruction n. 教學、指示;
instructive adj. 有教育意義的;
instructor n. 指導者;
instructively adv. 教育地
同 educate 教育
近 construct 建造
片 instruct sb. in... 教導某人某事

19 teach
-taught-taught

vi. 教、講授、當老師　vt. 教、講授、訓練

- He taught his class how to add and subtract.
他教學生如何算加法與減法。
- I remember teaching you how to be a good student.
我記得教過你如何做個好學生。
- Teaching is a kind of career, and teacher is a kind of job.
教育是一種行業,而教師則是一種職業。

衍 teaching n. 教學、講授;
teachability n. 可教性;
teachable adj. 適於教學的;
teacher n. 教師
組 self-taught 自修的;
teach-in 辯論;
teaching staff 教育工作者
片 teach sb. a lesson 教訓某人

20 train
-trained-trained

vi. 接受訓練、鍛鍊　vt. 訓練、培養　n. 火車

- He trained his dog to heel.
他訓練他的狗隨行。
- Some dogs can be trained to guide the blind.
有些狗可以被訓練做導盲犬。

衍 training n. 訓練、鍛鍊、培養;
trainee n. 練習生;
trainable adj. 可訓練的
同 teach 教、講授、訓練
組 training camp 集訓營;
bullet train 高速火車;
non-stop train 直達列車
片 lose one's train of thought 遺忘

聯想學習Plus

- lose one's train of thought 是指某人的思路突然中斷，一時之間忘記自己正在想什麼或說什麼的意思，train of 是一連串、一系列的意思，thought 在這裡是「思考、想法」，為名詞。
- ride the gravy train 的 gravy 在此處不作「肉汁」解釋，而是「不花力氣而得來的錢財」，因此說一個人 ride the gravy train，意思是說對方沒有付出勞力就有很多財富的意思。

小試身手UP

( ) 1. Being _____ is still a dream for children in developing countries.
　　(A) educated　(B) teaching　(C) taught　(D) instructed

( ) 2. The animals in the circus are _____ to play tricks to amuse the audience.
　　(A) instructed　(B) trained　(C) teaching　(D) educated

1. (A) 受教育對於發展中國家的孩童而言仍是一種夢想。
2. (B) 馬戲團裡的動物被訓練雜耍以娛樂觀眾。

引領

🎧 MP3 2-05

conduct / direct / guide / head / lead / preside

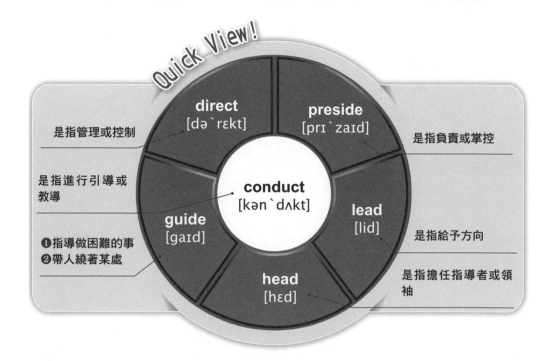

Quick View!

direct [də`rɛkt]
是指管理或控制
是指進行引導或教導

preside [prɪ`zaɪd]
是指負責或掌控

conduct [kən`dʌkt]

guide [gaɪd]
❶指導做困難的事
❷帶人繞著某處

lead [lid]
是指給予方向
是指擔任指導者或領袖

head [hɛd]

---

21 conduct
-conducted-conducted

vi. 引導、帶領　vt. 引導、帶領　n. 行為

- The guide conducted his members to their rooms in the hotel.
  導遊領著他的團員到飯店房間。
- The university is conducting a survey on students having part-time jobs.
  這所大學正在調查有打工的學生。

衍 conductive *adj.* 傳導（性）的；
conduction *n.* 傳導；
conductor *n.* 車掌、領導人、指揮、導體

同 lead 引導、領（路）

組 code of conduct 行為準則；
disorderly conduct 脫序、目無法紀的行為

direct
-directed-directed

vi. 指導、指揮　*vt.* 指揮、主持、管理　*adj.* 直接的

- The captain directed his men to prepare for starting off.
  船長命令手下準備啟航。
- My teacher directed me to hold a class meeting the next Friday.
  老師命我主持下週五的班會。

衍 direction *n.* 指導；
directional *adj.* 指向性的；
directive *adj.* 管理的；
director *n.* 導演
反 indirect 間接的
組 direct flight 直飛航線；
direct current 直流電
片 direct sb. to do sth. 命令某人做某事

guide
-guided-guided

vt. 引導、指導　*vi.* 擔任嚮導　*n.* 導遊

- The librarian guided us to the shelf displaying the books about Asian snakes.
  圖書館員帶我們到陳列亞洲蛇類的書架前。
- He was considered a hero for guiding his team to triumph.
  他帶領隊伍獲得勝利，被認為是英雄。

衍 guidance *n.* 指導、引導；
guidable *adj.* 可引導的；
guiding *adj.* 指導性的
反 misguide 把……引入歧途
組 guide dog 導盲犬；
guided missile 導向飛彈
片 guide sb. to a place 引導某人到某地

head
-headed-headed

vi. 出發　*vt.* 作為……的首領、率領　*n.* 頭

- He heads the children's reading program.
  他主導兒童閱讀的計畫。
- There is always a sled dog heading the other dogs to their destination.
  總有一隻領頭的雪橇犬帶領其他狗兒前進方向。

衍 heading *n.* 頁首文字；
headed *adj.* 有頭的
同 lead 領導
組 head-hunting 獵人頭、挖角；
head office 總公司、總部；
headline 頭條新聞
片 head the list 名列首位；
head for 走向

生活常用

學校工作

情緒心智

社會萬象

25 lead
-led-led

vi. 領導　vt. 領導、指揮、率領　n. 指導、鉛

- He led us through the woods.
  他帶領我們穿越樹林。
- Carelessness may lead to accidents.
  粗心會導致意外。
- What a close call. Their team led only by one point.
  多麼驚險啊！他們的隊伍只以一分領先。

衍 leading *adj.* 領導的；
leader *n.* 領導者、指揮者；
leadership *n.* 領導
反 follow 跟隨
組 leading role 主角
片 lead astray 把……引入歧途；
lead the way 帶路；
follow sb.'s lead 效法某人

26 preside
-presided-presided

vi. 管轄、指揮、主持

- Ms. Hawkes presides over all the staff meetings.
  霍克絲女士掌控所有的員工會議。
- Mr. Lin will preside over B&F Company from March 20th.
  林先生從三月二十號開始掌管 B&F 公司。

衍 presidence *n.* 管理；
presidency *n.* 美國總統職位；
president *n.* 總統、董事長；
presider *n.* 主宰者
同 direct 指揮、主持、管理
片 preside at / over 主持、負責

小試身手UP↑

( ) 1. He _____ us through the hotel to our room.
    (A) led　(B) leading　(C) presided　(D) presides
( ) 2. His car is _____ south now.
    (A) led　(B) leading　(C) presided　(D) heading
( ) 3. It's my turn to _____ over the group meeting this time.
    (A) conduct　(B) guide　(C) preside　(D) head

1. (A) 他帶我們穿過飯店到達我們的房間。
2. (D) 他的車正往南行駛。
3. (C) 這次輪到我主持小組會議。

支配

🎧 MP3 2-06

control / dominate / predominate / reign / rein / rule / sway

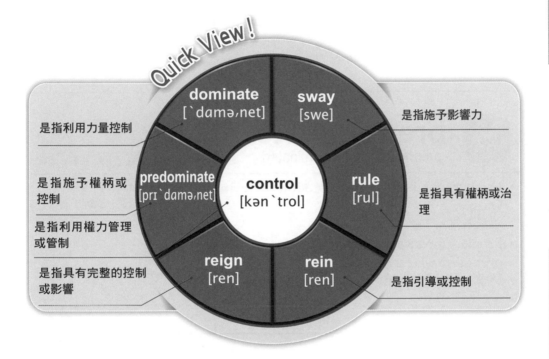

Quick View!

- **dominate** [`dɑmə,net] — 是指利用力量控制
- **sway** [swe] — 是指施予影響力
- **predominate** [prɪ`dɑmə,net] — 是指施予權柄或控制；是指利用權力管理或管制；是指具有完整的控制或影響
- **control** [kən`trol]
- **rule** [rul] — 是指具有權柄或治理
- **reign** [ren]
- **rein** [ren] — 是指引導或控制

---

27 | ## control
-controlled-controlled

vt. 控制、支配、管理　n. 指揮部

- It's common for the ruling party to gain control of the council or even the congress.
  由執政黨來控制議會甚至國會的情況還挺常見的。
- Don't be mad. Please control your temper.
  不要生氣。請控制你的脾氣。

衍 controlled *adj.* 被控制的；
controller *n.* 控制器

組 remote control 遙控（器）；
control tower 塔台；
self-control 自制；
birth control 生育控制；
gun control 槍支管理法

片 control over 控制

28 | dominate
-dominated-dominated

vi. 處於支配地位　*vt.* 支配、統治、控制

- For most women, family always dominates their life.
  對大多數女性而言，家庭永遠是她們的生活重心。
- Do not dominate your children. They are not subordinate to you.
  別對你的孩子展現控制欲，他們不是你的附屬品。

衍 dominance *n.* 優勢；
dominant *adj.* 統治的；
domination *n.* 支配；
dominative *adj.* 統治的；
dominator *n.* 支配者
同 rule 支配
組 male-dominated 男權的

29 | predominate
-predominated-predominated

vi. 占主導（或支配）地位　*vt.* 主宰、支配

- French-speaking people predominate in Quebec.
  說法語的人在魁北克占大多數。
- People who are for this proposal predominate over those who are against it.
  贊成這項提議的人壓倒性超過反對的人。

衍 predominant *adj.* 占優勢的；
predominance *n.* 卓越；
predominantly *adv.* 占主導地位地
同 rule 支配
片 predominate over 壓倒

30 | reign
-reigned-reigned

vi. 支配、盛行、占優勢　*n.* 支配

- Terror reigned over this area during a long time of war.
  長期的戰爭下，這地區已被恐懼所主宰。
- During the reign of the queen, turbulence and famine no longer existed.
  在女王的治領之下，動亂與飢荒不復在。

衍 reigning *adj.* 統治的
同 rule 統治、管轄、控制、支配
組 reign of terror 恐怖統治
片 reign over 統治

31 | rein
-reined-reined

vi. 勒馬、勒住牲口　vt. 駕馭、控制、統治　n. 韁繩

- When I was angry, I would take a deep breath and rein in my temper.
  當我生氣的時候，我會深呼吸，控制我的脾氣。
- The boss gives me free rein as long as I can finish the work he assigns me.
  只要我能完成老闆交代給我的任務，他願意放手讓我去做。

衍 reins *n.* 感情的源泉
同 control 控制、支配、管理
組 bearing rein 勒馬的韁繩
片 draw rein 慢下來；
keep a tight rein on 對……嚴加約束；
rein in 控制、駕馭

---

32 | rule
-ruled-ruled

vi. 統治、管轄　vt. 控制、支配　n. 規則

- In Africa, it's the animal that rules the land.
  在非洲，動物才是統治者。
- Dad makes it a rule to take a walk before breakfast.
  父親有吃早餐前去散步的習慣。

 make it a rule to-V 是指「養成……習慣、習慣於」的意思。

衍 ruler *n.* 統治者、直尺
同 control 控制
組 rule of law 法規；
golden rule 指導原則；
home rule 地方自治
片 rule of thumb 經驗法則；
as a rule 通常；
rule the roost 當家；
against the rules 違反規則

---

33 | sway
-swayed-swayed

vi. 支配、統治　vt. 搖動、影響　n. 搖擺

- Their feelings were powerfully swayed by the speech.
  他們的感受深深被演講影響了。
- That candidate's remarks always held sway over people's hearts.
  那位候選人的言詞總是能左右民眾的心緒。

同 guide 管理、操縱
片 sway back and forth 來回搖擺；under the sway of sb. / sth. 受到……的影響；sway from side to side 左右搖擺；hold sway 占統治地位

 聯想學習Plus

- sway 除了「統治、支配」的意思外，還有「擺盪、搖晃」的意思，想要表達前後、來回、左右搖晃的話，有很多替換詞語如 to and fro（前後）、backwards and forwards（前後）、back and forth（來回、前後）、side to side（左右）等等。
- 跟著音樂擺動身體，可以說 sway to the music。

小試身手UP

（　）1. Due to his cruelty and tyranny, his ＿＿＿＿ was finally overthrown by his people.
　　　(A) reign　(B) dominate　(C) predominate　(D) ruler
（　）2. Everyone should follow the ＿＿＿＿. There is no exception.
　　　(A) controls　(B) dominators　(C) rules　(D) reins

 Ans
1. (A)　由於他殘酷暴虐，他的統治最終被人民推翻了。
2. (C)　每個人都要遵守規定。沒有例外。

7 Lesson 管理

🎧 MP3 2-07

administer / govern / manage / regulate

Quick View!

govern [`gʌvɚn]
是指管理或領導
是指管理、照顧或負責

administer [əd`mɪnəstɚ]

regulate [`rɛgjəˌlet]
是指以法律或方法控制

manage [`mænɪdʒ]
是指指引或控制

---

34 administer
-administered-administered

vi. 擔任管理者　vt. 管理、掌管、經營

• The girl scout leader administers the troop.
女童子軍隊長管理整個小隊。

• He has a head for business management. That's why he is able to administer chain steakhouses.
他很有經商的頭腦。這也是為什麼他可以經營連鎖牛排館。

衍 administrative *adj.* 行政的；administration *n.* 管理
同 manage 管理
組 self-administer 自我管理
片 administer to 幫助、給予

govern
-governed-governed

- The sheik and his family governed the emirate.
  阿拉伯酋長與家人統治這個酋長國。
- The new government repealed the old law.
  新政府廢除了這條舊法。

衍 governable *adj.* 可統治的；
governance *n.* 統治權；
government *n.* 政府、內閣；
governor *n.* 州長
同 regulate 管理、控制
反 misrule 對……治理不當
組 self-governed 獨立的、自治的；
coalition government 聯合政府

manage
-managed-managed

- She manages a bookstore.
  她管理一家書局。
- Sandy was fired because she talked back to her manager.
  珊蒂由於和經理頂嘴被開除了。

衍 management *n.* 管理；
manageable *adj.* 可管理的；
manager *n.* 經理
同 conduct 引導、帶領
組 managing editor 總編輯；
general manager 總經理
片 manage with 用……設法應付過去

regulate
-regulated-regulated

- The government regulates the sale of guns.
  政府管控槍枝的交易。
- Traffic signs regulate efficiently the flow of traffic.
  交通號誌有效控制交通流量。

衍 regulation *n.* 管理、規定；
regulative *adj.* 管制的；
regulator *n.* 管理者
近 regular *adj.* 有規律的、規則的
組 well-regulated 有規則的；
be regulated by law 受法律制約；
rules and regulations 規章制度

**聯想學習Plus**

- 不論是官員（officer）、州長（governor）、市長（mayor）、議員（senator）或是各級部長（minister），都是人民的公僕（public servant）。
- 即便你現在只是一個行政助理（administrative assistant），以後也有機會成為經理（manager）。

小試身手UP

( ) 1. It takes brains to _____ a company, so we need a consultant.
   (A) rule   (B) manage   (C) governor   (D) dominate

Ans　1. (B) 管理一間公司是很花腦力的，所以我們需要管理顧問。

執行

🎧 MP3 2-08

act / enact / execute / function / officiate / operate / perform

Quick View!

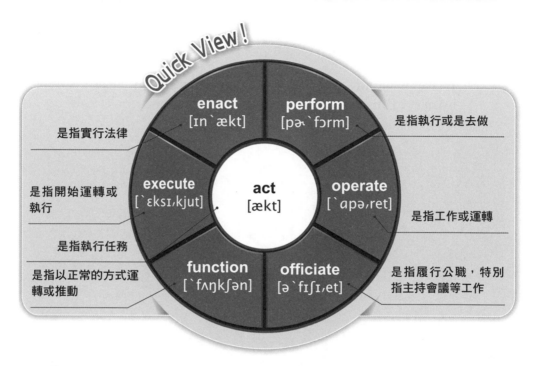

- **enact** [ɪn`ækt] 是指實行法律
- **perform** [pɚ`fɔrm] 是指執行或是去做
- **execute** [`ɛksɪˌkjut] 是指開始運轉或執行；是指執行任務
- **act** [ækt]
- **operate** [`ɑpɚˌret] 是指工作或運轉
- **function** [`fʌŋkʃən] 是指以正常的方式運轉或推動
- **officiate** [ə`fɪʃɪˌet] 是指履行公職，特別指主持會議等工作

---

38 act
-acted-acted

vi. 做事、行動   vt. 裝出、舉動像   n. 行動

- He acted as leader and quickly gave us orders.
  他做起指揮，迅速地給我們下指令。
- Richard decided to act on what his father said to study hard.
  理查決定聽父親的話，好好讀書。
- Acting on impulse will get you in trouble.
  意氣用事只會替你招來麻煩。

衍 acting *n.* 演戲；action *n.* 行動；actor *n.* 男演員；actress *n.* 女演員

同 perform 履行

組 act of God 不可抗力、天災

片 act for 代理；
act upon 對……起作用；
Act your age! 成熟點！

enact
-enacted-enacted

vt. 制定（法律）、實施、頒布

- Congress enacted a bill to protect the water supply.
  國會頒布一項保護水源的法案。
- A package of economic revitalization policies will be enacted in the coming year.
  來年預計實施一系列的經濟振興政策。

衍 enactive *adj.* 制定法律的；enactment *n.* （法律的）制定、律法；enactory *adj.* 制定法律的

同 perform 履行

組 re-enact 重新制定

生活常用

execute
-executed-executed

vt. 實施、實行、執行、處刑

- The gymnast executed her routine perfectly.
  體操選手完美地執行她的固定動作。
- Those who commit serious crimes should be executed.
  那些犯重罪的人應被處死。

衍 executer *n.* 實行；execution *n.* 完成；executive *adj.* 執行的；

組 carry into execution 實施；executive officer 執行官；chief executive officer (= CEO) 執行長

學校工作

function
-functioned-functioned

vi. 運轉、起作用　n. 作用

- The city cannot function without electricity.
  城市沒有電無法運轉。
- A stone can function as a weapon.
  石頭可以用來做武器。
- If the television doesn't function, check out the antenna.
  如果電視不能看，檢查天線看看吧。

衍 functional *adj.* 在起作用的；functionality *n.* 官能、機能；functionally *adv.* 功能地

同 operate 運作

組 function key 功能鍵；multi-function 多功能的；function word 功能詞；bodily functions 生體機能

情緒心智

社會萬象

officiate
-officiated-officiated

vi. 執行職務　vt. 行使（職務）、主持

- The mayor of the town officiates at the meeting once a month.
  鎮長每個月主持會議一次。
- The groom and bride officiated at their wedding by themselves.
  這對新人自己舉行自己的婚禮。

衍 officiary *n.* 一群官員；
　official *n.* 公務員、官員
組 official leave 公假
片 officiate as 擔任

---

operate
-operated-operated

vi. 作出、工作、運作、運轉　vt. 操作

- This battery-powered sewing machine can operate for several hours.
  這個電池驅動的縫紉機可以運轉好幾個小時。
- Sam has a great capacity for mechanics. He can easily operate different kinds of electronic devices.
  山姆對機械很在行，他可以很輕鬆地操縱不同類型的電子儀器。

衍 operating *adj.* 操作的；
　operation *n.* 操作；
　operator *n.* 操作者
組 operating room 手術室；
　co-operate 合作；
　standard operating procedure (= SOP) 標準作業程序
片 operate on sb. 替某人開刀

---

perform
-performed-performed

vi. 行動、表現　vt. 履行、執行、完成、做

- He performed all the assigned tasks.
  他執行所有被交辦的任務。
- Judging from his poor performance, he'll be fired soon.
  從他差勁的表現可知，他快要被開除了。

衍 performance *n.* 演出；
　performer *n.* 表演者
同 act 做事、行動
反 neglect 忽略
片 perform an operation 動手術；
　perform a miracle 製造奇蹟

聯想學習Plus

- 機器要常常保養（maintain），才不會發生故障（malfunction）。
- 中華民國的五院分別為行政院（Executive Yuan）、立法院（Legislative Yuan）、司法院（Judical Yuan）、考試院（The Examination Yuan）、監察院（The Control Yuan）。行政院下常見的部會有內政（Interior）、交通（Transportation and Communication）、文化（Culture）、外交（Foreign Affairs）、國防（National Defense）、教育（Education）、法務（Justice）、經濟（Economic Affairs）、衛福（Health and Welfare）、財政（Finance）等。

小試身手UP

（　）1. Computers which exceeds humans in calculation can ＿＿＿＿ a variety of tasks at the same time
　　　 (A) operation　(B) perform　(C) conduct　(D) construct

（　）2. Being short of battery, the portable radio doesn't ＿＿＿＿.
　　　 (A) be operated　(B) be executed　(C) process　(D) function

1. (B)　運算方面優於人腦的電腦可以同時執行多項工作。
2. (D)　由於電池耗盡，手提收音機沒辦法收聽了。

Lesson 9

計算

MP3 2-09

count / calculate / estimate / evaluate / figure / number / reckon

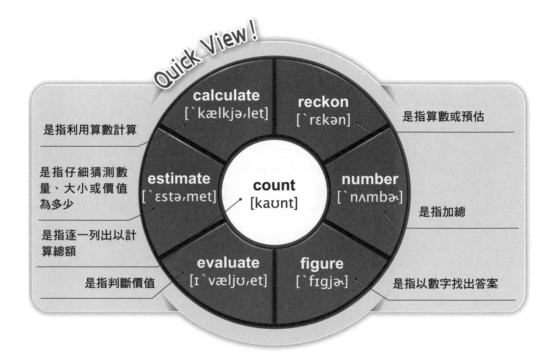

Quick View !

calculate [`kælkjə,let]
是指利用算數計算

reckon [`rɛkən]
是指算數或預估

estimate [`ɛstə,met]
是指仔細猜測數量、大小或價值為多少

count [kaʊnt]

number [`nʌmbɚ]
是指加總

是指逐一列出以計算總額

evaluate [ɪ`væljʊ,et]
是指判斷價值

figure [`fɪgjɚ]
是指以數字找出答案

---

45 | count
-counted-counted

vi. 總計 *vt.* 計算、數 *n.* 計算

- The five-year-old boy could count from 1 to 100.
  這五歲男童可以從 1 數到 100。
- I don't want to count on my parents any more.
  我不想再依靠父母了。
- Can you count how many fireflies there are in this field?
  你可以數出這片田野裡有多少隻螢火蟲嗎？

衍 counter *n.* 計算者；
counting *n.* 計數；
countable *adj.* 可數的
同 total 合計為
組 count noun 可數名詞；
countdown 倒數
片 count in 把……算入；
count out 不把……算在內

calculate
-calculated-calculated

vi. 計算　*vt.* 計算

- He calculated the cost of a dozen oranges at twenty-nine cents each.
  他計算 12 顆柳丁，每顆成本為 29 分美金。
- As a boss, you should know how to calculate tax precisely.
  身為老闆，你應該要知道該如何精確計算稅額。

衍 calculating *adj.* 計算的；
calculation *n.* 計算；
calculator *n.* 計算機
同 count 計算
組 calculating machine 計算機
片 calculate on / upon 指望

estimate
-estimated-estimated

vi. 估計、估價　*vt.* 估計、估量　*n.* 估價、評價

- We estimated our grocery bill before we got to the cashier.
  去結帳前我們先估算了結帳金額。
- It's estimated that the number of people committing suicide goes up year by year.
  據估計，每年自殺的人數都在上升。
- The police estimated there could be five burglars.
  警方估計可能有五名盜賊。

衍 estimable *adj.* 可估價的；
estimation *n.* 評價；
estimative *adj.* 估計的
同 evaluate 估價、評估
片 estimate the cost at + 數字
估算成本為；
make an estimate 估算；
by one's estimate 按估計

evaluate
-evaluated-evaluated

vt. 對……評價、為……鑑定

- Before the new product is on the market, you need to evaluate how it can stand up to wear and tear.
  新產品在上市前，需要評估其耐磨損度。
- Without knowing the cause, we can't evaluate its consequences.
  不知道理由的話，我們無法評估後果。

衍 evaluation *n.* 估價；
evaluative *adj.* 估價的
同 value 估價
組 re-evaluate 再估價；
self evaluate 自我評估

49 figure
-figured-figured

vi. 計算　*vt.* 計算　*n.* 外形、人物、數字

- I am used to figuring how many calories I consume per meal.
  我習慣計算每餐吃進的熱量。
- I infer Jane is poor from her skinny figure.
  我從珍骨瘦如柴的身材，推斷出她很窮困。
- They hire an actuary to figure tax for them.
  他們僱用精算師幫他們計算稅額。

衍 figurative *adj.* 比喻的；
figuration *n.* 成形；
figurable *adj.* 可以定形的

組 full-figured 肥胖的；
father figure 父親般的人物；
figure of speech 修辭

片 figure out 想出、料想；
figure in 把⋯⋯計算在內

---

50 number
-numbered-numbered

vi. 計入、算作　*vt.* 計入、算作　*n.* 數字

- The guests at the party numbered twenty.
  參加派對的賓客有二十人。
- The number of students who fail in exams has reduced since last year.
  考試不及格的學生人數從去年開始已經減少。

衍 numberless *adj.* 無數的；
Numbers *n.*（聖經）民數記

組 number plate 牌照；
number one 自己的利益；
even number 偶數；
odd number 奇數

片 number among 把⋯⋯算作；
number in 把⋯⋯算作

---

51 reckon
-reckoned-reckoned

vi. 計算、數、測量　*vt.* 計算、數

- He reckoned how much he would need to save for a new skateboard.
  他算了一下買新滑板要存多少錢。
- The movie *Titanic* is reckoned to be one of the most romantic movies made.
  電影《鐵達尼號》被視為最浪漫的電影之一。

衍 reckoning *n.* 計算；
reckoner *n.* 計算者

同 judge 判斷

組 day of reckoning 清算時候

片 reckon in 把⋯⋯計算在內；
reckon with 對付；
reckon on 仰賴；
a force to be reckoned with 重要人士

聯想學習Plus

- 一個人的價值（value）是無法用金錢去評估（evaluate）的。
- number 泛指任何數字，如 0、1、2、3……9999 等；figure 也可指「數字」，但大多只指 0、1、2、3……9，超過 10 的話多不用此字；digit 也是另一個描述「數字」的單詞，與其說是數字，卻較常用於表達「……位數」，如 one digit（個位數）、double digit（兩位數）、triple digit（三位數）等，用法上略有差異。
- 學數學，首先要認識加（plus）減（minus）乘（multiply）除（divide）怎麼說喔！

小試身手UP

（　　）1. Teachers use tests to ＿＿＿＿ how much their students have learned.
　　　　 (A) evaluate　 (B) number　 (C) figure　 (D) calculate
（　　）2. Circle 6 ＿＿＿＿ from 1 to 49. If you are lucky, you might hit the jackpot.
　　　　 (A) calculators　 (B) numbers　 (C) digits　 (D) figures

1. (A) 老師利用考試來評量學生學習的程度。
2. (B) 從 1 到 49 的號碼中圈出 6 個號碼。如果你夠幸運，就能中頭彩。

證實

🎧 MP3 2-10

affirm / assure / certify / confirm / ensure / justify / testify

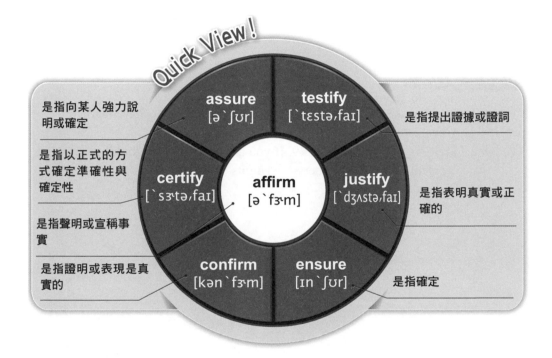

Quick View!

是指向某人強力說明或確定	**assure** [əˋʃʊr]
是指以正式的方式確定準確性與確定性	**certify** [ˋsɝtəˏfaɪ]
是指聲明或宣稱事實	
是指證明或表現是真實的	**confirm** [kənˋfɝm]

testify [ˋtɛstəˏfaɪ]	是指提出證據或證詞
affirm [əˋfɝm]	
justify [ˋdʒʌstəˏfaɪ]	是指表明真實或正確的
ensure [ɪnˋʃʊr]	是指確定

---

52 | affirm
-affirmed-affirmed

vi. 斷言　vt. 證實、確認

- It was affirmed he had a tumor in his lungs.
  他被確診肺部長腫瘤。
- The fortuneteller affirmed that he would get married the next month.
  算命師斷言他下個月就會結婚。

衍 affirmable *adj.* 可斷言的；
　affirmance *n.* 斷言；
　affirmative *adj.* 肯定的；
　affirmation *n.* 斷言
同 confirm 證實、確定
反 deny 否定、否認
近 firm *v.* 使穩固

53 **assure**
-assured-assured

- The hijackers assured the police of the safety of the hostage.
  劫機犯向警方保證人質的人身安全。
- I assure you that you will have my full support.
  我向你保證你可以得到我全力支援。

Tip assure sb. of sth. 是指「向某人保證某事」之意。

衍 assured *adj.* 確定的；
assurer *n.* 保證人；
assurance *n.* 保證
同 guarantee 保證
近 insure 投保、確保；
ensure 保證、擔保
組 rest assured 放心；
life assurance 人壽保險

54 **certify**
-certified-certified

vi. 證明、保證　vt. 證明、證實

- He certified a check with his signature.
  他以簽名保證支票為真。
- See, this is our boss' signature. It certifies that he has agreed.
  看，這是我們老闆的簽字，證明他已經同意了。

衍 certified *adj.* 有保證的；
certification *n.* 證明；
certifier *n.* 保證書；
certificate *n.* 證書、執照
同 testify 作證
組 certificate master 文憑教師；
certified mail 掛號信

55 **confirm**
-confirmed-confirmed

vt. 證實、確定

- You had better call the airline to confirm your flight 48 hours before departure.
  你最好在起飛前 48 小時向航空公司確認你的航班。
- According to the news report, two men were confirmed injured in that accident.
  據新聞報導，目前已證實有兩人在那場意外中受傷。

衍 confirmed *adj.* 確定的；
confirmation *n.* 確定；
confirmative *adj.* 確定的
同 verify 證明、證實
反 deny 否定、否認
組 confirmed case 確診病例

生活常用

學校工作

情緒心智

社會萬象

56 ensure
-ensured-ensured

vt. 保證、擔保

- Those dark clouds ensure rain.
  那些烏雲表示等一下會下雨。
- Wearing the helmet ensures us against getting hurt.
  戴安全帽確保我們不受傷害。

同 assure 保證；
guarantee 保證

近 ensue 接著發生

片 ensure from / against 保護、使安全；ensure sb. sth. 對某人保證某事

57 justify
-justified-justified

vi. 證明合法、辯解　vt. 使正當、替辯護

- The photograph justified his claim that he had met the president.
  照片證實他的確曾與總統會面。
- Every accused has the right to justify himself in court.
  每個被告在法庭上都有為自己辯解的權利。

衍 justified *adj.* 有正當理由的；
justifier *n.* 證明者；
justice *n.* 正義

同 warrant 擔保

反 condemn 宣告有罪、譴責

組 self-justifying 自己辯白的；
justifiable homicide 正當殺人

片 justify oneself 為自己辯解

58 testify
-testified-testified

vi. 作證　vt. 表明、證明

- The witness testified that she had seen the suspect enter the building.
  證人出席作證曾看見嫌犯進入大樓。
- Copernicus' heliocentricism was testified to be true.
  哥白尼的地動說證實為真。

衍 testifier *n.* 證明者；
testification *n.* 證據；
testimony *n.* 證言

片 testify against 作對……不利的證明；
testify to 證實；
testify for 為……作證

 **聯想學習Plus**

- 正義（justice）是經過明確證據（evidence）給證明（justified）出來的，也印證了 Justice has long arms.（法網恢恢，疏而不漏。）這句古諺。

- Justice has long arms. 字面上解讀為「正義有長手臂」，也就是說正義無處不在，犯法便難逃法網制裁，也就是「法網恢恢，疏而不漏」的意思。若把 justice 替換成 kings，寫成 Kings have long arms.，國王有長手臂，就是指國王的權力很大，可以伸及統轄的各個地方，也就是「王權及四海」的意思。

小試身手UP

( ) 1. The document was ＿＿＿＿ with an official seal.
    (A) confirmed   (B) confirm   (C) ensure   (D) certified

( ) 2. I called the airline to ＿＿＿＿ my seat on the flight.
    (A) confirm   (B) certified   (C) confirmed   (D) ensure

 Ans
1. (D) 這份文件有蓋關防加以確認。
2. (A) 我打電話給航空公司確認機位。

聯合

🎧 MP3 2-11

associate / combine / connect / merge / unite

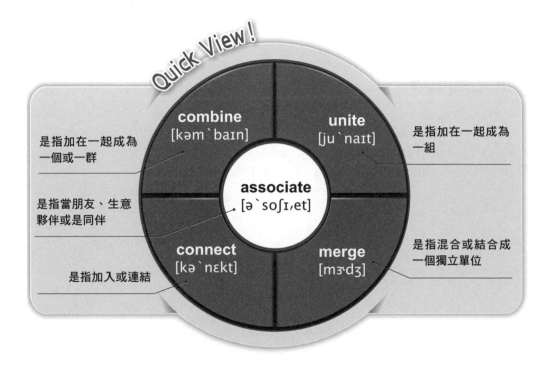

Quick View !

combine [kəm`baɪn]
是指加在一起成為一個或一群

unite [ju`naɪt]
是指加在一起成為一組

associate [ə`soʃɪ,et]

是指當朋友、生意夥伴或是同伴

是指加入或連結

connect [kə`nɛkt]

merge [mɝdʒ]
是指混合或結合成一個獨立單位

---

59 associate
-associated-associated

vi. 結交、交往　*vt.* 使聯合　*n.* 合夥人

• Ms. Black associates with them only at work.
布萊克女士只有工作時跟他們往來。

• If you don't remind me of that matter, I'll never associate these signs with it.
如果你沒有提醒我那件事的話，我絕不會將這些徵兆跟此事聯想在一起的。

衍 associated *adj.* 聯合的；
association *n.* 聯盟；
associative *adj.* 聯合的

反 dissociate 使分離

組 Associated Press 美聯社；
associate professor 副教授

片 associate with 連結、與……有關聯

combine
-combined-combined

- He combined dirt with water to make mud.
  他將土與水和在一起做成泥巴。
- This learning software combines knowledge with amusement.
  這套學習軟體結合了知識和娛樂。

Tip combine A with B 是指「將 A 與 B 結合在一起」。

衍 combined *adj.* 聯合的；
combination *n.* 聯盟；
combinative *adj.* 結合的
反 separate 分隔
組 combining weight 化合量；
combining form 化合體；
combination lock 暗碼鎖
片 combine against 聯合反對

connect
-connected-connected

- I connected the plug to an extension cord.
  我將插頭接到延長線上。
- Trade connections will be helpful to the growth of the economy.
  貿易往來對經濟成長將有所幫助。

Tip connect A to B 是指「將 A 與 B 連接起來」。

衍 connecter *n.* 連接之人或物；
connected *adj.* 有關聯的；
connectible *adj.* 可聯結的；
connection *n.* 銜接
反 disconnect 使分離
片 connect up 接通；
connect with 連接；
in connection with 有⋯⋯連繫、關於

merge
-merged-merged

- The two roads merged into one.
  這兩條路最後併成一條。
- Our company will be merged into a big business group next month.
  我們公司下個月要併入一個大集團。

衍 merger *n.* 合併；
mergence *n.* 結合
同 combine 使結合
組 hostile merger 惡意併吞
片 merge into 使合併；
merge together 混合起來；
merge with 結合

生活常用

學校工作

情緒心智

社會萬象

63 unite
-united-united

- The prime minister united the members of her party.
  總理將黨內成員團結一起。
- United we stand, divided we fall.
  團結則存，分裂則亡。

衍 unit *n.* 單元；
united *adj.* 聯合的；
unitable *adj.* 可聯合的
同 combine 使結合
反 divide 劃分
組 United Arab Emirates 阿拉伯聯合大公國；
United Nations 聯合國

 聯想學習Plus

- connect the dots 其實是一種將點與點連成線後，得出一個圖形的小遊戲，中文就是連線遊戲的意思。賈伯斯曾在演講中數度使用這個片語，當然並非指連線遊戲，而是說，將事情點滴串連起來後，再推敲出答案、線索的意思。

小試身手UP

(　) 1. The remarks he made _____ the panic crowd together.
　　(A) emerged　(B) united　(C) combined　(D) connected
(　) 2. If I have a screw, I can make these two pieces of wood _____ into a whole one.
　　(A) merge　(B) associate　(C) connect　(D) divide

 Ans
1. (B)　他做的演說讓驚慌的群眾團結起來。
2. (A)　如果我有螺絲釘，我就能把這兩片木板接在一起。

12 Lesson 混合

🎧 MP3 2-12

blend / fuse / mingle / mix / stir

Quick View!

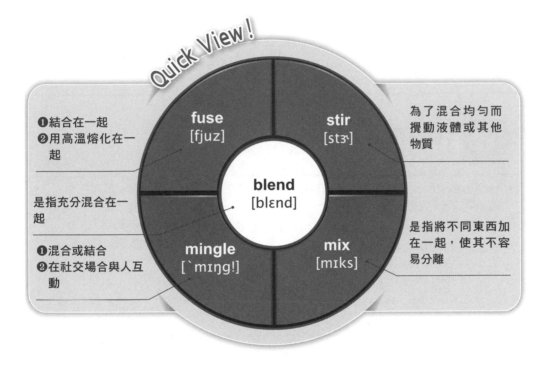

- ❶結合在一起
- ❷用高溫熔化在一起

fuse [fjuz]

stir [stɝ]

為了混合均勻而攪動液體或其他物質

是指充分混合在一起

blend [blɛnd]

❶混合或結合
❷在社交場合與人互動

mingle [`mɪŋgl̩]

mix [mɪks]

是指將不同東西加在一起，使其不容易分離

---

64 blend
-blended-blended

vi. 混和、混雜　vt. 使混和、使交融　n. 交融

- Blend the yellow pigment and the blue pigment to make green.
  將黃色與藍色顏料混合做成綠色顏料。
- Your skirt blends in with this pair of shoes.
  你的裙子和這雙鞋子十分搭配。

Tip blend in with sth. 是指「與某物非常協調」之意。

衍 blended *adj.* 數種混合的；
blender *n.* 合群的人、攪拌器；
blending *n.* 混合
同 mix 使混和、攪和
反 sort 把……分類
組 blended family 繼親家庭
片 blend (sth.) in 融入；
blend with 和……混合在一起

65 fuse
-fused-fused

vi. 熔合、混合　*vt.* 熔合、混合　*n.* 保險絲

- They fused their ideas to come up with a plan.
  他們將各種想法結合在一起變成一個計畫。
- The blacksmith fused steel with iron to forge a sword.
  鐵匠將鋼與鐵熔製鑄成一把劍。
- The fuse blew and caused the blackout.
  保險絲燒斷造成停電。

衍 fused *adj.* 接上保險絲的
同 blend 使混和、使混雜、使交融
組 fuse box 保險絲盒；
  fuse sky radiation 漫天輻射；
  short fuse 暴躁性子
片 blow a fuse 大怒；
  fuse with 融合

66 mingle
-mingled-mingled

vi. 相混合、交往、往來　*vt.* 使混合、使相混

- He's too shy to mingle at parties.
  他太害羞以致無法融入派對中。
- The writing style of this work of fiction mingles humor with irony.
  這本小說的寫作風格幽默中帶著諷刺。

衍 minglement *n.* 混合
同 mix 使混和、攪和
組 mingle-mangle 混合
片 mingle with 混合

67 mix
-mixed-mixed

vi. 相混合、相溶合　*vt.* 使混和　*n.* 結合

- If you mix yellow and blue, you will have green.
  如果你將黃色與藍色混在一起，就會變成綠色。
- Don't mix with the wrong people, or you'll be in trouble.
  交友須謹慎，否則你會惹禍上身的。

衍 mixable *adj.* 可混合的；
  mixed *adj.* 摻雜的；
  mixture *n.* 混合
反 separate 分隔
組 mixed-blood 混血兒；
  mixed blessing 好壞參半之事
片 mix up 拌和；
  mix in 摻入

68 | **stir**
-stirred-stirred

vi. 攪動、拌和 vt. 激動、煽動 n. 轟動

- Can we stir up their interest in the idea?
  我們可以激起他們對這個想法的興趣嗎？
- What he said stirred my anger greatly.
  他的話激起我極大的憤怒。
- She used her finger to stir the water and made some ripples.
  她用手指攪動水面，激起些許漣漪。

衍	stirring *adj.* 激動人心的； stirrer *n.* 挑撥離間者； stirrings *n.* 萌芽
反	still 靜止、平靜
組	shit stirrer 攪屎棍； stir fry 快炒
片	stir up 激起； stir one's blood 使人熱血沸騰

 聯想學習Plus

- 因為雞湯味道太淡而無味（bland）了，媽媽在湯裡添加了些祕方，然後用勺子（ladle）慢慢攪拌（stir），好讓湯入味。

小試身手UP

( ) 1. We _____ flour, eggs, sugar, and milk to make cake batter.（複選）
(A) unite　(B) mix　(C) blend　(D) mingle
( ) 2. Separate yolk from egg white, whip it and then add it to the _____ of step one.
(A) mixure　(B) fuse　(C) blender　(D) stirrer

 Ans

1. (B)(C)(D) 我們將麵粉、蛋、糖與牛奶混在一起做成蛋糕糊狀物。
2. (A) 將蛋白與蛋黃分離，打發蛋白後，再添入步驟一的混合物中。

提出

🎧 MP3 2-13

finance / offer / present / submit / tender

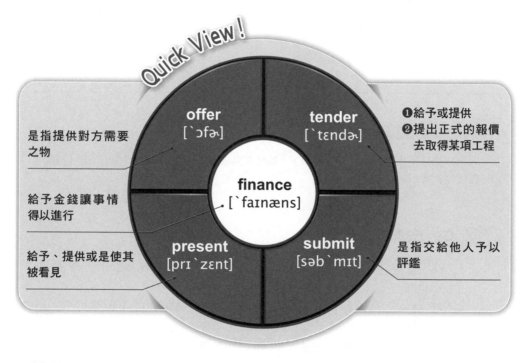

Quick View!

offer [`ɔfɚ`]
是指提供對方需要之物

tender [`tɛndɚ`]
❶給予或提供
❷提出正式的報價去取得某項工程

finance [`faɪnæns]

present [prɪ`zɛnt]
給予、提供或是使其被看見

submit [səb`mɪt]
是指交給他人予以評鑑

給予金錢讓事情得以進行

---

69 finance
-financed-financed

vi. 籌措資金　vt. 供資金給　n. 財政、金融

- Tax money financed the construction of the new freeway.
  稅收補助新高速公路的興建。
- Crowdfunding is an approach that people finance from other people to fulfill their goal.
  群眾集資是向他人籌措資金以達成自身目標的一種方式。

衍 financial *adj.* 財政的
同 support 支撐
組 finance company 貸款公司；
　 finance house 金融公司；
　 financial management 財務管理；
　 financial aid 貸款

70 offer
-offered-offered

vi. 提議　vt. 給予、提供　n. 提議

- The entrepreneur offered me a job.
  那位企業家給了我一個工作機會。
- Many people offered help to the families of the victims.
  許多人提供幫助給受害者的家庭。

衍 offering *n.* 貢獻
同 present 贈送
反 receive 收到
組 special offer 特別優惠；
　 job offer 工作邀請
片 on offer 供出售的；
　 make sb. an offer 向某人提出建議

71 present
-presented-presented

vt. 贈送、呈獻　adj. 在場的　n. 目前、禮物

- The judge presented a blue ribbon to the winner.
  裁判向優勝者頒發藍彩帶。
- After all the evidence was presented, Allen confessed to his crime.
  所有的證據都呈上後，艾倫承認了自己的罪行。

衍 presence *n.* 出席；
　 presentation *n.* 贈送、表現；
　 presentable *adj.* 可提出的
反 receive 收到
組 presence of mind 鎮定；
　 present arms 舉槍致敬；
　 present participle 現在分詞
片 at present 目前

72 submit
-submitted-submitted

vi. 屈從、忍受、甘受　vt. 提交、呈遞

- Jason submitted his resignation to his supervisor and left the office immediately.
  傑森向上司提交離職信，然後立即離開了辦公室。
- Please submit the application form by 5:00 p.m.
  請在下午五點前提交申請表。

衍 submissive *adj.* 服從的；
　 submission *n.* 屈從；
　 submissiveness *n.* 柔順；
　 submissively *adv.* 順從地
同 yield 使屈服、使投降
反 resist 抵抗、反抗、抗拒
片 submit oneself to 屈服於；
　 submit to 提交、臣服於

生活常用

學校工作

情緒心智

社會萬象

73 | **tender**
-tendered-tendered

vi. 提出、提供、投標 *adj.* 柔軟的 *n.* 照料人

- The premier and all the cabinet members tendered their resignations to the president.
  行政院院長與全體閣員向總統請辭。
- My company tendered a bid for the construction of the new museum.
  本公司投標了新博物館的興建工程。

衍 tenderize *v.* 使軟化
反 receive 收到
組 tender-hearted 性情溫和的；
   door tender 門房；
   legal tender 法定貨幣；
   bartender 酒保
片 tender for 投標；
   tender to（正式）提出、提供

聯想學習Plus

- 我們給（offer）每一位在辦公室（office）的警察（officer）一個禮物（present）。
- 財政（finance）部主要負責擬定經濟（economics）方面的政策，央行則負責執行貨幣（monetary）政策。

小試身手UP

( ) 1. Please pull over and _____ your ID card and driver's license.
      (A) present (B) offer (C) submit (D) tender
( ) 2. If you want to take a sick leave, you also have to _____ a doctor's medical record.（複選）
      (A) admit (B) submit (C) offer (D) finance

1. (A) 請靠邊停車，並出示你的身分證與駕照。此處應該只是要求顯示證件，無須交出證件，因此 offer、submit 和 tender 都不合題意。
2. (B)(C) 如果你想請病假，你也必須要檢附醫生診斷證明。

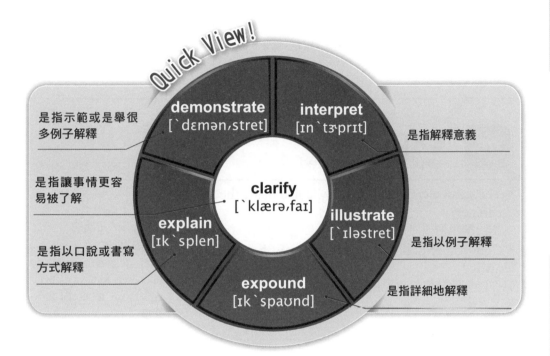

解說

🎧 MP3 2-14

clarify / demonstrate / explain / expound / illustrate / interpret

Quick View!

demonstrate
[ˈdɛmənˌstret]
是指示範或是舉很多例子解釋

interpret
[ɪnˈtɝprɪt]
是指解釋意義

clarify
[ˈklærəˌfaɪ]

是指讓事情更容易被了解

explain
[ɪkˈsplen]
是指以口說或書寫方式解釋

illustrate
[ˈɪləstret]
是指以例子解釋

expound
[ɪkˈspaʊnd]
是指詳細地解釋

---

74 clarify
-clarified-clarified

vi. 得到澄清、變得明晰　vt. 澄清、闡明

- She drew a map to clarify the directions.
  她畫了地圖讓方向更清楚。
- After listening to his explanation, we all got clarified.
  在聽完他的解釋後，我們所有人都恍然大悟。

衍 clarification n. 說明；
　clarity n. 清楚明晰
同 explain 解釋；
　make clear 使變得清楚
組 clarified butter 淨化奶油

75 demonstrate
-demonstrated-demonstrated

vi. 示威　*vt.* 示範、教學、顯示、證明

- The dance teacher demonstrated the jumps she wanted us to learn.
舞蹈老師親自示範我們要學習的跳躍動作。
- Cathy demonstrated that the bike Tony was riding was actually hers.
凱西證明了東尼在騎的腳踏車確實是她的。

衍 demonstrant *n.* 示威者；
demonstration *n.* 示範；
demonstrative *adj.* 示範的
同 illustrate 用圖例闡明、圖解
組 demonstrative pronoun 指示代名詞

76 explain
-explained-explained

vi. 解釋、說明　*vt.* 解釋、說明、闡明

- The carpenter explained how he had made the cabinets.
木匠解說他如何打造這些櫃子。
- Can you explain why you took my bicycle away?
你能解釋為何要拿走我的腳踏車嗎？

衍 explainable *adj.* 可說明的；
explanation *n.* 說明；
explanatory *adj.* 辯明的
反 obscure 使難理解
片 explain away 通過解釋消除；
explain oneself 解釋自己的行為；explain sth. to sb. 向某人解釋某事

77 expound
-expounded-expounded

vt. 解釋、詳細述說

- This statement is not clear; perhaps you could expound on it.
這份聲明不是很清楚，或許你可以詳細解釋。
- I don't get your point. Can you expound on it for me?
我不了解你的重點，你可以再詳細描述一下嗎？

同 explain 解釋
片 expound on sth. 詳細說明某事

78 illustrate
-illustrated-illustrated

vt.（用圖、實例等）說明

- By using a prism, the teacher illustrated how rainbows were formed.
  老師利用稜鏡來解釋彩虹是如何形成的。
- English teachers like to illustrate new words with pictures.
  英語老師喜歡用圖解說新單字。

衍 illustration *n.* 說明、圖解；
illustrative *adj.* 說明的；
illustrator *n.* 插圖畫家
同 clarify 澄清
片 illustrate with 用……來說明

79 interpret
-interpreted-interpreted

vi. 作解釋 vt. 解釋、翻譯、詮釋

- How do you interpret his latest book?
  你如何詮釋他最新寫的書？
- We always interpret a nod as a sign of agreement.
  我們總是把點頭當成是贊成的意思。

衍 interpretable *adj.* 可解釋的；
interpretation *n.* 解釋；
interpreter *n.* 口譯員
組 visual interpretation 視覺判讀；
simultaneous interpreter 同步翻譯員
片 interpret as 把……理解為；
interpret for 為……翻譯

小試身手UP

( ) 1. The physical education teacher _____ some warm-ups before letting students swim.
(A) demonstrated (B) interpreted (C) explained (D) illustrated

( ) 2. People _____ for women's rights.
(A) illustrated (B) interpreted (C) demonstrated (D) clarified

Ans
1. (A) 讓學生游泳前，體育老師先示範了一些暖身運動。
2. (C) 人們為女權上街頭示威。

面臨

🎧 MP3 2-15

confront / dare / encounter / face / meet

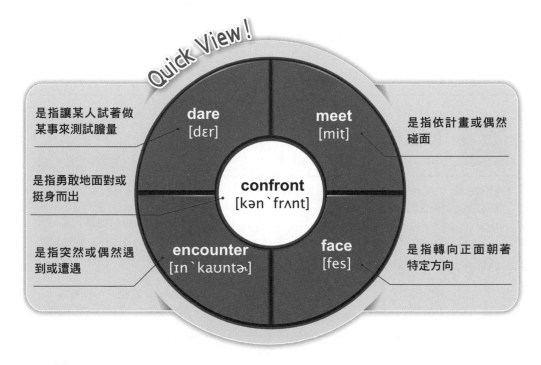

Quick View!

是指讓某人試著做某事來測試膽量 — **dare** [dɛr]

是指依計畫或偶然碰面 — **meet** [mit]

confront [kən`frʌnt]

是指勇敢地面對或挺身而出

是指突然或偶然遇到或遭遇 — **encounter** [ɪn`kaʊntɚ]

face [fes] — 是指轉向正面朝著特定方向

---

80 | # confront
-confronted-confronted

vt. 迎面遇到、面臨、遭遇

- Never say never though life is confronted with many difficulties.
  雖然人生面臨許多難關也絕不要輕言放棄。
- Sally was confronted by an old friend on the street in Greece.
  莎莉在希臘的街上遇到她的一位舊識。

衍 confrontation *n.* 對抗；
confrontational *adj.* 對抗的；
confrontationist *n.* 支持或主張對抗的人

同 face 面對；encounter 遭遇

片 be confronted by / with 面臨、遇到

81 dare
-dared-dared

vt. 敢於面對、敢冒（險）　　*n.* 果敢行為

- I dared her to eat a bug.
  我激她吃蟲。
- No one dares to object to our manager's proposal.
  沒有人敢反對經理的提議。

Tip object to + N 是表示「反對做某事」之意。

衍 daring *adj.* 大膽的；
daringly *adv.* 大膽地

反 hesitate 躊躇、猶豫

組 I dare say 可能

片 dare sb. to do sth. 激某人做某事；You wouldn't dare. 你不敢。

82 encounter
-encountered-encountered

vi. 偶然相遇　*vt.* 遭遇　*n.* 衝突、偶遇

- We encountered a bear in the woods!
  我們在樹林突然遇到一隻熊！
- Stay calm when you encounter an earthquake.
  遇到地震時請保持冷靜。
- Girls always dream of having a romantic encounter in foreign countries.
  女孩總是夢想能有浪漫的異國邂逅。

同 meet 遭遇、經歷

組 re-encounter 重逢

片 an encounter with 與……相遇

83 face
-faced-faced

vi. 朝、向　*vt.* 面向、正對　*n.* 面孔

- Our house faces the road.
  我們房子面對著馬路。
- My boss will ask you some questions face to face.
  我老闆要當面問你一些問題。

衍 faceless *adj.* 無個性的；
facial *adj.* 面部的

組 two-faced 雙面的；face-lift 整容；facial mask 面膜

片 be faced with 面臨；
face to face 面對面；
face away 轉頭；
make a face 扮鬼臉

84 meet
-met-met

- We decided to meet at the restaurant at seven o'clock.
  我們決定七點在餐廳碰面。
- They are looking for a house that meets their needs.
  他們正在尋找符合他們需求的房子。

衍 meeting *n.* 集會
同 join 會合、相遇
片 meet halfway 妥協；
make (both) ends meet 收支平衡；
meet one's need 滿足某人需求

聯想學習Plus

- 水面（surface）上浮著一張臉（face）。
- 形容人膽量大可用 daring（大膽的）、brave（勇敢的）、courageous（有勇氣的）、bold（大膽的）等。

小試身手UP

(　) 1. I wasn't having any fun at the park until I _____ a friend of mine.
　　(A) confronted　(B) meet　(C) encountered　(D) faced
(　) 2. We _____ the bad weather on our trip.
　　(A) faces　(B) encountered　(C) affronted　(D) dared
(　) 3. Please _____ me when I talk to you.
　　(A) face　(B) faces　(C) meet　(D) dare

Ans
1. (C)　我在公園百無聊賴之際，突然遇到一位朋友。
2. (B)　我們在旅途中遭遇到壞天氣。
3. (A)　當我跟你說話時，請面對我。

學校工作

情緒心智

社會萬象

16 Lesson 裁判

🎧 MP3 2-16

arbitrate / intercede / judge / mediate / referee / umpire

Quick View!

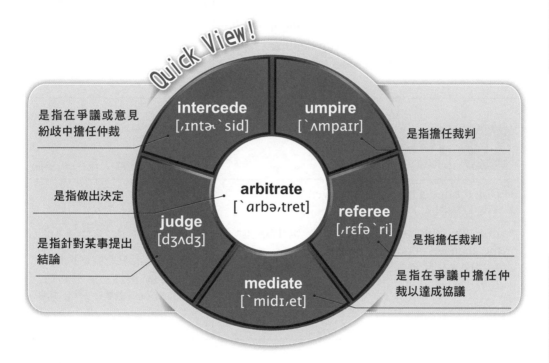

是指在爭議或意見紛歧中擔任仲裁 — **intercede** [ˌɪntɚˈsid]

umpire [ˈʌmpaɪr] — 是指擔任裁判

是指做出決定 — **arbitrate** [ˈɑrbəˌtret]

是指針對某事提出結論 — **judge** [dʒʌdʒ]

referee [ˌrɛfəˈri] — 是指擔任裁判

mediate [ˈmidɪˌet] — 是指在爭議中擔任仲裁以達成協議

---

85 arbitrate
-arbitrated-arbitrated

vi. 進行仲裁   vt. 裁決

- If you have any question about the contract, you can ask for arbitration anytime.
  如果你對這份合約內容有異議，你隨時可以要求進行公斷。

- The opposing sides agreed to ask the third party to arbitrate their dispute.
  對立的雙方同意請第三方仲裁他們的爭端。

衍 arbitrary *adj.* 獨斷的；
   arbitration *n.* 仲裁；
   arbitrator *n.* 仲裁人
同 umpire 仲裁、裁判
片 go to arbitration 提請裁決；
   arbitrate between 擔任……仲裁

191

intercede
-interceded-interceded

vi. 仲裁、說情

- He was hesitant about interceding in a quarrel between two such hostile opponents.
  他對於在如此有敵意的雙方之間擔任仲裁的工作很猶豫。
- The mother interceded with the judge for her son who was involved in drug dealing.
  那位母親替她涉及販毒的兒子向法官求情。

衍 intercession *n.* 仲裁、求情、調解
同 mediate 調停解決
片 intercede with sb. 向某人求情

judge
-judged-judged

vi. 審判　vt. 審判、判決　n. 法官

- Don't judge a book by its cover.
  不要以貌取人。
- In some countries, it is the jury that judges if the accused is guilty or not.
  有些國家採陪審團制，由陪審團來判定被告是否有罪。

衍 judgement *n.* 判決；
judgmatic *adj.* 有分辨力的
組 guest judge 嘉賓評委；
well-judged 判斷正確的；
judge-made 法官制定的
片 judge by 根據……來判斷；
judge from 根據……作出判斷

mediate
-mediated-mediated

vi. 調解、斡旋　vt. 調停解決　adj. 居間的

- The lawyer mediated an agreement between the two sides.
  律師為雙方調解協議。
- The police succeeded in mediating an end to the gunfight.
  警方斡旋成功，結束了槍戰。

衍 mediation *n.* 調解、斡旋；
mediative *adj.* 調停的；
mediatize *v.* 作調解人；
mediator *n.* 調停者
同 intercede 仲裁
片 mediate between A and B 替 A 和 B 調解

89 referee
-refereed-refereed

vi. 擔任裁判、仲裁　vt. 仲裁、調停　n. 裁判

- The coach's assistant offered to referee the game.
  教練助理提出擔任比賽裁判的要求。
- They lost the game because the referee had a bias in favor of the opposing team.
  由於裁判偏袒對手，讓他們輸了比賽。

Tip have a bias in favor of + N 是表示「偏袒著……」之意。

衍 reference *n.* 參考
同 judge 審判
近 refugee *n.* 難民

90 umpire
-umpired-umpired

vi. 做仲裁、當裁判　vt. 仲裁、裁判　n. 裁決者

- We still need to find someone who is willing to umpire our game on Saturday.
  我們仍需找一位願意在週六比賽擔任裁判的人。
- I'll umpire a baseball game this afternoon.
  今天下午我要當棒球比賽的裁判。

衍 umpireship *n.* 裁判之職權；
　umpirage *n.* 仲裁
同 judge 判斷
組 base umpire 壘審

生活常用

學校工作

情緒心智

社會萬象

小試身手UP↑

(　) 1. These two men who fought all the time ended up _____ their dispute.
(A) arbitrating　(B) interceding　(C) judging　(D) meditating
(　) 2. You are a good _____ of character.
(A) arbitration　(B) judge　(C) referee　(D) umpire

1. (A) 一直有嫌隙的兩人最終將他們的爭議訴諸仲裁。meditate 是「冥想」之意。
2. (B) 你對於品格有很好的評斷力。be a good judge of 是「善於判斷……」之意。

供應

🎧 MP3 2-17

equip / furnish / outfit / provide / supply

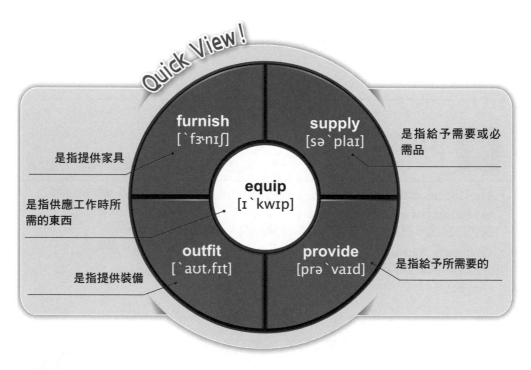

Quick View！

furnish
[ˋfɝnɪʃ]

是指提供家具

supply
[səˋplaɪ]

是指給予需要或必
需品

equip
[ɪˋkwɪp]

是指供應工作時所
需的東西

outfit
[ˋaʊtˌfɪt]

是指提供裝備

provide
[prəˋvaɪd]

是指給予所需要的

91

equip
-equipped-equipped

vt. 裝備、配備

- She equipped herself for work with a new briefcase.
  她為了工作買了一個新公事包。
- Good professional training will equip you for your job.
  良好的職業訓練能讓你勝任你的工作。

Tip 物 + equip sb. for + N 是表示「具備某物能讓某人
有……能力」之意。

衍 ill-equipped *adj.* 裝備不良的；
equipment *n.* 裝備

同 furnish 供應、提供

組 mobile terminal equipment 行
動終端設備

片 equip with 給……裝備、配備

92 furnish
-furnished-furnished

- They still have not furnished their apartment.
  他們的公寓目前還沒有布置家具。
- The book furnished me with quite a bit of information about science.
  這本書提供我很多科學方面的資訊。

衍 furnishing *n.* 裝備；
furnisher *n.* 供給者；
furniture *n.* 家具
同 supply 提供
組 street furniture 城市設施
片 furnish with 用……裝備、提供……

93 outfit
-outfitted-outfitted

- The latest model of the car has been outfitted with the self-driving system.
  這輛車的最新款已經裝備了自動駕駛系統。
- The soldiers are outfitted with the best weapons.
  士兵們配備了最好的武器。

衍 outfitter *n.* 裝飾用品商店
同 equip 配備
片 outfit with 裝備……

94 provide
-provided-provided

- The rescue team provided the victims with water and food.
  救難隊提供災民水與食物。
- Parents provide children with food, clothing and education.
  父母為孩子提供食物、衣服和教育。

衍 provided *conj.* 假如；
provider *n.* 供應者；
providing *conj.* 假如
同 supply 供給、供應、提供
反 consume 消耗、花費、耗盡
片 providing that 假若；
provide for 為……作準備；
provide with 供給

生活常用

學校工作

情緒心智

社會萬象

95 | supply
-supplied-supplied

vt. 供給、供應、提供　n. 供應

- The teacher supplied the students with pens and paper.
  老師給予學生筆與紙。
- Food is in short supply in Africa.
  非洲糧食短缺。

衍 supplied *adj.* 備有……的；
　supplier *n.* 供應者

反 demand 需求

組 supply and demand 供需；
　power supply 供電

片 in short supply 稀少的；
　supply with 提供；
　supply to 提供

聯想學習Plus

- provide with 是指提供東西（例如 provide with clothes），provide to 是拿東西給人（例如 provide food to them），provide for 是指父母親的養育（例如 provide for her child）。

小試身手UP

(　) 1. She _____ herself for the camping trip with a backpack and a sleeping bag.
　　(A) equipped　(B) supplied　(C) provided　(D) offered
(　) 2. The encyclopedia _____ people with varied information they need.
　　(A) offers　(B) fulfills　(C) outfits　(D) provides

Ans

1. (A)　她為了露營準備了背包與睡袋。
2. (D)　百科全書提供人們所需要知道的各種資訊。offer 是及物動詞，直接接受詞；outfit 主要是提供設備或服裝而言。

分類

🎧 MP3 2-18

classify / catalog / marshal / methodize / systematize

生活常用

Quick View !

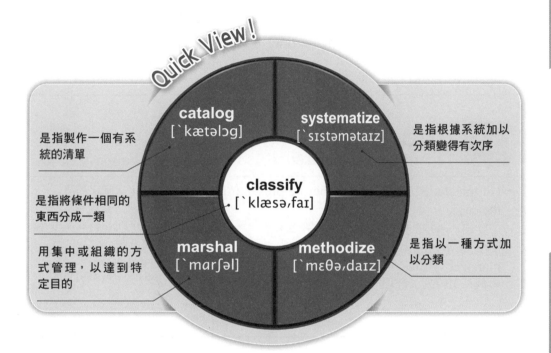

catalog
[`kætəlɔg]
是指製作一個有系統的清單

systematize
[`sɪstəmətaɪz]
是指根據系統加以分類變得有次序

classify
[`klæsə,faɪ]

是指將條件相同的東西分成一類

marshal
[`marʃəl]
用集中或組織的方式管理，以達到特定目的

methodize
[`mεθə,daɪz]
是指以一種方式加以分類

學校工作

情緒心智

---

96 classify
-classified-classified

vt. 將……分類、將……分等級

- People classify trees by the kind of leaves they have.
  人們以樹葉辨別樹種。
- The document has been classified top secret. No one except the president can read it.
  這份文件被列為最高機密。除了總統，沒有任何人有權限閱讀。

衍 classified *adj.* 分類的；
classifieds *n.* 分類廣告；
classifiable *adj.* 可分類的；
classification *n.* 分級
同 organize 組織、安排
組 classified directory 黃頁電話簿；
classified ad 分類廣告

社會萬象

catalog
-cataloged-cataloged

vt. 將……編入目錄　n. 目錄（簿）

- It's quite easy to shop online. You just read the catalog and click the item you want to buy, and you'll get it in 2 or 3 days.
  網路購物很容易。只要翻閱商品目錄，點選你想買的物品，兩至三天貨物就會送到你手上。
- Many living beings become extinct before they are cataloged.
  許多生物在被編入目錄前就已絕種。

衍 catalogue n. 目錄；
cataloger n. 編製目錄的人；
catalogic adj. 目錄似的

同 classify 將……分類、將……分等級

組 catalog marketing 目錄行銷；
catalog store 商品目錄商店；
card catalog 圖書館裡的卡片目錄

marshal
-marshaled-marshaled

vt. 排列、統帥、整理、引領　n. 元帥

- He marshaled his evidence before presenting the case.
  他在陳述案情前先將物證一一列舉出來。
- The new employee was marshaled into the manager's office.
  新員工被帶到了經理的辦公室。

衍 marshalcy n. 元帥之職位

同 arrange 整理、布置

組 Marshal of the Royal Airforce 皇家空軍元帥

片 marshal together 組織；
be marshaled into 被引領到

methodize
-methodized-methodized

vt. 為……定順序、使有條理

- Please methodize the books on the shelf in order.
  請將架上的書按順序排列好。
- Making a list to do before acting can methodize your thoughts.
  行動之前先列出待辦事項，可以幫你釐清思緒。

衍 method n. 方法、辦法；
methodical adj. 有條理的

100 | systematize
-systematized-systematized

vi. 系統化、構成體系　vt. 將……分類

- You should systematize the way you speak.
  你說話應該要有條理。
- It's necessary to be more systematic when you conduct a team.
  你指揮團隊時需要更有組織性。

衍 systematizer *n.* 組織者；
　system *n.* 系統；
　systemic *adj.* 組織的、全身的
同 organize 組織、分配
組 systemic disease 全身性疾病

 聯想學習Plus

- marshal 是「元帥」之意，也就是陸軍最高階的將領，那其他軍階又該怎麼說呢？
  現在就來認識我們經常聽到各個軍階的英文吧！由高至低階分別為：marshal（元帥）→ general（將軍）→ colonel（上校）→ captain（上尉）→ lieutenant（中尉）→ sergent（中士）→ soldier（士兵、大頭兵）。

小試身手UP

(　) 1. They ordered a table and chairs from the furniture _____.
　　　(A) catalog　(B) classified　(C) marshal　(D) classification
(　) 2. He _____ his coin collection according to type and age.
　　　(A) catalog　(B) classified　(C) catalogs　(D) marshaled

 Ans

1. (A) 他們從家具型錄訂購桌子跟數張椅子。
2. (B) 他將收集的錢幣依類型與年代分類、排列。marshal 有集中管理以達到特定目的的意思，較無分門別類的意含。

宣稱

🎧 MP3 2-19

advocate / announce / assert / broadcast / declare / proclaim / state

Quick View!

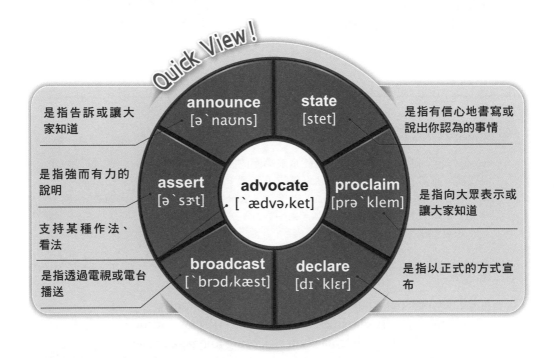

是指告訴或讓大家知道

announce
[ə`naʊns]

state
[stet]

是指有信心地書寫或說出你認為的事情

是指強而有力的說明

assert
[ə`sɝt]

advocate
[`ædvə͵ket]

proclaim
[prə`klem]

是指向大眾表示或讓大家知道

支持某種作法、看法

是指透過電視或電台播送

broadcast
[`brɔd͵kæst]

declare
[dɪ`klɛr]

是指以正式的方式宣布

---

101 | # advocate
-advocated-advocated

vt. 擁護、提倡、主張　n. 擁護者

- He advocates buying fruits and vegetables grown on local farms.
  他提倡購買當地農場種植的蔬果。
- Many parents advocated reforming the education system.
  許多家長主張改革教育制度。

Tip advocate + V-ing 是「提倡、主張做……」之意。

衍 advocacy n. 提倡；
advocator n. 擁護者
同 support 扶持
組 devil's advocate 故意唱反調的人
片 play the devil's advocate 唱反調

announce
-announced-announced

- They announced the birth of their first baby.
  他們宣布有了第一個小孩。
- I'm pleased to announce that we have 15% of growing profit this season.
  我很高興向大家宣布本季我們收益成長了 15%。

衍 announcement *n.* 宣告；
announcer *n.* 宣告者

反 conceal 隱瞞

片 announce for 宣稱支持某人競選、宣布參與；
announce to 宣布

assert
-asserted-asserted

vt. 斷言、聲稱

- He asserted his alibi for that night.
  他聲稱自己當晚有不在場證明。
- The police asserted that the case was closed.
  警方宣布這起案件已經結案。

衍 asserted *adj.* 聲稱的；
assertion *n.* 言明；
assertive *adj.* 肯定的；
assertor *n.* 堅持者

同 declare 宣布、宣告、聲明

近 asset *n.* 資產

片 assert oneself 堅持自己的主張、表現堅定

broadcast
-broadcast(ed)-broadcast(ed)

vi. 廣播、播放　vt. 播送、散播

- The radio station broadcasts the news at seven o'clock.
  電台七點時會播報新聞。
- The death of the diplomat was broadcasted to every person immediately.
  那名外交官的死訊馬上被播送給大眾知道。

衍 broadcasting *n.* 播放；
broadcaster *n.* 廣播電台

同 announce 宣布

組 broadcasting station 廣播電台；
outside broadcast 實況廣播；
live broadcast 實況轉播

生活常用

學校工作

情緒心智

社會萬象

declare
-declared-declared

- Japan's attack on Pearl Harbor led to the United States' declaration of war against Japan and entry into World War Ⅱ.
日本偷襲珍珠港事件是導致美國對日宣戰並參與二戰的主因。
- The mayor declared that he would do his best to serve the public.
市長表示會盡其所能地為民服務。

衍 declared *adj.* 公開宣布的；
declarer *n.* 宣告者；
declaration *n.* 宣言
同 state 陳述、聲明、說明
組 Declaration of Independence 美國獨立宣言
片 declare against 宣布反對；
declare war against 向……宣戰

proclaim
-proclaimed-proclaimed

- The king proclaimed the day a national holiday.
國王將那天定為國定假日。
- The government proclaimed a new law that all passengers in the car should fasten the seatbelt.
政府頒布新的交通法，規定車上的乘客都要繫安全帶。

衍 proclamation *n.* 公布
同 declare 聲明
組 self-proclaimed 自稱的

state
-stated-stated

- She stated her opinion.
她表達了她的看法。
- Each time I take an exam, I get into a state. I think I'm too nervous.
我每次考試都緊張不安，我想我太緊張了。

衍 stated *adj.* 交待明白的；
statehood *n.* 國家地位；
statement *n.* 聲明
同 declare 宣布、宣告
片 lie in state 瞻仰遺容；
state of affairs 情況、局勢；
in a state 緊張或焦躁的情緒

- 我很確定（assert）這件東西必須插進（insert）屁股（ass）裡。
- state 有「州、邦、國家」的意思，有明顯的政權、政府體制的意涵；nation 是強調民族性的國家而言；country 則偏重地理方面的國家，使用上還是略有差異的喔！

小試身手UP

( ) 1. When emergency occurs, you will hear the air-raid alarm _____ across the country.
　　(A) declared　(B) pronounced　(C) talked　(D) broadcast
( ) 2. He _____ his love to me.
　　(A) declared　(B) pronounced　(C) broadcast　(D) statement

1. (D) 當發生緊急情況時，空襲警報將響徹全國。
2. (A) 他向我表達他的愛。

限制

MP3 2-20

confine / define / hamper / impede / limit / restrain / restrict

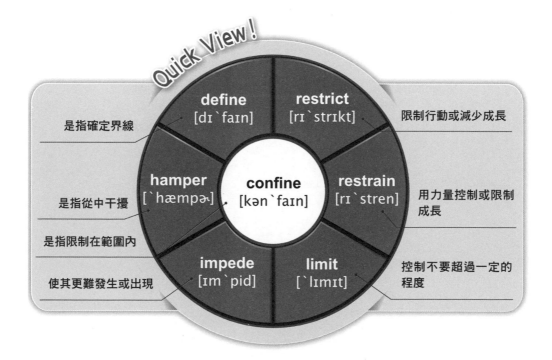

Quick View！

是指確定界線 — **define** [dɪ`faɪn]

restrict [rɪ`strɪkt] — 限制行動或減少成長

是指從中干擾 — **hamper** [`hæmpɚ]

confine [kən`faɪn]

restrain [rɪ`stren] — 用力量控制或限制成長

是指限制在範圍內

使其更難發生或出現 — **impede** [ɪm`pid]

limit [`lɪmɪt] — 控制不要超過一定的程度

---

108 confine
-confined-confined

vt. 限制、使局限　n. 範圍

- The storm confined me to the house.
暴風雨將我困在屋內。
- Please confine your remarks to what everyone is interested in.
請把你要說的話限定在大家都有興趣的話題上。

Tip sb. be confined to bed / a wheelchair 是指「某人臥病在床、離不開輪椅」之意。

衍 confined *adj.* 監禁的；
confinement *n.* 限制；
confining *adj.* 受限的
同 restrain 抑制、遏制
片 confine to 限制在……；
confine within 在……界限內

109 define
-defined-defined

vt. 界定、限定、下定義、立界限

- The boundaries of the farm are easily defined.
  農場的邊界很容易認定。
- The grand justices are in charge of defining the ambiguity of constitutions.
  大法官負責解說憲法的模糊地帶。

衍 defined *adj.* 清晰的；
definable *adj.* 可限定的；
definite *adj.* 明確的；
definition *n.* 定義、規定

組 well-defined 定義明確的；
ill-defined 不明確的

片 define as 把……定義為……

---

110 hamper
-hampered-hampered

vt. 妨礙、阻礙　*n.* 障礙物、籃子

- The bad weather hampered our mountain climbing.
  壞天氣破壞了我們爬山的計畫。
- Hunger and cold hampered my thinking.
  飢寒交迫使我無法思考。

同 impede 妨礙、阻止

反 assist 幫助、協助

近 hammer *n.* 槌頭

組 top-hamper 多餘礙事的東西；
clothes hamper 洗衣籃；
food hamper 裝食物的籃子

---

111 impede
-impeded-impeded

vt. 妨礙、阻礙、阻止

- The cascades of snow impeded the rescue's progress.
  大雪紛飛影響了搜救進度。
- The lack of resources has become an impediment to educational progress in the remote area.
  資源匱乏已經成為偏鄉教育發展上的一大阻礙了。

衍 impedance *n.* 阻抗；
impediment *n.* 妨礙；
impeditive *adj.* 足以阻礙的

同 hinder 妨礙、阻礙

近 centipede *n.* 蜈蚣

片 impede the progress of 延誤

112 limit
-limited-limited

- We limited our game to two hours.
  我們限制比賽時間為兩小時。
- Dno't go over the speed limit on the highway.
  公路開車不要超速。

衍 limited *adj.* 有限的；
limitation *n.* 限制；
limitative *adj.* 限制的
同 restrict 限制
組 limited company 股份有限公司
片 off-limits 禁止的；
limit to 限制；
within limits 有限度地

---

113 restrain
-restrained-restrained

vt. 抑制、遏制

- Try to restrain your temper.
  試著控制你的脾氣。
- The customers were restrained from leaving when the shopkeeper found something lost.
  當店家發現少了東西時，便不讓顧客離開。

衍 restrained *adj.* 受限制的；
restrainedly *adv.* 抑制地；
restraint *n.* 抑制
反 impel 推進、推動
組 restraints of trade 貿易障礙；
legally restrained 法律禁止的
片 restrain from 限制

---

114 restrict
-restricted-restricted

vt. 限制、限定、約束

- His parents restricted him to his room.
  他的父母親限制他待在房間內。
- The club is restricted to those who are 25 or above.
  這個俱樂部限制二十五歲以上的人才能進入。

衍 restricted *adj.* 受限制的；
restrictedly *adv.* 有限地；
restriction *n.* 限制
同 confine 限制、使局限
片 restrict to 限制；
restrict access to 限制進入

 聯想學習Plus

- limited 是指有被限制的，因此不寬或不廣闊，unlimited 則是指沒有界線。
- 他承認（admit）剛剛已經違反了開車速限（speed limit）。

小試身手UP

(　) 1. The reporters were asked to _____ their questions to the major issue.
　　(A) impede　(B) restrict　(C) confine　(D) hamper

(　) 2. That accident _____ him to the wheelchair for the rest of his life.
　　(A) confined　(B) limited　(C) hampered　(D) interfered

(　) 3. People under 18 are _____ access to bars or night clubs.
　　(A) limited　(B) hampered　(C) restricted　(D) impeded

 Ans

1. (C) 記者被要求盡量針對主題發問。
2. (A) 那場意外讓他後半輩子都要靠輪椅行動了。
3. (C) 未滿十八歲的人禁止進入酒吧或夜店。

完成

🎧 MP3 2-21

accomplish / achieve / complete / effect / finish / fulfill

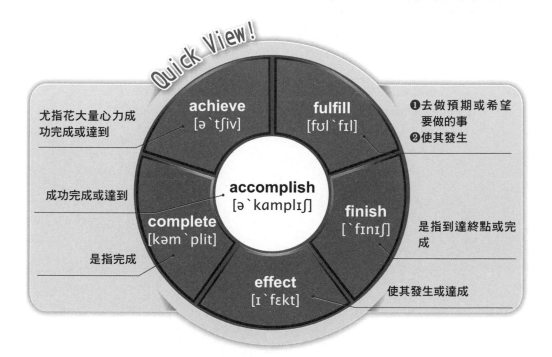

Quick View!

尤指花大量心力成功完成或達到

achieve
[ə`tʃiv]

fulfill
[fʊl`fɪl]

❶去做預期或希望要做的事
❷使其發生

成功完成或達到

accomplish
[ə`kamplɪʃ]

complete
[kəm`plit]

finish
[`fɪnɪʃ]

是指到達終點或完成

是指完成

effect
[ɪ`fɛkt]

使其發生或達成

---

115 **accomplish**
-accomplished-accomplished

vt. 完成、實現、達到

- I was lazy yesterday, but I accomplished a lot of work today.
  我昨天偷懶，但是今天完成很多事情。
- Mr. Fogg accomplished his traveling around the world in 80 days with his servant.
  佛格跟他的僕人完成了用八十天環遊世界。

衍 accomplished *adj.* 已實現的；
accomplishable *adj.* 可完成的；
accomplishment *n.* 成就、完成
同 complete 完成、結束
近 accompany *v.* 陪伴；
accomplice *n.* 共犯、幫兇

116 achieve
-achieved-achieved

vi. 達到目的　vt. 完成、實現

- He wanted to become famous, and then he achieved his goal.
  他想要成名，然後他達到目標。
- The writer achieved fame after he wrote an interesting novel called "*Shock*"!
  這個作家由於寫了一本叫《震駭》的有趣小說而出名！

衍 achievable *adj.* 可完成的；
achievement *n.* 完成、成就
反 fail 不及格、失敗
組 Achievement Medal 成就勳章；
underachieve 未發揮水平

117 complete
-completed-completed

vt. 完成、結束　adj. 全部的、完全的

- He completed the test in one hour.
  他用一個小時完成考試。
- The construction of the boy's dormitory will be completed at the end of the year.
  男子宿舍的興建將在今年年底完工。

衍 completed *adj.* 完整的；
completely *adv.* 完整地、徹底地；
completeness *n.* 完整；
completion *n.* 完成
反 incomplete 不完全的

118 effect
-effected-effected

vt. 實現、達到（目的）　n. 結果

- As a politician, he is working on effecting pension reforms.
  身為一位政治人物，他一直致力於實現年金改革。
- The new traffic rules will be carried into effect next month.
  新的交通法規下個月生效。

衍 effective *adj.* 有效的；
effectively *adv.* 實際上；
effectiveness *n.* 有效
組 greenhouse effect 溫室效應；
butterfly effect 蝴蝶效應
片 come into effect 生效；
in effect 實際上

生活常用

學校工作

情緒心智

社會萬象

119 finish
-finished-finished

vi. 結束　*vt.* 結束、完成

- The movie finishes at eleven, and then we can have lunch nearby.
  電影 11 點結束，之後我們可以在附近用餐。
- Amanda usually finishes up with a mint candy after meals.
  用完餐後，亞曼達通常會吃一顆薄荷糖作結束。

衍 finished *adj.* 完成的；
finishing *adj.* 最後的；
finisher *n.* 完工者
反 begin 開始
組 finishing line 終點線
片 finish with 完成；
finish up with 以……告終；
from start to finish 自始至終

120 fulfill
-fulfilled-fulfilled

vt. 完成、實現、達到、使結束

- He fulfilled his duty of caring for the child.
  他實現照顧孩子的責任。
- An honest man always fulfills his promise.
  正直的人總是信守諾言。

衍 fulfilled *adj.* 滿足的；fulfilling *adj.* 能實現個人抱負的；fulfillment *n.* 實現
同 finish 結束、完成
組 self-fulfilling 實現自己抱負的；fulfill an engagement 實現承諾

小試身手UP

（　）1. The Taiwanese soap opera starts at 8:00 and ＿＿＿＿＿ at 10:00 from Monday to Friday.
　　　(A) accomplishes　(B) finishes　(C) completes　(D) fulfills
（　）2. After making so much effort, he eventually ＿＿＿＿＿ his goal.（複選）
　　　(A) finished　(B) completed　(C) accomplished　(D) achieved

Ans

1. (B)　這齣台語連續劇週一至週五從 8 點播到 10 點。
2. (C)(D)　在付出這麼多的努力之後，他終於實現他的目標。

查驗

MP3 2-22

audit / censor / explore / inspect / review / scrutinize / detect

Quick View!

censor [`sɛnsɚ]
將不合時宜的內容進行篩除或過濾

detect [dɪ`tɛkt]
用特殊方法找出隱含或不清楚的地方

explore [ɪk`splor]
為了更加了解而去思索或討論

audit [`ɔdɪt]

scrutinize [`skrutn͵aɪz]
是指仔細地觀察

是指檢查紀錄或帳戶以確保無誤

inspect [ɪn`spɛkt]
是指仔細地看並找出問題

review [rɪ`vju]
是指再次研究或觀察

---

121 | # audit
-audited-audited

vi. 審計、查帳　vt. 審計、查帳

- The Internal Revenue Service often audits a company or individual that claims a great number of tax deductions.
  稅務局針對提出大量減稅的公司或個人都會進行稽核。
- All companies are required to have an audit every year.
  所有的公司每年都需進行一次審計。

衍 auditor *n.* 查帳員；
auditorial *adj.* 查帳的；
audition *n.* 試鏡

組 performance audit 績效審計；
internal auditing 內部稽核；
audit program 稽核項目；
financial audit 財務審計

片 do an audit 進行審計

122 censor
-censored-censored

vt. 審查　n. 審查員

- Although our college is open-minded, the student newspapers still need censoring.
  雖然我們校風開放，但校刊還是需要接受審查。
- Even now publishing a book still needs censoring by the authorities in some countries.
  即便到了現在，在某些國家出書仍需要接受當局審查。

衍 censorable *adj.* 須受檢查的；
censorship *n.* 審查（制度）
同 examine 檢查、細查、診察
近 sensor *n.* 感應器

123 explore
-explored-explored

vi. 探索、探險　vt. 探測

- Let's explore this idea.
  讓我們來探討這個想法吧。
- We human beings always dream of exploring outer space because we believe there are some living things out there.
  我們人類一直以來都夢想能夠探索外太空，因為我們深信有外太空生物的存在。

衍 explorer *n.* 勘探者；
explorative *adj.* 探險的；
exploration *n.* 探索、調查
同 search 搜查、搜尋
近 explode *v.* 使爆炸

124 inspect
-inspected-inspected

vi. 檢查、視察　vt. 檢查、審查

- He inspected the engines to make sure they would function well.
  他仔細檢查引擎以確保正常運作。
- The doctor made a quick inspection of the wound.
  醫生快速地檢查了傷口。

衍 inspection *n.* 檢查、審視；
inspective *adj.* 注意的；
inspector *n.* 檢查員
同 examine 檢查

125 review
-reviewed-reviewed

vi. 再檢查、複審　vt. 再檢查、複習

- I reviewed my notes before the test.
  我考試前複習了自己的筆記。
- The film, which was about religion, received mixed reviews.
  這部關於宗教的電影評價兩極。

衍 reviewable *adj.* 可回顧的；
reviewal *n.* 覆查；
reviewer *n.* 檢閱人

組 under review 複查或重新考慮中；
reviewing stand 閱兵台；
judicial review 司法審查；
a rave review 極高的評價
book review 書評

126 scrutinize
-scrutinized-scrutinized

vi. 作詳細檢查　vt. 詳細檢查、細看

- The detective scrutinized every inch of the crime scene.
  警探仔細地觀察案發現場的每一個角落。
- The editor's duty is to scrutinize every word and its spelling in the copy.
  編輯的責任就是仔細檢查稿子上的每一個字與拼寫。

衍 scrutineer *n.* 檢查者、監票人；
scrutinous *adj.* 細察的；
scrutiny *n.* 詳細的檢查

同 inspect 檢查、審查

反 glance 瀏覽、掃視

127 detect
detected-detected

vt. 發現、察覺、查出、看穿

- The gate has a sensor which can detect any metal substance.
  閘門有能夠偵測任何金屬物品的感應器。
- The alarm will go off immediately when smoke is detected.
  一旦偵測到煙，警報器就會立刻響起。

衍 detective *n.* 偵探
detection *n.* 偵查

同 discover *v.* 發現；
perceive *v.* 察覺

反 conceal *v.* 隱藏

- explore 是從拉丁字而來，意指調查或尋找之意，原意中還有大聲喊叫的意思，是說
  獵人為了將躲藏起來的動物嚇出巢穴的做法。
- 他們苦苦哀求（implore）我們去調查（explore）這樁爆炸案（explosion）發生的原因。

小試身手UP

(   ) 1. I'm just _____ the course because I haven't decided to take the course or
not.
    (A) auditing   (B) censoring   (C) inspecting   (D) detecting
(   ) 2. _____ an unknown area in the deep forest needs a lot of preparation.
    (A) Testing   (B) Exploring   (C) Auditing   (D) Reviewing

1. (A) 我只是旁聽而已，因為我還沒決定是否要修這堂課。
2. (B) 要探索森林祕處未知的地帶需要充分準備才行。

23 Lesson 操練

🎧 MP3 2-23

drill / discipline / exercise / rehearse

Quick View !

discipline [ˈdɪsəplɪn]
教育使其行為端正

drill [drɪl]

rehearse [rɪˈhɝs]
是指為戲劇或表演進行練習

是指以紀律或重複的方式訓練或教導

exercise [ˈɛksɚˌsaɪz]

是指鍛鍊身體

---

128 drill
-drilled-drilled

vt. 操練、訓練　*n.* 鑽頭、訓練

- His father drilled him in spelling words before the quiz.
  他的父親在他小考前給他拼字訓練。
- Every man should do his military service and get drilled well there.
  男人都應該服兵役，在軍中好好鍛鍊自己。

衍 drilling *n.* 訓練；
driller *n.* 鑽床；
drillable *adj.* 可訓練的

組 fire drill 消防演習；
military drill 軍事演練；
anti-terrorist drill 反恐演習

片 drill in 訓練；
drill down 深層探究

129 discipline
-disciplined-disciplined

vt. 訓練、使有紀律　n. 紀律

- He disciplined his dog for jumping on people.
  他的狗因為撲向人所以被他處罰。
- Can you teach me how to discipline a child? It's tough for me.
  你能教我該如何管教小孩嗎？我覺得很棘手。

衍 disciplinary *adj.* 紀律的、懲戒的

組 self-disciplined 能律己的

片 discipline sb. for 為……處罰某人

130 exercise
-exercised-exercised

vi. 練習、運動　vt. 鍛鍊、練習

- I exercise in the gym every morning.
  我每天早上都會上健身房運動。
- Students hate exercise books, let alone exams.
  學生討厭寫練習本，更不用說考試了。
- My auntie's coming did exercise our minds greatly.
  我阿姨的來訪著實令我們傷腦筋。

衍 exerciser *n.* 做運動的人；exercisable *adj.* 可運用的

同 practice 練習、學習

組 exercise bike 健身腳踏車；anaerobic exercise 無氧運動

片 take exercise 做運動；exercise one's mind 使煩惱、不安

131 rehearse
-rehearsed-rehearsed

vi. 練習、演習　vt. 練習、演習、訓練

- Let's rehearse those dance steps one more time.
  讓我們再練習一次舞步吧。
- The students are rehearsing in the auditorium for the commencement.
  學生們正在禮堂內為畢業典禮排練。

衍 rehearsal *n.* 排練、試演、練習

同 practice 練習、學習

組 dress rehearsal 預演彩排

片 rehearse for 為……排練

聯想學習Plus

- drill 有「鑽子」的意思，其他常見的工具還包括槌頭（hammer）、槓桿（lever）、鋸子（saw）與螺絲起子（screwdriver）。
- Bill 雖然經過不斷的訓練（drill），他的病情（ill）依舊（still）沒有好轉。

小試身手UP

( ) 1. Military _____ are one of manifestations to show a nation's military forces.
   (A) disciplines   (B) exercises   (C) training   (D) drills

( ) 2. These performers conducted the _____ numerous times so they performed perfectly on the stage.
   (A) exercises   (B) drills   (C) disciplines   (D) rehearsal

1. (D) 軍事演練是一國展現自我武力的一種表現。
2. (D) 這些表演者進行了無數次的排練，因而能在正式演出時完美表現。

遏止

🎧 MP3 2-24

curb / leash / persecute / quell / quench

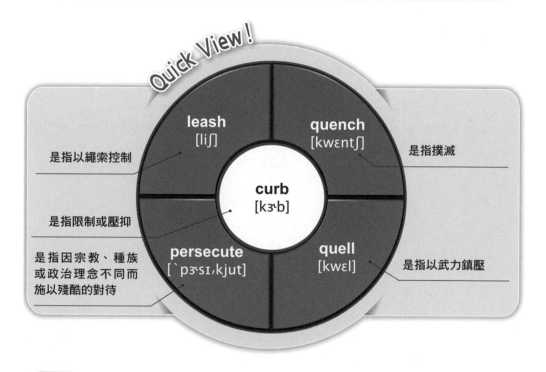

Quick View!

leash
[liʃ]
是指以繩索控制

quench
[kwɛntʃ]
是指撲滅

curb
[kɝb]

是指限制或壓抑

是指因宗教、種族
或政治理念不同而
施以殘酷的對待

persecute
[`pɝsɪˌkjut]

quell
[kwɛl]
是指以武力鎮壓

---

132 | # curb
-curbed-curbed

vt. 控制、遏止 n. 勒馬繩

- If you don't curb your dog, you'll be asked to leave.
  如果你不管好你的狗，我們就要請你離開。
- The government must take action immediately to curb street vendors.
  政府必須立即採取行動，取締街頭攤販。

同 restrain 抑制、遏制
近 curd v. 使凝結；
  cub n. 幼獸

leash
-leashed-leashed

vt. 約束、控制　**n.** 鏈條、皮帶

- They leashed the dog before walking it outdoors.
  他們在帶狗出門散步前會幫牠繫上狗鍊。
- Some parents are used to leashing their children in every decision. Sometimes they should learn to let go, or the kids will never grow up.
  有些家長習慣插手孩子們的每一個決定。有時候也要學會放手，否則孩子永遠也長不大。

同 chain 拘禁、束縛
組 strain at the leash 迫不及待；
leash law 拴狗條例；
phone leash 手機吊帶
片 on a tight leash 被嚴格控制；
keep a dog on a leash 用繩索牽狗

persecute
-persecuted-persecuted

vt. 迫害、殘害、困擾、為難

- Some governments persecute people who oppose their policies.
  有些政府會迫害反對他們政策的人。
- A large number of refugees persecuted by wars and conflicts have raised international concerns.
  受到戰爭衝突迫害的大量難民已經引起國際關切。

衍 persecution n. 迫害、困擾；
persecutor n. 迫害者
同 oppress 壓迫、壓制
組 persecution complex 被迫害妄想

quell
-quelled-quelled

vt. 鎮壓、平息、壓制

- The police were given an order to quell the demonstration.
  警方奉命鎮壓示威活動。
- The speech the president made yesterday could not quell the growing doubts about the future of the nation.
  總統昨日的演說也無法平息人們對國家未來與日俱增的疑慮。

同 calm 使鎮定、使平靜

生活常用

學校工作

情緒心智

社會萬象

136 quench
-quenched-quenched

vt. 熄滅、撲滅、平息、壓抑、解渴

- A bucket of water quenched the fire.
  一桶水就將火給撲滅了。
- A cup of tea will quench my thirst.
  一杯茶就能解我的渴。

衍 quenchable *adj.* 可以壓制的；
　quencher *n.* 熄滅的人（物）；
　quenchless *adj.* 難鎮靜的
同 suppress 鎮壓、平定、壓制
組 quench steel 淬鋼
片 quench one's thirst 解渴

 聯想學習Plus

- leash 當名詞是指「牽狗的鏈條」，on a short / tight leash 是指用很短、很緊繃的鏈子牽著狗走，就像用很短的狗鏈限制住狗的行動，狗兒無法走遠，一走遠就會被鏈子勒住脖子。而 have sb. on a short / tight leash 這句話，就是說人的行動完全被限制住，無法自由行動的意思，白話來說就是「把某人管得死死的」。

小試身手UP

( ) 1. Thinking of the homework that has to be done _____ me.
　　(A) leashed　(B) quelled　(C) quenched　(D) depresses
( ) 2. Adolf Hitler _____ the Jewish people.（複選）
　　(A) quelled　(B) oppressed　(C) persecuted　(D) quenched

 Ans
1. (D)　想到要做的功課就讓我心情沉重。
2. (B)(C)　阿道夫‧希特勒迫害猶太人。

25 Lesson

壓制

🎧 MP3 2-25

repress / suppress / withhold / oppress

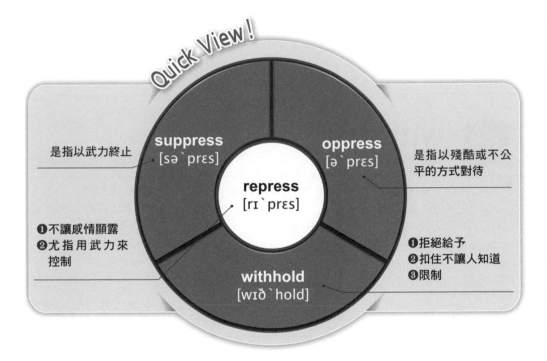

Quick View!

是指以武力終止

suppress
[sə`prɛs]

oppress
[ə`prɛs]

是指以殘酷或不公
平的方式對待

repress
[rɪ`prɛs]

❶不讓感情顯露
❷尤指用武力來
　控制

❶拒絕給予
❷扣住不讓人知道
❸限制

withhold
[wɪð`hold]

---

137 repress
-repressed-repressed

vi. 抑制、鎮壓　*vt.* 抑制、壓制、約束

- The army quickly repressed the uprising.
  軍隊迅速地鎮壓了暴動。
- He repressed his desire to talk to her.
  他壓抑自己想跟她說話的衝動。

衍 repressed *adj.* 受壓抑的；
repressible *adj.* 可鎮壓的；
repression *n.* 抑制、壓制；
repressive *adj.* 鎮壓的

同 restrain 抑制、遏制

反 incite 激勵、激起、煽動

suppress
-suppressed-suppressed

vt. 鎮壓、平定、壓制

- The government suppressed the rebellion.
政府鎮壓叛亂。
- "The revolt should be suppressed in an hour," said the president.
總統說：「必須在一個小時內鎮壓叛變。」

衍 suppressed *adj.* 抑制的；
suppresser *n.* 鎮壓者；
suppression *n.* 壓抑、禁止
同 curb 控制、約束、抑制

withhold
-withheld-withheld

vi. 克制、自制　vt. 保留、阻擋

- Your boss withholds money from your pay for taxes and insurance.
你的老闆從你的薪水預扣了稅與保險費。
- Angela knew that Kevin was the thief but she withheld information.
安琪拉知道凱文就是小偷，但是她隱瞞了真相。

衍 withheld *adj.* 被扣留的
同 preserve 保護、維護、維持
近 withdraw 提領、收回
組 withholding tax 代扣所得稅；
withholding period 停藥期
片 withhold from 保留、隱瞞

oppress
-oppressed-oppressed

vt. 壓迫、壓制、使沉重

- Many dictators oppress their people by force.
許多獨裁者會用武力壓迫自己的人民。
- The oppressed will fight for their rights.
受迫害者要為他們的權利而戰。

衍 oppressed *adj.* 受壓迫的；
oppression *n.* 壓迫、壓制；
oppressive *adj.* 壓迫的；
oppressor *n.* 壓制者
同 burden 加重壓於、加負擔於

聯想學習Plus

• 她去 ATM 提領（withdraw）薪水的時候，發現被公司用許多名義扣掉（withhold）了錢，讓她很沮喪（depressed）。

小試身手UP

(   ) 1. My boss is bossy, and he _____ we employees to work not only overtime but also on holidays.
    (A) oppresses   (B) withholds   (C) suppresses   (D) represses

(   ) 2. The landlord _____ my deposit until I returned the key.
    (A) oppressed   (B) withheld   (C) suppressed   (D) repressed

1. (A) 我老闆很跋扈，他壓迫我們員工不僅加班還要假日上班。
2. (B) 房東在我歸還鑰匙後才退還押金。

生活常用

學校工作

情緒心智

社會萬象

激發

🎧 MP3 2-26

activate / induce / motivate / spur / stimulate / urge

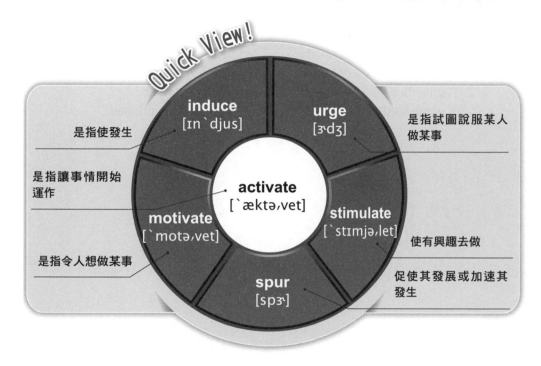

Quick View!

induce
[ɪn`djus]
是指使發生

urge
[ɝdʒ]
是指試圖說服某人做某事

是指讓事情開始運作

activate
[`æktə͵vet]

motivate
[`motə͵vet]

stimulate
[`stɪmjə͵let]
使有興趣去做

是指令人想做某事

spur
[spɝ]

促使其發展或加速其發生

---

141 | activate
-activated-activated

vt. 使活動起來、使活化、觸發

- You will activate the alarm if you open the door without inputting the correct code.
  你如果沒有輸入正確密碼就開門的話，就會觸動警報器。

- Adequate caffeine can activate my slowing-down brain.
  適量的咖啡因能激活我那變遲緩的腦袋。

衍 active *adj.* 活躍的；
activation *n.* 活化作用；
activator *n.* 激活劑

反 deactivate 使無效；
inactivate 使不活躍

組 voice-activated 聲控的；
activated charcoal 活性碳

142 induce
-induced-induced

vt. 引起、導致、引誘

- That cold potion will induce drowsiness.
  那款感冒藥水會引發嗜睡。
- Don't induce me to do something illegal.
  不要引誘我做非法的事。

Tip induce sb. to-V 是指「誘使某人去做某事」之意。

衍 induced *adj.* 由……引起的；
inducer *n.* 誘導物；
inducement *n.* 誘因
同 cause 導致、使發生、引起
近 seduce *v.* 勾引；
deduce *v.* 推論；
reduce *v.* 減少

143 motivate
-motivated-motivated

vt. 給……動機、刺激、激發

- A good teacher motivates students to learn.
  好的老師會激發學生學習的意願。
- The teacher motivated students to study hard by giving candy.
  老師用發糖果來激勵學生努力學習。

衍 motivated *adj.* 有積極性的；
motivation *n.* 刺激；
motivational *adj.* 動機的；
motivator *n.* 激發因素；
motive *n.* 動機
片 be motivated by 被激起

144 spur
-spurred-spurred

vi. 給予刺激　vt. 鞭策、鼓勵　n. 刺激

- Her enthusiasm spurred me on.
  她的熱情激勵了我。
- On the spur of the moment, she bought ten hats in the department store.
  她一時衝動，在百貨公司買了十頂帽子。

衍 spurred *adj.* 裝有馬刺的
同 urge 催促、激勵
片 earn one's spurs 贏得榮譽；
on the spur of the moment 一時衝動；
spur on 催促、鞭策

145 | stimulate
-stimulated-stimulated

vi. 有刺激之作用　vt. 刺激、使興奮

- That book stimulated his interest in monsters.
  那本書激起他對怪獸的好奇。
- A good manager stimulates the workers to work diligently.
  好的經理會激勵員工勤奮工作。

衍 stimulant *n.* 興奮劑；
stimulation *n.* 刺激；
stimulative *adj.* 刺激性的；
stimulus *n.* 刺激

反 deaden 緩和、使變弱

片 stimulate to 刺激某人做某事

146 | urge
-urged-urged

vi. 極力主張　vt. 催促、力勸、慫恿

- They urged us to stay at home because of the snowstorm.
  因為暴風雪的緣故，他們勸我們留在家裡。
- Tom's mother urged that he (should) marry as soon as possible.
  湯姆的母親催促他趕快結婚。

衍 urgency *n.* 緊急；
urgent *adj.* 急迫的；
urgently *adv.* 急迫地

同 push 逼迫、促使

組 urgent request 急迫要求

片 urge (sb.) on 鼓勵某人做某事

小試身手UP

(　) 1. There is nothing that could _____ me to accept your offer.
　　(A) induce　(B) stir　(C) spur　(D) seduce

(　) 2. The rider _____ his horse to jump over the fence.
　　(A) induced　(B) urged　(C) spurred　(D) stimulated

1. (A) 沒有任何事可以說服我接受你的提議。
2. (C) 騎士策馬跳過柵欄。

27 Lesson

驅使

🎧 MP3 2-27

compel / force / impel / propel / push

Quick View!

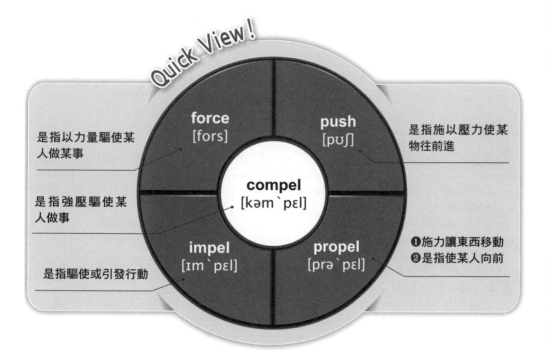

- 是指以力量驅使某人做某事

force
[fors]

push
[pʊʃ]

- 是指施以壓力使某物往前進

compel
[kəm`pɛl]

- 是指強壓驅使某人做事

- 是指驅使或引發行動

impel
[ɪm`pɛl]

propel
[prə`pɛl]

❶施力讓東西移動
❷是指使某人向前

---

147 **compel**
-compelled-compelled

vt. 強迫、使不得不

- His violent actions compelled the teacher to call the police.
  他的暴力舉動迫使老師打電話報警。

- My boss never compels me to work overtime.
  我老闆從不強迫我加班。

衍 compelling *adj.* 強制的；
compellent *adj.* 引人注目的
反 persuade 說服、勸服
組 compelling evidence 有利證據
片 compel to 強迫

148 force
-forced-forced

- Ivan forced her to tell the truth.
  艾凡強迫她說實話。
- Women used to be forced to quit when they were to give birth.
  過去婦女要待產時都會被迫離職。

衍 forced *adj.* 強迫的；
forceful *adj.* 強有力的；
forcefully *adv.* 強有力地
同 compel 強迫、使不得不
組 g-force 重力；
Air Force One 空軍一號
片 force in 強迫進入；
force down 往下壓

149 impel
-impelled-impelled

vt. 推進、推動、驅使、迫使

- The final pay cut impelled the workers to go on strike.
  因為最後減薪迫使工人罷工抗議。
- What reason impelled him to robbing the bank?
  什麼原因迫使他去搶銀行？

Tip impel sb. to N / Ving / VR 是指「迫使某人做某事」之意。

衍 impellent *adj.* 推動的、驅使的；
impeller *n.* 推動器
同 force 強迫、迫使

150 propel
-propelled-propelled

vt. 推動、驅策、激勵

- The sailing boat is propelled by wind.
  帆船靠風力推進。
- His curiosity propelled him into the deserted factory.
  好奇心驅使他進入那座廢棄的工廠。

衍 propellant *n.* 推進者、發射火箭；propellent *adj.* 推進的；
propeller *n.* 推進器、螺旋槳
同 push 推、推動
組 jet-propelled 噴氣推進式的；
propeller-driven aircraft 螺旋槳飛機

151 push
-pushed-pushed

vi. 推　vt. 推、推進　n. 推進

- I pushed my bed against the wall.
  我將床往牆邊靠。
- My wife always pushes me to buy beautiful clothes for her.
  我妻子總是要我買漂亮衣服給她。
- The wind pushed the door open.
  是風推開了門。

衍 pushed *adj.* 為難的；
pushing *adj.* 推的；
pusher *n.* 推進者
反 pull 拉、拖
組 push-up 伏地挺身
片 push away 推開；
when it comes to push 當有急需時

 聯想學習Plus

- 跟能量有關的名詞除了力（force）外，還有功率（power）、能量（energy）與力量（strength）。
- 這門是自動門（automatic），不須向外推（push）或往內拉（pull）。

小試身手UP

(　) 1. _____ the dresser against the wall, please.
　　(A) Force　(B) Propel　(C) Push　(D) Compel
(　) 2. The remote plane is _____ by electricity.
　　(A) propelled　(B) pushed　(C) forced　(D) stimulated

 Ans
1. (C)　請把梳妝台靠牆放。
2. (A)　這架遙控飛機由電所驅動。

推遲

🎧 MP3 2-28

defer / delay / detain / postpone / shelve / stay / suspend

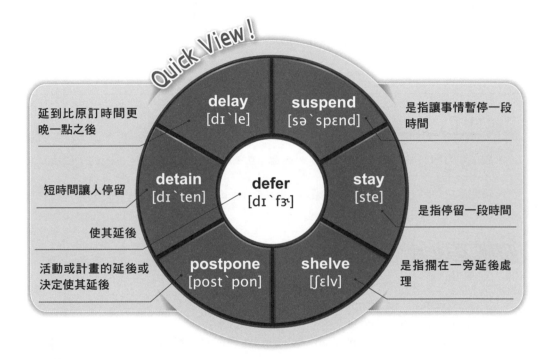

Quick View !

delay [dɪ`le]	**suspend** [sə`spɛnd]
detain [dɪ`ten]	**defer** [dɪ`fɝ]	**stay** [ste]
postpone [post`pon]	**shelve** [ʃɛlv]

- 延到比原訂時間更晚一點之後
- 是指讓事情暫停一段時間
- 短時間讓人停留
- 使其延後
- 是指停留一段時間
- 活動或計畫的延後或決定使其延後
- 是指擱在一旁延後處理

152 | defer
-deferred-deferred

vi. 推遲、延期 *vt.* 推遲、使展期

- We deferred our trip until Mom felt better.
  我們將旅遊延後直到媽媽身體好一點。
- You should defer to the elderly because they are full of experience and wise.
  你應該多聽長輩的話，因為他們既有經驗又有智慧。

衍 deferred *adj.* 延期的；
deferrer *n.* 延期者；
deferrable *adj.* 可延期的
反 hurry 使趕緊、催促
組 deferred payment 延期付款；
deferred charges 遞延費用
片 defer to 聽從、遵從

153 delay
-delayed-delayed

vi. 拖延　vt. 延緩、使延期　n. 耽擱

- We delayed our vacation until we saved more money.
  我們將假期延後直到我們存到更多錢為止。
- Our boss asked me to finish the task soon and not to delay.
  我的老闆要我立刻完成工作，不得拖延。

同 detain 拘留、扣留
反 hurry 使趕緊、催促
組 delay-action 延遲的；
　　delaying tactics 拖延戰術
片 without delay 立即

154 detain
-detained-detained

vt. 留住、使耽擱

- The police detained the suspect.
  警方扣留嫌犯。
- I am sorry to detain you so long.
  很抱歉耽擱你這麼久的時間。

衍 detainee n. 被拘留者；
　　detainer n. 非法占有；
　　detainment n. 拘留
同 delay 耽擱、延誤；
　　detention 拘留、滯留
反 free 使自由、解放

155 postpone
-postponed-postponed

vi. 延遲、延緩　vt. 使延期

- The umpire postponed the baseball game because of rain.
  裁判因下雨將球賽延後。
- Please postpone the test date until next Monday.
  請把考試時間延到下週一。

Tip postpone + Ving 是「延後去做某事」之意。

衍 postponement n. 延期
反 advance 使向前移動、推進、促進
片 postpone until 推延到

156 shelve
-shelved-shelved

vt. 擱置、暫緩考慮

- Let's shelve this matter until we get more information.
  讓我們先擱置這個問題，等到有更多資訊再說吧。
- This case has been shelved for years because no new information has been received.
  這個案件已經被擱置好幾年了，因為一直沒有獲得新情報。

衍 shelving *n.* 斜坡；
shelvy *adj.* 成傾斜狀的；
shelf *n.* 書架、擱板
組 continental shelf 大陸棚

157 stay
-stayed-stayed

vi. 停留、保持　vt. 延緩、延後

- She stayed at our house for five days.
  她待在我們家五天。
- The lawyer asked the judge to stay the sentence till the evidence was all collected.
  律師要求法官延緩判決，直到證據全數收齊為止。

衍 stayer *n.* 滯留者
反 move 使移動、搬動
片 stay away from 遠離；
stay on 留下繼續；
stay behind 仍留在原地；
stay with 同……住在一起；
stay up 熬夜

158 suspend
-suspended-suspended

vi. 懸掛、吊　vt. 使中止

- They suspended the game until the rain stopped.
  他們將球賽延至雨停。
- My driver's license was suspended for three months because I was over the speed limit on the highway.
  我的駕照被吊銷三個月，因為我在公路上超速行駛。

衍 suspender *n.* 懸掛物；
suspense *n.* 掛慮；
suspension *n.* 懸掛；
suspenseful *adj.* 緊張的
組 suspended sentence 緩刑；
suspense novel 懸疑小說
片 suspend from 從……懸掛；
suspend by 以……懸掛

聯想學習Plus

- 村民向政府申請建造一座連接兩個村落的吊橋（suspension bridge），但這個請求一直被擱置（shelve）在議會中，懸（suspended）而未決。

小試身手UP

( ) 1. The flight to Kinmen was _____ due to the bad weather.（複選）
    (A) delayed   (B) deferred   (C) detained   (D) shelved
( ) 2. His plate was _____, so he could not drive temporarily.
    (A) postponed   (B) delayed   (C) deferred   (D) suspended

Ans

1. (A)(B) 飛往金門的班機由於氣候不佳而延誤。
2. (D) 他的車牌被吊銷了，所以他暫時不能開車。

超越

🎧 MP3 2-29

better / exceed / excel / surpass / top

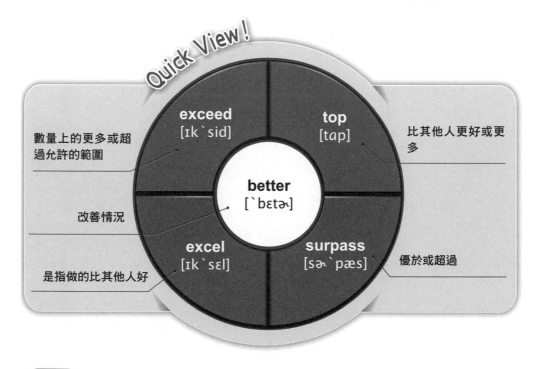

Quick View!

exceed
[ɪk`sid]

數量上的更多或超過允許的範圍

top
[tɑp]

比其他人更好或更多

better
[`bɛtɚ]

改善情況

excel
[ɪk`sɛl]

是指做的比其他人好

surpass
[sɚ`pæs]

優於或超過

159

better
-bettered-bettered

vi. 變得較好 vt. 超過、勝過

- She bettered her previous record.
  她超越了她之前的紀錄。
- After three months of training, Judy finally got the better of her opponents in the dance competition.
  經過三個月的訓練，茱蒂最終在舞蹈比賽中打敗了對手。

組 better half 配偶；
better-off 更有餘裕

片 get better 改善；
all the better 更好；
get the better of 打敗；
couldn't be better 再好不過了

exceed
-exceeded-exceeded

- Don't exceed the speed limit.
  不要超越速限。
- Your grades exceeded mine in math.
  你的數學成績比我好。

衍 exceeding *adj.* 極度的；
　 exceedingly *adv.* 非常地

同 surpass 超過

片 exceed in 在某事超越

excel
-excelled-excelled

- The Brazilian national team excels at football.
  巴西隊的足球實力是頂尖的。
- The excellence of the car consists in its engine.
  汽車的優越與否在於它的引擎。

衍 excellence *n.* 優秀、傑出；
　 excellency *n.* 優點；
　 excellent *adj.* 出色的

同 surpass 勝過、優於

組 par excellence 出類拔萃的；

片 excel at / in 擅長

surpass
-surpassed-surpassed

- This year's milk supply surpasses last year's.
  今年牛奶供應量超過去年。
- Tom's ability surpassed expectations.
  湯姆的能力超出預期。

衍 surpassing *adj.* 非凡的；
　 surpassingly *adv.* 超群地

同 excel 勝過他人

片 surpass in 在……方面勝過

生活常用

學校工作

情緒心智

社會萬象

163 top
-topped-topped

vi. 高出、超越　vt. 高於、超過

- He topped his brother in swimming.
  他在游泳上勝過他的哥哥。
- Write down your name and ID NO. at the top of the test paper.
  在考卷上方寫上名字和身分證號碼。

衍 topping *n.* 最高的；
tops *adj.* 最上等的；
topper *n.* 第一流人物

組 top-secret 最高機密的；
lap-top 筆記型電腦

片 at the top of 在……上面

 聯想學習Plus

- better 是 good 或 well 的比較級，除了當形容詞或副詞之外，還能當動詞和名詞，意思上都脫離不了「更好、較好」的範疇。當名詞時，就是「較佳者、較優者」；當動詞時，就是「好於、優於、勝於、強過」之意。另一個有相似用法的字就是 lower，可以做修飾語或是動詞。
- top banana 本意是指喜劇演員，以前舞台劇演出者講了一個笑話後，別人就會給他一根香蕉，因此就沿用這習俗，將 top banana 指稱最滑稽的演員，久而久之，除了喜劇演員外，公司總裁、最高級的政府官員也能用 top banana 來指稱。

小試身手UP

(　) 1. Working conditons nowadays have ＿＿＿ a lot. Don't you think so?
　　 (A) exceeded　(B) exceed　(C) surpassed　(D) bettered

(　) 2. Don't make your cost ＿＿＿ your budget.（複選）
　　 (A) excel　(B) surpass　(C) exceed　(D) top

 Ans
1. (D) 如今，工作條件已經改善許多。你不這麼認為嗎？
2. (B)(C)(D) 不要讓成本超出你的預算。

競爭

🎧 MP3 2-30

battle / compare / compete / contest / contrast / fight / match

Quick View!

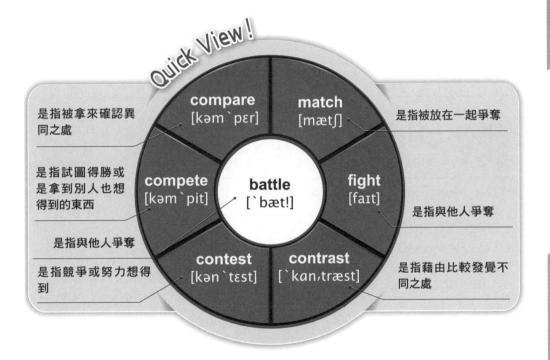

compare [kəm`pɛr]
是指被拿來確認異同之處

match [mætʃ]
是指被放在一起爭奪

compete [kəm`pit]
是指試圖得勝或是拿到別人也想得到的東西

battle [`bæt!]

fight [faɪt]
是指與他人爭奪

contest [kən`tɛst]
是指與他人爭奪
是指競爭或努力想得到

contrast [`kan,træst]
是指藉由比較發覺不同之處

---

164 | # battle
-battled-battled

vi. 作戰、戰鬥　vt. 與……作戰

- The firefighters battled the fire.
  消防員與火搏鬥。
- Firemen battled to save the child from the burning house.
  消防員奮力把孩子從著火的房子中救了出來。

Tip battle to do sth. 是指「奮力做某事」之意。

同 fight 打仗

組 battleship 戰艦；
battlefield 戰場

片 battle for 為……奮鬥；
do battle against / with 跟……對戰

237

compare
-compared-compared

- The police compared the two sets of fingerprints and found that they didn't match.
  警方比對了兩組指紋結果發現不吻合。
- The poet likes to compare a sly guy to a fox.
  詩人喜歡把狡猾的人比作狐狸。

衍 compared *adj.* 比較的；
comparison *n.* 比較；
comparative *n.* 相對的
同 match 使比賽
組 beyond compare 無與倫比
片 compare with 與……相比；
compare to 把……比作

compete
-competed-competed

vi. 競爭、對抗、比賽

- The two friends competed for first place in the class.
  這兩個朋友彼此競爭班上的第一名。
- Several companies competed to get the construction contract of the new bridge.
  幾個公司在爭奪新大橋的工程契約。

衍 competition *n.* 競爭；
competitive *adj.* 競爭性的；
competitor *n.* 敵手
同 contest 爭奪、競爭
組 competent woman 有能力的女人
片 compete against / with 與……競爭；compete for 為……競爭

contest
-contested-contested

vi. 競爭　vt. 爭奪、與……競賽

- The field that the armies contested for was soon littered with the dead and wounded.
  軍隊原本要爭奪的戰場，立刻堆滿成堆的屍體與傷者。
- One of the judges didn't show up for the swimming contest.
  其中一個裁判沒有出席游泳比賽。

衍 contestable *adj.* 可爭的；
contestant *n.* 參加競賽者；
contestation *n.* 爭論
組 beauty contest 選美；
bidding contest 競標
片 not going to win any beauty contests 醜的；
enter a contest 參加比賽

168 contrast
-contrasted-contrasted

vi. 形成對照　**vt.** 使對比、使對照

- The book contrasted the lives of women one hundred years ago with those today.
  這本書對照了一百年前的女人跟現今女人的生活。
- By contrast, this bike is better than that one.
  相比之下，這輛腳踏車比那輛好。

衍 contrasting *adj.* 截然不同的；
contrastive *adj.* 對比的
同 compare 比較、對照
片 in contrast with 與……相比；
by contrast 相比之下；
contrast with 與……形成對照

169 fight
-fought-fought

vi. 打仗、奮鬥　**vt.** 與……作戰

- He is fighting for the championship tonight.
  他今晚將爭奪冠軍。
- The two countries decided to cease fire after fighting for many years.
  經年戰爭後，兩個國家協議停火。

衍 fighting *adj.* 戰鬥的；
fighter *n.* 戰士
組 fighting game 格鬥遊戲；
gunfight 槍戰；
fighting word 挑釁的話
片 fight with 爭奪某物；
fight back 反擊

170 match
-matched-matched

vi. 相配　**vt.** 使較量、使比賽

- Do you know who you'll be matched against in the semifinal?
  你知道你將會與誰在準決賽中對決嗎？
- We will have a tennis match against them next week.
  下週我們將和他們進行網球比賽。

衍 matched *adj.* 相配的；
matching *adj.* 一致的；
matchless *adj.* 無與倫比的
組 match point 決勝點；
love match 戀愛結婚
片 match up 相配；
match up to 比得上；
match for 比得上
be matched against sb. 與某人比賽

- 除了 fighter 有「鬥士、戰士、勇士」的意思，也可以用 warrior（戰士）、solider（勇士、士兵）、knight（騎士）、chevalier（騎士、武士）、samurai（武士）等說法喔！
- firefighter 是指「打火者、消防員」，bullfighter 是指「鬥牛士」。

小試身手UP

(　　) 1. The teacher ＿＿＿＿ the climate in the U.S. with that in Mexico.
(A) compared　(B) contrasted　(C) fought　(D) matched

(　　) 2. Most male species have the habit to ＿＿＿＿ for their territory.
(A) contrast　(B) compete　(C) fight　(D) match

Ans

1. (A)　老師比較了美國跟墨西哥的氣候。
2. (C)　多數雄性物種都有爭奪地盤的習性。

PART 3

情緒心智
Emotions & Mind

衍 衍生字　同 同義字　反 反義字　近 近型字　組 組合字　片 片語

認為

🎧 MP3 3-01

consider / fancy / imagine / suppose / think

Quick View !

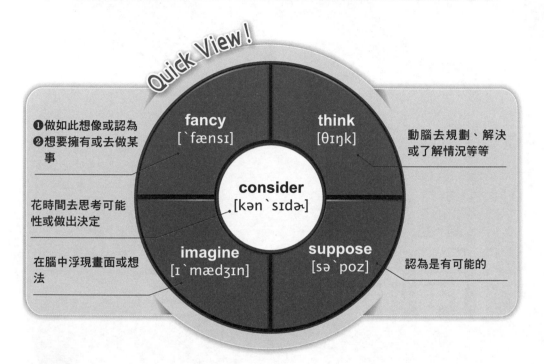

❶做如此想像或認為
❷想要擁有或去做某事

fancy
[`fænsɪ]

think
[θɪŋk]

動腦去規劃、解決或了解情況等等

consider
[kən`sɪdɚ]

花時間去思考可能性或做出決定

在腦中浮現畫面或想法

imagine
[ɪ`mædʒɪn]

suppose
[sə`poz]

認為是有可能的

consider
-considered-considered

vi. 考慮、細想　vt. 考慮、認為

- She is considering being an exchange student in Australia.
  她正在考慮去澳洲當交換學生。
- All of us considered him the last hope of mankind.
  我們全都視他為人類最後的希望。

Tip consider + Ving 考慮……

衍 considering *prep.* 考慮到；
considered *adj.* 經過深思熟慮的；
consideration *n.* 考慮；
considerate *adj.* 體貼的
同 think 思索
反 disregard 不顧
組 all things considered 從全面考慮、總的來說

2 | **fancy**
-fancied-fancied

- Fancy living in Paris. How romantic it is!
  想想在巴黎生活的畫面！多浪漫啊！
- He took a great fancy to the girl with a ponytail.
  他極度迷戀那位綁馬尾的女孩。

Tip fancy + Ving 想像、喜愛……

衍 fancier *n.* 空想家；
  fanciful *adj.* 想像的
同 imagine 想像
反 plain 樸素的
組 fancy ball 嘉年華會
片 fancy sb.'s chances 有信心；
  fancy as 想像、認為

---

3 | **imagine**
-imagined-imagined

vi. 想像、猜想　vt. 想像

- Can you imagine hitting a jackpot and being a billionaire?
  你能想像中頭彩並成為億萬富翁嗎？
- You can't imagine how disappointed I was at that time.
  你無法想像我當時有多失望。

Tip imagine + Ving 想像……

衍 image *n.* 影像；
  imagism *n.* 意象派；
  imaginary *adj.* 虛構的
同 envision 展望
片 Imagine that! 很難想像！
  imagine as 想像成

---

4 | **suppose**
-supposed-supposed

vi. 猜想、料想　vt. 猜想、以為

- I suppose that he must be in the lab now.
  我猜想他現在一定在實驗室。
- He won't show up, I suppose.
  我料想他不會出現。

衍 supposed *adj.* 假定的；
  supposing *conj.* 如果；
  supposedly *adv.* 可能；
  supposition *n.* 想像、假定
同 believe 認為
片 be supposed to-V 應該

5 | think
-thought-thought

vi. 認為　vt. 想、思索

- I can't answer yet. I'm still thinking about your question.
  我答不上來，因為我還在想你的問題。
- I think the novel is very interesting.
  我認為這部小說非常有趣。

衍 thinking *adj.* 好思考的；
thinker *n.* 思想家；
thought *n.* 思考

同 suppose 猜想、以為

組 think big 立大志、眼光放遠

片 think little of 不重視；
think about 考慮；
think nothing of 把……視為平常

聯想學習Plus

- think about 是指「思考」，比如 think about your future；think of 是「認為、思念」，比如 think of the new manager；think as 則是指「認為」，比如 think of my parents as good people。

小試身手UP

(　) 1. She is _____ moving to Alaska.
(A) considering　(B) thinking　(C) supposing　(D) imagining to

(　) 2. I can't _____ that people will live on the moon.
(A) imagine　(B) think　(C) consider　(D) fancy

Ans 1. (A) 她正在考慮搬到阿拉斯加。
2. (A) 我無法想像人類會住在月球上。

回想

🎧 MP3 3-02

memorize / recall / recollect / remember / reminisce

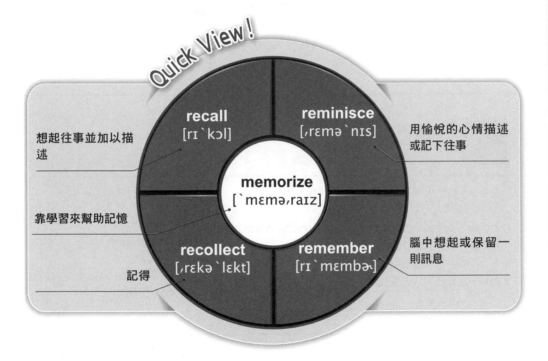

Quick View!

recall
[rɪ`kɔl]
想起往事並加以描述

reminisce
[ˌrɛmə`nɪs]
用愉悅的心情描述或記下往事

memorize
[`mɛməˌraɪz]

靠學習來幫助記憶

recollect
[ˌrɛkə`lɛkt]
記得

remember
[rɪ`mɛmbɚ]
腦中想起或保留一則訊息

---

6 | # **memorize**
-memorized-memorized

vt. 記住、背熟

- He memorized the song lyrics.
  他記得這首歌的歌詞。
- It's hard for me to memorize new vocabulary.
  我很難記住新字彙。

衍 memorization n. 熟記；
memory n. 記憶；
memorialize v. 紀念
同 remember 記得
片 take a walk down memory lane
追憶往昔

7 recall

-recalled-recalled

vi. 記得、回想　*vt.* 回想、召回

- The company recalled thousands of cars for the sake of security.
  為了安全起見，公司召回了數千台汽車。
- I remember his face but I cannot recall where I met him and what his name is.
  我記得他的長相，但是想不起來在什麼地方見過他以及他叫什麼名字。

衍 recallable *adj.* 可回憶的、可召回的
組 recall an order 撤銷訂貨單；have some recall 有些記憶
片 beyond recall 無法挽回的、想不起來

8 recollect

-recollected-recollected

vi. 回憶、記憶　*vt.* 回憶、追憶

- I can't recollect when I last saw him.
  我想不起上次什麼時候見過他。
- I can't recollect having had dinner with him before.
  我記不得以前曾跟他用過晚餐。

Tip recollect + Ving 回想起⋯⋯

衍 recollected *adj.* 回憶到的；recollection *n.* 記憶；recollective *adj.* 記起的
同 remember 記得
反 forget 忘記
片 to the best of my recollection 如果我沒記錯

9 remember

-remembered-remembered

vi. 記得、記住　*vt.* 想起、回憶起

- I finally remembered his name.
  我終於記起他的名字。
- Remember to ring me when you are back.
  當你回來的時候記得打電話給我。

衍 remembrance *n.* 記憶力
同 recollect 使記起
反 forget 忘記
組 Remembrance Day 陣亡將士紀念日
片 remember to 向⋯⋯致意

10 | reminisce
-reminisced-reminisced

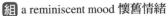 vi. 追憶、回想　vt. 追憶、緬懷

- He doesn't like to reminisce about his miserable childhood.
  他不喜歡回憶他悲慘的童年。
- We have plenty of time to reminisce about our precious short lives.
  我們有足夠的時間來回憶珍貴且短暫的一生。

衍 reminiscence *n.* 舊事、回憶錄；reminiscent *adj.* 懷舊的

組 a reminiscent mood 懷舊情緒

片 reminisce about 回憶；be reminiscent of 使人想起

生活常用

學校工作

情緒心智

社會萬象

聯想學習Plus

- member 是「會員」的意思，前面加 re 就形成動詞 remember（記得）；mind 是「心智」，前面加 re 就形成動詞 remind（提醒、使記起）。

小試身手UP

(　) 1. She has a poor _____. That's why she always forgets to bring her key.
   (A) memorize　(B) recollect　(C) remember　(D) memory

(　) 2. Those old soldiers always get together and _____ those good old days.
   (A) recollect　(B) memorize　(C) remember　(D) reminisce

 Ans
1. (D) 她記憶力很差，這是她為何總是忘記帶鑰匙的原因。
2. (D) 那些老兵總是聚在一起追憶美好的往日時光。

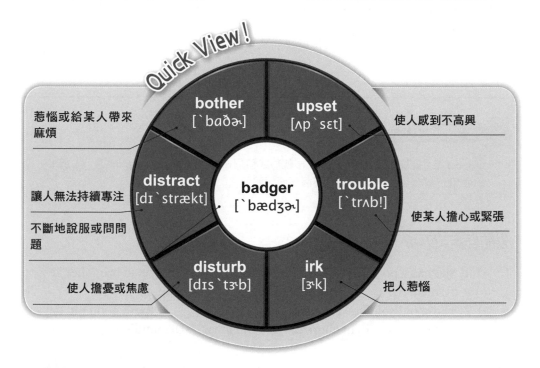

Quick View!

惹惱或給某人帶來麻煩	**bother** [`bɑðɚ]
	upset [ʌp`sɛt] — 使人感到不高興
讓人無法持續專注	**distract** [dɪ`strækt]
不斷地說服或問題	**badger** [`bædʒɚ]
	trouble [`trʌbl̩] — 使某人擔心或緊張
使人擔憂或焦慮	**disturb** [dɪs`tɝb]
	irk [ɝk] — 把人惹惱

---

11 badger
-badgered-badgered

vt. 困擾、糾纏　n. 獾

- The beggar badgered me to give him some change.
  乞丐一直纏著我要零錢。
- The kid badgered his mother into buying that toy in the store.
  小孩一直在店裡纏著媽媽買玩具。

[同] question 詢問
[組] badger game 美人計；Badger State 獾州（美國威斯康辛州別名）
[近] badge n. 徽章
[片] badger into + Ving 纏著要……

12 bother
-bothered-bothered

vi. 煩惱、擔心　vt. 煩擾、打擾

- The loud noise is bothering us.
  這吵雜的噪音正打擾我們。
- John: Do you mind if I sit here?
  Jane: Doesn't bother me at all.
  約翰：妳介意我坐在這兒嗎？
  珍：我不介意。

衍 bothersome *adj.* 令人厭煩的
同 trouble 使煩惱、使憂慮
片 hot and bothered 相當生氣的、
　心急如焚的

13 distract
-distracted-distracted

vt. 使分心、困擾

- Noise from the street distracted him from his work.
  街上的吵雜聲干擾他工作。
- The rumor that he is having an affair with a married woman distracts him a lot.
  他跟已婚女性婚外情的謠傳令他十分困擾。

衍 distraction *n.* 干擾分心；
　distracted *adj.* 心煩意亂的
同 disturb 打擾、妨礙
片 distract from 使分心

14 disturb
-disturbed-disturbed

vi. 打擾、妨礙　vt. 擾亂、搞亂

- The party next door disturbed our sleep.
  隔壁的派對妨礙我們睡覺。
- I'm sorry to disturb you with these trifles.
  抱歉拿這些瑣事來煩你。

衍 disturbance *n.* 擾亂、打擾；
　disturbing *adj.* 令人覺得厭煩的
同 bother 煩擾、打攪
近 turbulence *n.* 亂流、動亂

15 irk
-irked-irked

vt. 使厭倦、使苦惱

- Drivers were irked by the rising price of gasoline.
  汽油價格上漲讓駕駛相當頭痛。
- No one replying to their complaints irked the customers.
  沒人回應他們的投訴令顧客氣惱。

衍 irksome *adj.* 令人厭煩的
同 annoy 煩擾、生氣
反 please 使高興

16 trouble
-troubled-troubled

vi. 煩惱　vt. 使煩惱　n. 憂慮

- What is troubling you?
  什麼事令你操煩？
- Can I trouble you about a room booking problem?
  我可以請教你一個有關訂房的問題嗎？
- I didn't mean to cause anyone trouble.
  我並不想給任何人添麻煩。

衍 troublesome *adj.* 麻煩的；
　troublemaker *n.* 製造問題者；
　troubleshoot *v.* 解決問題、偵錯
同 upset 煩擾、打擾
反 comfort 使安逸舒適
片 trouble sb. about sth. 用某事叨擾別人

17 upset
-upset-upset

vi. 翻倒、傾覆　vt. 使心煩意亂

- Their complaints upset her.
  他們的抱怨困擾著她。
- Milk upsets his stomach.
  牛奶令他的腸胃不適。

衍 upsetting *adj.* 心煩的
同 trouble 使煩惱、使憂慮
反 calm 使鎮定
組 an upset stomach 肚子不舒服
片 upset the apple cart 破壞計畫

聯想學習Plus

- bothersome（令人討厭的、麻煩的）同義詞有：tiresome（煩人的、討厭的）；annoying（討厭的、使人煩惱的）；irksome（令人厭煩的、令人惱恨的）；troublesome（令人煩惱的、討厭的）。

小試身手UP

( ) 1. A blow of wind _____ the surface of the pond.
   (A) troubled　(B) disturbed　(C) badgered　(D) distracted

( ) 2. A: If I have time, I will pay a visit to your new apartment.
   B: You don't need to _____ to come by.
   (A) disturb　(B) trouble　(C) badger　(D) bother

( ) 3. A mosquito kept hovering around me last night, and that really _____ me.（複選）
   (A) disturbed　(B) troubled　(C) annoyed　(D) distracted

1. (B)　一陣風吹撥動了池水。
2. (D)　A: 如果我有時間，我會去拜訪你的新公寓。
   　　　B: 你不必特意來一趟。
3. (A)(B)(C)　昨晚有一隻蚊子在我身邊盤旋，令我覺得煩。

想要

MP3 3-04

desire / expect / hope / plan / want / wish

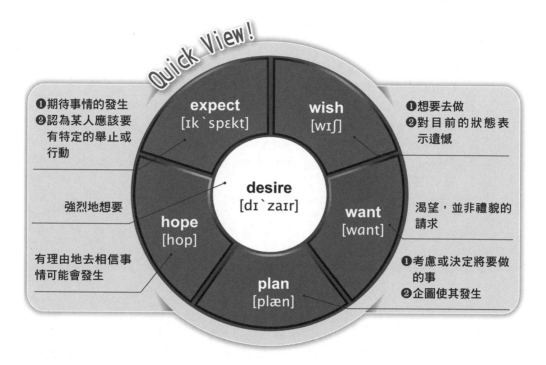

Quick View!

expect
[ɪk`spɛkt]
❶期待事情的發生
❷認為某人應該要有特定的舉止或行動

wish
[wɪʃ]
❶想要去做
❷對目前的狀態表示遺憾

desire
[dɪ`zaɪr]

hope
[hop]
強烈地想要
有理由地去相信事情可能會發生

want
[want]
渴望，並非禮貌的請求

plan
[plæn]
❶考慮或決定將要做的事
❷企圖使其發生

---

18 desire
-desired-desired

vt. 渴望、要求 n. 欲望

- Both countries desire peace after years of war.
  經過幾年的戰亂後，兩國都渴望和平。
- She's a material girl. What she desires most is money.
  她是拜金女，最渴望金錢。

衍 desirous *adj.* 渴望的；
desirable *adj.* 值得嚮往的；
desirably *adv.* 合意地
同 wish 但願
反 hate 討厭
組 sexual desire 性渴望
片 a desire for sth. 渴望某物；
desire to-V 想要

19 expect
-expected-expected

vi. 期待、預期　**vt.** 期待、盼望

- They expected more letters from their son.
  他們期盼收到兒子更多的來信。
- He didn't expect to see his coming.
  他沒預期會見到他過來。
- The novel *Great Expectations* was written by Charles Dickens.
  小說《孤星血淚》是由狄更斯所著。

衍 expected *adj.* 期待中的；
expectative *adj.* 期望的；
expectation *n.* 期望、預料；
expectancy *n.* 預期
同 anticipate 預期
反 despair 絕望
組 life expectancy 預期壽命
片 expect for 期盼

20 hope
-hoped-hoped

vi. 希望、期待　**vt.** 希望、盼望

- I hope that I can get the job.
  我希望能獲得那份工作。
- Many people hope to reform the education system.
  許多人希望改革教育體制。
- They hope against hope that no one is dead or injured.
  他們仍抱持無人死傷的一線希望。

衍 hopeful *adj.* 抱有希望的；
hopeless *adj.* 不抱希望的；
hopelessness *n.* 不抱希望
同 desire 渴望、要求
反 despair 絕望
組 white hope 承擔著艱鉅任務的人、被寄予厚望的人
片 hope against hope 抱一線希望

21 plan
-planned-planned

vi. 計劃、打算　**vt.** 計劃、打算

- He planned to send his children to college.
  他打算送他的孩子上大學。
- Did you make any plans for your trip?
  你有為你的旅行做任何安排嗎？

衍 planned *adj.* 有計劃的；
planning *n.* 制定計劃；
planner *n.* 計劃者
同 propose 提出
組 family planning 家庭計劃
片 plan out 縝密計劃；
plan for 為……作計劃

22 want

-wanted-wanted

vi. 缺乏、需要　*vt.* 想要、通緝

- What do you want from me?
  你想從我這裡得到什麼？
- My iPad wants repairing.
  我的平板該送修了。
- All he wanted was luck, so he failed at last.
  他缺少的就是運氣，所以最終失敗了。

衍 wanted *adj.* 被通緝的；
　 wanting *adj.* 缺少的；
　 wantage *n.* 缺少
同 desire 渴望、要求
反 plenty 豐富
組 want ad 徵聘廣告
片 want out of sth. 想要退出

23 wish

-wished-wished

vi. 希望、想要　*vt.* 祝願、希望

- We wish you a merry Christmas.
  我們願你聖誕快樂。
- As you wish, ma'am.
  夫人，如您所願。
- I wish (that) I hadn't been there.
  我真希望我那時候沒去那裡。

衍 wishful *adj.* 願望的；
　 wishfully *adv.* 希望地
同 want 要、想要
組 wish list 願望清單；
　 wishful thinking 如意算盤
片 wish on 把……強加於

小試身手UP

(　) 1. Close your eyes, make a _____, and then blow out the candle.
　　　(A) desire　(B) hope　(C) want　(D) wish
(　) 2. Children all _____ Santa Claus will come and give them gifts.
　　　(A) want　(B) desire　(C) expect　(D) plan

Ans　1. (D) 閉上眼睛，許個願，再吹熄蠟燭。
　　　2. (C) 孩子們全都期待聖誕老人過來送禮物。

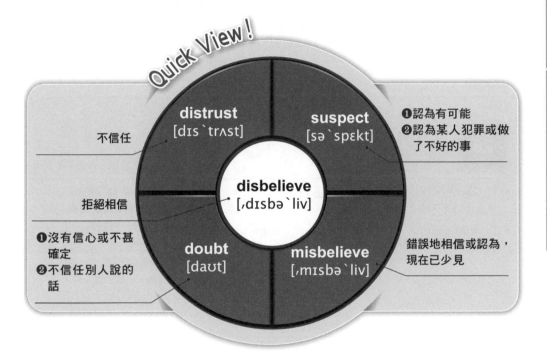

Lesson **5** 不信 🎧 MP3 3-05

disbelieve / distrust / doubt / misbelieve / suspect

Quick View!

distrust [dɪs`trʌst] 不信任

suspect [sə`spɛkt] ❶認為有可能 ❷認為某人犯罪或做了不好的事

disbelieve [ˌdɪsbə`liv] 拒絕相信

doubt [daʊt] ❶沒有信心或不甚確定 ❷不信任別人說的話

misbelieve [ˌmɪsbə`liv] 錯誤地相信或認為，現在已少見

---

24 **disbelieve**
-disbelieved-disbelieved

vi. 不信、懷疑　vt. 不相信

- No one can disbelieve facts.
  沒有人可以否認事實。
- Though he defended himself with efforts in court, the jury disbelieved him.
  儘管他在法庭上努力為自己辯護，陪審團依然不相信他。

衍 disbelief *n.* 懷疑
同 doubt 懷疑
反 believe 相信

25 distrust
-distrusted-distrusted

vt. 不信任、懷疑　n. 不信任

- We had a slight distrust of him after seeing him sneak into our room.
  見過他偷溜進我們房間後，我們就對他有些不信任了。
- He looked at his friend with distrust.
  他用懷疑的眼光看著他朋友。

衍 distrustful *adj.* 不信任的；
distrustfully *adv.* 懷疑地
同 mistrust 不信任、懷疑
反 trust 信任

26 doubt
-doubted-doubted

vi. 懷疑　vt. 懷疑、不相信

- He doubts if he could pass the test.
  他懷疑自己能否通過考試。
- I doubt that he is hiding something from us.
  我懷疑他對我們有所隱瞞。

衍 doubting *adj.* 懷疑的；
doubtless *adj.* 無疑的；
doubtful *adj.* 可疑的
同 mistrust 不信任
反 confidence 信賴
片 in doubt 不確定的；
no doubt 無疑地；
beyond doubt 無庸置疑

27 misbelieve
-misbelieved-misbelieved

vi. 信奉異教　vt. 不信

- He misbelieved what we told him.
  他不信我們跟他說的話。

衍 misbelieving *adj.* 信仰錯誤的；
misbeliever *n.* 信仰錯誤的人

28 | suspect
-suspected-suspected

vi. 懷疑、猜疑　vt. 懷疑、不信任

• The police suspected him of being involved in two different crimes.
警方懷疑他涉嫌兩宗不同的罪。

• The cat suspected danger approaching and fled away.
貓查覺到危險靠近，馬上逃走了。

衍 suspicion *n.* 疑心；
　　suspecter *n.* 猜疑者；
　　suspicious *adj.* 猜疑的
同 distrust 不相信
反 trust 信任
組 suspected case 疑似病例
片 suspect of 懷疑

 聯想學習Plus

• 有關情緒的單字，包括滿足（satisfaction）、憂愁（sorrow）、懷疑（doubt）與驕傲（pride）。
• 我很懷疑（doubt）你能把錢變成兩倍（double）。
• distrust 的語氣比 mistrust 強，但兩者意思相同，只是 mistrust 可用來描述自己，而 distrust 不行。

小試身手UP

（　）1. The judge didn't accept the _____ testimony because he couldn't prove it.
(A) doubt's　(B) distrust's　(C) suspect's　(D) misbelieve's

（　）2. The scientist _____ anything but things that could be proved by science.（複選）
(A) believed　(B) suspected　(C) trusted　(D) doubted

 Ans
1. (C) 法官沒有採信嫌犯的供辭，因為他沒辦法證明。
2. (B)(D) 科學家只相信能被科學證明的事物。

猜想

🎧 MP3 3-06

assume / conceive / deem / guess / presume

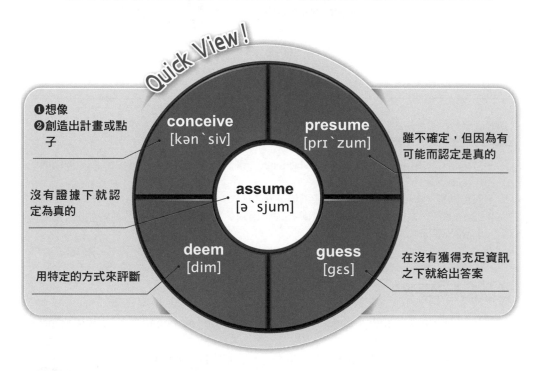

Quick View!

conceive
[kən`siv]

❶想像
❷創造出計畫或點子

presume
[prɪ`zum]

雖不確定，但因為有可能而認定是真的

assume
[ə`sjum]

沒有證據下就認定為真的

deem
[dim]

用特定的方式來評斷

guess
[gɛs]

在沒有獲得充足資訊之下就給出答案

---

29 | ## assume
-assumed-assumed

vi. 裝腔作勢　*vt.* 以為、假定為

- Everyone assumed they were rich because they had a big house, many luxurious cars, and a swimming pool.
  每個人認為他們住豪宅、開名車，還有游泳池，他們就是有錢人。

- He assumed a look as if he didn't know me.
  他裝出一副好似不認識我的樣子。

衍 assumed *adj.* 假裝的；
assuming *adj.* 僭越的；
assumption *n.* 假定
同 suppose 猜想
反 conclude 斷定
組 assumed name 化名

conceive
-conceived-conceived

vi. 構想、設想　vt. 構想出、想像

- I cannot conceive how our house will look when painted purple.
  我無法想像房子漆成紫色是什麼模樣。
- He conceived it his responsibility to fix the problem.
  他認為解決這個問題是他的責任。
- Who can conceive an idea like this?
  誰能想出像這樣的點子？

衍 conceivable *adj.* 可相信的；
　 conceiver *n.* 構想者
同 think 思索
組 ill-conceived 計劃不周的
片 conceive of 設想

deem
-deemed-deemed

vi. 持某種看法　vt. 認為、以為、視作

- He deemed it too great a risk.
  他認為這樣風險太大。
- David deemed it his responsibility to save the animals from being abused.
  大衛認為保護動物免於受虐是他的責任。

Tip deem it + N + to-V 視……為……

同 consider 考慮到
片 be deemed to-V 被認為是……

guess
-guessed-guessed

vi. 猜、推測　vt. 猜測、推測

- Can you guess how many pennies there are in this jar?
  你可以猜一下罐子裡有多少錢嗎？
- Guess who I saw on the street.
  猜猜看我在街上遇到誰了。

衍 guessable *adj.* 可推測的；
　 guessingly *adv.* 憑猜測
同 think 認為
反 prove 證明
組 second-guess 事後評論
片 at a guess 依猜測

生活常用

學校工作

情緒心智

社會萬象

33 | presume
-presumed-presumed

- I presume John will win the swimming competition.
  我認為約翰會贏得游泳比賽。
- He has been missing for years, so he is presumed dead.
  他失蹤好幾年了，所以被認為死了。

衍 presuming *adj.* 專橫的；
　presumedly *adv.* 推測上；
　presumable *adj.* 可推測的
同 suppose 猜想
反 prove 證明
片 presume on 利用

聯想學習Plus

- sume 結尾的動詞有：assume（假定、設想）、consume（消費、吃喝）、presume（假定、推測）、resume（重新開始、繼續）。
- 妻子欺騙（deceive）先生懷孕（conceive）的消息。

小試身手UP

(　) 1. The judge can't ＿＿＿＿＿ any suspect guilty before evidence tells.
　　　(A) assume　(B) suppose　(C) guess　(D) conceive
(　) 2. He ＿＿＿＿＿ a wonderful wedding, so both the bride and groom appreciated that.
　　　(A) conceived　(B) presumed　(C) guessed　(D) deemed

Ans　1. (A) 在罪證確鑿前，法官不能評斷任何嫌犯是有罪的。
　　　2. (A) 他構思出一個完美的婚禮，所以新人都很感激。

理解

🎧 MP3 3-07

comprehend / know / perceive / realize / sense / understand

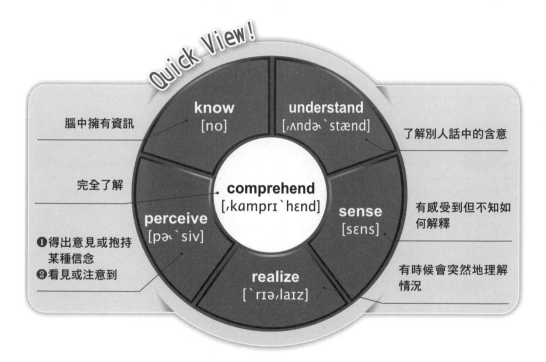

Quick View!

腦中擁有資訊	**know** [no]
完全了解	**understand** [ˌʌndɚˋstænd] 了解別人話中的含意
comprehend [ˌkɑmprɪˋhɛnd]	**sense** [sɛns] 有感受到但不知如何解釋
perceive [pɚˋsiv] ❶得出意見或抱持某種信念 ❷看見或注意到	**realize** [ˋrɪəˌlaɪz] 有時候會突然地理解情況

---

34 comprehend
-comprehended-comprehended

vt. 理解、了解、包含

- Thanks to your specific explanation, I comprehend what the poem says.
多虧你明確的解說，我才明白這首詩在講什麼。

- This reading tests students' comprehension.
這篇文章在測驗學生的理解力。

衍 comprehensibility *n.* 可了解性；
comprehension *n.* 理解力；
comprehensible *adj.* 可理解的

同 understand 理解

片 beyond one's comprehension 難以理解的

35 know
-knew-known

vi. 知道、了解　vt. 知道、辨別

- Not until a few days later did she know what had happened.
  直到幾天後，她才知道發生什麼事。
- The ambitions and desires of aggressors know no bounds.
  侵略者的野心和欲望是無邊無界的。

衍 knowable *adj.* 可知的；knowing *adj.* 有知識的、有意的

組 know one's business 精明能幹；know the time of day 消息靈通；know-nothing 一無所知的；know-how 技術

片 be known to 為……所熟知

36 perceive
-perceived-perceived

vt. 察覺、感知、理解

- He perceived smoke coming out of the kitchen and soon called the fire department.
  他察覺到有煙從廚房冒出來，立即打電話給消防局。
- I always perceive obstacles as challenges.
  我總是把阻礙當作考驗。

衍 perceivably *adv.* 可知覺地；perceivable *adj.* 可察覺的

同 sense 感覺

片 perceive as 把……看作

37 realize
-realized-realized

vt. 領悟、了解、認識到、實現

- Do you realize how hard it is to find a job?
  你知道要找一份工作有多困難嗎？
- He needs money urgently, so he is trying to realize on his house.
  他急需用錢，所以他正試著變賣房子。

衍 realization *n.* 領悟；realizable *adj.* 可實現的；reality *n.* 真實

同 understand 理解

組 self-realization 自我實現

片 realize on 變賣；realize from 知道

38 sense
-sensed-sensed

vt. 感覺到、理解　n. 感官、感覺

- Susan sensed the cold as soon as Rick opened the window.
  當瑞克一打開窗戶，蘇珊就感到寒冷。
- Kevin was out of his senses when he saw the terrifying scene.
  凱文看到這可怕的一幕時，失去了理智。

衍 senseless *adj.* 不省人事的；
sensible *adj.* 明理的；
sensitive *adj.* 敏感的

同 feel 感覺

組 sense of smell 嗅覺；
sense of humor 幽默感

片 sensible of 察覺；
sensitive to 對……敏感

---

39 understand
-understood-understood

vi. 理解　vt. 理解、懂、熟諳

- Do you understand what you are reading?
  你懂你在讀的東西嗎？
- It's hard for her to make herself understood.
  她很難令自己被他人理解。

衍 understanding *n.* 認識；
understandably *adv.* 可理解地；
understandable *adj.* 可理解的

同 grasp 領會、理解

反 misunderstand 曲解

片 be given to understand 得知、
聽說

生活常用　學校工作　情緒心智　社會萬象

小試身手UP

(　) 1. I heard of James, but I didn't _____ him well.
(A) follow　(B) realize　(C) grasp　(D) know
(　) 2. It's common for fans to _____ their idol's news.
(A) grasp　(B) understand　(C) realize　(D) follow
(　) 3. With the teacher's interpretation, students all _____ this poem.
(A) comprehend　(B) realize　(C) sense　(D) perceive

1. (D) 我聽說過詹姆士這號人物，但我不太認識他。
2. (D) 粉絲會追蹤偶像新聞是很常見的。
3. (A) 藉由老師的解釋，學生們全都理解這首詩的含意。

喜愛

cherish / enjoy / prize / relish / treasure / value / worship

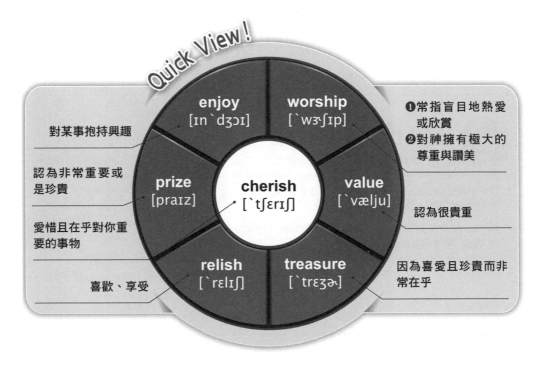

Quick View!

enjoy [ɪn`dʒɔɪ]
對某事抱持興趣

worship [`wɝʃɪp]
❶常指盲目地熱愛或欣賞
❷對神擁有極大的尊重與讚美

prize [praɪz]
認為非常重要或是珍貴

cherish [`tʃɛrɪʃ]

value [`vælju]
認為很貴重

relish [`rɛlɪʃ]
愛惜且在乎對你重要的事物
喜歡、享受

treasure [`trɛʒɚ]
因為喜愛且珍貴而非常在乎

---

40 | cherish
-cherished-cherished

vt. 珍愛、撫育、愛護

- The thing Grandma cherishes most is the letter from her first love.
  祖母最珍惜的一件東西就是初戀給她的信。
- Friendship is highly cherished.
  友誼是最珍貴的。

同 adore 愛慕、熱愛
反 neglect 忽視、忽略
組 cherish a belief 珍惜理念

41 enjoy
-enjoyed-enjoyed

- The French term "bon appétit" means "enjoy the meal."
  「Bon appétit」這個法文詞語的意思是「用餐愉快」。
- The young generation tends to enjoy living alone.
  年輕世代有享受單身生活的趨勢。

衍 enjoyable *adj.* 有樂趣的；
enjoyably *adv.* 有樂趣地；
enjoyment *n.* 享受
同 like 喜歡
反 dislike 不喜愛
片 enjoy oneself 過得愉快；
Enjoy your meal! 用餐愉快！

---

42 prize
-prized-prized

- He prized his family above everything else.
  他把他的家人看得比其他一切更寶貴。
- Believe it or not, I got first prize in the speech competition.
  信不信由你，我在演講比賽中拿了冠軍。

衍 prized *adj.* 被看作最有價值的；prizeman *n.* 得獎人
同 treasure 珍愛、珍視
組 Nobel Prize 諾貝爾獎；
prizewinning 得獎的

---

43 relish
-relished-relished

- To be honest, I didn't relish chatting with him.
  老實說，我並不喜歡跟他聊天。
- Seeing the baby sipping milk with relish melts my heart.
  看見寶寶津津有味地喝奶融化了我的心。

同 enjoy 欣賞
反 loathe 厭惡
組 sweet pickle relish 甜酸黃瓜醬
片 with relish 高興

生活常用

學校工作

情緒心智

社會萬象

44 | **treasure**
-treasured-treasured

vt. 珍愛、珍視　*n.* 財富

- The movie is about pirates who are looking for buried treasure.
  電影是在講述海盜尋寶的故事。
- Treasure those who you love.
  珍惜你所愛的人。

衍 treasurable *adj.* 貴重的；
treasurer *n.* 財務主管；
treasury *n.* 國庫

同 cherish 珍愛

組 treasure hunt 尋寶遊戲

片 One man's trash is another man's treasure. 各人看法不同。

45 | **value**
-valued-valued

vt. 尊重、重視、珍視、估價

- I value the bike at 1,500 dollars.
  我估計這台腳踏車值一千五百元。
- My father values family beyond anything.
  我父親把家庭看得比任何東西都要重要。

衍 valued *adj.* 貴重的；
values *n.* 價值標準；
valueless *adj.* 無價值的

同 worth 價值

組 value asset 價值資產；
value added tax 增值稅

片 take sth. at face value 從表面來看某物；value as 尊重

46 | **worship**
-worshiped-worshiped

vi. 敬神、拜神　*vt.* 崇拜、敬重

- Many people come to this church to worship on Sundays.
  很多人週日會來這座教堂禮拜。
- Worshiping our ancestors is a Chinese tradition.
  祭祖是我們中國的一項傳統。

衍 worshiper *n.* 禮拜者；
worshipful *adj.* 虔誠的；
worshipingly *adv.* 崇敬地

同 respect 敬重、尊敬

反 contempt 輕視

組 self-worship 自我崇拜；
celebrity worship syndrome 哈名人症候群

聯想學習Plus

- prize 當名詞時，有「獎品、獎金」的意思，其他相似意思的還有：award（獎、獎品、獎狀）、reward（報酬）、medal（獎牌）、trophy（獎品、戰利品）。
- 說到 treasure（財寶、金銀珠寶），就要認識相關用語：gold（黃金）、silver（銀）、jewel（寶石）、diamond（鑽石）、pearl（珍珠）等。

小試身手UP

( ) 1. The sculpture is priceless. It can't be _____ at any price.
　　　(A) prized　(B) enjoyed　(C) worshiped　(D) valued

( ) 2. The sausage _____ of honey. How amazing.
　　　(A) prizes　(B) enjoys　(C) worships　(D) relishes

( ) 3. My father is honest, decent, and never breaks his words. He is the one I
　　　_____ most in the world.
　　　(A) cherish　(B) treasure　(C) worship　(D) relish

1. (D) 這座雕刻是無價的，無法用任何價格來估算。
2. (D) 這香腸有花蜜的味道。真令人吃驚。
3. (C) 我父親為人老實、正直，又守信用，是這世上我最敬重的人。

讚賞

🎧 MP3 3-09

acclaim / admire / applaud / appreciate / commend / laud / praise

Quick View!

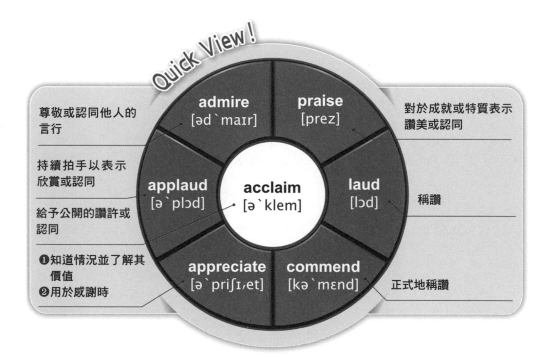

尊敬或認同他人的言行 — **admire** [əd`maɪr]

praise [prez] — 對於成就或特質表示讚美或認同

持續拍手以表示欣賞或認同 給予公開的讚許或認同 — **applaud** [ə`plɔd]

acclaim [ə`klem]

laud [lɔd] — 稱讚

❶知道情況並了解其價值 ❷用於感謝時 — **appreciate** [ə`priʃɪˌet]

commend [kə`mɛnd] — 正式地稱讚

---

47 acclaim
-acclaimed-acclaimed

vi. 歡呼、喝采　vt. 歡呼、喝采、稱讚

- You can see people acclaim those athletes for their excellent performances at the Taipei 2017 Universiade.
在 2017 台北世大運中，四處可見人們為選手的傑出表現喝采。

- The Nobel laureates are widely acclaimed for their contribution to human beings.
諾貝爾得主們因為對人類的貢獻獲得眾人的讚譽。

衍 acclaimed *adj.* 受到讚揚的；
acclamation *n.* 歡呼、喝采；
acclamatory *adj.* 歡呼的
同 applaud 稱讚、贊成
組 poet laureate 桂冠詩人
片 by acclamation 通過口頭表決方式

admire
-admired-admired

- I admire the hard work you do.
  我感謝你辛苦的付出。
- We'll admire Johnson for his profound knowledge.
  我們佩服強森知識淵博。

衍 admiring *adj.* 讚美的；
admirable *adj.* 值得讚揚的；
admiration *n.* 羨慕

同 honor 尊敬

反 despise 看不起

片 admire for 因……稱讚

applaud
-applauded-applauded

- The audience applauded when the play ended.
  當戲劇結束後，觀眾報以掌聲。
- Let's applaud to welcome our special guest.
  讓我們鼓掌來歡迎我們的特別來賓。

衍 applause *n.* 鼓掌歡迎；
applausive *adj.* 拍手喝采的

同 approve 贊成

組 self-applause 自己誇讚

片 applaud sb. to the echo 大聲讚美、喝采

appreciate
-appreciated-appreciated

- Andrea appreciated her sister's help with the children.
  安德莉雅感激她妹妹幫忙照顧小孩。
- No one appreciates my paintings. That hurts.
  沒有人欣賞我的畫作。真令人傷心。

Tip appreciate + Ving 感激做……

衍 appreciation *n.* 賞識；
appreciative *adj.* 有欣賞力的；
appreciator *n.* 欣賞者

同 value 尊重

反 depreciate 輕視、貶值

commend
-commended-commended

- The principal publicly commended him for helping other people.
  校長公開表揚他的樂於助人。
- The book has a good reputation, and it's highly commended to read.
  這本書評價很好，極力推薦大家去閱讀。

衍 commendable *adj.* 值得讚美的；
commendation *n.* 推薦；
commendatory *adj.* 推薦的
同 praise 讚揚、稱讚
片 commend itself to sb. 給某人好印象；
commend for 稱讚

---

laud
-lauded-lauded

vt. 讚美　n. 讚美

- At our school, the sports stars were more lauded than the academic achievers.
  在我們學校，比起功課好的學生，運動明星更受讚揚。
- Our boss seldom lauds his employees' performances.
  我們老闆甚少誇讚員工的表現。

衍 laudable *adj.* 值得讚賞的；
laudably *adv.* 值得讚賞地；
laudative *adj.* 表示讚美的
同 praise 稱讚

---

praise
-praised-praised

vt. 讚美、表揚、歌頌　n. 讚揚

- The coach praised the players for their hard work.
  教練表揚球員辛苦的練習。
- The manager praised Ted for his diligence.
  經理表揚泰德的勤奮。

衍 praiseworthiness *n.* 值得讚揚；
praiseworthy *adj.* 可嘉獎的
同 compliment 讚美
反 blame 指責
片 in praise of 為讚揚；
praise for 因某特性讚揚

聯想學習Plus

- 單親媽媽辛苦扶養（raise）孩子，因此受到眾人的讚揚（praise）。
- applaud（鼓掌喝采）是指持續地拍手（clap）並製造聲響，以表示認同。
- 跟 commend（推薦）有關的動詞還有：recommend（推薦）、advise（建議、忠告）、suggest（建議）、propose（建議、提議）等。

小試身手UP

（　）1. Since I can't _____ art, I do not comment on it.
　　　(A) praise　(B) applaud　(C) commend　(D) appreciate
（　）2. Albee _____ her dog with treats when it behaves well.
　　　(A) praises　(B) appreciates　(C) admires　(D) applauds

Ans
1. (D)　由於我不懂欣賞藝術，我對此便不做評論。
2. (A)　當狗狗表現好的時候，艾比會用點心當作獎勵。

鄙視

🎧 MP3 3-10

depreciate / despise / disdain / disrespect / scorn

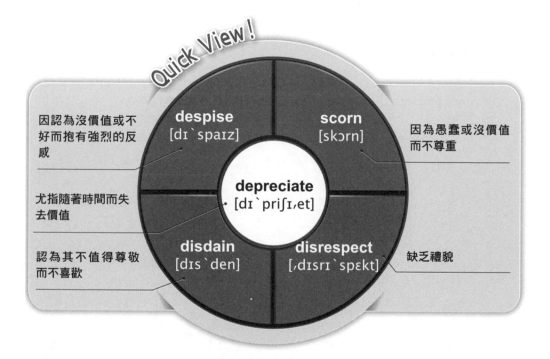

Quick View!

despise
[dɪ`spaɪz]

因認為沒價值或不好而抱有強烈的反感

尤指隨著時間而失去價值

disdain
[dɪs`den]

認為其不值得尊敬而不喜歡

depreciate
[dɪ`priʃɪ͵et]

scorn
[skɔrn]

因為愚蠢或沒價值而不尊重

disrespect
[͵dɪsrɪ`spɛkt]

缺乏禮貌

---

54 | ## depreciate
-depreciated-depreciated

vi. 貶值　vt. 輕視、貶低

• The way he spoke to that beggar teemed with depreciation.
他對那個乞丐的說話方式充滿了輕視。

• The shares I bought last year have depreciated 8 %.
我去年買的股票貶值了 8 %。

衍 depreciation *n.* 貶值；
depreciatory *adj.* 跌價的；
depreciable *adj.* 可折舊的
反 appreciate 賞識、增值
組 accelerated depreciation 加速折舊

55 | **despise**
-despised-despised

vt. 鄙視、看不起

- I despise anyone who is mean to animals.
  我看不起任何對動物殘忍的人。
- He despised himself for not fighting for his own rights.
  他因沒有替自己爭取權利而自我厭惡。

衍 despicably *adv.* 卑劣地；
despicable *adj.* 卑劣的
同 hate 憎恨
反 respect 尊敬
片 despise for 因某事輕視

56 | **disdain**
disdained-disdained

vt. 蔑視、鄙棄　n. 輕蔑、鄙視

- He disdains anyone whose position is below him.
  他瞧不起職務比他低的人。
- I disdain to hang out with those people.
  我不屑與那些人為伍。

Tip disdain to-V 不屑去做某事

衍 disdainful *adj.* 驕傲的；
disdainfulness *n.* 藐視

57 | **disrespect**
disrespected-disrespected

vt. 不尊敬　n. 輕蔑、無禮

- Don't disrespect the handicapped or the elderly.
  不要對身障者或老人無禮。
- The official's remarks show disrespect for women.
  官員的言論顯示對女性的不尊重。

衍 disrespectful *adj.* 無禮的；
disrespectable *adj.* 不值得尊敬的
片 disrespect for 對……輕蔑無禮；
no disrespect (to sb.) 沒有不敬之意

58 scorn
-scorned-scorned

vi. 表示輕蔑　vt. 輕蔑、藐視　n. 鄙視

- They scorned the idea of dressing in silly costumes.
  他們反對穿著愚蠢的戲服。
- The manager poured scorn on Tina's new plan.
  經理對蒂娜的新計畫不屑一顧。

衍 scornful *adj.* 嘲笑的；
scornfully *adv.* 藐視地；
scornfulness *n.* 輕蔑

同 contempt 蔑視

片 pour scorn on 對……不屑一顧；treat sb. with scorn 嘲弄某人

聯想學習Plus

- 形容人的言行無禮，有幾種說法：disrepectful（無禮的）、rude（粗魯的）、impolite（沒有禮貌的）、rough（粗野的、粗暴的）、coarse（粗糙的、粗魯的）等等。

小試身手UP

(　) 1. The student showed _____ to his teachers, so he was given a major demerit.
(A) depreciation　(B) despite　(C) disrespect　(D) respect

(　) 2. Once a new car lands, its value _____.
(A) depreciates　(B) scorns　(C) despises　(D) disdains

1. (C) 那名學生因為對師長無禮，所以被記了一支大過。
2. (A) 新車一落地，它就折舊了。

11 Lesson 感謝

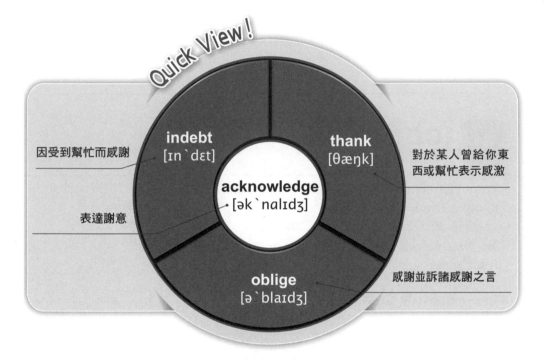

🎧 MP3 3-11

acknowledge / indebt / oblige / thank

Quick View !

indebt [ɪn`dɛt]
因受到幫忙而感謝

acknowledge [ək`nɑlɪdʒ]

表達謝意

thank [θæŋk]
對於某人曾給你東西或幫忙表示感激

oblige [ə`blaɪdʒ]
感謝並訴諸感謝之言

---

59 acknowledge
-acknowledged-acknowledged

vt. 對……表示謝忱、承認

- Her grandmother wrote a note of thanks to acknowledge my help.
  她的祖母寫了一張謝卡感謝我的幫忙。
- I acknowledge that your decision was right.
  我承認你那時的決定是對的。

衍 acknowledged *adj.* 公認的；
acknowledgement *n.* 答謝的表示
同 recognize 認識、承認
反 deny 否定
組 acknowledge the corn 認錯

60 | indebt
-indebted-indebted

vt. 使負債、使受惠

- We are indebted to her for her generosity.
  我們很感激她的慷慨解囊。
- PIIGS are universally recognized as indebted countries.
  歐豬五國被公認為債台高築。

Tip be indebted to sb. for sth. 因某事而感激某人

衍 indebted *adj.* 感激的、負債的；
indebtedness *n.* 受惠

近 debt *n.* 負債

61 | oblige
-obliged-obliged

vi. 施恩惠、幫忙　vt. 使感激、迫使

- I'm much obliged to my aunt for her support to my education.
  我非常感激我阿姨對我學業上的資助。
- He was obliged to do a thing that he doesn't want to do.
  他被迫做一件他不想做的事。

Tip be obliged to-V 被迫做某事

衍 obliging *adj.* 樂於助人的；
obliger *n.* 施惠於人者

同 require 需要

反 free 使解脫

片 much obliged 感謝

62 | thank
-thanked-thanked

vt. 感謝　n. 感謝

- I thanked him for doing me a favor.
  我感謝他的幫忙。
- I'm thankful for your kind help when I was in need.
  我很感激你在我需要幫忙時，好心地幫助我。

衍 thanks *n.* 道謝；
thankful *adj.* 欣慰的；
thankfully *adv.* 感激地

同 acknowledge 就……表示謝忱

片 I can't thank you enough. 我對你真是感激不盡。
thanks to 由於

 聯想學習Plus

- thank for 表示感謝某事如 thank for his help；thankful 是對某人表達感謝之意；thankless 是指困難而且很難被認同的。
- 我們對於他傳授這麼多知識（knowledge）表示謝意（acknowledge）。
- 表達「感謝」的單字有：appreciate（感激、感謝）、acknowledge（表示感謝、承認）、oblige（使感激、施恩於）、grateful（感激的）。

小試身手UP

(　　) 1. She is self-confident, so she would not _____ her mistake.
　　　　(A) acknowledge　(B) oblige　(C) thank　(D) allow

(　　) 2. I am really _____ for her invitation.
　　　　(A) appreciated　(B) thanked　(C) acknowledged　(D) indebted

 Ans　1. (A)　她很自負，所以不願承認錯誤。
　　　　2. (D)　我真的很感謝她的邀請。

威脅

🎧 MP3 3-12

harass / intimidate / menace / terrorize / threaten

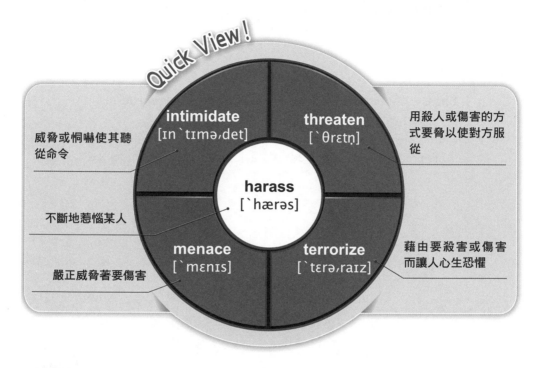

Quick View!

intimidate
[ɪn`tɪmə,det]
威脅或恫嚇使其聽從命令

threaten
[`θrɛtn̩]
用殺人或傷害的方式要脅以使對方服從

harass
[`hærəs]

不斷地惹惱某人

menace
[`mɛnɪs]
嚴正威脅著要傷害

terrorize
[`tɛrə,raɪz]
藉由要殺害或傷害而讓人心生恐懼

---

63 | **harass**
-harassed-harassed

vt. 不斷騷擾、使煩惱

- I saw a girl harassed by a guy on the MRT.
  我看見一位女孩在捷運上被人騷擾。
- Women's groups urge the authorities to enact a law to ban sexual harassment at the workplace.
  女性團體呼籲當局制定法律,遏止職場性騷擾。

衍 harassment *n.* 煩惱、騷擾;
harassed *adj.* 疲憊焦慮的
同 trouble 使憂慮、使煩惱
組 sexual harassment 性騷擾

64 | intimidate
-intimidated-intimidated

vt. 威嚇、脅迫

- Shop owners were intimidated by gangsters who were running a protection racket.
流氓威脅店家索取保護費。
- The clerk was intimidated into opening the safe by the robbers.
店員被搶匪脅迫打開保險箱。

衍 intimidated *adj.* 受到恐嚇的；
intimidating *adj.* 令人生畏的；
intimidation *n.* 恫嚇
同 threaten 威脅
片 intimidate sb. into Ving 威脅某人做……

65 | menace
-menaced-menaced

vi. 進行恐嚇　*vt.* 威脅、恐嚇、危及

- He was menaced by a bully after school.
他放學後遭到惡棍威脅。
- A pest is a menace to the plants.
害蟲有害植物。

衍 menacing *adj.* 威脅的、險惡的；menacingly *adv.* 威脅地
同 threaten 威脅
片 menace sb. with sth. 用某物來威脅某人

66 | terrorize
-terrorized-terrorized

vt. 使恐怖、恐嚇

- The little boy was terrorized by the snarling dog.
小男孩被這隻狂吠的狗嚇到了。
- ISIS's terrorist attacks have terrorized the residents in the U.S.
ISIS 恐怖攻擊讓美國人民驚慌不安。

衍 terrorist *n.* 恐怖分子；
terrorism *n.* 恐怖主義；
terror *n.* 恐懼
組 counter-terrorism 反恐怖主義
片 terrorize into Ving 威脅做……

生活常用

學校工作

情緒心智

社會萬象

67 threaten
-threatened-threatened

vi. 威脅、恐嚇　*vt.* 威脅、恐嚇

- The judge threatened to send him to jail.
  法官揚言要將他送去坐牢。
- Kevin threatened to sue you.
  凱文威脅要告你。
- The girl threatens to commit suicide if her boyfriend breaks up with her.
  男友如果要跟她分手，女孩就威脅要自殺。

衍 threatened *adj.* 受到威脅的；
　threatening *adj.* 險惡的；
　threat *n.* 威脅
同 warn 警告
片 be threatened with 受到……威脅

聯想學習Plus

- warn、alert、caution 是用來提醒別人的警告；而 threaten 和 menace 則是用來威脅、恐嚇別人；harass 則是指侵擾、騷擾別人。

小試身手UP

(　) 1. The plague was once a lethal ＿＿＿＿ to the people in the Middle Ages.
　　(A) harassment　(B) terrorism　(C) threatening　(D) menace

(　) 2. Stop ＿＿＿＿ me. I am concentrating on my report which is due tomorrow.
　　(A) threatening　(B) harassing　(C) terrorizing　(D) menacing

Ans
　1. (D)　瘟疫曾是中世紀人們的致命威脅。
　2. (B)　別再騷擾我了。我要專心做明天要交的報告。

警告

🎧 MP3 3-13

admonish / alert / caution / warn

Quick View !

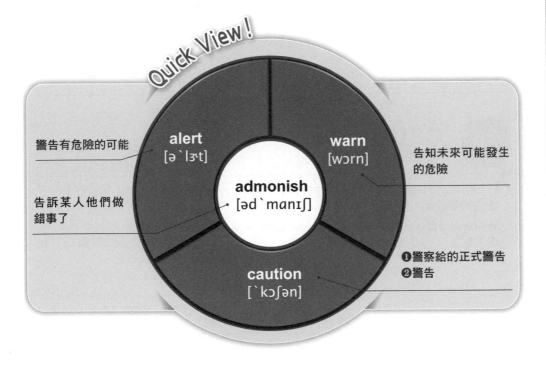

警告有危險的可能

alert
[ə`lɜ·t]

告訴某人他們做錯事了

admonish
[əd`manɪʃ]

warn
[wɔrn]
告知未來可能發生的危險

❶警察給的正式警告
❷警告

caution
[`kɔʃən]

68

admonish
-admonished-admonished

vt. 告誡、警告、提醒

- The teacher admonished the children to be careful when they crossed the street.
  老師告誡孩子們過街時要小心。

- My parents always admonish me against doing something illegal.
  我父母常常告誡我不要犯法。

Tip admonish sb. against Ving 勸告某人不要做某事

衍 admonishment n. 警告、勸告；
admonition n. 警告；
admonitor n. 告誡者

片 admonish for / against 警告、告誡

69 alert
-alerted-alerted

vt. 向……報警、使警覺、使注意

- The mayor alerted the citizens to the danger of the hurricane.
  市長提醒市民注意颶風的侵襲。
- An anonymous e-mail alerted the police to the explosive in the city hall.
  一封匿名郵件向警方舉報市政廳有炸裂物品。

衍 alertly *adv.* 機警地；
alertness *n.* 警覺
組 highest alert 一級戒備
片 on the alert 警戒；
alert sb. to sth. 提醒某人戒備某事

70 caution
-cautioned-cautioned

vt. 警告、告誡、使小心

- I cautioned her about the slippery floor.
  我提醒她小心地板溼滑。
- Without glasses, he walks with caution.
  沒了眼鏡，他走路走得很小心。

衍 cautionary *adj.* 警告的；
cautioner *n.* 警告者；
cautious *adj.* 十分小心的
同 alert 向……發出警報
反 carelessness 粗心大意
組 caution money 保證金
片 throw caution to the winds 魯莽行事、不顧一切

71 warn
-warned-warned

vi. 發出警告 vt. 警告、告誡、提醒

- They warned us of the landslide.
  他們提醒我們小心土石流。
- The teacher always warns us not to cheat on exams.
  老師總是警告我們考試不要作弊。

 Tip warn sb. about / for / of sth. 提醒某人提防某事

衍 warning *n.* 警報；
warner *n.* 警告者
同 inform 通知
組 warning sign 警告標誌
片 warn off 警告……不得靠近

 **聯想學習Plus**

• 氣象專家警告（warn）寒流來襲，請民眾記得做好保暖（warm）工作。

小試身手UP

（　　）1. The young man ignored the hunter's _____ and went into the forest.
　　　　(A) caution　(B) alert　(C) warn　(D) admonish
（　　）2. Keep _____ when you walk home at night.
　　　　(A) caution　(B) admonish　(C) alert　(D) warn

 Ans

1. (A) 年輕人忽視獵人的警告，往森林走去。caution 可當名詞，為「口頭警告」之意，alert 是警戒、警報，是一種戒備的狀態或是訊號之意，較不符合題意。
2. (C) 當你深夜走路回家時，記得保持警戒。

厭惡

🎧 MP3 3-14

disgust / displease / revolt / sicken / spite

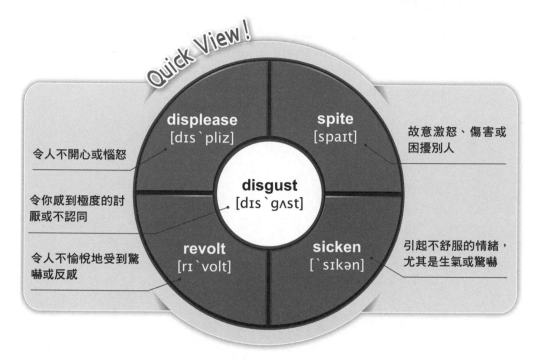

Quick View !

displease [dɪsˋpliz]
令人不開心或惱怒

spite [spaɪt]
故意激怒、傷害或困擾別人

disgust [dɪsˋgʌst]
令你感到極度的討厭或不認同

revolt [rɪˋvolt]
令人不愉悅地受到驚嚇或反感

sicken [ˋsɪkən]
引起不舒服的情緒，尤其是生氣或驚嚇

---

72 disgust
-disgusted-disgusted

vt. 使厭惡、使討厭　n. 作嘔、厭惡

- Seeing the dead animal on the road disgusted her.
  看見馬路上有動物的屍體令她噁心。
- I was disgusted with the way you treated your "rich" friends.
  你對待「有錢」朋友的方式令我反感。

衍 disgusting *adj.* 令人作嘔的；
disgusted *adj.* 感到噁心的
同 sicken 使作嘔
反 please 使高興
片 be disgusted at / with 對……感到厭惡、反感

displease
-displeased-displeased

vi. 使人生氣　*vt.* 得罪、觸怒、使討厭

- Because he displeased his boss by failing to obey his order, he got a pay cut.
  他因為不順從而惹怒老闆，所以被扣薪了。
- The boss was displeased with his employees' low work efficiency.
  老闆不滿意員工低落的工作效率。

衍 displeased *adj.* 感到不開心的；
displeasing *adj.* 令人不愉快的；
displeasure *n.* 不滿
同 anger 使發怒
反 please 使滿意

revolt
-revolted-revolted

vi. 厭惡、反感　*vt.* 使厭惡、使反感

- The news that the father abused his child revolted every parent.
  傳出父親虐待孩子的新聞令每位父母極度不齒。
- She felt revolted by staying overnight in the wild.
  她對於要在野外過夜感到厭惡。

衍 revolting *adj.* 背叛的、造反的
反 obey 服從
組 Arab Revolt 阿拉伯大起義
片 in revolt 嫌惡地

sicken
-sickened-sickened

vi. 生病　*vt.* 使生病

- The pornographic pictures sickened us.
  這些色情圖片使我們感到噁心。
- I sicken of listening to your excuses.
  我聽煩了你的藉口。
- He was sickened by his roommate's loud snoring at midnight.
  他受夠室友在半夜發出的打鼾巨響。

衍 sickening *adj.* 使人噁心的；
sickener *n.* 過量的藥物；
sick *adj.* 生病的、厭煩的
片 sicken of 厭煩

生活常用

學校工作

情緒心智

社會萬象

76 spite
-spited-spited

vt. 惡意對待、刁難、使惱怒　n. 惡意

- He did it just to spite her.
  他那樣做只是為了激怒她。
- Out of spite, Adam stole Andy's bag and threw it into the lake.
  出於怨恨，亞當偷了安迪的包包，並把它扔進湖裡。

衍 spiteful *adj.* 惡意的；
　　spitefully *adv.* 懷有惡意地；
　　spitefulness *n.* 懷恨在心
同 malice 怨恨
片 in spite of 儘管；
　　out of spite 出於惡意

聯想學習Plus

- 間諜（spy）一直吐口水（spit），令人覺得厭煩（spite）。
- dis- 表示「否定、相反、不、分離」的意思，例如：disgrace（丟臉、恥辱）、discourage（使洩氣）、displease（使不開心）、dishearten（使灰心）等。

小試身手UP

(　) 1. In _____ of cold, you still can see many girls wear short skirts on the street.
(A) disgust　(B) revolt　(C) spite　(D) sick

(　) 2. His aggressive remarks on the relations between the straits _____ the party leader.
(A) displeased　(B) revolted　(C) disgusted　(D) sickened

Ans 1. (C) 儘管天冷，還是能看到許多女孩穿著短裙上街。
2. (A) 他那激進的兩岸關係言論惹惱了黨的領導人。

15 Lesson

羞辱

🎧 MP3 3-15

affront / disgrace / humiliate / insult / shame

Quick View!

因為做了不好的事情使自己或家人不再被尊重

disgrace
[dɪs`gres]

shame
[ʃem]

令人感到羞辱、沒有尊嚴

侮辱或冒犯的言行

affront
[ə`frʌnt]

令人感到丟臉或失去尊嚴

humiliate
[hju`mɪlɪˌet]

insult
[ɪn`sʌlt]

無禮或冒犯的言行

---

77 | # affront
-affronted-affronted

vt. 公開侮辱、有意冒犯　n. 公然侮辱

• Burning the national flag was regarded as an affront to the country.
焚燒國旗的行為被視為侮辱國家。

• I felt affronted by the discrimination on the grounds of color.
因為膚色受到歧視讓我感到被冒犯。

Tip on the grounds of N 以……為由

同 insult 侮辱
片 an affront to N 對……的侮辱、冒犯

78 disgrace
-disgraced-disgraced

vt. 使蒙羞、使丟臉　n. 恥辱、丟臉的事

- He is such an outstanding person that he won't want to disgrace the family.
  他是如此傑出的人，所以絕不願意令家族蒙羞。
- He disgraced the team by cheating.
  他由於作弊讓整個團隊丟臉。

衍 disgraced *adj.* 失寵的、遭貶謫的；disgraceful *adj.* 不名譽的、可恥的

片 disgrace oneself 使名譽受損；in disgrace 失寵

79 humiliate
-humiliated-humiliated

vt. 使蒙恥辱、羞辱、使丟臉

- It was humiliating that I forgot my wallet when I wanted to pay the check.
  我要買單時發現忘記帶錢包，真是超丟臉。
- Being scolded by the teacher in front of his classmates humiliated him a lot.
  在同班同學面前被老師斥責令他十分難堪。

衍 humiliation *n.* 蒙羞；humiliator *n.* 羞辱者；humiliatory *adj.* 丟臉的

同 embarrass 使難堪

80 insult
-insulted-insulted

vt. 侮辱、羞辱　n. 辱罵

- He thinks his job is so easy that it's an insult to his intelligence.
  他認為他的工作超簡單，實在有辱他的智商。
- The man insulted the clerk for trivialities, so he was sued for deliberate humiliation.
  男子因為小事辱罵店員，所以被控告公然侮辱。

Tip an insult to sb.'s intelligence 侮辱某人的智商

衍 insulting *adj.* 無禮的、侮辱的；insultingly *adv.* 無禮地

同 offend 冒犯

組 pocket an insult 忍氣吞聲

片 add insult to injury 更糟糕的是

81 shame
-shamed-shamed

vt. 蒙羞、感到羞愧　n. 羞恥、恥辱

- Her hard work put me to shame.
  她的勤奮令我羞愧。
- To my shame, I never said thank you to my parents and hugged them.
  令我羞愧的是，我從來沒有跟父母說句感謝，給他們擁抱。

衍 shameful *adj.* 丟臉的、可恥的；
shameless *adj.* 無恥的；
shamefulness *n.* 可恥

組 shamefaced *adj.* 臉帶愧色的；
shame-making 引起羞恥感的

片 put to shame 使蒙羞；
shame on you 應該感到羞恥

 聯想學習Plus

- insult 源自拉丁語，在 1600 年代，是指以粗暴的方式對待，現在則是指口語上的羞辱居多。
- 你在他門前（front）尿尿，對他們是種侮辱（affront）。

小試身手UP

( ) 1. I didn't mean to ＿＿＿＿ you by saying that. Can you forgive me?
　　　(A) insult　(B) humiliate　(C) affront　(D) shame
( ) 2. To some extent, calling someone idiot is a(n) ＿＿＿＿. They may sue you.
　　　(A) shame　(B) humiliate　(C) insult　(D) disgrace

 Ans
1. (C) 我那樣說不是有意要冒犯你的，可以原諒我嗎？
2. (C) 某種程度上，叫人白癡算是一種羞辱。對方可以告你的。

生活常用

學校工作

情緒心智

社會萬象

驚懼 (1)

🎧 MP3 3-16

alarm / appall / awe / daunt / dread / fear / frighten

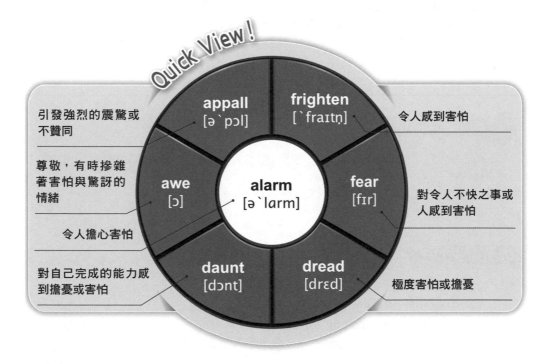

Quick View!

引發強烈的震驚或不贊同 — **appall** [ə`pɔl]

frighten [`fraɪtn̩] — 令人感到害怕

尊敬，有時摻雜著害怕與驚訝的情緒 — **awe** [ɔ]

alarm [ə`lɑrm]

fear [fɪr] — 對令人不快之事或人感到害怕

令人擔心害怕

對自己完成的能力感到擔憂或害怕 — **daunt** [dɔnt]

dread [drɛd] — 極度害怕或擔憂

---

82 **alarm**
-alarmed-alarmed

vt. 使驚慌不安、使恐懼　n. 警報

- The child's violent behavior alarmed his parents.
  這小孩的暴力行為令家長擔心。
- The alarm system detected the burglar.
  警報系統偵測到竊賊侵入。

衍 alarmed *adj.* 受驚的；
alarming *adj.* 驚人的；
alarmingly *adv.* 令人掛慮地

同 startle 使驚嚇

組 alarm clock 鬧鐘；
fire alarm 火警

片 take alarm at 因……而驚恐；
in alarm 驚慌地

83 appall
-appalled-appalled

vt. 使驚恐、使膽寒

- The gunshot case appalled the whole town.
  槍擊事件使整個城鎮陷入恐慌。
- The photos taken in the battlefield are really appalling.
  這些在戰場拍的照片非常駭人。

衍 appalled *adj.* 驚駭的、喪膽的；
appalling *adj.* 可怕的；
appallingly *adv.* 駭人聽聞地
同 horrify 使驚懼

84 awe
-awed-awed

vt. 使敬畏、使畏怯　n. 敬畏

- The size of the elephant awed the little boy.
  大象的龐大體型令小男孩心生畏懼。
- He looked at me in awe as if he had seen a monster.
  他用畏懼的眼神看著我，就好像看到怪物一樣。
- Mortals should be in awe of the immortals.
  凡人應要敬畏眾神。

衍 awed *adj.* 充滿敬畏的；
awing *adj.* 飛翔著地；
awesome *adj.* 令人敬畏的
同 respect 尊敬
反 contempt 蔑視
組 awe-inspiring 令人敬畏的；
awe-strike 使敬畏
片 stand / be in awe of 敬畏……

85 daunt
-daunted-daunted

vt. 嚇倒、使畏縮、使氣餒

- He was daunted by the difficulty of the task.
  他被任務的困難度給嚇到了。
- Jessie was daunted when her boyfriend yelled at her.
  當男友對潔西大吼的時候，她被嚇呆了。

衍 daunting *adj.* 使人氣餒的；
dauntingly *adv.* 令人生畏地；
dauntless *adj.* 嚇不倒的
同 discourage 使氣餒
片 nothing daunted 無所畏懼、毫不氣餒

dread
-dreaded-dreaded

vi. 懼怕、擔心　vt. 懼怕、擔心

- Some people dread flying.
  有些人害怕搭飛機。
- Students who don't do their homework dread going to school.
  沒有做作業的學生不敢去學校。

Tip dread + Ving / to-V 害怕……

衍 dreaded *adj.* 令人畏懼的；
dreadful *adj.* 令人恐懼的
同 fear 害怕
組 penny dreadful 廉價驚險小說
片 A burnt child dreads the fire. 一朝被灼燒，三年怕火光。
I dread to think. 我不敢想。

fear
-feared-feared

vi. 害怕　vt. 害怕、畏懼、擔心　n. 懼怕、擔憂

- I fear high places.
  我怕高。
- Please keep quiet for fear of disturbing other people.
  請保持安靜，以免干擾別人。

衍 fearful *adj.* 可怕的；
fearfully *adv.* 可怕地；
fearless *adj.* 無畏的
同 dread 擔心
反 courage 英勇
組 inflation fear 通膨恐慌
片 for fear of 唯恐；
without fear or favour 公正地

frighten
-frightened-frightened

vi. 驚恐、害怕　vt. 使驚恐、使駭怕

- It's said that lighting up firecrackers can frighten away the man-eating monster called "Nian."
  據說放鞭炮可以嚇跑吃人年獸。
- Do not show up suddenly like that. I'm frightened to death.
  不要那樣突然出現。我魂都嚇飛了。

衍 frightened *adj.* 受驚的；
frightening *adj.* 使人驚嚇的；
frightful *adj.* 可怕的
同 scare 使恐懼
反 compose 使安定
片 frighten sb. into doing sth. 使某人嚇得做某事；
frighten to death 嚇死人

聯想學習Plus

- 與情緒有關的單字包括焦慮（anxiety）、關切（concern）、憐憫（pity）與害怕（dread）。
- 當小朋友讀到（read）這一篇關於很多死人（dead）的文章時，都覺得很害怕（dread）。
- 常見令人害怕的人物有：terrorist（恐怖分子）、demon（惡魔、惡人）、vampire（吸血鬼）、ghost（鬼）、phantom（幽靈）、Lucifer（魔王、撒旦）、Satan（魔鬼、撒旦）等。

小試身手UP

（　）1. Since seeing the movie, I've been ＿＿＿＿ to open the closet.
　　　(A) fear　(B) frightened　(C) dreading　(D) alarming
（　）2. The dictator ＿＿＿＿ his people by force suppression.
　　　(A) awes　(B) fears　(C) daunts　(D) dreads

1. (B) 自從看過那部電影後，我就一直很怕打開衣櫥。
2. (A) 獨裁者靠武力鎮壓手段使人民心生畏懼。

驚懼 (2)

🎧 MP3 3-17

funk / horrify / panic / terrify / scare / startle

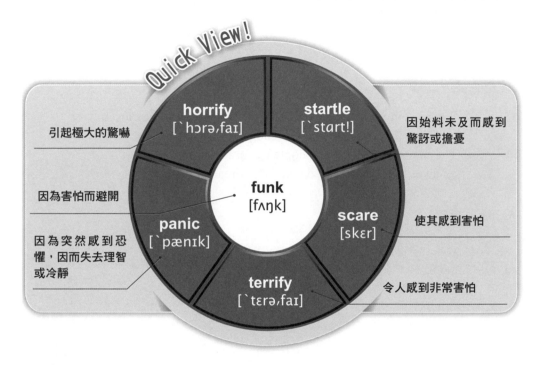

Quick View!

引起極大的驚嚇 — **horrify** [`hɔrə,faɪ]

startle [`start!] — 因始料未及而感到驚訝或擔憂

因為害怕而避開 — **funk** [fʌŋk]

panic [`pænɪk]

scare [skɛr] — 使其感到害怕

因為突然感到恐懼，因而失去理智或冷靜 —

terrify [`tɛrə,faɪ] — 令人感到非常害怕

---

89 | funk
-funked-funked

vi. 畏縮　vt. 畏縮、使恐懼

- I funked to tell him the truth.
  我怕跟他說實話。
- The wife has been in a blue funk because of all her housework.
  這位太太一直很害怕因為家事太多。

衍 funky *adj.* 驚恐的
同 fear 害怕
組 blue funk 極大的恐懼
片 be in a funk 沮喪、消沉、嚇壞

90 horrify
-horrified-horrified

vt. 使恐懼、使驚懼

- The sight of the dead animal horrified us.
  看到死掉動物的景象令我們恐懼。
- We were all horrified by that piece of news.
  那則新聞令我們恐懼。

衍 horrifying *adj.* 使人驚駭的；
horrific *adj.* 可怕的；
horrible *adj.* 可怕的；
horror *n.* 恐懼

組 horror film 恐怖片

91 panic
-panicked-panicked

vi. 十分驚慌　vt. 使恐慌　n. 驚慌

- The fire alarm panicked all the students and teachers.
  火災警報引發全體師生的驚慌。
- Don't panic. We will find the way out of here.
  不要慌。我們會找到出路的。

衍 panicky *adj.* 驚慌失措的；
panic-stricken *adj.* 驚慌失措的

同 fear 害怕

組 panic buying 恐慌性搶購

片 be seized with panic 驚慌失措；
in a panic 驚慌的

92 terrify
-terrified-terrified

vt. 使害怕、使恐怖

- Big, hairy spiders terrified my dad.
  又大又有毛的蜘蛛嚇到我父親。
- The police found the hostage huddled in the corner like a terrified child.
  警方發現人質像個受驚的小孩般蜷縮在角落裡。

衍 terrifying *adj.* 嚇人的；
terrifically *adv.* 非常地；
terrific *adj.* 可怕的、極好的

同 frighten 使害怕

片 be terrified at 被……嚇一跳；
terrify the life out fo sb. 把某人嚇得魂飛魄散

93 **scare**
-scared-scared

vi. 受驚　*vt.* 驚嚇、使恐懼　*n.* 驚恐

- The horror movie scared me.
  恐怖片嚇到我了。
- I'm scared to see the horror films.
  我很怕看恐怖電影。
- The flying roaches really scare me to death.
  會飛的蟑螂真的令我嚇破膽。

衍 scared *n.* 恐懼的；
　scarer *n.* 嚇人之事物；
　scary *adj.* 可怕的
同 frighten 使驚恐
反 calm 使鎮靜
片 scare away 把……嚇跑；scare
　one out of one's wit 把某人嚇呆

94 **startle**
-startled-startled

vi. 驚嚇、驚奇　*vt.* 使驚嚇、使嚇一跳

- The cat startled me when it jumped up on my lap.
  這隻貓突然跳到我的腿上，使我嚇一跳。
- He is so cowardly that every sudden sound startles him.
  他很膽小，每個突然的聲響都會驚動到他。

衍 startled *adj.* 受驚嚇的；
　startling *adj.* 令人吃驚的；
　startler *n.* 令人吃驚的人或物
同 frighten 驚嚇
組 startle reflex 驚跳反射

小試身手UP↑

（　）1. The bolt of thunder _____ me out of bed.
　　(A) horrified　(B) panics　(C) startled　(D) funked
（　）2. Hearing that there is a bomb on the plane, all passengers are in a _____.
　　(A) panic　(B) startle　(C) fear　(D) scare

Ans
1. (C) 打雷聲把我嚇到彈出床外。
2. (A) 當聽到機上有炸彈時，乘客全都很驚恐。

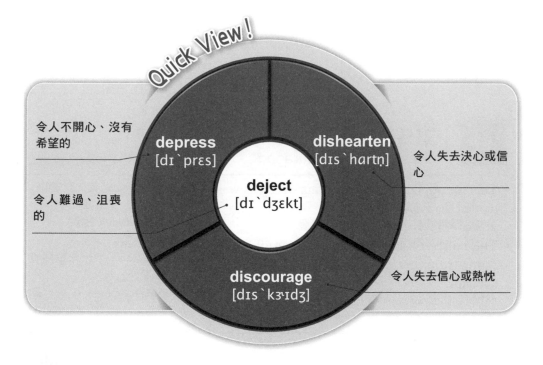

沮喪

🎧 MP3 3-18

deject / depress / discourage / dishearten

Quick View!

- 令人不開心、沒有希望的 — **depress** [dɪ`prɛs]
- 令人難過、沮喪的
- **deject** [dɪ`dʒɛkt]
- **dishearten** [dɪs`hɑrtn̩] — 令人失去決心或信心
- **discourage** [dɪs`kɝɪdʒ] — 令人失去信心或熱忱

---

95 | deject
-dejected-dejected

vt. 使沮喪、使灰心

- The team's fifth loss in a row dejected its fans.
  球隊連續第五次的輸球，令球迷很沮喪。
- Tim was a little dejected to hear he wasn't hired by that company.
  提姆聽到自己沒有被那間公司錄用時，感到有些失落。

衍 dejected *adj.* 情緒低落的；
dejectedly *adv.* 灰心地、沮喪地；
dejection *n.* 洩氣
反 encourage 鼓勵

depress
-depressed-depressed

vt. 使沮喪、使消沉、使心灰意冷

- This failure depressed him a lot.
  這次的失敗令他相當沮喪。
- Parents feel depressed if their children performed poorly in studies.
  如果孩子課業表現不佳，父母會很失望。
- Many people were out of work during the depression.
  不景氣時，許多人失業了。

衍 depressed adj. 沮喪抑鬱的；depression n. 意氣消沉、蕭條；depressive adj. 壓抑的
同 sadden 使難過
反 encourage 鼓勵
組 depressive neurosis 抑鬱型精神官能症；depression angle 俯角

discourage
-discouraged-discouraged

vt. 使洩氣、使沮喪

- That his application for working overseas was denied discouraged him.
  他申請調職海外被拒，令他沮喪。
- The police officer discouraged that old man from transferring money to a stranger's account.
  員警試圖勸阻老翁不要把錢轉給陌生帳戶。

衍 discouraging adj. 使人洩氣的；discouraged adj. 氣餒的；discouragement n. 洩氣
反 encourage 鼓勵
組 discouraged workers 未積極尋找工作的人
片 discourage sb. from 打消、勸阻

dishearten
-disheartened-disheartened

vt. 使沮喪、使氣餒、使灰心

- He was disheartened by several rejections from the publishers.
  他因為受到出版社好幾次的退件而感到灰心。
- It disheartens everyone that the proposal wasn't accepted.
  提案沒通過這件事令大夥沮喪。

衍 disheartened adj. 灰心的；disheartenment n. 沮喪
同 discourage 使沮喪
反 hearten 使振奮
片 be disheartened by sth. 因某事而灰心

聯想學習Plus

- 以 ject 當字尾的詞有：deject（使沮喪）、eject（吐出、噴射）、abject（悲慘的）、reject（拒絕）。
- 他天生心臟有缺陷（defect），但他不沮喪（dejected），仍抱持希望。

小試身手UP↑

(　　) 1. Because of the economic _____, people were out of a job, stores shut down, and the GDP kept shrinking.
　　　(A) depression　(B) disheartening　(C) dejection　(D) discouragement

(　　) 2. Her parents _____ her from studying abroad.
　　　(A) depressed　(B) dejected　(C) discouraged　(D) disheartened

Ans　1. (A)　由於經濟不景氣，使得人民失業、店家關門，GDP 持續下降。
　　　2. (C)　她的父母親勸她不要出國留學。

Lesson 19　悲傷

🎧 MP3 3-19

distress / grieve / lament / moan / mourn / sadden

Quick View!

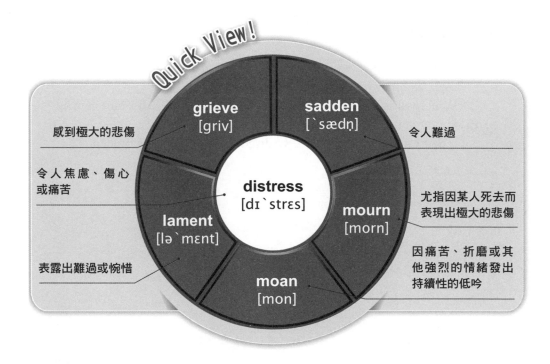

grieve [griv]　感到極大的悲傷

令人焦慮、傷心或痛苦

lament [lə`mɛnt]　表露出難過或惋惜

distress [dɪ`strɛs]

sadden [`sædn̩]　令人難過

mourn [morn]　尤指因某人死去而表現出極大的悲傷

因痛苦、折磨或其他強烈的情緒發出持續性的低吟

moan [mon]

99　distress
-distressed-distressed

vt. 使悲痛、使苦惱、使憂傷　n. 悲痛

- The way she had been treated in her husband's family caused her mental distress.
  她在夫家所受到的對待給她帶來心理上的痛苦。
- Her parents' death in the airplane crash distressed her.
  她的父母墜機身亡令她悲痛不已。

衍 distressed *adj.* 痛苦的；
distressing *adj.* 令人煩惱的
同 hurt 使受傷
反 comfort 安逸
片 in distress 在貧苦、貧困、悲痛中

100 grieve
-grieved-grieved

vi. 悲傷、哀悼　vt. 使悲傷、使苦惱

- Grandmother grieved over the death of her husband.
  祖母因為失去祖父而憂傷。
- The whole country is grieving for those soldiers who died on the battlefield.
  全國都在哀悼那些戰死沙場的士兵。

衍 grieved *adj.* 悲痛的；
grievance *n.* 牢騷；
grievous *adj.* 令人悲痛的
同 sadden 使悲傷
反 please 使開心
片 grieve for / over 因某事而悲傷

101 lament
-lamented-lamented

vi. 哀悼、悲痛　vt. 哀悼、痛惜

- She lamented the loss of her youth.
  她哀嘆已逝的青春。
- Kevin lamented over the death of his wife, Karen.
  凱文對妻子凱倫的死感到悲痛。

衍 lamented *adj.* 被悼念的；
lamentable *adj.* 令人惋惜的；
lamentably *adv.* 令人惋惜地
同 mourn 哀悼
反 rejoice 高興
片 lament over 為……而悲痛

102 moan
-moaned-moaned

vi. 呻吟、嗚咽　vt. 悲嘆、抱怨

- He moaned about his bad luck.
  他抱怨自己運氣不好。
- The patient always moans at night.
  晚上總會聽到病人呻吟著。

衍 moaner *n.* 抱怨者；
moanful *adj.* 悲歎的
同 wail 嚎啕
片 bitch and moan 抱怨呻吟

103 **mourn**
-mourned-mourned

vi. 哀痛、哀悼　vt. 為……哀痛

- Mr. Diaz mourned the death of his friend.
  狄亞茲先生憑弔他友人的逝世。
- Citizens are mourning for their mayor, who died in a car accident this morning.
  市民哀悼今天早上車禍身亡的市長。

衍 mourning *n.* 悲傷；
mournfully *adv.* 悲哀地；
mourner *n.* 悲傷者
同 grieve 使悲傷
組 mourning dove 北美斑鳩；
mourners' bench 懺悔席
片 in mourning 戴孝

104 **sadden**
-saddened-saddened

vi. 悲哀、悲痛　vt. 使悲傷、使難過

- It saddens me that I have to say goodbye to you guys.
  必須跟你們這群夥伴道別讓我難過。
- We are all saddened by what just happened to you.
  對你剛發生的事我們全都感到很難過。

衍 sad *adj.* 難過的；
sadness *n.* 悲哀、悲傷

（　）1. He _____ with pain when he was hit by a motorcycle, and then lost consciousness.
(A) distressed　(B) moaned　(C) lamented　(D) saddened

（　）2. Every citizen wore a white ribbon to _____ the victims of that campus gunshot case.
(A) depressed　(B) moaned　(C) mourned　(C) distressed

1. (B) 他被摩托車撞到時發出痛苦的呻吟，然後便失去了意識。
2. (C) 每個市民繫上白絲帶，悼念那起校園槍擊事件的受害者。

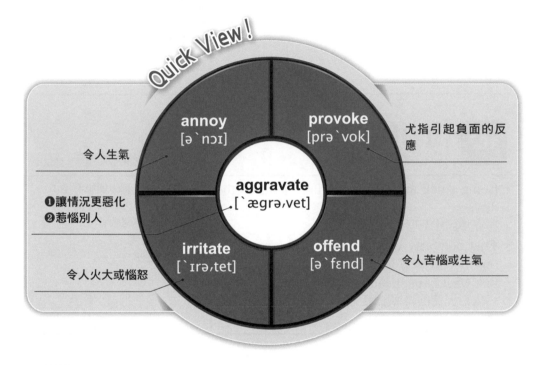

Lesson 20 惹惱

🎧 MP3 3-20

aggravate / annoy / irritate / offend / provoke

Quick View !

annoy [ə`nɔɪ] — 令人生氣

provoke [prə`vok] — 尤指引起負面的反應

aggravate [`ægrə,vet] — ❶讓情況更惡化 ❷惹惱別人

irritate [`ɪrə,tet] — 令人火大或惱怒

offend [ə`fɛnd] — 令人苦惱或生氣

---

105 aggravate
-aggravated-aggravated

vt. 加重、增劇、使惡化、激怒

- Drinking coffee aggravates my stomachache.
  喝咖啡會令我胃更痛。
- Continuous ejection of pollutant smoke aggravates our air quality.
  不斷排出廢氣使我們空氣品質更惡化。
- The way he looks at me aggravates me.
  他看我的方式令我生氣。

衍 aggravated *adj.* 加重的；
aggravating *adj.* 惡化的；
aggravation *n.* 惡化
同 infuriate 使大怒
組 aggravated assault 重傷害

106 annoy
-annoyed-annoyed

vi. 令人討厭　vt. 惹惱、使生氣

- Do you know a web series whose main character is an orange annoying other fruits or vegetables?
  你知道那部以煩人的柳丁為主角的網路影集嗎？
- Your snoring is really annoying.
  你的打呼聲真的很令人討厭。

衍 annoying *adj.* 討厭的、煩人的；
annoyed *adj.* 惱怒的；
annoyance *n.* 煩惱
同 bother *v.* 煩擾、打擾
反 please 使高興
片 be annoyed at 被……惹惱

107 irritate
-irritated-irritated

vi. 引起惱怒　vt. 惱怒、使煩躁

- Being stuck in traffic sometimes irritates the drivers.
  困在車陣中有時會令駕駛抓狂。
- That celebrity was irritated by the made-up report and decided to file a lawsuit against that weekly publication.
  名人對捏造的報導感到生氣，因此決定向週刊提告。

衍 irritatingly *adv.* 使憤怒地；
irritation *n.* 激怒；
irritator *n.* 刺激者
同 annoy 惹惱
反 appease 平息

108 offend
-offended-offended

vi. 引起不舒服　vt. 冒犯、觸怒

- I tried to mention that in an easy way for fear of offending him.
  我試圖用輕鬆的方式來提那件事，以免惹他不開心。
- She felt offended for she wasn't invited.
  她因為沒被邀請而感到不悅。

衍 offensive *adj.* 冒犯的；
offender *n.* 惹人生氣的人；
offense *n.* 冒犯
同 displease 使不高興
反 appease 撫慰
組 a first offender 初犯
片 offend against 違反、觸犯、違背……

provoke
-provoked-provoked

vt. 對……挑釁、煽動、激怒、激起

- Her speech provoked much protestation.
  他的演講激起許多反彈。
- The dog will attack if it gets provoked.
  這隻狗如果被挑釁，就會攻擊人。

衍 provoking *adj.* 令人生氣的；
provocative *adj.* 氣人的；
provocation *n.* 激怒

同 anger 使發怒

反 appease 撫慰

組 provoke hatred 激起仇恨

片 provoke into 鼓動去做

 聯想學習Plus

- 表示惡化的單字有：aggravate（加劇、惡化）、deteriorate（惡化、使退化）、worsen（變糟、惡化）。

小試身手UP

( ) 1. The burning smoke _____ my eyes and makes me cry.
   (A) offends (B) aggravates (C) irritates (D) annoys

( ) 2. Stop teasing me. It is _____.
   (A) aggravating (B) irritating (C) provoking (D) annoying

 Ans
1. (C) 燃燒的煙霧刺激我的眼，讓我淚流不止。
2. (D) 別再逗弄我了，很煩的。

生活常用

學校工作

情緒心智

社會萬象

忍受

🎧 MP3 3-21

abide / bear / endure / stand / forbear / tolerate

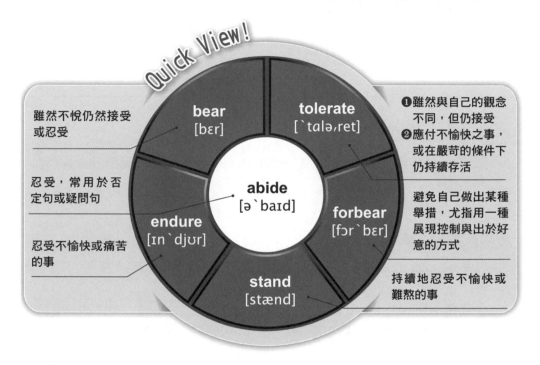

Quick View!

雖然不悅仍然接受或忍受 — **bear** [bɛr]

忍受，常用於否定句或疑問句 — **endure** [ɪn`djʊr]

忍受不愉快或痛苦的事

abide [ə`baɪd]

tolerate [`talə‚ret] — ❶雖然與自己的觀念不同，但仍接受 ❷應付不愉快之事，或在嚴苛的條件下仍持續存活

forbear [fɔr`bɛr] — 避免自己做出某種舉措，尤指用一種展現控制與出於好意的方式

stand [stænd] — 持續地忍受不愉快或難熬的事

110 **abide**
-abided-abided

vi. 持續　*vt.* 忍受、容忍

- She cannot abide her husband's vulgar language.
  她無法忍受她先生滿口髒話。
- Every driver and pedestrian should abide by the traffic laws.
  每位駕駛和行人都要遵守交通法規。

Tip can't abide + Ving 不能容忍……

衍 abiding *adj.* 不變的；
　 abidingly *adv.* 不變地；
　 abidance *n.* 居住、遵守
同 endure 忍受
組 law-abiding citizen 守法公民
片 abide by 遵守

bear
-bore-borne

vt. 忍受、經得起、承受　n. 熊

- I can't bear to see you cry.
  我不忍看到你哭。
- The chair can't bear your weight, so it collapses.
  這張椅子無法承受你的重量，所以塌了。

衍 bearing *n.* 忍耐；
bearish *adj.* 粗魯的；
bearer *n.* 持有者；
bearable *adj.* 可忍受的
同 withstand 禁得起
組 bear hug 熊抱
片 bear with 忍受；bear on 有關；
bear up 不氣餒、支持下去

---

endure
-endured-endured

vi. 忍受、持續　vt. 忍耐、忍受

- The fabric is said to be able to endure fire.
  這種布料據說可以耐火。
- I can no longer endure a boring life like this.
  我無法再忍受像這樣的無聊生活了。

衍 enduring *adj.* 耐久的；
endurable *adj.* 耐久的；
endurance *n.* 耐久力
同 last 持續
片 What can't be cured must be endured. 盡人事聽天命。（無能為力的事就只能忍耐了）

---

stand
-stood-stood

vi. 站立　vt. 經得起　n. 攤子

- I can't stand the heat. I sweat in summer.
  我怕熱，夏天時都會流汗。
- Real friendship can stand the test of time.
  真正的友誼經得起時間的考驗。

衍 standing *adj.* 長期的
同 endure 忍受
組 standing committee 常務委員會；
stand pat 堅持己見；
standby 待命信號【海】

114 | **forbear**
-forbore-forborne

vi. 克制、忍耐、避免做　vt. 克制、忍耐

- She could not forbear weeping.
  她止不住啜泣。
- I asked myself to forbear from punching him in the face.
  我要求自己克制住往他臉上揍一拳的衝動。

Tip forbear from Ving / N 避免做某事

衍 forbearing *adj.* 有耐心的；
forbearance *n.* 寬容

同 abstain 戒

---

115 | **tolerate**
-tolerated-tolerated

vt. 忍受、容忍、寬恕

- She tolerates her child's messy room although she does not like it.
  雖然她不喜歡她孩子髒亂的房間，但是她還能忍受。
- I won't tolerate school bullying to happen.
  我不會容忍校園霸凌的發生。

衍 toleration *n.* 忍受；
tolerance *n.* 寬大；
tolerable *adj.* 可容忍的

同 allow 容許

組 ability to tolerate 忍受力

(　) 1. It's too painful for me to _____ a child.
　　(A) bear　(B) tolerate　(C) stand　(D) abide

(　) 2. No one can _____ his sin for he massacred a family.
　　(A) stand　(B) tolerate　(C) endure　(D) bear

1. (A)　對我來說，生小孩太痛苦了。
2. (B)　由於他殘殺一家人，沒人會寬恕他的罪孽。

deride / flout / jeer / mock / ridicule

Quick View!

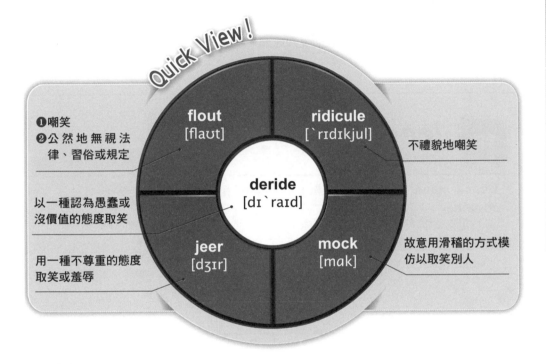

❶嘲笑
❷公然地無視法律、習俗或規定

flout
[flaʊt]

ridicule
[`rɪdɪkjul]

不禮貌地嘲笑

以一種認為愚蠢或沒價值的態度取笑

deride
[dɪ`raɪd]

用一種不尊重的態度取笑或羞辱

jeer
[dʒɪr]

mock
[mɑk]

故意用滑稽的方式模仿以取笑別人

---

116 | **deride**
-derided-derided

vt. 嘲笑、嘲弄

- They derided him for his unorthodox beliefs.
  他們笑他不正統的信仰。
- His accent was derided as provincial.
  他的口音被笑說是鄉下來的人。

衍 deridingly *adv.* 嘲弄地；
derisive *adj.* 嘲笑的；
derision *n.* 嘲弄
同 ridicule 奚落

117 flout
-flouted-flouted

vi. 藐視、嘲笑　vt. 藐視、嘲笑

- The man was under arrest for flouting authority.
男子因公然藐視公權力而遭到逮捕。
- The boy was punished for flouting the way his classmate walked.
男孩因為嘲笑同學走路的方式而受到處罰。

同 sneer 嘲笑

118 jeer
-jeered-jeered

vi. 嘲笑、嘲弄　vt. 嘲笑、嘲弄

- I can't stand people's jeering my taste of costume.
我不能忍受別人嘲笑我的服裝品味。
- Jeering at people's defects is not kind.
取笑別人的缺點並不仁慈。

衍 jeering *adj.* 嘲弄的；
jeerer *n.* 嘲笑者；
jeeringly *adv.* 揶揄地
同 scoff 嘲弄
反 respect 敬重
片 jeer at 嘲弄

119 mock
-mocked-mocked

vi. 嘲弄、嘲笑　vt. 嘲弄、嘲笑、模仿

- She mocks the way her mother talks.
她模仿她母親說話的方式。
- Don't mock those who study slowly.
不要嘲笑學習慢的人。

衍 mocker *n.* 嘲弄者；
mockery *n.* 嘲弄；
mocking *adj.* 嘲弄的
同 ridicule 嘲笑
組 mock exams 模擬考
片 mock at 嘲弄；
mock up 仿製

120 ridicule
-ridiculed-ridiculed

vt. 嘲笑、戲弄　　*n.* 嘲笑

- The bully ridiculed the new kid because of his eyeglasses.
  惡霸嘲笑新同學戴的眼鏡。
- He became an object of ridicule.
  他成為被嘲笑的對象。

衍 ridiculous *adj.* 可笑的；
　 ridiculously *adv.* 荒謬地；
　 ridiculousness *n.* 荒謬

同 mock 嘲笑

反 respect 敬意

組 an object of ridicule 被嘲笑的
　 對象

片 hold sb. up to ridicule 嘲笑某人

 聯想學習Plus

- mock 源自拉丁文，是指擤鼻子，當時這種舉動被視為嘲笑。
- 這個學生模仿（mock）和尚（monk）邊走路邊騎（ride）大象，畫面實在很荒謬
  （ridiculous）。

小試身手UP

( ) 1. The student _____ the school regulation that wearing long hair was
banned, so he was given a demerit.
(A) mocked　(B) jeered　(C) scorned　(D) flouted

( ) 2. A well-educated man never _____ the handicapped but helps them
instead.
(A) mocks　(B) scolds　(C) ridiculous　(D) absurd

 Ans
1. (D) 那名學生公然蔑視學校禁止留長髮的規定，因此遭記過處分。
2. (A) 有教養的人絕不會嘲笑身體有缺陷的人，反而會出手幫忙。

生活常用

學校工作

情緒心智

社會萬象

鎮定

🎧 MP3 3-23

alleviate / calm / moderate / pacify / tranquilize

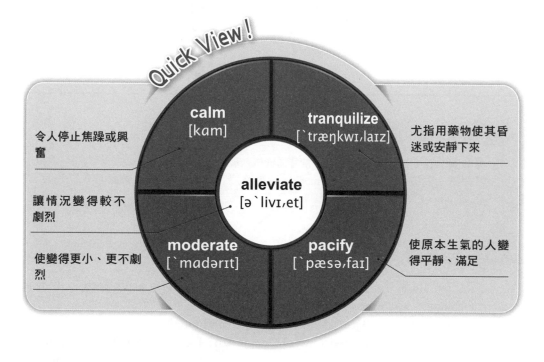

Quick View !

令人停止焦躁或興奮

calm
[kam]

tranquilize
[`træŋkwɪ͵laɪz]

尤指用藥物使其昏迷或安靜下來

讓情況變得較不劇烈

alleviate
[ə`livɪ͵et]

使原本生氣的人變得平靜、滿足

使變得更小、更不劇烈

moderate
[`mɑdərɪt]

pacify
[`pæsə͵faɪ]

---

121 alleviate
-alleviated-alleviated

vt. 減輕、緩和

- A good nurse alleviates the patient's suffering.
  好的護士可以減輕病患的痛苦。
- Painkillers are often used to alleviate the pain when one has a headache.
  人們頭痛時，常吃止痛藥減輕痛苦。
- Sometimes crying might alleviate sorrow.
  有時候哭泣能緩解悲傷。

衍 alleviation *n.* 鎮痛物；
alleviative *adj.* 緩和的
同 mitigate 使緩和
組 alleviate the pain 減輕痛苦

122 **calm** -calmed-calmed	*vi.* 鎮定、平靜　*vt.* 使鎮定、使平靜
• The speaker calmed the angry crowd. 演講者安撫激動的群眾。 • After a storm comes a calm. 雨過天晴。	衍 calmative *adj.* 鎮靜的； calmly *adv.* 平靜地； calmness *n.* 安寧 同 quiet 使安靜 反 excite 使激動 片 calm down 冷靜下來

123 **moderate** -moderated-moderated	*vi.* 變溫和、變弱　*vt.* 使和緩、減輕
• This air-conditioner can moderate the temperature automatically. 這台冷氣會自動調節溫度。 • The storm has moderated. 暴雨已經趨緩了。	衍 moderately *adv.* 有節制地； moderation *n.* 穩健； moderator *n.* 仲裁者 組 moderate breeze 和風 片 in moderation 適度地、節制地

124 **pacify** -pacified-pacified	*vt.* 使平靜、使安靜、撫慰
• Using force could not pacify the rioters. 使用武力無法平息暴動。 • The mother pacified her baby by humming a lullaby until the baby fell asleep. 媽媽哼著搖籃曲哄寶寶直到入睡。	衍 pacifist *n.* 和平主義者； pacifier *n.* 鎮靜劑； pacifically *adv.* 和平地 同 calm 使平靜 反 offend 觸怒

125 tranquilize
-tranquilized-tranquilized

vi. 使平靜、使鎮定　*vt.* 使平靜

- The cheetah was tranquilized with a dart gun and was transferred to another reserve.
  獵豹被麻醉槍迷昏後，移送到另一個保護區。
- Drinking warm milk befor going to bed always tranquilizes me.
  睡前喝杯溫牛奶總能令我放鬆。

衍 tranquilization *n.* 平靜；
tranquilizer *n.* 精神安定劑；
tranquillity *n.* 穩定；
tranquil *adj.* 平靜的

組 minor tranquilizer 弱效鎮定劑

聯想學習Plus

- The Pacific Ocean（太平洋）的 pacific 就是從 pacify 變化而來，同學在記單字時，就能舉一反三。the Atlantic Ocean（大西洋）的 Atlantic 則從 Atlantis（亞特蘭提斯，沉沒於大西洋的島嶼）變化而來；the Indian Ocean（印度洋）的 Indian 就跟 India 有關；至於 the Arctic Ocean（北冰洋）與 the Antarctic Ocean（南冰洋）都有出現的 arctic 是「北極圈」，因此 antarctic 就是相反的「南極圈」。

小試身手UP

(　) 1. If we say the lake is _____, it means its surface is still and has no wind.
　　　(A) calm　(B) pacified　(C) tranquilized　(D) moderate
(　) 2. My headache hurts badly, but it _____ after I took the pill.
　　　(A) calmed　(B) alleviated　(C) pacified　(D) moderated

1. (A)　當我們說湖是風平浪靜的，就是說湖水表面是靜止的，也沒有風。
2. (B)　我頭痛地厲害，但吃完藥後就舒緩多了。

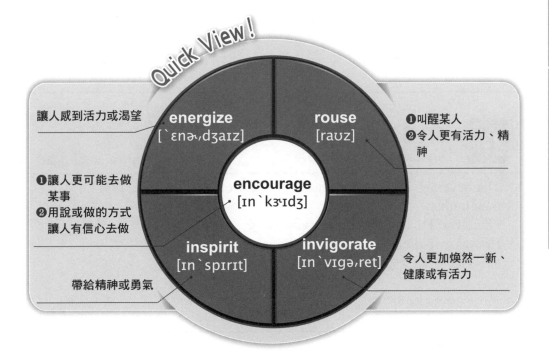

24 Lesson 激勵

MP3 3-24

encourage / energize / inspirit / invigorate / rouse

Quick View !

energize [`ɛnɚˌdʒaɪz]
讓人感到活力或渴望

rouse [raʊz]
❶叫醒某人
❷令人更有活力、精神

encourage [ɪn`kɝɪdʒ]

❶讓人更可能去做某事
❷用說或做的方式讓人有信心去做

inspirit [ɪn`spɪrɪt]
帶給精神或勇氣

invigorate [ɪn`vɪgəˌret]
令人更加煥然一新、健康或有活力

126 encourage
-encouraged-encouraged

vt. 鼓勵、慫恿、支持

- Her praise encouraged me to continue playing the piano.
  她的稱讚促使我繼續彈琴。
- Parents should encourage their children to learn more.
  父母應該鼓勵孩子們多學一點。

衍 encouraged adj. 受到鼓舞的；
  encouragement n. 鼓勵；
  encouraging adj. 鼓勵的

同 support 扶持

反 discourage 勸阻、不鼓勵

片 encourage in 鼓勵投入；
  encourage to 鼓勵去做

127 | energize
-energized-energized

vi. 精力充沛地做　vt. 激勵、使精力充沛

- A can of iced Coke always energizes me after a jog.
  慢跑完後來罐冰可樂總能讓我恢復精力。
- I feel energized after these days off.
  這幾天休假過後，我感到精力充沛。

衍 energetics *n.* 能量學；
energetic *adj.* 精力旺盛的；
energy *n.* 能量、活力

組 energy drinks 能量飲料；
high energy food 高能量食物

128 | inspirit
-inspirited-inspirited

vt. 激勵精神、鼓舞、使振作

- The beverage inspirited them for the rest of their journey.
  喝完這杯飲料，讓他們又能繼續後面的旅程。
- He was inspirited by the letter from his son.
  他受到兒子寄來的信的鼓勵。

同 cheer 振奮、鼓勵
近 spirit *n.* 精神、心靈；
inspire *v.* 鼓舞、激勵

129 | invigorate
-invigorated-invigorated

vt. 賦予精神、鼓舞

- He'd been bored with his work, but this new project invigorated him.
  他已經厭煩他的工作，但是這項新計畫讓他重燃活力。
- The team was invigorated by the cheerleaders.
  球隊受到啦啦隊的打氣。

衍 invigorated *adj.* 生氣勃勃的；
invigoration *n.* 精神充沛；
invigorative *adj.* 有精神的
近 vigor *n.* 精力、活力

130 | rouse
-roused-roused

vi. 奮發起來　vt. 激起、激怒、使激動

- The comedy roused me to laughter.
  這齣喜劇讓我捧腹大笑。
- He was roused from sleep by the fire alarm.
  他從睡夢中被火警驚醒。

衍 roused *adj.* 發怒的；
　rousing *adj.* 使覺醒的；
　rouser *n.* 喚醒者
同 stir 攪動
組 rabble-rousing 煽動暴民的
片 rouse from / out 叫醒

聯想學習Plus

- 表示「力」的單字有：energy（活力、能量）、power（力量、電力、權力）、strength（力量、力氣、體力）、force（力量、武力、暴力）、vigor（精力、活力、體力）。

小試身手UP

(　) 1. The boss ＿＿＿＿ his workers not to work overtime in order to save electricy.
　　(A) encourages　(B) stimulates　(C) inspires　(D) energizes

(　) 2. The smell of cooking ＿＿＿＿ my appetite.
　　(A) encourages　(B) stimulates　(C) invigorates　(D) inspirits

Ans
1. (A) 為了省電，老闆鼓勵員工不要加班。
2. (B) 煮飯的香味引發我的食欲。

沉思

🎧 MP3 3-25

brood / contemplate / deliberate / meditate / muse / reflect

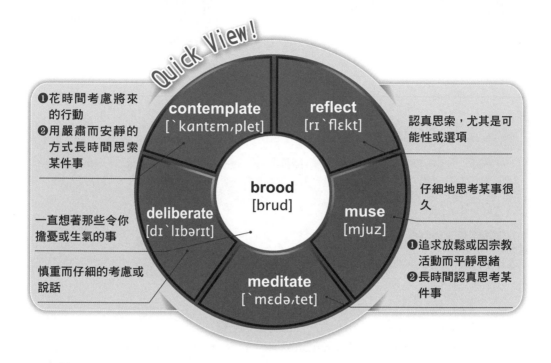

Quick View!

❶花時間考慮將來的行動
❷用嚴肅而安靜的方式長時間思索某件事

contemplate
[`kɑntɛmˌplet]

reflect
[rɪ`flɛkt]

認真思索，尤其是可能性或選項

brood
[brud]

仔細地思考某事很久

一直想著那些令你擔憂或生氣的事

deliberate
[dɪ`lɪbərɪt]

muse
[mjuz]

❶追求放鬆或因宗教活動而平靜思緒
❷長時間認真思考某件事

慎重而仔細的考慮或說話

meditate
[`mɛdəˌtet]

131 brood
-brooded-brooded

vi. 考慮、擔憂　*vt.* 盤算、細想

- She brooded over her future all day.
  她整日都在憂思她的未來。
- He likes to stroke his chin when he broods.
  當他在思索時，喜歡摸著下巴。

衍 brooding *adj.* 徘徊不去的；
　brooodily *adv.* 鬱鬱不樂地；
　broody *adj.* 想不開的
同 meditate 沉思
組 brood patch 孵卵斑【鳥】
片 brood about 擔憂、考慮

contemplate
-contemplated-contemplated

vi. 冥思苦想　*vt.* 思忖、思量、仔細考慮

- She contemplated the problem and finally solved it.
  她思考這個問題很久，最後終於將它解決了。
- Lucy contemplated quitting her present job.
  露西考慮辭掉現在的工作。

Tip comtemplate + Ving 打算做……

衍 contemplable *adj.* 可考慮的；
contemplation *n.* 冥想；
contemplator *n.* 好沉思的人

同 consider 細想

近 template *n.* 樣板、範本

片 contemplate one's navel 陷入冥想

---

deliberate
-deliberated-deliberated

vi. 仔細考慮、思考　*vt.* 仔細考慮

- The committee deliberated on the issue for some time before reaching a consensus.
  委員會在達成共識前，考慮這個議題很長一段時間。
- The couple are deliberating whether or not to give birth to a baby.
  這對夫妻正在考慮是否要生孩子。

衍 deliberately *adv.* 慎重地；
deliberation *n.* 深思熟慮；
deliberative *adj.* 慎重的

同 consider 細想

片 deliberate about / over / on 仔細討論、考慮……

---

meditate
-meditated-meditated

vi. 沉思、冥想　*vt.* 計劃、打算

- She meditates before yoga class.
  開始瑜珈課前她會先冥想。
- The detective meditated on the words everybody said.
  偵探思索每個人講過的話。

Tip meditate + Ving 考慮做……

衍 meditation *n.* 默想；
meditative *adj.* 愛沉思默想的；
meditator *n.* 冥想者

同 think 思索

片 meditate on 考慮

135 | muse
-mused-mused

vi. 沉思、冥想　*vt.* 若有所思地說　*n.* 冥想

- My father looked at the photographs and mused about the old days.
  我父親望著照片，想著過往時光。
- The model is the muse of the artist. All his works are inspired by her.
  這個模特兒是這位藝術家的靈感泉源，他所有的創作靈感都來自於她。

衍 musing *adj.* 沉思的；
musingly *adv.* 冥想地

同 think 思索

片 muse on / over / about 冥想、沉思……

136 | reflect
-reflected-reflected

vi. 深思、反省　*vt.* 思考、反省

- He reflected on the consequences of his action.
  他反省這次行動的後果。
- The boss is reflecting on whether to hire more people or not.
  老闆正在考慮是否要多僱用一點人手。

衍 reflecting *adj.* 引起反射的；
reflection *n.* 反射；
reflective *adj.* 沉思的

同 think 思索

組 reflective index 光線折射係數；
reflected glory 借重他人得來的榮耀

片 reflect on 仔細考慮

小試身手UP↑

(　) 1. The people you hang out with can _____ your characters.
(A) deliberate　(B) muse　(C) contemplate　(D) reflect

(　) 2. Julie's parents _____ about her future because she masters no skills.
(A) deliberate　(B) contemplate　(C) meditate　(D) brood

1. (D) 你結識的人能反映你的性格。
2. (D) 茱莉沒有專長，她的父母很擔心她的未來。

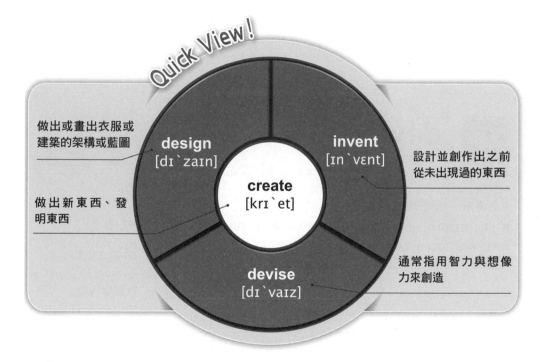

26 Lesson

創造

🎧 MP3 3-26

create / design / devise / invent

Quick View!

做出或畫出衣服或
建築的架構或藍圖

design
[dɪ`zaɪn]

invent
[ɪn`vɛnt]

設計並創作出之前
從未出現過的東西

做出新東西、發
明東西

create
[krɪ`et]

devise
[dɪ`vaɪz]

通常指用智力與想像
力來創造

---

137 | # create
-created-created

vt. 創造、創作、設計、引起

- The chef created a new dish.
  主廚創造了新菜色。

- In the beginning, God created the heaven and
  the earth.
  起初神創造天地。

- All men are created equal.
  人生而平等。

衍 creation *n.* 創立；
creative *adj.* 創造的；
creatively *adv.* 有創造力地
同 make 建造
反 destroy 破壞
組 self-created 自己創造的；
job creation 創造就業機會；
all creation 全世界

138 | design
-designed-designed

vi. 設計　vt. 設計、構思、繪製

- She designs and makes her own clothes.
  她設計及製作自己的衣服。
- We commissioned an interior designer to design our living room.
  我們委託室內設計師幫我們設計客廳。

衍 designed *adj.* 設計好的；
designation *n.* 指定；
designer *n.* 設計者
同 draw 描寫
組 designated hitter 指定打擊手
片 by design 故意；
design for 設計；
have designs on 覬覦

139 | devise
-devised-devised

vt. 設計、發明、策劃、想出　n. 遺贈

- She devised a plan to earn money.
  她想出一個賺錢的方法。
- The mausoleum has devices that will shoot arrows once its triggered.
  這座陵寢有一經觸動就會射出箭弩的裝置。

衍 deviser *n.* 設計者；
device *n.* 裝置；
devisable *adj.* 可設計的
同 invent 創造
組 device driver 設備驅動程式
片 leave one to one's own devices
讓某人自行處理問題

140 | invent
-invented-invented

vt. 發明、創造

- Do you know who invented the television?
  你知道誰發明了電視？
- Please don't invent an excuse.
  請不要找藉口。
- He didn't invent the story. What he told you is true.
  他沒有胡說，他跟你說的都是真的。

衍 inventible *adj.* 可發明的；
invention *n.* 發明；
inventive *adj.* 創造的
同 devise 設計
反 imitate 模仿
片 invent an excuse 找藉口

聯想學習Plus

- 在他發明（devise）東西之前，他不斷地修訂（revise），最後設計出（design）這套象徵特殊符號（sign）的作品。
- 發明是無中生有、原創的意涵，發明的相反就是模仿、複製別人，所以反義詞有：copy（複製、影印、模仿）、duplicate（複製品）、replicate（複製）、imitate（仿造）、mimic（模仿）。

小試身手UP

(   ) 1. J. K. Rowling's novels are full of _____ and imagination. People of all ages love them.
　　　　(A) invention　(B) design　(C) creator　(D) device

(   ) 2. I like the _____ of this onepiece for its cutting and fabric are so special.
　　　　(A) creation　(B) design　(C) devise　(D) invention

1. (A) J. K. 羅琳的小說充滿創造力與想像力，老少咸宜。
2. (B) 我喜歡這件一件式洋裝的設計，它的剪裁與布料如此特別。

預測

🎧 MP3 3-27

forecast / foretell / predict / prophesy

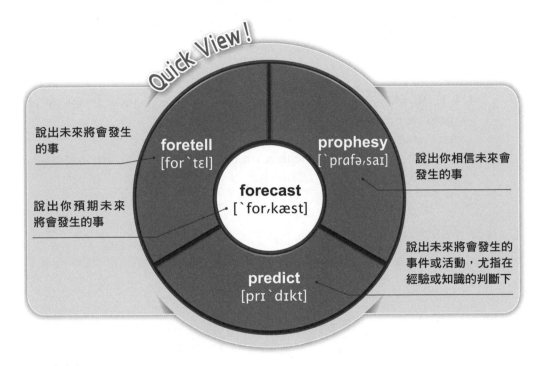

Quick View!

說出未來將會發生的事
foretell
[for`tɛl]

說出你預期未來將會發生的事

forecast
[`for͵kæst]

prophesy
[`prɑfə͵saɪ]
說出你相信未來會發生的事

predict
[prɪ`dɪkt]
說出未來將會發生的事件或活動，尤指在經驗或知識的判斷下

---

141 # forecast
-forecast-forecast

vi. 作預測   vt. 預測、預報   n. 預報

- The economic forcasts for the coming year stay pessimistic.
  來年的經濟預報仍然不樂觀。
- The weather forecast said there would be no rain during the Spring Festival.
  天氣預報說春節期間不會下雨。

衍 forecaster *n.* 預測者
近 broadcast 廣播
組 weather forecast 天氣預測；
affective forecasting 情感預測；
daily forecast 每日預報

142 foretell
-foretold-foretold

vt. 預言、預示

- No one could foretell that the movie would be a blockbuster.
  沒人預料到這部電影能變成賣座強片。
- So far people still can't foretell when an earthquake will occur.
  到目前為止人們還無法預測地震發生的時間。

同 predict 預言

143 predict
-predicted-predicted

vi. 作預言　*vt.* 預言、預料、預報

- They predicted that it would rain today.
  他們預測今天會下雨。
- The doomsday was predicted to take place in 2012.
  曾有人預言 2012 年會發生世界末日。

衍 predictability *n.* 可預測性；
predictable *adj.* 可預料的；
prediction *n.* 預報；
unpredictable *adj.* 出乎預料的
同 foresee 預見

144 prophesy
-prophesied-prophesied

vi. 預言、預告　*vt.* 預言、預告

- She prophesied the Great Fire of London and her own death in 1561.
  她預言了 1561 年倫敦大火還有她自己的死期。
- These prophecies of doomsday were considered somewhat exaggerated.
  這些對末日的預言被認為有些誇大了。

衍 prophecy *n.* 預言能力；
prophet *n.* 先知；
prophetic *adj.* 預言性的
同 predict 預報
組 self-fulfilling prophecy 心理暗示；Minor Prophets《小預言書》

生活常用

學校工作

情緒心智

社會萬象

 **聯想學習Plus**

- predictable 是指可以被預測的，unpredictable 則是指難以預測、出乎意料、無法捉摸的。
- foretell 的 fore 有「前部的、向前的」的意思，因此 foretell 是在事情發生之前就說出，也就是「預測、預示」。forecast 也是在之前就投擲，就成了「預測、預報」。相同字首的單字還有：forehead（前額）、forearm（前臂）、foresee（預見、預知）、foreshadow（預兆）、forethought（先見、事先考慮）等。

小試身手UP

( )1. The route of the typhoon is more _____ now than before, so the authorities can warn the people in advance.
　　(A) forecasting　(B) foretelling　(C) predictable　(D) broadcasting

( )2. I am used to listening to the weather _____ on the radio when driving.
　　(A) prediction　(B) forecast　(C) foretelling　(D) prophesy

 Ans
1. (C) 比起過去，現在要預測颱風路徑容易多了，所以有關當局能提前警告民眾。
2. (B) 我習慣開車的時候收聽廣播的天氣預報。

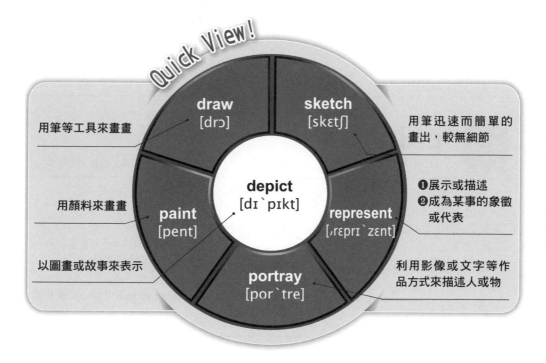

描繪

🎧 MP3 3-28

depict / draw / paint / portray / represent / sketch

生活常用

學校工作

情緒心智

社會萬象

Quick View!

draw [drɔ]
用筆等工具來畫畫

sketch [skɛtʃ]
用筆迅速而簡單的畫出，較無細節

paint [pent]
用顏料來畫畫

depict [dɪ`pɪkt]

represent [ˌrɛprɪ`zɛnt]
❶展示或描述
❷成為某事的象徵或代表

以圖畫或故事來表示

portray [por`tre]
利用影像或文字等作品方式來描述人或物

---

145 **depict**
-depicted-depicted

vt. 描畫、雕出、描述

- The author depicts vividly the world a hundred years in the future.
  作家生動地描述了一百年後的世界。
- The painting depicts the lives of ordinary people in the Song Dynasty.
  這張畫描繪出宋朝小老百姓的生活。

衍 depiction n. 敘述
同 portray 把……描繪成
片 depict as 描述成

146 draw
-drew-drawn

vi. 畫圖　vt. 畫、繪製、描寫　n. 抽籤

- The little girl drew some flowers for her mother.
  小女孩給她媽媽畫了一些花。
- The train will draw in the station in five minutes.
  火車過五分鐘就會到站。

衍 drawing *n.* 製圖；
drawers *n.* 內褲；
drawer *n.* 抽屜

同 pull 拉

組 bottom drawer 嫁衣
top-drawer 最高級的

片 draw attention 吸引注意力

---

147 paint
-painted-painted

vi. 油漆　vt. 油漆、塗顏色　n. 油漆

- We painted the roof white so that everyone could see it at first sight.
  我們將屋頂漆成白色，好讓每個人都能第一眼就瞧見。
- The students of the art school have to practice painting on the canvas.
  美術學院的學生必須練習在畫布上作畫。

衍 painting *n.* 上油漆；
painted *adj.* 刷上油漆的；
painter *n.* 畫家

同 cover 覆蓋

組 wet paint 油漆未乾；
gloss paint 亮光漆

片 paint a picture of sth. 描述某事

---

148 portray
-portrayed-portrayed

vt. 畫人物或風景等、用語言描寫

- The court artist had to finish portraying the Duchess in 3 months.
  宮廷畫師必須在三個月內完成公爵夫人的肖像。
- The main character was portrayed as a great heroine.
  主角被描述成一位偉大的女英雄。

衍 portrayal *n.* 描繪；
portrayer *n.* 肖像畫家；
portraitist *n.* 人像攝影師

同 picture 想像

片 portray as 描述成

represent
-represented-represented

vi. 代表、代理　vt. 描繪、抽象地表現

- People say that red roses represent the feeling of love.
  據說玫瑰花的花語是愛情。
- The picture represented a corner in the garden in the afternoon.
  這張圖描繪出午後時光的花園一角。

衍 representable *adj.* 能被描繪的；
  representation *n.* 代理；
  representative *adj.* 典型的
同 portray 畫
組 make representations 提出抗議；
  sales representative 推銷員
片 represent to 向……指出

sketch
-sketched-sketched

vi. 畫素描、畫速寫　vt. 寫生、速寫

- This author always sketches the plot before she begins to write a book.
  這位作家先概述情節後再開始寫成書。
- He did several sketches of the same scene to practice.
  為了練習，他會素描同一個景色很多次。

衍 sketchily *adv.* 大略地；
  sketchiness *n.* 大概
同 draw 描寫
組 sketchbook 寫生簿；
  a thumbnail sketch 簡單描述

小試身手UP

（　）1. The _____ is still wet. Don't sit on the chair.
　　(A) drawer　(B) sketch　(C) representative　(D) paint
（　）2. He will _____ the scenes he likes and paint them later at his studio.
　　(A) paint　(B) sketch　(C) represent　(D) portray

1. (D) 油漆還未乾，別坐那張椅子。
2. (B) 他會把喜歡的景色速寫下來，然後回畫室再上色。

生活常用

學校工作

情緒心智

社會萬象

MEMO

PART

4

社會萬象
Social Phenomenon

衍 衍生字　　同 同義字　　反 反義字　　近 近型字　　組 組合字　　片 片語

傷害 (1)

🎧 MP3 4-01

ache / harm / harrow / hurt / pain

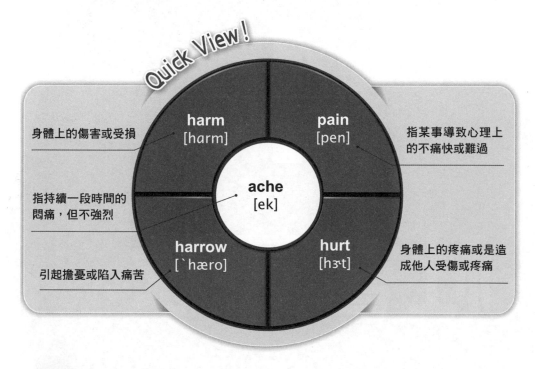

Quick View !

harm [harm]	**pain** [pen]
身體上的傷害或受損	指某事導致心理上的不痛快或難過
ache [ek]	
指持續一段時間的悶痛，但不強烈	
harrow [`hæro]	**hurt** [hɜt]
引起擔憂或陷入痛苦	身體上的疼痛或是造成他人受傷或疼痛

ache
-ached-ached

vi. 疼痛　n. 疼痛

- Tom's legs ached after a long walk.
  湯姆在走了很長一段路後雙腿疼痛。
- I have a headache. May I ask for leave?
  我頭痛，我可以請假嗎？

衍 aching *adj.* 疼痛的
組 face ache 面部神經痛；
　　backache 背痛；
　　toothache 牙痛
片 ache for 渴望

2 | **harm**
-harmed-harmed

vt. 損害、傷害、危害　*n.* 危害

- Too much sun does harm the skin.
  曬太多太陽確實會傷害皮膚。
- Eating night snacks once in a while will never do you harm.
  偶爾吃宵夜對你無害。

衍 harmful *adj.* 有害的；
harmless *adj.* 無害的
反 benefit 有益於
組 penal harm 刑罰傷害；
self-harm 自我傷害
片 come to harm 受損害；
wouldn't harm a fly 好人；
do sb. harm 對某人有害

---

3 | **harrow**
-harrowed-harrowed

vt. 使痛苦、折磨　*n.* 耙子

- The fire at the school harrowed the whole town.
  學校發生大火使得城鎮陷入憂傷中。
- The farmer drew a harrow over the farm in the sun.
  農夫頂著烈日用耙子耙地。

衍 harrowed *adj.* 苦惱的；
harrowing *adj.* 痛心的、悲慘的
同 wound 傷害
近 hollow *v.* 挖空、變空
組 disc harrow 圓盤耙

---

4 | **hurt**
-hurt-hurt

vi. 疼痛　*vt.* 使受傷　*n.* 創傷

- I didn't mean to hurt you.
  我不是有意要傷害你的。
- He is in pain because he hurt his left leg yesterday.
  他昨天傷了左腿所以現在很痛。

衍 hurter *n.* 引起損害之人或事物；hurtful *adj.* 有害的
反 heal *v.* 癒合、痊癒
組 free from hurt 免受痛苦
片 get hurt 受傷；
hurt feelings 傷害感情；
cry before one is hurt 無病呻吟

5 pain
-pained-pained

vt. 使煩惱、使痛苦　n. 痛苦、辛苦

- It pains me to see him fail.
  看到他失敗我很難過。
- Parents take great pains to take care of their children.
  父母費心照顧孩子。

衍 pains *n.* 千辛萬苦；
　painless *adj.* 不痛的
同 suffer 遭受、經歷
組 acute pain 急性疼痛
片 pain in the ass 討厭的人；
　take (great) pains 費力；
　spare no pains 不遺餘力

小試身手UP

(　) 1. Did you _____ yourself when you fell off the ladder?
　　(A) hurt　(B) pain　(C) ached　(D) harrow

(　) 2. Polluted water expelled from the factory does _____ the river.
　　(A) hurt　(B) pain　(C) ache　(D) harm

1. (A)　當你從梯子上跌下來的時候，有傷到自己嗎？
2. (D)　工廠排放的汙水危害河水。

rack / suffer / torment / torture / wound

Quick View !

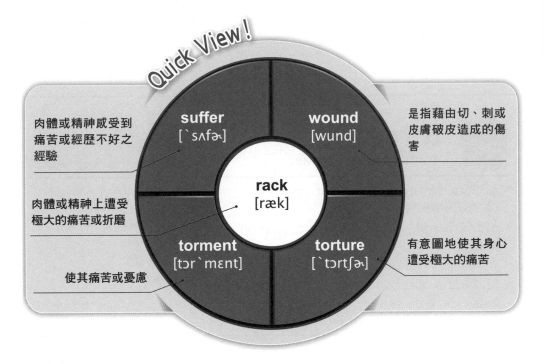

肉體或精神感受到痛苦或經歷不好之經驗

suffer
[`sʌfɚ]

wound
[wund]

是指藉由切、刺或皮膚破皮造成的傷害

rack
[ræk]

肉體或精神上遭受極大的痛苦或折磨

torment
[tɔr`mɛnt]

torture
[`tɔrtʃɚ]

有意圖地使其身心遭受極大的痛苦

使其痛苦或憂慮

6 | **rack**
-racked-racked

vt. 使受極大痛苦、折磨　n. 網架

- Pain racked his body.
  痛苦穿透他全身。
- The suspect was tied up on the rack and racked by whipping.
  嫌犯被綁在拷問台上，受到鞭刑拷打。

衍 racking *adj.* 折磨人的
同 hurt 使受傷
組 nerve-racking 傷腦筋的、使人不安的
片 rack up 傷害、累計

7 **suffer**
-suffered-suffered

vi. 受苦、患病　vt. 遭受、經歷

- She suffers from headaches.
  她飽受頭痛之苦。
- Since you're getting fat, you may suffer from high blood pressure.
  因為你變胖了，可能會得高血壓。

衍 suffering *n.* 苦惱；
sufferer *n.* 受難者；
sufferance *n.* 忍受
同 endure 忍耐、忍受
組 not suffer fools gladly 對愚蠢的人缺乏耐心
片 suffer from 受……之苦；
suffer through 挨過

8 **torment**
-tormented-tormented

vt. 使痛苦、折磨、煩擾　n. 痛苦

- The cruel guard tormented the prisoners.
  殘忍的警衛折磨囚犯。
- Many people in Africa are tormented by hunger.
  非洲許多人為飢餓所苦。
- Making a speech in public is a torment to him.
  公開發表演說對他來說是個折磨。

衍 tormenting *adj.* 令人痛苦的；
tormentor *n.* 使苦痛的人；
tormentress *n.* 女性折磨者
同 torture 拷問
反 comfort 舒適
組 self-torment 自我虐待

9 **torture**
-tortured-tortured

vt. 折磨、使為難　n. 拷問

- The soldiers tortured their prisoners until they revealed military secrets.
  士兵虐待囚犯直到他們吐露軍事機密。
- In ancient times, suspects were tortured until they made a confession.
  在古代，嫌犯會受到嚴刑拷打直到招供為止。

衍 torturer *n.* 虐待者；
torturous *adj.* 折磨人的
同 torment 使痛苦
組 self-torture 苦修；
torture chamber 刑求室

10 wound
-wounded-wounded

vi. 傷害　vt. 使受傷、傷害　n. 傷口

- He wounded his knee by falling on a rock.
  他跌倒撞到石頭造成膝蓋受傷。
- The man died from a gunshot wound to the head.
  那名男子死於頭部槍傷。

衍 wounded *adj.* 受傷的；
　wounding *adj.* 傷人感情的
同 hurt 使受傷
組 wound dressing 敷料；
　flesh wound 皮肉傷
片 wound up 興奮的、緊張的；
　lick one's wounds 自舔傷口

 聯想學習Plus

- 什麼時候需要先用到急救（first aid），是受傷（wound）、曬傷（sunburn）或是感到疼痛（pain）時？
- 你知道該如何清理（clean）、包紮（dress）、縫合（suture）、擦拭（swab）傷口（wound）嗎？

小試身手UP

（　）1. She _____ from headaches.
　　　(A) hurt　(B) racked　(C) suffers　(D) wounds
（　）2. She _____ her brains trying to remember.
　　　(A) hurt　(B) racked　(C) suffered　(D) tortured

1. (C)　她頭痛難耐。
2. (B)　她因極力回想而頭痛欲裂。rack one's brains to-V / Ving 是指絞盡腦汁去做某事之意。

生活常用　學校工作　情緒心智　社會萬象

租借

🎧 MP3 4-03

borrow / lend / let / owe / rent

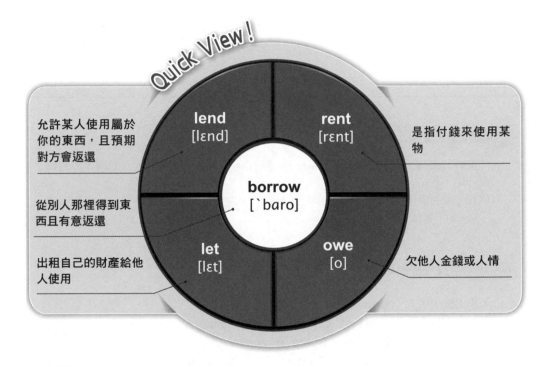

Quick View !

lend [lɛnd]
允許某人使用屬於你的東西，且預期對方會返還

從別人那裡得到東西且有意返還

rent [rɛnt]
是指付錢來使用某物

borrow [`baro]

let [lɛt]
出租自己的財產給他人使用

owe [o]
欠他人金錢或人情

---

11 **borrow**
-borrowed-borrowed

vi. 借（東西、錢） *vt.* 借、借入

- May I borrow your notes for a few days?
  我可以向你借幾天筆記嗎？
- The money Grace borrowed from the bank may approach five thousand dollars.
  葛瑞絲向銀行借的錢可能接近五千美金了。

Tip borrow sth. from sb. 從某人借來某物

衍 borrowing *n.* 借用；
borrower *n.* 借用人
同 take 拿、取、握、抱
反 lend 借給
組 borrowing powers 借款權限；
borrow trouble 杞人憂天

12 **lend**
-lent-lent

vi. 貸款　vt. 把……借給

- It was raining hard, so I lent her my umbrella.
  當時下大雨，所以我把傘借給她。
- I dread that Alex will ask me to lend him money next Monday.
  我怕艾力克斯下週一會開口向我借錢。

衍 lending *n.* 出借；
lender *n.* 出借人；
lendable *adj.* 可貸放的
同 loan *v.* 借出、貸與
反 borrow 借、借入
組 lending library 租賃圖書店
片 lend oneself to 有助於；
lend itself to 適合

---

13 **let**
-let-let

vi. 出租　vt. 出租、租給　n. 出租

- My brother owns the cottage, and we're letting it from him for this summer.
  我哥哥擁有這棟小屋，我們這個夏天要跟他租借小屋使用。
- Anita replied that her father didn't let her travel with us.
  安妮塔回覆說她父親不讓她和我們去旅行。

衍 letting *n.* 租金
同 allow 允許、准許
片 let alone 更不必說；
let down 使失望；
let in 讓……進來；
let off 寬恕；
let go 放開、忘掉

---

14 **owe**
-owed-owed

vi. 欠錢　vt. 欠（債等）

- I owe 500 dollars to my landlord.
  我欠房東五百元。
- I owe you $100 USD, right? May I pay you back next Friday?
  我欠你一百美元，對吧？我可以下週五再還你嗎？

衍 owing *adj.* 欠著的
同 indebted 負債的
反 pay 付、支付、付款給
片 owing to 由於；
I owe you one. 欠你一次人情。

生活常用

學校工作

情緒心智

社會萬象

15 | rent
-rented-rented

vi. 出租　vt. 租用、租入　n. 租金

- We rent our apartment. We don't own it.
  我們的公寓是租的，不是我們自己的。
- It's strongly recommended that you rent a car rather than take a bus in Okinawa.
  去沖繩玩，與其搭公車，不如租輛車四處玩更好。

衍 rental *n.* 租金；
rentable *adj.* 可租的；
renter *n.* 承租人；
同 let 出租、租給
組 rent-free 免租金的；
rent bank 租金銀行
片 rent out 出租；
for rent 出租中

聯想學習Plus

- 約翰在繳交房租（rent）的路上看到一台販賣機（vending machine），把錢用光後，只能回家把錢寄（sent）給房東。

小試身手UP

（　）1. He promised to _____ me his helmet for the bike race this Saturday.
(A) lend　(B) borrow　(C) let　(D) owe

（　）2. I had enough money to buy the game after my sister _____ me 5,000 dollars.
(A) rents　(B) let　(C) lent　(D) borrowed

（　）3. I'm a landlady, and _____ one flat of my apartment downtown.
(A) borrowing　(B) letting　(C) renting　(D) lending

Ans
1. (A) 他答應借我安全帽參加本週六的自行車比賽。
2. (C) 我姊姊借我五千元後，我就有錢買遊戲。
3. (B) 我是包租婆，我把位於市區公寓的其中一層出租出去。

掏空

🎧 MP3 4-04

empty / extract / hollow / void

Quick View !

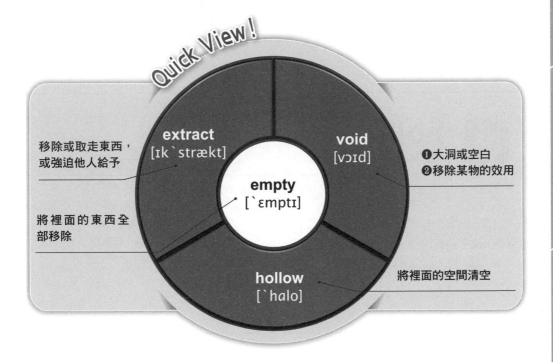

移除或取走東西，
或強迫他人給予

extract
[ɪk`strækt]

empty
[`ɛmptɪ]

void
[vɔɪd]

❶大洞或空白
❷移除某物的效用

將裡面的東西全
部移除

hollow
[`halo]

將裡面的空間清空

---

16 | empty
-emptied-emptied

vi. 成為空的　*vt.* 使成為空的　*adj.* 空的

- Please empty the garbage can.
  請清空垃圾桶。
- The police emptied out Jim's pockets and found my lost watch.
  員警翻了吉姆的口袋，找到我那只遺失的手錶。

衍 empties *n.* 空瓶；
emptily *adv.* 空空地；
emptiness *n.* 空虛

同 vacate *v.* 空出

反 full 滿的

組 empty calorie 沒營養價值的食物

片 be empty of 缺乏

17 extract
-extracted-extracted

vt. 用力取出、使勁拔出、抽出　n. 提取物

- The dentist extracted my wisdom tooth.
  牙醫拔了我的智齒。
- The teacher extracted some sentences from chapter ten and explained how they were written.
  老師從第十章中選出一些句子，並解釋它們的結構。

衍 extractable *adj.* 可拔出的；
　extraction *n.* 抽出；
　extractive *adj.* 提取的
同 extirpate 使連根拔起
反 restore 恢復
組 yeast extract 酵母提取物
片 extract from 提取、抽出

18 hollow
-hollowed-hollowed

vi. 變空　vt. 挖空　adj. 中空的　adv. 空洞地

- The woodcarver hollowed out a block of wood.
  木雕師傅挖空了一段木頭。
- Knock on the wall, and it sounds hollow.
  敲敲牆壁，聽起來是中空的。

衍 hollowly *adv.* 凹陷地；
　hollowness *n.* 凹陷
同 empty 使成為空的
組 hollow-eyed 眼窩凹陷的
片 hollow out 清空、挖空

19 void
-voided-voided

vt. 使空出、退出、離開　adj. 空的　n. 空白

- The book is void of knowledge and interest.
  這本書缺乏知識和趣味性。
- They voided a room for storing their extra furniture.
  他們空出一個房間存放額外的家具。

衍 voided *adj.* 有空間的；
　voider *n.* 取消者；
　voidable *adj.* 可使無效的
反 occupied 被占用的
組 air void 空氣洞；
　void check 無效支票
片 null and void 無效的

• 你要避免（avoid）成為一個內在空無一物（void）的人。
• 村長疏散（evacuate）村民後，整個村空無一人（empty），便辭去職位（vacate）了。

小試身手UP↑

( ) 1. Mom let me _____ out the garbage can in the kitchen last night because it was already full.
  (A) empty (B) extract (C) void (D) hollow

( ) 2. The judge _____ some information from the witness of the car accident.
  (A) extracted (B) voided (C) emptied (D) hollowed

( ) 3. She _____ the check because she had made a mistake.
  (A) emptied (B) extracted (C) voided (D) hollowed

1. (A) 昨晚媽讓我清空廚房的垃圾桶，因為它早已經滿了。void 有清空或空出的意思，但通常多用於撤出、排泄、使無效之意。hollow 是指物體表面向內或向下彎曲，也就是凹陷之意。extract 有利用化學或工業過程從某物中取得另一物質，或是指把東西拿出、拉出來的動作。
2. (A) 法官從車禍目擊者的身上取得資訊。
3. (C) 因為失誤，所以她使這張支票失效。

Lesson 5

抓捕

🎧 MP3 4-05

arrest / catch / grasp / seize

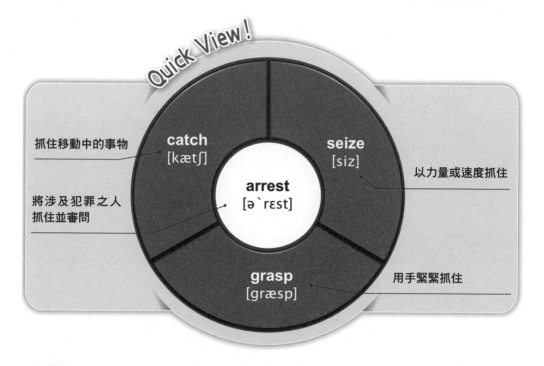

Quick View !

catch [kætʃ] — 抓住移動中的事物
— 將涉及犯罪之人抓住並審問

arrest [ə`rɛst]

seize [siz] — 以力量或速度抓住

grasp [græsp] — 用手緊緊抓住

---

20 | arrest
-arrested-arrested

vt. 逮捕、拘留 n. 拘留

- The police arrested the criminal and brought him to jail.
  警方將罪犯逮捕並送他入獄。
- The one who stole my purse last week is under arrest.
  上週偷我錢包的人被捕了。

衍 arresting *adj.* 引人注意的;
arrestive *adj.* 引人注意的;
arrestment *n.* 阻止;
arrestor *n.* 逮捕者

同 stop 阻止、阻擋

反 release 釋放、解放

組 arrest warrant 逮捕令、拘票;
cardiac arrest 心搏停止

catch
-caught-caught

vi. 被鉤住、被卡住　**vt.** 接住、抓住　**n.** 接球

- My brother caught the ball hit by the professional player.
  我弟弟接到了職業選手擊出的球。
- He hastened to catch the flying saucer.
  他趕緊去接住飛盤。

衍 catching *adj.* 傳染性的；
catcher *n.* 捕手
同 seize 抓住、捉住
反 release 釋放、解放
組 catch-22 進退兩難的；
window catch 窗栓
片 catch up with 趕上；
catch fire 著火

grasp
-grasped-grasped

vi. 抓　**vt.** 領會、理解　**n.** 領會

- Dazed, he could not grasp her meaning.
  他一臉迷糊樣，可見他不懂她的意思。
- You have to grasp every opportunity of a job interview.
  你要把握每一次求職面試的機會。
- Grasp the rope swinging to you.
  快抓住盪向你的繩索。

衍 grasping *adj.* 緊緊抓住的
同 seize 捉住
反 abandon 遺棄
組 grasp the nettle 迎著困難上
片 grasp at 攫取

seize
-seized-seized

vi. 抓住、捉住、奪取　**vt.** 抓住、捉住

- The police seized the stolen property.
  警方查獲到被偷的東西。
- She seized me by the arm when I was walking past her.
  在我經過她時候，她抓住了我的手臂。

衍 seizable *adj.* 可捉捕的；
seizer *n.* 扣押者；
seizor *n.* 占有者；
seizure *n.* 抓住
同 grab 攫取、抓取
反 loose 解開
組 seize the opportunity 把握機會
片 seize on 把握

生活常用

學校工作

情緒心智

社會萬象

- 警方在逮捕（arrest）到嫌犯後，就開始休息（rest）了。
- RIP 就是 Rest in Peace（安息）的縮寫。
- 當他抓住機會（seize / grasp an opportunity）獲得權力（seize power）後，便下令軍隊停火（cease fire）。

小試身手UP

（　）1. The police succeeded in _____ the wanted man before he sneaked out of the country.
(A) arrest　(B) catching　(C) seizure　(D) holding

（　）2. He was _____ for a hit and run accident.
(A) arrested　(B) catching　(C) seized　(D) grasped

（　）3. A man of ambition will _____ any chance to succeed.
(A) arrest　(B) seize　(C) catch　(D) cease

1. (B) 警方在通緝犯潛逃出境前成功抓住他。
2. (A) 他因為一起肇事逃逸事件遭到逮捕。
3. (B) 有企圖心的人會抓住任何成功的機會。

Lesson 6 追求

🎧 MP3 4-06

court / hunt / pursue / trail

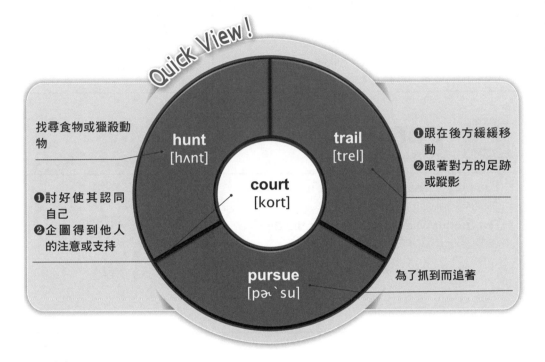

Quick View!

找尋食物或獵殺動物

hunt
[hʌnt]

❶討好使其認同自己
❷企圖得到他人的注意或支持

court
[kort]

trail
[trel]

❶跟在後方緩緩移動
❷跟著對方的足跡或蹤影

pursue
[pɚˋsu]

為了抓到而追著

---

24 **court**
-courted-courted

vt. 奉承、討好、設法取得、招致　n. 法庭

- The single mother courted sympathy in order to get financial support.
  這名單親媽媽博取同情以取得經濟支援。
- If you settle your lawsuit out of court, you will end up saving yourself a lot of money.
  如果你在庭外和解訴訟，你就能省下一大筆錢。
- Carelessness courts accidents.
  疏忽會釀成意外。

衍 courteous *adj.* 有禮貌的；
courtesy *n.* 好意
同 pursue 追求
組 court-martial 軍事法庭；
court tennis 室內網球
片 appear in court 出庭；
pay court to 向……獻殷勤

25 hunt
-hunted-hunted

vi. 打獵、搜尋　vt. 搜尋、獵取　n. 打獵

- The police have been hunting for an escaped convict for two days.
  警方從兩天前就一直持續追捕逃犯。
- The hunter always goes hunting with his retriever.
  獵人總是帶著他的獵犬去打獵。
- He's been hunting for a new job since he got fired.
  他從解僱以來一直在找新工作。

衍 hunter *n.* 獵人；
huntress *n.* 女獵師
同 pursue 追趕、追蹤、追捕
組 hunting ground 獵場；
hunt ball 獵人舞會；
head hunter 獵色人材的人
片 hunt out 找出；
hunt down 追捕到

26 pursue
-pursued-pursued

vi. 追趕　vt. 追趕、追求、追捕

- The prey eventually got rid of its pursuers.
  獵物最終擺脫了追捕者。
- Ted tried in vain to pursue after the thief.
  泰德盡力去追小偷，但是無功而返。

衍 pursuer *n.* 追求者；
pursuit *n.* 追蹤；
pursuant *adj.* 追趕的
同 chase 追逐
反 flee 逃、逃走
片 pursue after 追趕

27 trail
-trailed-trailed

vi. 拖、曳　vt. 跟蹤、追獵　n. 足跡

- The slower cars trailed the faster ones.
  比較慢的車跟在比較快的車後面。
- If you don't want to be spoiled, don't watch the trailer before seeing the movie.
  如果你不想被劇透，看電影前就不要看預告。

衍 trailing *adj.* 蔓延的；
trailer *n.* 拖車、預告；
trailless *adj.* 無路徑的
同 pursue 追趕
組 trailer park 拖車屋停駐場；
film trailer 電影預告；
trailer camp 拖車營地
片 on the trail of 尋找、跟蹤

 **聯想學習Plus**

- 古時候的人有三種生活方式：打獵（hunting）、採集（gathering）與耕種（cultivating）。
- 當她發現尾隨者（pursuer / follower / stalker）是誰後，氣地去提告（sue）。

小試身手UP

（　　）1. She decided to ＿＿＿＿ her dream of studying abroad after her children all grew up.
　　　　(A) court　　(B) pursue　　(C) hunt　　(D) trail

（　　）2. Although John ＿＿＿＿ Jane for years and finally they got married, they still ended up in divorce.
　　　　(A) pursued　　(B) hunted　　(C) caught　　(D) trailed

（　　）3. Linus always ＿＿＿＿ a blanket after him when he goes out.
　　　　(A) courts　　(B) hunts　　(C) pursues　　(D) trails

生活常用

學校工作

情緒心智

社會萬象

 Ans
1. (B) 在小孩都已長大成人後，她決定追尋出國留學的夢想。
2. (A) 儘管約翰追求珍好多年，兩人也終於結婚，但最後卻以離婚收場。
3. (D) 奈勒斯出門時總會將一條毯子拖在身後。

7 Lesson

准許

🎧 MP3 4-07

admit / allow / authorize / endorse / permit / ratify

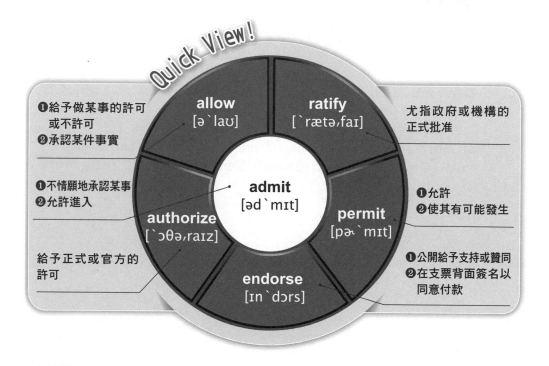

Quick View!

allow [ə`laʊ]
❶給予做某事的許可或不許可
❷承認某件事實

ratify [`rætəˌfaɪ]
尤指政府或機構的正式批准

authorize [`ɔθəˌraɪz]
❶不情願地承認某事
❷允許進入
給予正式或官方的許可

admit [əd`mɪt]

permit [pɚ`mɪt]
❶允許
❷使其有可能發生
❶公開給予支持或贊同
❷在支票背面簽名以同意付款

endorse [ɪn`dɔrs]

---

28 | **admit**
-admitted-admitted

vi. 承認 *vt.* 承認

- This movie ticket admits one.
  這張電影票只允許一個人觀賞。
- She admitted that she was cheating on the final exam.
  她承認期末考有作弊。

衍 admission *n.* 門票、進入許可；
admittable *adj.* 可容許的；
admittance *n.* 入場許可；
admittedly *adv.* 無可否認地
同 consent 同意
反 exclude 排除

29 allow
-allowed-allowed

vi. 容許　vt. 允許、准許

- His mother said no at first, but later she allowed him to go to the late movie.
他母親一開始不答應，但是後來還是答應讓他看晚場電影。
- Please allow me to go with you.
請允許我和你一起去。

衍 allowable *adj.* 正當的、允許的；
allowance *n.* 零用錢
同 consent 同意
反 disallow 不許、駁回
組 allowable error 容許誤差
片 allow for 考慮到；
allow of 容許有……的可能

---

30 authorize
-authorized-authorized

vt. 批准、認可、允許

- The mayor authorized a parade through downtown.
市長允許在市區遊行。
- Only the bank account holder can authorize the bank to pay.
只有銀行帳戶持有者可以授權銀行付款。

衍 authorized *adj.* 公認的；
authorization *n.* 授權；
authoritatively *adv.* 權威地；
authority *n.* 職權、權力
同 legalize 使合法化
反 forbid 禁止；
ban 禁止

---

31 endorse
-endorsed-endorsed

vt. 贊同、認可、背書

- He endorsed her for governor.
他支持她擔任州長。
- This bill is endorsed by most of the legislators.
這項法案受到大多數立委的認同。

衍 endorsee *n.* 原收款人自己背書以讓渡的對象；endorsement *n.* 背書；endorser *n.* 背書人
同 approve 贊成
組 blank endorsement 空白背書；
endorse a check 支票背書
片 endorse over 背書

32 permit
-permitted-permitted

vi. 允許　vt. 允許、准許　n. 許可證

- The hospital does not permit any visitors after nine o'clock.
  醫院九點後不允許會客。
- Her boss permitted her to leave the office earlier.
  她的老闆允許她提早下班。

衍 permittivity *n.* 電容率；
　permission *n.* 許可
同 allow 允許、准許
反 prohibit 禁止
片 permit of 允許；
　obtain permission 取得許可

33 ratify
-ratified-ratified

vt. 批准、認可

- The Congress ratified the treaty.
  國會同意了條約。
- Many member countries ratified an agreement to boycott the country that tried to develop nuclear weapons.
  許多會員國批准一項抵制發展核武國家的協議。

衍 ratifier *n.* 批准者；
　ratification *n.* 承認
同 confirm 批准、確認

(　) 1. If you want to visit the castle, you need to obtain ＿＿＿＿ from the owner.
　　(A) admission　(B) authorities　(C) allowance　(D) permission
(　) 2. After being questioned, she eventually ＿＿＿＿ killing her baby by accident.（複選）
　　(A) admitted　(B) permitted　(C) acknowledged　(D) ratified

Ans

1. (D)　如果想參觀這座城堡，你需要先取得城堡主人的同意。
2. (A)(C)　在被質問後，她終於坦承失手打死孩子。admit 和 acknowledge 都有承認的意思，兩者也可直接接 V-ing，表示承認做過某事而言。

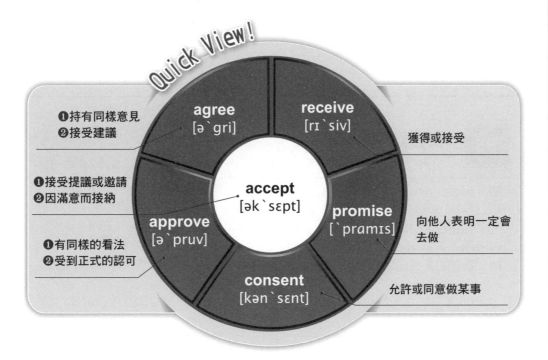

Lesson 8 接受

🎧 MP3 4-08

accept / agree / approve / consent / promise / receive

Quick View!

- **agree** [ə`gri]
  - ❶持有同樣意見
  - ❷接受建議
- **receive** [rɪ`siv]
  - 獲得或接受
- **accept** [ək`sɛpt]
- **approve** [ə`pruv]
  - ❶接受提議或邀請
  - ❷因滿意而接納
  - ❶有同樣的看法
  - ❷受到正式的認可
- **promise** [`pramɪs]
  - 向他人表明一定會去做
- **consent** [kən`sɛnt]
  - 允許或同意做某事

34 accept
-accepted-accepted

vi. 接受、應允　vt. 接受、答應、同意

- She accepted the job offer.
  她接受了這份工作。
- Please accept the invitation to my wedding on September 25.
  請接受參加我九月二十五日婚禮的邀請。

衍 acceptable *adj.* 可接受的；
acceptation *n.* 承認；
acceptive *adj.* 可接受的；
acceptance *n.* 接受

同 approve 贊成

反 refuse 拒絕

片 gain acceptance with 受歡迎；
accept as 接受成為

35 | agree
-agreed-agreed

vi. 同意、贊同 *vt.* 同意

- I agree with my friends about most things.
  對於大多數的事情，我和朋友看法都相同。
- I agreed to work overseas since my boss offered me double pay.
  因為老闆給我兩倍的薪水，我同意去海外工作。

衍 agreement *n.* 同意、一致、協議；agreeable *adj.* 宜人的
同 accept 承認、認可
反 disagree 意見不合
組 agree to disagree 同意可以有不同的意見
片 agree on 同意某選擇；agree to 同意；agree with sb. 同意某人

36 | approve
-approved-approved

vi. 贊成、贊許 *vt.* 贊成、同意、贊許

- The bank approved Sam's loan application.
  銀行核准山姆的貸款申請。
- His father will never approve of his going swimming alone.
  他父親絕對不會同意他獨自去游泳。

衍 approval *n.* 批准、認可；approver *n.* 贊成者
同 endorse 贊同、認可
反 disapprove 不贊同
片 approve of 核准

37 | consent
-consented-consented

vi. 同意、贊成、答應 *n.* 答應

- They consented to her going on a trip with her friends.
  他們同意讓她跟朋友去旅行。
- I consent to your proposal of buying more machines.
  我同意你採購更多機器的提議。

衍 consenting *adj.* 准許的；consenter *n.* 同意者
同 permit 允許
反 dissent 持異議
片 consent to 同意；by common consent 普遍認可

38 | promise
-promised-promised

vi. 允諾、保證　*vt.* 允諾、答應　*n.* 諾言

- The children promised to come home before dark.
  孩子們承諾天黑前會回家。
- An honest man always keeps his promise.
  誠實的人總是信守諾言。

衍 promising *adj.* 大有可為的；
　promiser *n.* 許諾者；
　promisor *n.* 立約人
同 agree 同意
組 Promised Land 應許之地
片 keep a promise 履行諾言；
　break a promise 毀約

39 | receive
-received-received

vi. 得到、接收　*vt.* 收到、接到

- He received many cards while he was in the hospital.
  他在醫院時收到很多慰問卡。
- Mr. Wang received a letter to the effect that his son had been kidnapped.
  王先生收到一封信，大意是說他兒子被綁架了。

Tip to the effect that 是「大意是」之意。

衍 reception *n.* 接待；
　receivable *adj.* 可承認的；
　receiver *n.* 聽筒
同 accept 接受；get 得到
反 give 送出
片 receive with open arms 熱烈歡迎

小試身手UP

(　) 1. He is a(n) _____ man who is considered the next successor.
　　　(A) acceptable　(B) promising　(C) approval　(D) agreeable
(　) 2. He turned down the job offer. In other words, he didn't _____ the position.
　　　(A) accept　(B) agree　(C) consent　(D) promise
(　) 3. If anyone _____ on this proposal, please raise your objection on the spot.
　　　(A) disapproves　(B) denies　(C) disagrees　(D) dissents

1. (B) 他是前途看漲的人，被認為是下一任接班人。
2. (A) 他拒絕了這個工作邀約。換言之，他不接受這個職務。
3. (C) 如果有人不認同這項提議，請當場提出異議。

禁止

🎧 MP3 4-09

ban / forbid / inhibit / limit / prevent / prohibit

Quick View!

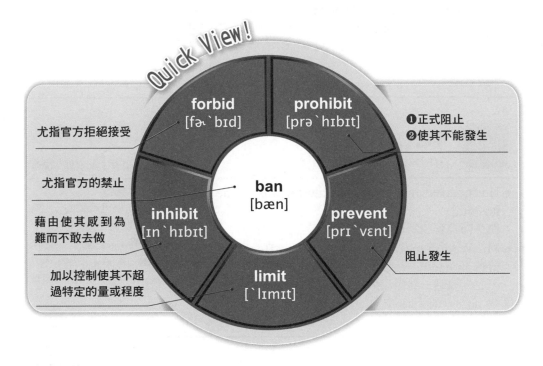

forbid [fɚˋbɪd]
尤指官方拒絕接受

prohibit [prəˋhɪbɪt]
❶正式阻止
❷使其不能發生

尤指官方的禁止

ban [bæn]

inhibit [ɪnˋhɪbɪt]
藉由使其感到為難而不敢去做

prevent [prɪˋvɛnt]
阻止發生

加以控制使其不超過特定的量或程度

limit [ˋlɪmɪt]

---

40 | **ban**
-banned-banned

vt. 禁止、取締　n. 禁止

- The law bans drunk driving.
  法律禁止喝酒開車。
- That country put a ban on people under 18 drinking alcohol.
  那個國家禁止未滿十八歲的人喝酒。
- Any TV program involving violence or adult content will be banned in the near future.
  任何有關暴力或成人內容的電視節目不久後都將遭到禁播。

衍 banned *adj.* 被禁的；
banner *n.* 旗幟、橫幅

組 banned film 禁映影片；
test ban 禁止核子武器試爆

片 ban from 禁止做

forbid
-forbade-forbidden

vt. 禁止、不許

- Her parents forbid her to smoke.
  她的父母禁止她吸菸。
- The regulations forbid eating or drinking on the MRT.
  明文規定禁止在捷運上飲食。
- God forbid that something bad should ever happen.
  但願壞事不會發生。

衍 forbidden *adj.* 被禁的；
forbiddance *n.* 禁止；
forbidding *adj.* 嚴峻的
同 prohibit 禁止
反 permit 允許
組 forbidden fruit 禁果；
the Forbidden City 紫禁城
片 God forbid that... 但願不會

inhibit
-inhibited-inhibited

vt. 抑止、阻礙

- The law inhibits the transfer of these rights to others.
  法律禁止將這些權利轉移給其他人。
- Fear inhibits the girl from telling the truth.
  恐懼使女孩說不出真相。

衍 inhibition *n.* 禁止；
inhibitive *adj.* 禁止的；
inhibitor *n.* 約束者
同 restrain 抑制、遏制
組 feedback inhibition 反饋抑制
片 inhibit from 禁止

limit
-limited-limited

vt. 限制、限定　n. 界限

- You should follow the speed limit when you drive on the highway.
  在公路上開車時須遵守速限。
- Water resources are limited, so we should develop a habit of saving water.
  水資源有限，所以我們應該要養成節約用水的習慣。

衍 limited *adj.* 有限的；
limitation *n.* 限制；
limitative *adj.* 限制的；
同 restrict 限制
組 limited company 股份有限公司；public limited company 有限公司
片 off-limits 禁止入內的

生活常用

學校工作

情緒心智

社會萬象

44 | **prevent**
-prevented-prevented

vi. 妨礙、阻止　vt. 防止、預防

- Washing hands often can help prevent illness.
  勤洗手可以預防疾病。
- You can't prevent me from marrying Tom.
  你不能阻止我和湯姆結婚。

衍 preventable *adj.* 可預防的；
preventer *n.* 妨礙者；
preventible *adj.* 可阻止的；
prevention *n.* 妨礙
同 forbid 禁止、不許
反 permit 允許
片 prevent from 制止

45 | **prohibit**
-prohibited-prohibited

vt. 禁止

- State law prohibits smoking on buses.
  州法律禁止在公車上抽菸。
- My parents prohibit me from swimming in the river.
  父母不許我在河裡游泳。

衍 prohibiter *n.* 禁止者；
prohibition *n.* 禁止；
prohibitive *adj.* 禁止性的
同 forbid 禁止
反 allow 准許
組 prohibitive tariff 禁止性關稅；
prohibited airspace 禁航區
片 prohibit from 阻止

( ) 1. The _____ of funds is the main reason why the project failed.
(A) banner　(B) prevention　(C) limitation　(D) preservation
( ) 2. Lady's night is _____ to women only, who can go to the bar for free.
(A) banned　(B) prohibited　(C) prevented　(D) restricted

1. (C) 資金有限是這項企畫失敗的主因。
2. (D) 淑女之夜只限女性，女性可以免費進入酒吧。be restricted to sb. 只限於某人。

拒絕

🎧 MP3 4-10

decline / deny / refuse / reject

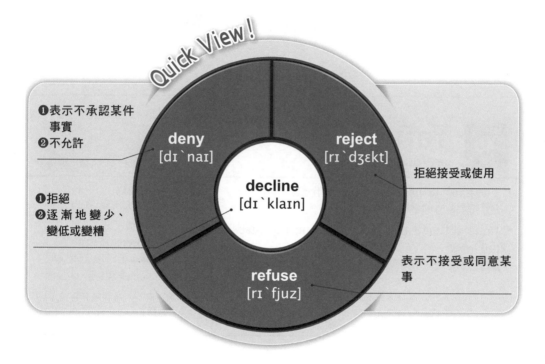

Quick View!

❶表示不承認某件事實
❷不允許

deny
[dɪ`naɪ]

reject
[rɪ`dʒɛkt]

拒絕接受或使用

decline
[dɪ`klaɪn]

❶拒絕
❷逐漸地變少、變低或變糟

refuse
[rɪ`fjuz]

表示不接受或同意某事

46 | decline
-declined-declined

vi. 謝絕　*vt.* 謝絕　*n.* 減少

- He declined to accept the award because he felt he didn't deserve it.
他拒絕接受這獎項，因為他覺得不配得到。
- Our profits have declined because of the drop in sales.
由於業績下滑，我們的營收已經減少了。

衍 declinable *adj.* 可變格的；
declination *n.* 謝絕；
declinatory *adj.* 謝絕的
同 refuse 拒絕
反 accept 同意
片 on the decline 衰退中；go into a decline 失去力量、影響等

47 deny
-denied-denied

vt. 否定、否認

- My boss denied my request for a raise.
  我的老闆否決了我加薪的請求。
- Cathy denied cheating on the exam.
  凱西否認考試有作弊。
- Your denial of her invitation hurt her feelings.
  你拒絕她的邀請傷了她的心。

衍 denial *n.* 否認、拒絕
同 renounce 拋棄
反 confirm 確定
組 access denied 拒絕存取
片 deny oneself 節制；
  There is no denying that... 不可
  否認的是……

48 refuse
-refused-refused

vi. 拒絕　vt. 拒絕　n. 渣滓

- The bank refused his request for a loan.
  銀行拒絕了他的貸款申請。
- Janet refused to work overtime because of low pay.
  由於薪水低，珍娜拒絕加班。

衍 refusal *n.* 拒絕；
  refusable *adj.* 可拒絕的
同 decline 謝絕
組 refuse collector 垃圾車；
  first refusal 第一優先購買權；
  refuse dump 垃圾場
片 an offer one cannot refuse 很誘
  人的條件

49 reject
-rejected-rejected

vt. 拒絕、抵制　n. 廢品

- Jasmine rejected the application for that prestigious university and went to a local one instead.
  茉莉拒絕去念那間知名大學，反而選擇就讀當地大學。
- All requests for a loan from my brother were rejected.
  向我哥借錢的要求全都被拒絕了。

衍 rejecter *n.* 否決者；
  rejection *n.* 拒絕；
  rejective *adj.* 拒絕的
同 bar 中止、禁止
反 accept 接受
組 reject goods 退貨

 **聯想學習Plus**

• 這個計畫（project）的本意是提供實習生替病患打針（inject）的機會，沒想到卻遭到駁回（reject）了。

小試身手UP

( ) 1. The show's popularity has _____ since the host was replaced.
(A) declined　(B) refused　(C) rejected　(D) denied

( ) 2. The minister issued a _____ that he was involved in the bribery, but he was forced to resign his office due to public opinion.
(A) decline　(B) denial　(C) refusal　(D) proposal

( ) 3. His application for a Thailand Visa is _____ for lack of some required documents.
(A) declined　(B) turned up　(C) refused　(D) reclaimed

 Ans
1. (A) 在主持人遭到替換後，這個節目受歡迎程度就開始下滑。
2. (B) 部長發表聲明，否認與賄賂一事有關，但因輿論壓力而被迫下台。
3. (C) 他申請泰國簽證，因為缺少必要文件而被退件。

升高

🎧 MP3 4-11

arise / boost / enhance / lift / promote / upgrade

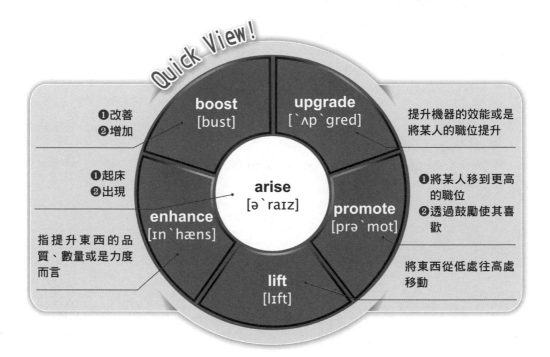

Quick View!

- **boost** [bust]
  - ❶改善
  - ❷增加
- **upgrade** [`ʌp`gred]
  - 提升機器的效能或是將某人的職位提升
- **arise** [ə`raɪz]
  - ❶起床
  - ❷出現
- **promote** [prə`mot]
  - ❶將某人移到更高的職位
  - ❷透過鼓勵使其喜歡
- **enhance** [ɪn`hæns]
  - 指提升東西的品質、數量或是力度而言
- **lift** [lɪft]
  - 將東西從低處往高處移動

---

50 arise
-arose-arisen

vi. 升起、上升、出現

- Steam arose from the boiling water.
  水蒸氣從沸水中升起。
- If any problem arises in the course of the experiment, call the professor.
  實驗過程中有出現任何問題，打電話給教授吧。

同 appear 出現、顯露
近 raise v. 舉起、升起
片 arise from 由……引起

boost
-boosted-boosted

- He boosted the child up.
  他將小孩抬起。
- The company boosted its sales by modifying its strategies.
  這間公司藉由調整策略來提高銷售量。
- Since signing this trade agreement, our country has had a boost in exports.
  簽署貿易協議後，我國出口量已大幅提高。

衍 booster *n.* 援助者；
boosterism *n.* 熱心擁護
同 lift 舉起、抬起
組 booster shot 後續疫苗注射
片 boost one's confidence 增強某人信心

enhance
-enhanced-enhanced

vt. 提高、增加

- The great sound system enhances his enjoyment of his new car.
  有了這套好的音響系統，增加他對新車的享受程度。
- Regular exercise can help enhance your physical strength.
  規律的運動能幫你強化體能。

衍 enhanced *adj.* 增大的；
enhancement *n.* 提高；
enhancer *n.* 美化
同 improve 改進

lift
-lifted-lifted

vi. 被提或舉起、升起　vt. 舉起

- The sick child lifted her head slowly.
  那個病童慢慢地抬起頭來。
- Can you help me lift the dresser to my bedroom?
  你可以幫我把這個衣櫥抬到臥室嗎？

衍 lifter *n.* 舉起的人；
liftable *adj.* 可以舉起的
同 raise 舉起、抬起
反 lower 放下、降下、放低
組 weight lifter 舉重者；
lift a finger 盡舉手之勞
片 lift up 舉起；
give sb. a lift 載某人一程

生活常用

學校工作

情緒心智

社會萬象

54 promote
-promoted-promoted

vt. 晉升、促進、宣傳

- The boss promoted Mr. Smith from clerk to supervisor.
  老闆將史密斯先生從店員晉升為主管。
- Paul was promoted to vice general manager last month.
  上個月保羅升職做了副總經理。

衍 promoter *n.* 促進者；
promotion *n.* 晉級、促銷；
promotional *adj.* 獎勵的；
promotive *adj.* 增進的
同 boost 提高、增加
反 degrade 使降級
組 promotion worker 推銷員
片 promote to 升級到

55 upgrade
-upgraded-upgraded

vt. 使升級、提高、提升　n. 升級

- She upgraded her computer by adding more memory.
  她增加記憶體讓電腦升級。
- Peter's English is on the upgrade with the help of his teacher.
  彼得的英語在老師的幫助下正在進步。

衍 upgradable *adj.* 可升級的
反 degrade 使降級
組 upgrade fever 升級熱
片 upgrade to 升級成……

( ) 1. Because of advanced technology, the global populatin has _____ in the past decades.
(A) promoted　(B) upgraded　(C) enhanced　(D) boosted
( ) 2. The doctor _____ his condition from fair to good. He will soon be discharged from hospital.
(A) graded　(B) upgraded　(C) rated　(D) classified

1. (D) 由於科技日新月異，過去數十年來全球人口數激增。
2. (B) 醫生將他的病況從普通提升到良好的程度。他很快就能出院了。

分歧

contradict / differ / disagree / dissent

🎧 MP3 4-12

Quick View !

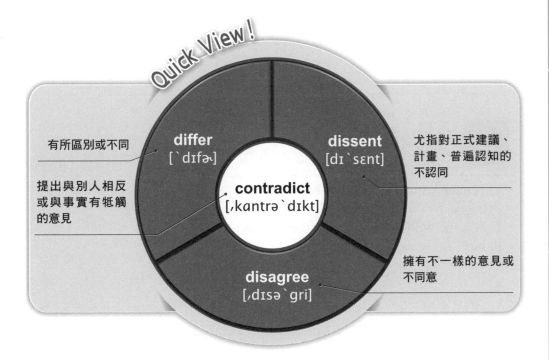

有所區別或不同

differ
[ˋdɪfɚ]

提出與別人相反
或與事實有牴觸
的意見

contradict
[ˌkɑntrəˋdɪkt]

dissent
[dɪˋsɛnt]

尤指對正式建議、
計畫、普遍認知的
不認同

擁有不一樣的意見或
不同意

disagree
[ˌdɪsəˋgri]

---

56 | **contradict**
-contradicted-contradicted

vi. 發生矛盾　*vt.* 否定、反駁

- I'm sorry to contradict you, but those aren't the facts of the case.
  我很抱歉持不同看法,但是事實並非如此。
- The latest discovery contradicted that professor's hypothesis.
  最新的發現跟那位教授的假設相悖。

衍 contradiction *n.* 矛盾;
contradictive *adj.* 傾向於矛盾的;
contradictory *adj.* 對立的
同 deny 否定
反 admit 承認
組 self-contradictory 自相矛盾的

57 differ
-differed-differed

vi. 不同、相異

- The twins look alike but they differ in many ways.
  這對雙胞胎看起來很像，但其實很多地方不一樣。
- Mom and Dad differ on my education.
  我爸媽對我的教育有不同的看法。

衍 difference *n.* 差別；
different *adj.* 不同的；
differentiable *adj.* 可區分的
同 contrast 對比
反 accord 符合
組 make no difference 沒有任何不同
片 differ from 與……不同；
differ with 與……意見不同

58 disagree
-disagreed-disagreed

vi. 意見不合、有分歧

- I disagree with you about the election.
  對於選舉，我跟你持不同的看法。
- I disagree with you about whether to eat out or not.
  是否出去吃飯，我和你意見不同。

衍 disagreeable *adj.* 不合意的；
disagreement *n.* 爭吵、不和
同 differ 相異
反 agree 意見一致
片 disagree with 與……意見不一、不同意

59 dissent
-dissented-dissented

vi. 不同意、持異議　n. 不同意

- Six of the judges agreed she should win the contest, and two dissented.
  六名裁判認為她應該獲勝，但是有兩位裁判持相反意見。
- We all approved of her arrangement without dissent.
  我們一致同意她的安排，沒有異議。

衍 dissenting *adj.* 持異議的；
dissenter *n.* 持異議者
同 disagree 不符、不一致
反 consent 答應
片 dissent from 與……意見不一

 **聯想學習Plus**

- I beg to differ. 或 I beg to disagree. 這兩句話的意思都一樣，都是用在不贊同別人意見的時候，是非常正式而客氣的說法，字面意思是「很抱歉與你持不同意見」，意思跟 I'm sorry, but I disagree. 一樣。也可從常見說法 I beg your pardon.（麻煩請你再說一遍。）來幫助記憶連結。

小試身手UP

( ) 1. Although their views on politics greatly _____, they still enjoyed talking with each other about the government.
(A) contradicted　(B) dissented　(C) differed　(D) agreed

( ) 2. Does anyone else have a _____ on this resolution? If not, we will go through next.
(A) contradiction　(B) dissent　(C) difference　(D) conflict

Ans

1. (C) 雖然他們的政治觀點非常不同，但他們還是喜歡一起談論政府。
2. (B) 還有其他人對這項決議有異議嗎？沒有的話，我們就要討論下一個。

反對

🎧 MP3 4-13

antagonize / counter / disaccord / object / oppose / protest

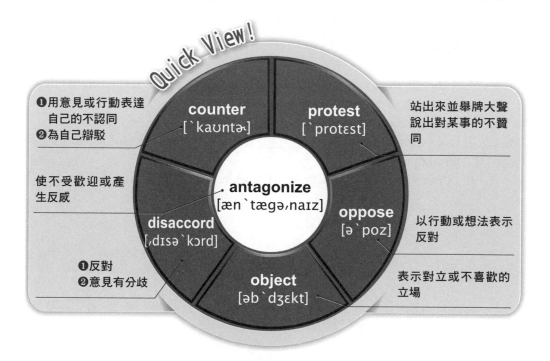

Quick View!

counter [`kaʊntɚ] ❶用意見或行動表達自己的不認同 ❷為自己辯駁

使不受歡迎或產生反感

disaccord [ˌdɪsəˈkɔrd] ❶反對 ❷意見有分歧

antagonize [ænˈtægəˌnaɪz]

protest [`protɛst] 站出來並舉牌大聲說出對某事的不贊同

oppose [əˈpoz] 以行動或想法表示反對

object [əbˈdʒɛkt] 表示對立或不喜歡的立場

---

60 antagonize
-antagonized-antagonized

vt. 使對抗、使敵對

- He antagonized the other players by cheating.
  他作弊所以成了其他選手的敵人。
- Timothy is such an easygoing man that his colleagues have no wish to antagonize him.
  提摩西的脾氣隨和，所以沒有同事有意與他為敵。

衍 antagonistic *adj.* 反對的；
antagonist *n.* 對手
同 oppose 妨礙

counter
-countered-countered

- When I suggested bike riding, he countered by saying that it was going to rain.
  當我提議騎單車,他以將會下雨表達反對。
- Her decision to work abroad instead of getting married ran counter to her family's expectation.
  她放棄結婚而打算去海外工作的決定與家裡的期待相悖。

衍 counteract *v.* 抵消
組 counter-culture 反傳統文化；
counter-attack 反擊
片 counter to 相反地；
under the counter 私下地

disaccord
-disaccorded-disaccorded

vi. 不一致、相爭　n. 不和、不一致

- At the end of every month, Mom checks whether the expenses disaccord with the account book.
  每個月月底時,媽總會確認支出跟帳簿有無出入。
- His statement of that incident disaccorded with the witness's testimony.
  他對事件的陳述跟目擊者的證詞有出入。

反 accord 一致、符合
片 disaccord with 反對

object
-objected-objected

vi. 反對　vt. 反對、抗議　n. 物體

- He objected to the prosecutor's accusation.
  他抗議原告的指控。
- No one dares to object to our manager's proposal.
  沒有人敢反對經理的提議。

衍 objection *n.* 反對；
objectless *adj.* 無目的的；
objective *adj.* 客觀的
同 disagree 意見不合
反 agree 意見一致
組 art object 藝術品；
money is no object 錢不是問題
片 object to 對……反對

生活常用

學校工作

情緒心智

社會萬象

64 oppose
-opposed-opposed

vi. 反對　*vt.* 反對、反抗、妨礙

- The faculty of the university opposed the idea of prolonging the school time.
那所大學的職員全都反對延長上課時間。
- Most students oppose smoking on campus.
大部分學生反對在校園吸煙。

衍 opposing *adj.* 反對的；
opposite *adj.* 對立的；
opposition *n.* 對抗

同 counteract 對抗

反 agree 同意

片 in opposition to 與……的意見相反；as opposed to 與……對照

65 protest
-protested-protested

vi. 抗議　*vt.* 抗議、聲明　*n.* 抗議

- Many workers went on strike to protest against the policy of one mandatory day off and one flexible rest day.
許多勞工罷工抗議一例一休這個政策。
- Residents gathered to protest against the planned incinerator nearby.
居民集結起來抗議附近興建焚化爐的計畫。

衍 protestation *n.* 抗議；
protester *n.* 反對者；
Protestant *adj.* 新教徒的

同 object 反對

反 support 支持

組 protest rally 抗議大會

片 protest against 反對

小試身手UP

（　）1. Lucy has a bias against studying abroad, and therefore she couldn't hold _____ opinions.
(A) objective　(B) subjective　(C) optimistic　(D) pessimistic

（　）2. As far as I'm concerned, I absolutely _____ abolishing the death penalty because of my belief in an eye for an eye.
(A) protest　(B) object　(C) oppose　(D) antagonize

1. (A) 露西對出國留學抱有偏見，因此無法做出客觀的意見。
2. (C) 就我來看，我絕對反對廢除死刑，因為我堅信以牙還牙。

改變

🎧 MP3 4-14

alter / change / convert / shift / transform / vary

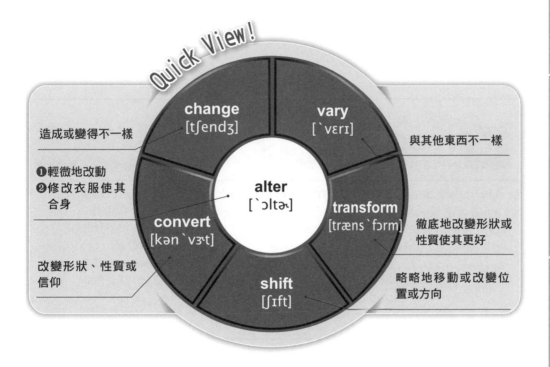

Quick View!

change [tʃendʒ] — 造成或變得不一樣

❶輕微地改動
❷修改衣服使其合身

vary [`vɛrɪ] — 與其他東西不一樣

alter [`ɔltɚ]

convert [kən`vɝt] — 改變形狀、性質或信仰

transform [træns`fɔrm] — 徹底地改變形狀或性質使其更好

shift [ʃɪft] — 略略地移動或改變位置或方向

---

66 alter
-altered-altered

vi. 改變、變樣　*vt.* 改變

- He altered the dress to make it shorter.
  他把洋裝改短。
- The skirt should be altered to fit your figure.
  裙子應該改一下才合身。
- The color of maple tree leaves alters with seasons.
  楓樹葉子的顏色會隨著季節改變。

衍 alternative *n.* 選擇；
　alterable *adj.* 可修改的；
　alternate *v.* 使交替
同 change 使變化
反 preserve 保存
組 alter ego 心腹朋友
片 Circumstances alter cases. 事隨境遷。

67　change
-changed-changed

vi. 變化　*vt.* 改變、交換　*n.* 變化

- They changed the color of their kitchen.
  他們將廚房的顏色換了。
- I've changed my mind. I quit!
  我改變主意了。我不幹了！

衍 changeable *adj.* 易變的；
　changeful *adj.* 不穩定的；
　changeless *adj.* 單調的
同 alter 改變
反 settle 使安寧
組 change gear 換檔；
　changing room 更衣室
片 change into 變成……

68　convert
-converted-converted

v. 轉變、兌換、改信　*n.* 改變信仰者

- My father decided to convert the yard into a garage in person.
  我父親決定親自將庭院改造成車庫。
- Excuse me, where can I convert U.S. dollars into Thailand bahts?
  請問，我可以去哪裡將美元兌換成泰銖？

衍 converted *adj.* 改變信仰的；
　converter *n.* 教化者；
　convertible *adj.* 可轉換的
同 transform 改成
組 convertible car 敞篷車
片 convert to / into 變成

69　shift
-shifted-shifted

vi. 變換、改變　*vt.* 替換　*n.* 輪班

- He always shifts his ground, so no one can pin him down on his position.
  他不停地改變立場，所以很難抓到他的重點。
- The night shift means working during the night period.
  值夜班是指在晚上時段工作的意思。

衍 shiftable *adj.* 可移動的；
　shiftless *adj.* 得過且過的；
　shifty *adj.* 機智的
同 change 使變化
組 day shift 日班；
　shift key 切換鍵
片 shift gear 換檔；
　shift for oneself 自謀生計

70 transform
-transformed-transformed

vi. 改變、改觀 *vt.* 使改變

- A fresh coat of paint transformed the old house.
  老屋塗上新漆後，有了新面貌。
- Andy transformed the living room into a guest room.
  安迪把客廳改成客房。

衍 transformable *adj.* 可改造的；
transformation *n.* 變化；
transformer *n.* 變壓器
同 alter 改變
組 transforming gene 轉化基因
片 transform to 變成

---

71 vary
-varied-varied

vi. 變化、呈多樣化 *vt.* 使不同、變更

- The weather has varied a lot more this time of year than in the past.
  一年這個時候的天氣跟過去相比變化很大。
- Sometimes my mood varies with the weather.
  有時候我的情緒會受天氣影響。

衍 varied *adj.* 不相同的；
variety *n.* 變化
同 change 更改
片 vary with 隨⋯⋯而變化；
vary from 與⋯⋯不同

小試身手UP

(　　) 1. I'm addicted to coffee. To me, nothing is a(n) _____ to coffee.
(A) alternative　(B) variety　(C) shift　(D) change

(　　) 2. Did you notice the moon _____ to the east little by little?
(A) change　(B) shift　(C) convert　(D) transform

(　　) 3. The weather recently is _____, so don't forget to bring a thin coat with you.
(A) changeable　(B) convertible　(C) alterable　(D) transformable

Ans
1. (A) 我是咖啡成癮者。對我而言，沒有東西能替代咖啡。
2. (B) 你有注意到月亮一點一點地往東邊移動嗎？
3. (A) 最近天氣多變化，所以別忘記隨身帶件薄外套。

生活常用

學校工作

情緒心智

社會萬象

包含

MP3 4-15

contain / cover / enclose / include / involve

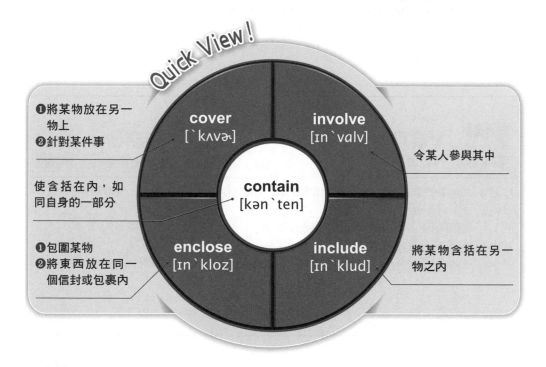

Quick View !

cover
[`kʌvɚ`]

❶將某物放在另一
物上
❷針對某件事

contain
[kən`ten]

使含括在內，如
同自身的一部分

involve
[ɪn`vɑlv]

令某人參與其中

enclose
[ɪn`kloz]

❶包圍某物
❷將東西放在同一
個信封或包裹內

include
[ɪn`klud]

將某物含括在另一
物之內

---

72 | contain
-contained-contained

vt. 包含、容納

- Many foods contain sugar.
  很多食物都含有糖分。
- This book contains the basic knowledge about the U.S.
  這本書裡有記載關於美國的基本常識。

衍 contained *adj.* 被控制的；
container *n.* 容器；
containment *n.* 包含
同 hold 握著、抓住、包含
反 release 釋放、解放
組 container ship 貨櫃船；
container car 貨櫃車
片 contain oneself 自制

cover
-covered-covered

vt. 蓋住、包含　*n.* 蓋子、封面

- The book is covered with a thick layer of dust. It must have been untouched for quite a long time.
這本書覆蓋著一層厚厚的灰塵。一定很久沒被人翻閱了。
- Under the cover of darkness, several prisoners fled last night.
在黑暗的掩護下，幾名囚犯昨晚逃獄了。

衍 covering *n.* 覆蓋物；
coverer *n.* 包裝工人；
coverage *n.* 覆蓋範圍
同 hide 隱瞞
反 uncover 揭露
片 be covered with 覆蓋著

enclose
-enclosed-enclosed

vt. 圍住、圈起、關閉住

- She enclosed a letter in the package.
她在包裹裡附了一封信。
- The village is enclosed by woods.
這座村莊被樹林環繞。

衍 enclosed *adj.* 與世隔絕的；
enclosure *n.* 圈住、圍欄、附件
同 surround 包圍、圍困
反 disclose 使顯露
組 enclosed fuse 封閉保險絲

include
-included-included

vt. 包括、包含、算入

- Value added tax is included in the price of every product or service we use every day.
我們每天用到的每一樣產品或服務的價格中都有包含增值稅。
- The price includes the accommodation and the transportation.
費用包括了住宿和交通。

衍 including *prep.* 包括；
inclusion *n.* 包含；
inclusive *adj.* 包含的
同 contain 包含、容納
反 exclude 排除在外
組 all-inclusive 包括一切的
片 include among 把……算入

生活常用

學校工作

情緒心智

社會萬象

76 involve
-involved-involved

vt. 涉入、包含、意味著、專注於

- Police work always involves danger.
  警察的工作總與危險相伴。
- Bill was so involved in studying that he didn't hear the alarm ring.
  比爾如此地投入讀書，以致於沒聽到警報聲響。
- The journalist involved me in that drug dealing.
  記者把我牽扯進那宗毒品交易中。

衍 involved *adj.* 複雜的；
involvement *n.* 連累；
involution *n.* 捲入
同 include 包含
片 involve in 介入；
involve with 引介；
be involved in 使專注、使專心

聯想學習Plus

- 帶有 tain 的字有：attain（得到）、certain（確定的）、captain（船長）、contain（包含）、detain（留校察看）、entertain（娛樂）、fountain（噴泉）、maintain（維持）、sustain（持續）、retain（保持）、obtain（得到）。

小試身手UP

( ) 1. A balanced diet should _____ dairy, bread, fruit, vegetable and soy.
　　(A) enclose　(B) contain　(C) involve in　(D) cover with
( ) 2. Your living room is big. I guess it can _____ dozens of people.
　　(A) involve　(B) enclose　(C) include　(D) hold
( ) 3. The postage isn't _____ in the fee. You need to pay 20 more dollars if you want to send the package.
　　(A) enclosed　(B) included　(C) contained　(D) involved

Ans

1. (B) 均衡的飲食應該包含乳製品、麵包、水果、蔬菜與大豆。
2. (D) 你家客廳真大。我猜可以容納好幾十人。
3. (B) 郵資不含在費用內。如果你想寄包裹，需要多付二十塊。

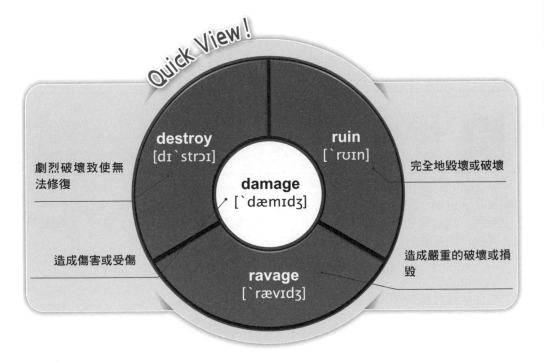

破壞

🎧 MP3 4-16

damage / destroy / ravage / ruin

Quick View!

destroy [dɪ`strɔɪ]

劇烈破壞致使無法修復

造成傷害或受傷

damage [`dæmɪdʒ]

ruin [`rʊɪn]

完全地毀壞或破壞

造成嚴重的破壞或損毀

ravage [`rævɪdʒ]

77 damage
-damaged-damaged

vt. 損害、毀壞　n. 損失、賠償金

- Extreme changes in the climate do cause damage to agriculture.
  劇烈的天氣變化確實會造成農損。

- If any accident happens to you on the way to work or from work, you can claim damages from your company.
  如果你上下班途中發生事故，你可以向公司要求賠償。

衍 damaging *adj.* 有害的；damageable *adj.* 易損壞的
同 harm 損害
反 benefit 有益於
組 damage control 損失控制
片 cause damage to 對……造成損害

78 | destroy
-destroyed-destroyed

vt. 毀壞、破壞

- Their barn was destroyed by a fire.
  一場火把他們的穀倉燒毀了。
- The typhoon finally died away, leaving many houses destroyed.
  颱風最後變弱，留下許多遭到肆虐的房子。

衍 destruction *n.* 破壞、毀滅
組 soul-destroying 十分單調的；
tank destroyer 反坦克裝甲車；
destroy a reputation 毀壞名譽；
destroyer escort 護航驅逐艦

79 | ravage
-ravaged-ravaged

vi. 毀滅、蹂躪　vt. 毀滅　n. 蹂躪

- We can imagine how cruel war is and what it is like after seeing the ravages of war.
  我們可以想像戰爭是如何地無情，以及受到戰爭蹂躪後的景象。
- The small village was ravaged by the fire overnight.
  這個小村莊被整夜的大火燒毀了。

同 damage 損害
反 preserve 保護
片 be ravaged by 受到……的摧殘

80 | ruin
-ruined-ruined

vi. 毀滅、毀壞　vt. 使毀滅　n. 廢墟

- A flood ruined the village.
  洪水沖毀了村子。
- The house was in ruins after a bomb killed three people there.
  那裡發生爆炸奪走三條人命後，房子便成了廢墟。

衍 ruinous *adj.* 毀滅性的；
ruination *n.* 毀滅；
ruinate *adj.* 墮落的、傾塌的
同 destroy 毀壞
反 repair 補救
片 in ruins 成為廢墟

聯想學習Plus

- 野火肆虐（rage）過後，整片森林被摧毀（ravage）地一乾二淨。
- 說到破壞，就會想到天災人禍，常見的災難有：catastrophe（大災難）、disaster（災難、不幸）、floods（水災）、drought（旱災）、earthquake（地震）、hurricane（颶風）、tornado（龍捲風）、tragedy（悲劇、災難）、plague（瘟疫、鼠疫）等。

小試身手UP↑

（　）1. Smoking is more likely to _____ your teeth than sweets.
　　　(A) destroy　(B) ruin　(C) ravage　(D) damage
（　）2. The sudden cut-in _____ our interest in chatting.
　　　(A) ravaged　(B) spoilt　(C) damaged　(D) destroyed

Ans　1. (D) 比起甜食，抽煙更可能傷害你的牙齒。
　　　2. (B) 突然的插話壞了我們談天的興致。

17 Lesson

保護

🎧 MP3 4-17

defend / guard / harbor / protect / refuge / shelter / shield

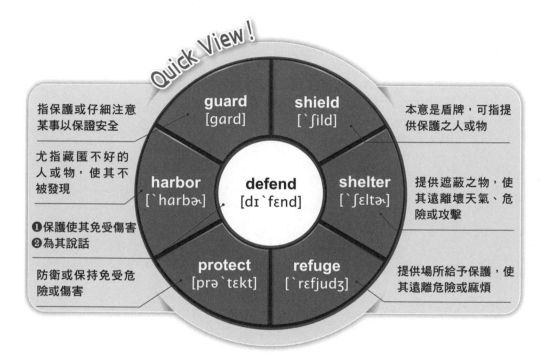

Quick View!

位置	單字	說明
指保護或仔細注意某事以保證安全	**guard** [gɑrd]	
	shield [`ʃild]	本意是盾牌，可指提供保護之人或物
尤指藏匿不好的人或物，使其不被發現	**harbor** [`hɑrbɚ]	
	defend [dɪ`fɛnd]	
	shelter [`ʃɛltɚ]	提供遮蔽之物，使其遠離壞天氣、危險或攻擊
❶保護使其免受傷害 ❷為其說話		
防衛或保持免受危險或傷害	**protect** [prə`tɛkt]	
	refuge [`rɛfjudʒ]	提供場所給予保護，使其遠離危險或麻煩

81

defend
-defended-defended

vi. 防禦、保衛　vt. 防禦、辯護

- The army defended the city against the intruders.
  軍隊防衛城市免受敵人侵入。
- The judge didn't believe what the defendant stated.
  法官不相信被告的陳述。

衍 defendant *n.* 被告；defender *n.* 辯護者；defense *n.* 保衛

同 protect 保護

反 attack 襲擊

組 self-defense 自衛；
   defend a case 辯護案子

片 defend against 防衛；
   defend with 以……保護

82 **guard**
-guarded-guarded

vi. 防範、警惕　vt. 看守　n. 守衛

- The shepherd dog guards the sheep from wolves.
  牧羊犬守護羊群遠離狼群。
- There is a soldier on guard in front of the gate of the military base.
  軍事基地大門前有士兵站哨。

衍 guarder *n.* 衛兵；
guardian *n.* 保護者；
guardless *adj.* 無人看守的
同 defend 防禦
組 guardian angel 守護神；
guard bar 護欄
片 on (one's) guard 提高警覺；
guard against 防範

生活常用

83 **harbor**
-harbored-harbored

vt. 庇護、藏匿　n. 海港、避難所

- The old inn harbored slaves escaping from the north.
  這棟老旅館藏匿從北方逃出的奴隸。
- The one who harbors a criminal is always regarded as an accomplice.
  窩藏犯人的人一律被視為共犯。

衍 harborage *n.* 停泊處；
harborless *adj.* 無避難所的
組 harbourmaster 港務長；
commercial harbor 商埠
片 harbor malice against 對……有敵意

學校工作

84 **protect**
-protected-protected

vt. 保護、防護

- A fence protects us from our neighbor's dog.
  圍欄保護我們免受鄰居狗的攻擊。
- Wearing sunscreen can protect you against ultraviolet rays.
  塗防曬霜可以避免紫外線。

衍 protection *n.* 保護；
protector *n.* 保護者
同 guard 保衛
反 endanger 危及
片 protect from / against 使免受

情緒心智

社會萬象

85 refuge
-refuged-refuged

vi. 避難、逃避　vt. 給予庇護　n. 庇護

- The political refugee sought political asylum from Belgium's Embassy.
  那名政治難民尋求比利時大使館的政治庇護。
- The climbers refuged from the cold in the cave overnight.
  登山客在洞穴中避寒過夜。

衍 refugee *n.* 難民
同 shelter 保護
組 women's refuge 婦女避難所；
　 economic refugee 經濟難民
片 take refuge 躲避

86 shelter
-sheltered-sheltered

vi. 躲避　vt. 保護　n. 避難所

- A canopy provided some shelter from the rain.
  遮雨棚擋了些雨。
- The Great Wall sheltered ancient China from invaders.
  長城在古代保護中國免受外患。

衍 shelterless *adj.* 沒有保護的；
　 sheltery *adj.* 保護的
同 shield 保衛
組 bomb shelter 防空壕
片 take shelter 避難

87 shield
-shielded-shielded

vi. 保護、防禦　vt. 保護、包庇　n. 盾

- The man shielded his eyes from the bright light.
  男子擋住亮光以保護眼睛。
- The police held up the riot shields against flying bullets.
  警方舉起防爆盾牌擋住飛來的子彈。

衍 shieling *n.* 小屋
同 defend 保護
組 shield law 新聞保障法
片 shield from 保護

聯想學習Plus

- 跟海港有關的單字有：port（港、港口、貿易港）、pier（觀光碼頭、防波堤）、wharf（碼頭、停泊處）、dock（船埠、碼頭）。
- 漫威電影宇宙中出現的神盾局（S.H.I.E.L.D）是「國土戰略防禦攻擊與後勤保障局」（Strategic Homeland Intervention, Enforcement and Logistics Division）的簡稱，在二戰期間為對抗九頭蛇（Hydra）而成立的組織。

小試身手UP

( ) 1. Syrian _____ are forced to flee from their country because of the Syrian Civil War and eager to seek international asylum.
　　(A) shelters　(B) safeguards　(C) shields　(D) refugees

( ) 2. The news said that a father _____ his child with his body from the fire.
　　(A) refuged　(B) harbored　(C) defended　(D) preserved

( ) 3. The shield is a good _____ against any physical attack.
　　(A) defendant　(B) guardian　(C) protection　(D) shelter

Ans
1. (D) 敘利亞難民因內戰問題被迫逃至國外，渴望尋求國際庇護。
2. (C) 新聞報導一名父親以身體替小孩擋火。
3. (C) 盾牌是很好的防護，可以抵擋任何物理攻擊。

發展

🎧 MP3 4-18

develop / germinate / grow / mature / sprout

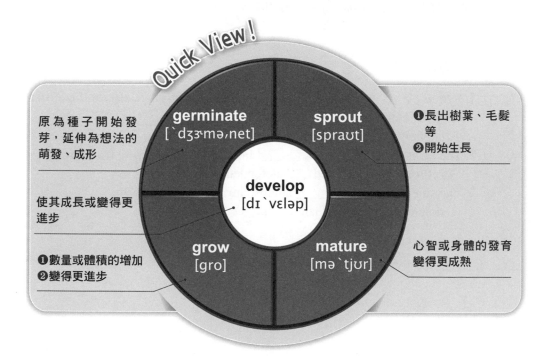

Quick View!

germinate
[`dʒɝməˌnet]

原為種子開始發芽，延伸為想法的萌發、成形

sprout
[spraʊt]

❶長出樹葉、毛髮等
❷開始生長

develop
[dɪ`vɛləp]

使其成長或變得更進步

grow
[gro]

❶數量或體積的增加
❷變得更進步

mature
[mə`tjʊr]

心智或身體的發育變得更成熟

88 **develop**
-developed-developed

vi. 發展　*vt.* 使成長、使發達、發展

- He wanted to develop his muscles.
  他想長出肌肉。
- Professor Lin made a speech on the development of science.
  林教授發表一場關於科學發展的演講。

衍 developed *adj.* 先進的；
developing *adj.* 開發中；
developer *n.* 開發者；
development *n.* 發展

同 grow 發育

反 decline 衰落

組 developed country 已開發國家

89 | germinate
-germinated-germinated

vi. 發芽、生長　vt. 使生長、形成

- The seed will germinate if it gets enough water and sunlight.
如果有足夠水分與陽光，種子就會發芽。
- The idea of publishing a book just germinated in his mind.
他心裡剛萌生出書這個念頭。

衍 germination n. 萌芽；
germinative adj. 發芽的；
germinator n. 使發芽的人或物
同 develop 使成長

90 | grow
-grew-grown

vi. 成長、生長　vt. 種植、使生長

- This plant can't grow in the shade.
這株植物在蔭涼處無法生長。
- Plants rely on soil, water, and sunlight to grow.
植物生長要依靠土壤、水和陽光。

衍 grown adj. 成熟的；
grower n. 栽培者；
growable adj. 可生長的；
growth n. 發育、生長
同 develop 發展
組 economic growth engine 經濟增長引擎
片 grow into 發展成、變成

91 | mature
-matured-matured

vi. 變成熟、長成　vt. 使成熟　adj. 成熟的

- Girls mature earlier than boys.
女孩子比男孩子早發育。
- Her background of growing up in a poor family made her mature faster than other kids.
她生長於貧困家庭的背景令她比其他孩子更早熟。

衍 maturative adj. 有助於成熟的；
maturely adv. 充分地；
maturity n. 完善
同 ripe 成熟的
反 immature 未成熟的
組 mature student 成年人大學生

92 | sprout
-sprouted-sprouted

vi. 發芽、快速生長　vt. 使萌芽　n. 嫩枝

- The buds on the trees sprout in spring.
  樹上的嫩芽在春天開始萌發。
- He found that he started to sprout a beard while going to high school.
  他發現上高中後開始長鬍子了。

同 grow 成長
組 bean sprout 豆芽
片 sprout up 快速成長

聯想學習Plus

- 表示熟的還有幾種說法：ripe（成熟的、熟透的）、full-grown（完全長成的、成熟的）、mellow（熟的、醇香的）。
- 說到熟，就會想到牛排幾分熟該如何表示，牛排熟度都以奇數來表示，從全生到全熟的說法如下：raw（全生的、未烹煮過）、blue rare（表面微煎過）、rare（一分熟、僅表面煎熟）、medium-rare（三分熟）、medium（五分熟、肉質開始變硬）、medium-well（七分熟）、well-done（全熟）。

小試身手UP

(　) 1. The little girl _____ into a fair lady several years later.
　　　(A) sprouted　(B) matured　(C) germinated　(D) grew
(　) 2. If you still behave like a child, you are not _____ enough.
　　　(A) grown　(B) developing　(C) matured　(D) germinated
(　) 3. The science teacher asked her students to observe how a bean _____ and take notes of the process of its growth.
　　　(A) grows up　(B) develops into　(C) blossoms　(D) germinates

Ans
1. (D)　小女孩幾年後長成一位窈窕淑女。
2. (A)　如果你行為還是像個孩子，就表示你還不夠成熟。
3. (D)　自然科老師要求學生觀察豆子發芽的經過，並記錄生長過程。

19 Lesson 繁盛

🎧 MP3 4-19

bloom / blossom / flourish / prosper / thrive

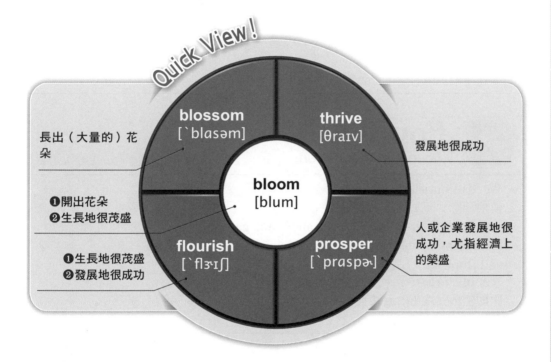

Quick View!

blossom [`blasəm]
長出（大量的）花朵

thrive [θraɪv]
發展地很成功

bloom [blum]

❶開出花朵
❷生長地很茂盛

❶生長地很茂盛
❷發展地很成功
flourish [`flɝɪʃ]

prosper [`praspɚ]
人或企業發展地很成功，尤指經濟上的榮盛

---

93 bloom
-bloomed-bloomed

vi. 開花、生長茂盛　n. 花

- The tulips bloom after the daffodils.
  鬱金香在水仙花之後開花。
- Hanami is an activity where the Japanese watch the cherry trees bloom and enjoy food as if they were on a picnic.
  賞花是日本人一邊欣賞櫻樹盛開一邊享用美食的活動，就像在野餐一樣。

衍 blooming *adj.* 開著花的；
　bloomer *n.* 開花植物；
　bloomy *adj.* 盛開的
同 flourish 繁茂
反 fade 枯萎
片 in bloom 盛開；
　in full bloom 盛開

blossom
-blossomed-blossomed

vi. 開花、生長茂盛　*n.* 花

- The apple trees blossom before they grow fruit.
  蘋果樹在結果前先開花。
- The small town has now blossomed into a modern city.
  那座小鎮如今已發展成為現代化城市。
- The orange blossom cologne you wore at the party smelled so good.
  你在派對上噴的橙花香氛味道真好聞。

衍 blossomy *adj.* 花盛開的
同 develop 使成長
組 orange blossom 橙花
片 blossom into 發展；
　 come into blossom 開花

flourish
-flourished-flourished

vi. 茂盛、繁盛　*vt.* 揮舞　*n.* 揮舞

- Weeds flourish in fertile soil.
  雜草在肥沃的土地上叢生。
- Art flourished in the Renaissance and gave birth to many talented men like Michelangelo and Raphael.
  文藝復興時期藝術十分興盛，也誕生出許多像米開朗基羅與拉斐爾這樣有才華的人。

同 thrive 興旺
反 decline 衰落

prosper
-prospered-prospered

vi. 繁榮、昌盛、成功　*vt.* 使繁榮

- The computer industry has prospered since the 1990s.
  電腦產業從 1990 年代開始興盛。
- He is good at analyzing what industry will prosper and invests in it.
  他擅長分析哪種產業有前景，然後投資它。

衍 prosperity *n.* 興旺；
　 prosperous *adj.* 興旺的；
　 prosperously *adv.* 繁榮地
反 decline 衰落
片 Cheaters never prosper. 靠欺騙，難發財。
　 prosper from 以……獲利

97 | thrive
-thrived-thrived

- Ferns like to thrive in the damp environment.
  蕨類植物喜歡生長在潮溼的環境中。
- As the saying goes, "He that will thrive must rise at five."
  俗話說得好，「五更起床，百事興盛。」

[同] prosper 成功
[反] languish 衰弱
[片] thriving and robust 蓬勃向上；
    thrive on 受⋯⋯成長

聯想學習Plus

- 植物會發芽（germinate / sprout）、開花（bloom / blossom）、結果（frutify），最後凋零（fade）。

小試身手UP

(　) 1. The furit farm ＿＿＿＿ with her considerate care, so she can harvest a lot every spring.
    (A) blossoms　(B) develops　(C) flourishes　(D) sprouts

(　) 2. Mr. Kuo's business has kept ＿＿＿＿ for decades. No one can beat him in this industry.
    (A) thriving　(B) maturing　(C) sprouting　(D) shrinking

1. (C) 果園在她的細心照顧下長得非常茂盛，所以她每年春天都能收成很多果實。
2. (A) 郭先生的事業持續蓬勃好幾十年。沒有人可以在這個產業上贏過他。

右側邊欄：生活常用　學校工作　情緒心智　社會萬象

遵從

🎧 MP3 4-20

behave / comply / follow / obey

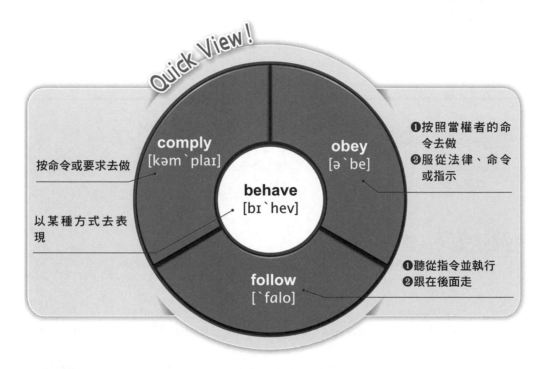

Quick View !

comply [kəm`plaɪ]
按命令或要求去做

obey [ə`be]
❶按照當權者的命令去做
❷服從法律、命令或指示

behave [bɪ`hev]

以某種方式去表現

follow [`falo]
❶聽從指令並執行
❷跟在後面走

---

98 # behave
-behaved-behaved

vi. 表現、舉止　vt. 使檢點、使守規矩

- Those children know how to behave in a restaurant.
  那些小孩子知道要在餐廳裡守規矩。
- Kids, behave yourselves when you are in a public place.
  孩子們，在公開場合要守規矩一點。

衍 behavior *n.* 舉止；
behavioral *adj.* 行為的

同 deport 持……舉止

組 well-behaved 行為端正的；
behavior pattern 行為模式

片 behave in an offensive manner
作出令人厭惡的行徑

comply
-complied-complied

- I complied with my teacher's request that I get permission from my parents.
我聽從老師的要求，先徵求父母親的同意。
- Everyone should comply with the rules of the factory.
每個人都應該遵守工廠的規定。

衍 compliance *n.* 順從、承諾
同 conform 遵照
反 refuse 拒絕
片 comply with 遵守

生活常用

 follow
-followed-followed

vi. 跟隨　*vt.* 跟隨

- Follow the instructions on the package before taking it.
在你服用前先遵照包裝上的指示。
- I found someone sneakily following me home.
我發現有人偷偷跟著我回家。

衍 following *adj.* 接著的；
　　follower *n.* 擁護者
同 succeed 接著發生
反 lead 引導
組 follow suit 跟著做
片 follow up 後續行動；
　　follow out 執行

學校工作

 obey
-obeyed-obeyed

vi. 服從、聽話　*vt.* 服從

- The soldier obeyed the officer's orders.
士兵聽從長官的命令。
- Obey the traffic rules, or you'll be fined.
遵守交通法規，否則你會被罰款。

衍 obeidance *n.* 服從；
　　obeidant *adj.* 順從的
同 comply 遵從
反 disobey 違反
組 obey orders 遵守命令
片 He that cannot obey cannot command. 領導之前要會服從。

情緒心智

社會萬象

- 除了 behavior 外，表示行為還有幾種說法：conduct（行為、品行）、manner（態度、舉止）、action（行動、行為）。

小試身手UP↑

( ) 1. It's interesting to study animals' _____.
　　　 (A) behaviors　(B) followers　(C) obeidance　(D) compliance

( ) 2. The man in a cape _____ me down the street.
　　　 (A) behaved　(B) followed　(C) trailed　(D) obeyed

( ) 3. The soldier must _____ commands no matter how irrational they may be.
　　　 (A) obey　(B) comply　(C) behave　(D) conduct

1. (A)　研究動物的行為很有趣。
2. (B)　穿斗篷的男子在街上跟著我。
3. (A)　士兵必須服從命令，不論命令有多不合理。

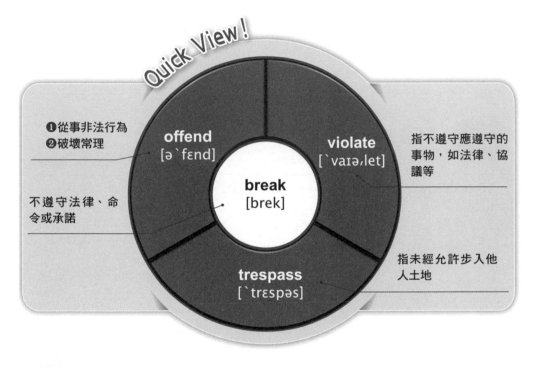

21 Lesson 違反

🎧 MP3 4-21

break / offend / trespass / violate

Quick View!

offend [ə`fɛnd]
❶從事非法行為
❷破壞常理

不遵守法律、命令或承諾

break [brek]

violate [`vaɪəˌlet]
指不遵守應遵守的事物，如法律、協議等

trespass [`trɛspəs]
指未經允許步入他人土地

---

102 | **break**
-broke-broken

vi. 中斷、中止　vt. 打破、折斷

- You can't make a promise and then break it.
  你不能承諾了之後又反悔。
- If you break the rules, you'll definitely be grounded.
  如果你違反規定，你必會被禁足。

衍 breaking *n.* 破壞；broken *adj.* 破碎的；breaker *n.* 打破的人

同 fracture 破裂

反 mend 縫補

組 broken-hearted 心碎的；
record-breaker 創紀錄者；
break jail 越獄

片 break up 分手

103 offend
-offended-offended

vi. 違反　vt. 冒犯

- The group claims that the new law would offend the Constitution.
  這個團體指稱新法律有違憲的問題。
- He felt offended by what his boss said.
  老闆說的話使他感到生氣。
- I didn't mean to offend you.
  我無意要冒犯你。

衍 offender *n.* 冒犯者；
offendress *n.* 女罪犯；
offensive *adj.* 冒犯的
同 hurt 使受傷
反 appease 撫慰
組 first offender 初犯
片 take the offensive 發動攻勢；
on the offensive 採取攻勢的

104 trespass
-trespassed-trespassed

vi. 擅自進入、冒犯　n. 擅自進入

- To rush home, we trespassed in the farmer's field.
  為了趕著回家，我們誤闖了農夫的田地。
- The sign says, "No trespassing!"
  牌子上寫著：「非請勿入」！

衍 trespasser *n.* 侵入者
同 intrude 闖入
組 trespass to chattel 財產侵害；
computer trespass 電腦入侵
片 trespass on 妨礙；
no trespassing 非請勿入

105 violate
-violated-violated

vt. 侵犯、違背、違反

- Those who violate the laws will get into trouble soon.
  犯法的人不久會為自己帶來麻煩。
- Though having a love affair with a third party doesn't violate the law, it's against our morals.
  雖然與第三者外遇並無不法，但卻不道德。

衍 violation *n.* 違犯；
violative *adj.* 違犯的；
violator *n.* 侵犯者
同 break 打破
反 keep 保有
組 violate a contract 違反契約

 **聯想學習Plus**

- 我想以繫上紫色的（violet）緞帶表示譴責暴力（violence）與一切違反（violate）公平正義的行為。

小試身手UP

( ) 1. She _____ the nutshell with a hammer.
  　(A) broke　(B) violated　(C) trespassed　(D) offended
( ) 2. She _____ the speed limit and got a ticket.
  　(A) defended　(B) broke　(C) violated　(D) trespassed
( ) 3. Do not _____ on private land, or the landlord may sue you.
  　(A) break　(B) violate　(C) trespass　(D) defend

生活常用　學校工作　情緒心智　社會萬象

 Ans
　　1. (A) 她用榔頭敲開核桃殼。
　　2. (C) 她違反速限，因此被開罰單。
　　3. (C) 不要擅闖私人土地，否則地主可能會告你。

Lesson 22

決定

🎧 MP3 4-22

decide / determine / resolve / settle

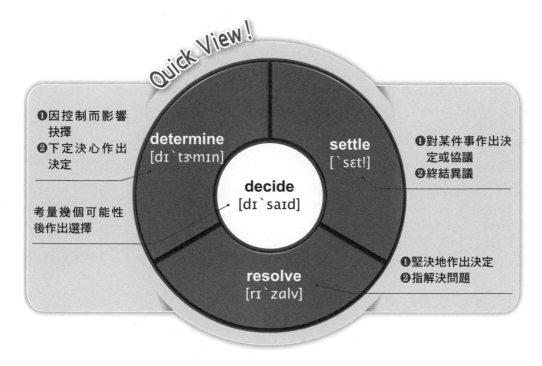

Quick View!

determine
[dɪ`tɝmɪn]

❶因控制而影響
抉擇
❷下定決心作出
決定

考量幾個可能性
後作出選擇

decide
[dɪ`saɪd]

settle
[`sɛt!]

❶對某件事作出決
定或協議
❷終結異議

❶堅決地作出決定
❷指解決問題

resolve
[rɪ`zalv]

106 decide
-decided-decided

vi. 決定　vt. 決定、決意

• The judges decided on the win going to that team.
裁判決定將優勝判給那支隊伍。

• Someday you may have to make a decision.
有一天你可能必須做出決定。

衍 decisive *adj.* 決定性的；
decision *n.* 決定；
decider *n.* 決勝局

同 settle 決定

反 waver 猶豫不決

組 decide in advance 提前決定

片 decide on 考慮後決定；decide against 作出不利於……的判決

107 determine
-determined-determined

vi. 決定　**vt.** 決定、影響

- We determined the date for our wedding.
  我們決定了婚禮日期。
- He is a man of determination. Nothing can change his mind.
  他是意志堅定的人。沒有什麼可以動搖他的心志。

衍 determined *adj.* 堅定的；
determinate *adj.* 確定的；
determination *n.* 決斷力；
determinant *n.* 決定因素

同 decide 決意

組 self-determination 自主、自決

片 determined by 由……決定；
determine to 決定

---

108 resolve
-resolved-resolved

vi. 決定、決議　**vt.** 決心　**n.** 決定

- They hoped the emergency could be resolved soon.
  他們希望可以盡快解決緊急狀況。
- Unlike the former manager in charge of this project, he resolved the problem without hesitation.
  跟前任專案負責人不同，他毫不遲疑地就解決了問題。

衍 resolvability *n.* 可溶解性；
resolvable *adj.* 可解決的；
resolved *adj.* 下定決心的；
resolution *n.* 決心、解析度

組 high-resolution 高解析的

片 resolve sth. into 使……變成

---

109 settle
-settled-settled

vi. 定居、確定　**vt.** 決定、解決

- They decided to settle their disagreement by asking for Tom's advice.
  他們決定徵詢湯姆的建議來解決他們之間的不和。
- To settle down in Taipei, William works very hard.
  為了在台北安頓下來，威廉很努力工作。

衍 settling *n.* 澄清；
settlement *n.* 安頓

同 determine 決定

反 unfix 使不穩定

組 settle disputes 解決爭端；
settlement house 睦鄰中心

片 settle down 安頓下來

- 他很確定（determinate）要終結（terminate）鬥爭，所以第一步先消滅（eliminate）異己。
- 這位阿兵哥決定（determine）阻止（deter）引爆埋在地下的地雷（mine）。

小試身手UP

（　）1. It's always hard for me to ＿＿＿＿ on which dress to put on since I have so many in my closet.
　　　(A) decide　(B) resolve　(C) settle　(D) determine

（　）2. The clerk cleverly ＿＿＿＿ the customer's anger.
　　　(A) settled　(B) decided　(C) determined　(D) resolved

1. (A) 我總是難以決定要穿哪件洋裝，因為我的衣櫥裡有太多件了。
2. (A) 這名店員聰明地平息了顧客的怒氣。

猶豫

🎧 MP3 4-23

falter / flounder / hesitate / stagger / waver

Quick View !

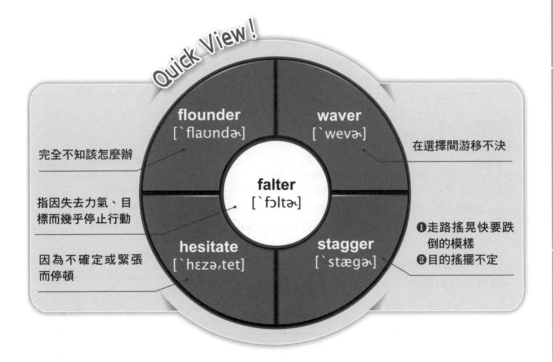

flounder [`flaʊndɚ]
完全不知該怎麼辦

waver [`wevɚ]
在選擇間游移不決

falter [`fɔltɚ]

指因失去力氣、目標而幾乎停止行動

❶走路搖晃快要跌倒的模樣
❷目的搖擺不定

hesitate [`hɛzə,tet]
因為不確定或緊張而停頓

stagger [`stægɚ]

---

110 falter
-faltered-faltered

vi. 動搖、猶豫、畏縮　vt. 結巴講出

- I will never falter in my quest for the truth.
  我對追求真理絕不遲疑。
- I felt her kind of falter when she was asked something personal.
  當她被問到私事時，我感受到她有點動搖。

衍 falteringly *adv.* 遲疑地
同 waver 猶豫不決
片 falter in 猶豫

111 flounder
-floundered-floundered

vi. 掙扎、困難重重、支吾　n. 比目魚

- He didn't warm up before swimming, so he was seized with a cramp, floundering in the water.
他游泳之前沒有暖身，所以腳抽筋，只能在水中苦苦掙扎。
- He wasn't well-prepared in advance. No wonder he floundered through his remarks.
他事先沒有做好準備。無怪乎演說說得七零八落。

衍 flounderingly *adv.* 掙扎地、總是失敗地

112 hesitate
-hesitated-hesitated

vi. 躊躇、猶豫　vt. 有疑慮、不願意

- I once hesitated over whether I should continue my current job or pursue my dream.
我曾猶豫過是否繼續現在的工作還是去追求我的夢想。
- Gary didn't hesitate to accept my proposal.
蓋瑞沒有猶豫就接受了我的提案。

衍 hesitation *n.* 猶豫；
hesitative *adj.* 支吾其詞的；
hesitant *adj.* 遲疑的
同 pause 暫停
反 dare 膽敢
片 He who hesitates is lost. 遲疑失良機。

113 stagger
-staggered-staggered

vi. 搖晃而行、猶豫、動搖　vt. 使搖晃、使猶豫

- She lost her balance, staggered back against the closet and toppled over.
她失去平衡，往後撞到櫃子而摔倒了。
- The girl staggered a moment and then screwed up her courage to step forward.
女孩猶豫了一下，然後鼓起勇氣走上前。

衍 staggerer *n.* 猶豫者、難題；
staggering *adj.* 搖晃欲倒的
片 stagger on / among 堅持進行；
stagger to one's feet 搖搖晃晃地站起來

waver
-wavered-wavered

vi. 動搖、猶豫不決   *n.* 搖擺

- Both of the candidates seem to waver on the election issues.
  兩位參選人似乎對選舉議題都猶豫不決。
- The flame of the candle wavered with the wind.
  蠟燭的火焰隨著風吹而搖曳著。

衍 waverer *n.* 動搖不定的人；
waviness *n.* 起伏
組 flag-waver 搖旗
片 waver between 猶豫不決

生活常用

學校工作

情緒心智

- 當吉姆跟他揮手（wave）致意時，他似乎遲疑（waver）著是要繼續手上編織（weave）毛衣的動作，還是回應回去。

小試身手UP

( ) 1. No matter what people think of, he never _____ in the belief he holds. He insists in his way.
  (A) falters   (B) waves   (C) hesitates   (D) staggers

( ) 2. When Maggie was lost in a foreign country, we could imagine how she _____ and felt helpless.
  (A) faltered   (B) wavered   (C) hesitated   (D) floundered

社會萬象

---

1. (A) 不管別人怎麼想，他對所持的信念毫不動搖，堅持自己的路。
2. (D) 當瑪姬在國外迷路時，我們可以想像她有多不知所措與無助。

放棄

🎧 MP3 4-24

abandon / desert / discard / disclaim / forego / resign

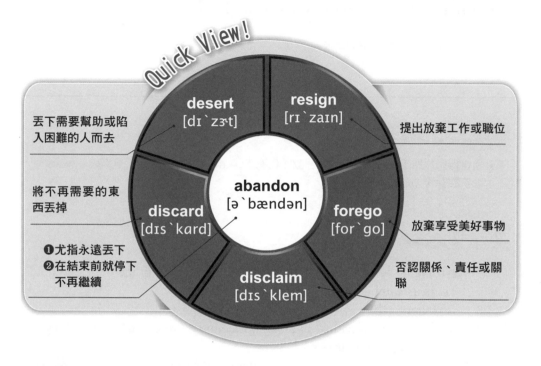

Quick View!

desert [dɪ`zɝt]
丟下需要幫助或陷入困難的人而去

resign [rɪ`zaɪn]
提出放棄工作或職位

discard [dɪs`kard]
將不再需要的東西丟掉
❶尤指永遠丟下
❷在結束前就停下不再繼續

abandon [ə`bændən]

forego [for`go]
放棄享受美好事物

disclaim [dɪs`klem]

否認關係、責任或關聯

---

115 ## abandon
-abandoned-abandoned

vt. 丟棄、拋棄、遺棄　n. 狂放

• The frightened thieves abandoned the stolen car and ran away.
驚慌失措的小偷丟下偷來的車溜了。
• Ben abandoned himself to drinking.
班沉溺於喝酒。

衍 abandoned *adj.* 被遺棄的；abandonee *n.* 受領被遺棄財物者；abandoner *n.* 放棄者；abandonment *n.* 放棄
同 desert 放棄
反 maintain 維持
片 abandon oneself to 沉溺於

116 | **desert**
-deserted-deserted

vi. 逃跑、開小差　vt. 拋棄　n. 沙漠

- He deserted his wife and children for his lover.
  他為了小三拋妻棄子。
- All my friends deserted me when I was in need of financial aid.
  在我需要經濟援助的時候，我的朋友都離我而去。

衍 deserter *n.* 背棄者；
desertion *n.* 拋棄；
desertification *n.* 沙漠化
同 abandon 遺棄
組 desert island 熱帶荒島；
desert habitat 沙漠棲息地
片 desert for 離棄另附他人

117 | **discard**
-discarded-discarded

vt. 拋棄、丟棄　n. 被拋棄的人或物

- We always discard old stuff when we do the cleanup at the end of a year.
  我們在年終的大掃除時總會清出老舊物品。
- Please discard this old shirt. It's worn out already.
  請把這件舊襯衫丟了吧，它已經很破舊了。

衍 discardable *adj.* 可丟棄的
同 reject 拒絕、抵制

118 | **disclaim**
-disclaimed-disclaimed

vi. 放棄權利、否認　vt. 放棄、否認

- He disclaimed all responsibility for the mistake.
  他否認這次失誤的一切責任。
- The agent issued a disclaimer that they had nothing to do with this scandal.
  經紀人發表與此件醜聞案無關的免責聲明。

衍 disclaimer *n.* 放棄；
disclamation *n.* 否認；
disclamatory *adj.* 否認的
同 deny 否定、否認
反 claim 要求
片 issue a disclaimer 發表免責聲明

生活常用

學校工作

情緒心智

社會萬象

119 forego
-forewent-foregone

vt. 放棄

- I'll have to forego our card game tonight because I have to get up early tomorrow.
  我必須放棄今晚的牌局遊戲，因為我明天必須早起。
- He forewent time spent with his family in order to be promoted at work.
  為了升遷，他放棄與家人相處的時光。

衍 foregoing *adj.* 前面的；
foregoer *n.* 前驅者
組 foregone conclusion 已成事實、可預期之結果

120 resign
-resigned-resigned

vi. 辭職　vt. 放棄、辭去

- The president of the company resigned.
  這家公司的總裁辭職了。
- Don't resign yourself to fate. You should overcome it.
  不要屈服於命運，你要克服它。

衍 resigned *adj.* 已辭職的；
resignation *n.* 辭職；
resignedly *adv.* 聽天由命地
同 relinquish 棄絕
片 resign oneself to 順從；
resign from 從……辭職

小試身手UP

(　) 1. He is an irresponsible father who _____ his family for good.
　　 (A) deserted　(B) resigned　(C) disclaimed　(D) abandoned
(　) 2. She _____ her job as a teacher to become a truck driver.
　　 (A) quit　(B) discarded　(C) forewent　(D) disclaimed

Ans　1. (D) 他是非常不負責任的父親，他棄家庭不顧。
　　　2. (A) 她放棄老師的工作，轉行當卡車司機。

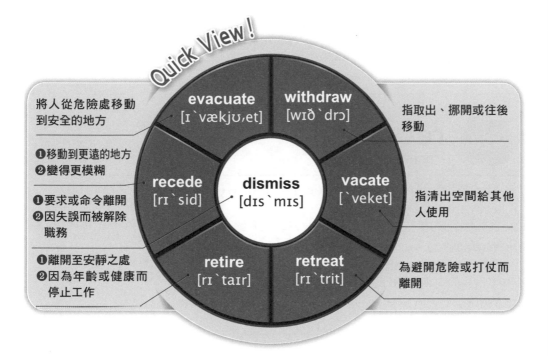

25 Lesson **撤退**　🎧 MP3 4-25

dismiss / evacuate / recede / retire / retreat / vacate / withdraw

Quick View!

- evacuate [ɪ`vækjʊˌet] — 將人從危險處移動到安全的地方
- withdraw [wɪð`drɔ] — 指取出、挪開或往後移動
- recede [rɪ`sid] — ❶移動到更遠的地方 ❷變得更模糊
- vacate [`veket] — 指清出空間給其他人使用
- retire [rɪ`taɪr] — ❶離開至安靜之處 ❷因為年齡或健康而停止工作
- retreat [rɪ`trit] — 為避開危險或打仗而離開
- dismiss [dɪs`mɪs] — ❶要求或命令離開 ❷因失誤而被解除職務

---

121 | **dismiss**
|-dismissed-dismissed

vt. 解散、遣散

- The company attempted to dismiss twenty workers to cut down on its personnel costs.
  這家公司打算資遣 20 名員工，以降低人事成本。
- Miss Liu was dismissed from her job because she was a contract worker.
  劉小姐是約聘人員，所以遭到解僱。

衍 dismissal *n.* 解僱；
　　dismissible *adj.* 可打發走的；
　　dismission *n.* 解散；
　　dismissive *adj.* 表現輕視的
同 discharge 使免除、使卸脫
反 employ 僱用
組 dismissal pay 資遣費
片 dismiss from 解僱、從……離開

405

122 | evacuate
-evacuated-evacuated

vt. 撤空、撤離、從……撤退

- The firefighters evacuated the burning building.
消防員將著火大樓裡頭的人都撤離了。
- The police evacuated all the people to the city park because of a bomb in the building.
因為大樓裡有炸彈，警方把所有人員都疏散到市立公園內。

衍 evacuation *n.* 疏散；
evacuative *adj.* 疏散的；
evacuator *n.* 撤退者
同 leave 遺棄、離棄
片 evacuate from... to 從……撤到

123 | recede
-receded-receded

vi. 收回、撤回

- The hills appeared to recede as we drove away from them.
當我們駛離山區後，山丘似乎離我們愈來愈遠。
- Whenever I see the waves hit the rocks and recede, I feel at peace.
每當我看著海浪拍打岩石並退去的畫面，我就感到平靜。

衍 recession *n.* 退回、衰退
同 retreat 撤退
反 proceed（做完某事後）接著做
組 recede from view 從視線消失
片 recede from 退回、撤回

124 | retire
-retired-retired

vi. 退休　vt. 使退休、撤回　n. 退隱

- The general commanded his troops to retire from the battlefield.
將軍下令軍隊從戰場撤退。
- Tom will take control of the shop when his father retires.
湯姆將在他父親退休後接管這家店。

衍 retiring *adj.* 退休的；
retired *adj.* 僻靜的；
retiredness *n.* 退隱；
retirement *n.* 退休
同 resign 放棄、辭去
組 retirement plan 退休計畫；
retired list 退役人員名單
片 retire into 隱居、遁入

125 retreat
-retreated-retreated

vi. 退避、撤退　vt. 使後退　n. 撤退

- When I vacuum the floor, the cat retreats to the closet.
  當我使用吸塵器吸地板時，貓咪躲到衣櫃裡。
- David beat a retreat when seeing his teacher coming.
  大衛一看到老師來了拔腿就跑。

衍 retreatant n. 參加天主教避靜者
同 retire 使退卻、撤回
反 advance 將……提前
片 beat a retreat 拔腳溜掉

126 vacate
-vacated-vacated

vi. 空出、離開、辭職　vt. 使撤退

- I plan to vacate just as soon as my new job is assured.
  等我新工作確認後，我就會辭職。
- Hotel guests are required to vacate their rooms before 11 am.
  飯店房客需要在上午十一點前退房。

衍 vacant adj. 神情茫然的；vacancy n. 空缺
組 vacant lot 空地
片 vacate one's seat 空出座位

127 withdraw
-withdrew-withdrawn

vi. 撤退、離開　vt. 抽回、撤退

- Martha withdrew money from her bank account.
  瑪莎從銀行帳戶領錢。
- Because her father was one of the judges, Helen decided to withdraw from the beauty contest.
  因為父親是評委之一，海倫決定退出選美比賽。

衍 withdrawn adj. 孤立的；withdrawal n. 收回、戒毒
同 retreat 撤退
組 withdrawal symptoms 戒斷症狀
片 withdraw from 退出、離開；withdraw into 縮入

生活常用

學校工作

情緒心智

社會萬象

- 班長對部隊下達了一連串的口令,像是集合(muster)、稍息(at ease)、立定(halt)、向右看(eyes right)、對齊(aline)、立正(attention)、報數(count off),最後才解散(dismiss)。

小試身手UP

( ) 1. After my husband _____, we took a long vacation.
  (A) retired (B) evacuated (C) retreated (D) receded

( ) 2. Students should stay in their seats until their teacher _____ class.
  (A) retires (B) dismisses (C) recedes (D) withdraws

1. (A) 我先生退休後,我們去度了個長假。
2. (B) 學生應待在位置上直到老師宣布下課才可以離開。

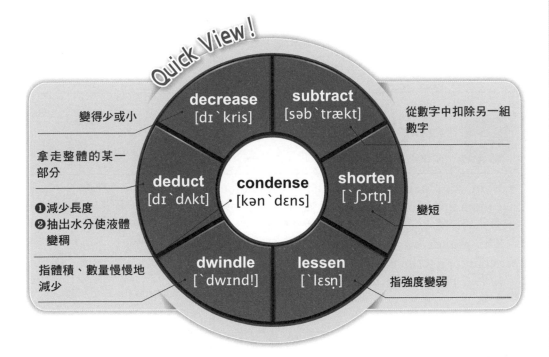

26 Lesson

縮減

🎧 MP3 4-26

condense / decrease / deduct / dwindle / lessen / shorten / subtract

Quick View!

- decrease [dɪ`kris] 變得少或小
- subtract [səb`trækt] 從數字中扣除另一組數字
- deduct [dɪ`dʌkt]
  - ❶減少長度
  - ❷抽出水分使液體變稠
- 拿走整體的某一部分
- condense [kən`dɛns]
- shorten [`ʃɔrtṇ] 變短
- dwindle [`dwɪnd!] 指體積、數量慢慢地減少
- lessen [`lɛsṇ] 指強度變弱

---

128 ## condense
-condensed-condensed

vi. 濃縮、凝結　vt. 壓縮、縮短

- She condensed the fruit juice by cooking it for a while.
  她煮了好一會兒濃縮果汁。
- Your article is too long. It has to be condensed into three lines.
  你的文章太長了，必須縮減為三行。

衍 condensed *adj.* 濃縮的；
condensation *n.* 縮短；
condensable *adj.* 可壓縮的；
condensate *n.* 濃縮物
同 compress 壓縮
反 expand 展開
組 condensed milk 煉乳
片 condense to 濃縮成

decrease
-decreased-decreased

vi. 減少　vt. 減少、減小　n. 減少

- The price of gasoline has decreased.
  汽油的價格下降了。
- Put an ice cube at room temperature, and it will decrease in size gradually.
  將冰塊置於常溫下，它會逐漸消融。

衍 decreasingly *adv.* 漸減地
同 lessen 變小
反 increase 增大
組 decreased appetite 食欲不振
片 on the decrease 逐漸減少的

deduct
-deducted-deducted

vt. 扣除、減除

- Some companies will deduct in advance certain taxes from employees' salaries.
  有些公司會先從員工的薪水扣掉一些稅。
- The player was deducted points from his score for a technical foul in the game.
  這名選手在比賽時因為技術性犯規所以被扣了些分數。

衍 deductible *adj.* 可扣除的；
  deduction *n.* 減除；
  deductive *adj.* 推論的
同 subtract 減去
組 deductible contribution 可扣除捐款
片 deduct sth. from sth. 將……從……扣除

dwindle
-dwindled-dwindled

vi. 漸漸減少、變小　vt. 使減少

- The crowd dwindled to none.
  人潮慢慢散去，最後空無一人。
- The couple's savings has dwindled away to nothing since both of them lost their jobs.
  自從兩人失去工作開始，夫妻倆的存款已經減少到分文不剩。

衍 dwine *v.* 衰退
同 shrink 退縮、畏怯
組 Spring dwindle 蜜蜂春季減少
片 dwindle away 逐漸消失

132 lessen
-lessened-lessened

vi. 變少、減輕　**vt.** 使變小、使變少

- The wind lessened as the storm ended.
  風暴停止後，風開始變小。
- In order to lessen the risk, the climber decided to take another path.
  為了減少風險，登山者決定走另外一條路。

衍 lesser *adj.* 較小的
同 abate 減少、減弱、減輕
反 increase 增強
組 lesser panda 小熊貓
片 lessen the price of 價值降低；
lessen the risk 減少風險

133 shorten
-shortened-shortened

vi. 變短、變小　**vt.** 使變短、減少

- I shortened the dress by three inches.
  我把洋裝修短三吋。
- The boy was asked to shorten the time spent in watching TV.
  男孩被要求減少看電視的時間。

衍 shortening *n.* 縮短
同 abbreviate 縮寫、使省略
反 lengthen 使加長、使延長

134 subtract
-subtracted-subtracted

vi. 做減法　**vt.** 減、減去、去掉

- Subtract your taxes from what you earn, and you'll get your net income.
  從你賺的錢中扣掉稅，就能得出你的淨收入。
- Three subtracted from nine equals six.
  九減掉三等於六。

衍 subtraction *n.* 減算；
subtractive *adj.* 減去的
同 deduct 扣除、減除
反 add 增加
組 subtraction sign 減號
片 subtract A from B 從 B 中扣除 A

- 這些句子（sentence）被濃縮成（condense）成一句，都是因為指揮家（conductor）要減少開銷（deduct）。
- 加減乘除的英文分別是 addition（加）、subtraction（減）、multiplication（乘）、division（除）。

小試身手UP

( ) 1. Pour a cap of this _____ detergent, I assure your laundry will become shining and bright.

　　(A) shortened　(B) condensed　(C) decreased　(D) lessened

( ) 2. When it gets darker and darker, people and cars on the street _____ to silence.

　　(A) lessen　(B) shorten　(C) deduct　(D) dwindle

( ) 3. Your luggage is overweight by 5 kilos, so you need _____ useless stuff from the luggage.

　　(A) divide　(B) shorten　(C) deduct　(D) dwindle

1. (B) 倒入一瓶蓋的濃縮洗衣精，我保證你的髒衣服變得閃亮潔白。
2. (D) 當天色愈來愈晚時，街上的人車漸漸散去，變得一片寂靜。
3. (C) 你的行李超重五公斤，所以你需要把不要的物品從行李中拿掉。

27 Lesson 降低

MP3 4-27

abase / degrade / diminish / lower / reduce / sink

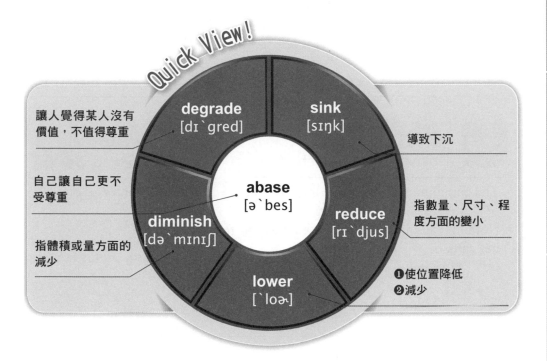

Quick View!

degrade [dɪ`gred]
讓人覺得某人沒有價值，不值得尊重
自己讓自己更不受尊重

sink [sɪŋk]
導致下沉

abase [ə`bes]

reduce [rɪ`djus]
指數量、尺寸、程度方面的變小
❶使位置降低
❷減少

diminish [də`mɪnɪʃ]
指體積或量方面的減少

lower [`loɚ]

---

135 abase
-abased-abased

vt. 使謙卑、使降低地位

- The way he talks with the man in the suit makes him abase himself.
  他跟穿西裝男子的講話方式很唯唯諾諾。
- It seems that you abase yourself before your wife.
  你在你老婆面前似乎沒有地位。

衍 abasement n. 身分低微
同 degrade 使降級、降低……的地位
反 exalt 高舉
組 self-abasement 自謙、自貶
片 abase oneself 自貶身分

degrade
-degraded-degraded

vi. 降低、降級　vt. 使降級、使丟臉

- Too much farming of this field has degraded its soil.
  這塊田地耕種太多次導致土壤受損。
- He degraded his parents for being caught red-handed when stealing women's underwear.
  他因為偷女性內衣當場被逮住而令父母蒙羞。

衍 degraded *adj.* 被降級的；
degradation *n.* 降級；
degradable *adj.* 可自然分解的；
degrading *adj.* 丟人的
同 reduce 減少、縮小、降低
反 uplift 使隆起
組 biodegrade 生物分解
片 degrade into 分解成

diminish
-diminished-diminished

vi. 變小、縮小　vt. 減少、縮減

- The pain diminished after he took aspirin.
  他服用阿斯匹靈後，疼痛減輕了。
- Nothing can diminish Jessie's enthusiasm for her career.
  什麼也不能澆熄潔西對她事業的熱忱。

衍 diminishingly *adv.* 逐漸減小地
同 decrease 減小
反 increase 增大
組 diminished responsibility 減輕的刑事責任

lower
-lowered-lowered

vi. 降低　vt. 減低、降下　adj. 較低的

- Please lower your voice in the library.
  在圖書館內請降低說話音量。
- The manager never lowers himself to ask for help.
  經理從來不放下身段尋求幫忙。

衍 lowering *adj.* 不高興的；
lowery *adj.* 陰暗的
同 drop 下降
反 heighten 增高
組 lower-class 下層社會的；
lower case 小寫字母；
Lower House 下議院
片 lower one's colors 放棄原來立場

139 reduce
-reduced-reduced

vi. 減少、降低　*vt.* 減少、降低

- He tried to reduce his expenses to make ends meet.
  他試著降低開銷以達到收支平衡。
- Hard life reduced the man to begging.
  艱苦的生活迫使這個人以乞討為生。

衍 reduced *adj.* 減少了的；
reducible *adj.* 可減少的；
reduction *n.* 減少
同 lessen 變小、變少、減輕
反 increase 增大
組 emission reduction 減排
片 reduce to 使淪於

140 sink
-sank-sunk

vi. 下沉、減弱　*vt.* 使陷入　*n.* 水槽

- The Titanic hit the iceberg and sank.
  鐵達尼號撞到冰山而沉沒。
- Her shouts echoed through the valley and sank at last.
  她的叫喊在山谷中迴盪，然後消失。

衍 sinking *n.* 下沉；
sinker *n.* 漁網上的鉛錘；
sinkage *n.* 下沉
同 fall 降落
反 float 浮
組 sinking fund 償債基金；
heat sink 散熱片
片 sink into 插入、陷入

生活常用

學校工作

情緒心智

社會萬象

小試身手UP

(　) 1. The helicopter _____ a ladder to help those villagers to get out of the floods.
(A) lowered　(B) sank　(C) reduced　(D) degraded

(　) 2. You need to upgrade your computer, or it will _____ in no time.
(A) sink　(B) reduce　(C) lower　(D) degrade

Ans

1. (A) 直升機降下梯子好讓那些村民從大水中脫困。
2. (D) 你需要升級你的電腦，否則它很快就會跟不上潮流。

取消

🎧 MP3 4-28

abolish / annul / cancel / repeal / revoke

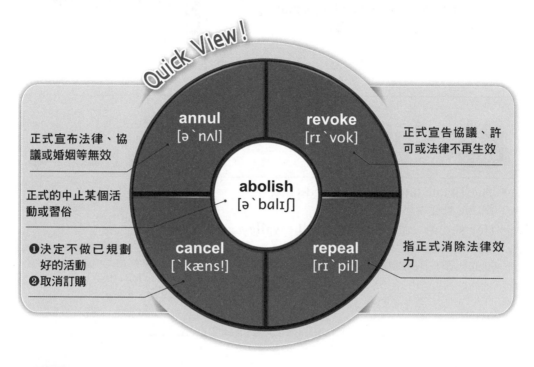

Quick View!

annul [ə`nʌl]
正式宣布法律、協議或婚姻等無效

正式的中止某個活動或習俗

❶決定不做已規劃好的活動
❷取消訂購

cancel [`kæns!]

abolish [ə`balɪʃ]

revoke [rɪ`vok]
正式宣告協議、許可或法律不再生效

指正式消除法律效力

repeal [rɪ`pil]

---

141 | abolish
-abolished-abolished

vt. 廢止、徹底破壞

- Last month parliament voted to abolish the death penalty overnight.
  議會於上個月花了一整晚議決廢除死刑。

- The governement decided to abolish a year-end bonus for most retired civil servants due to mounting public indignation.
  由於邊增的民怨，政府決定取消多數退休公務人員的年終獎金。

衍 abolishable *adj.* 可廢除的；abolishment *n.* 廢除
反 establish 建立
組 abolitionist movement 廢除奴隸制度運動

annul
-annulled-annulled

- The poor nation's debts were annulled.
  窮國的債務被免除了。
- That traffic regulation was annulled because it was out-of-fashion.
  那條交通規則因不合時宜已被廢除。

衍 annulment *n.* 廢除；
　annullable *adj.* 可被廢止的
同 disannul 使無效
近 annual *adj.* 每年的

cancel
-canceled-canceled

- She canceled the dental appointment because she couldn't get a ride there.
  因為沒有人載她，所以她取消了看牙診療。
- Because a typhoon was approaching, he was obliged to cancel his trip.
  由於颱風要來了，他不得不取消行程。

衍 cancelation *n.* 取消
同 delete 刪除
片 cancel out 消除、抵銷

repeal
-repealed-repealed

- If I have a right to vote, I must vote for the repeal of the death penalty.
  如果我有投票權，我一定支持廢除死刑。
- The new government repealed the old law.
  新政府廢除舊法律。

衍 repealer *n.* 廢止者；
　repealable *adj.* 能被取消的
同 withdraw 收回
組 repeal a law 廢除法律

生活常用

學校工作

情緒心智

社會萬象

145 revoke
-revoked-revoked

vt. 撤回、撤銷、廢除、取消

- His hunting license was revoked for hunting out of season.
  由於不在狩獵季節打獵，因此他的打獵執照被取消了。
- The officer had to revoke the order under pressure.
  軍官在壓力之下，只好撤銷了命令。

衍 revocable *adj.* 可廢止的；
revocatory *adj.* 廢除的；
revocation *n.* 廢止
同 repeal 撤銷
組 revoke one's license 吊銷執照

 聯想學習Plus

- 比賽取消用 cancel；比賽延後用 put off 或 postpone；約會改期可用 take a rain check；郵票蓋銷也用 cancel。
- 他廢除（annul）了一年一度的（annual）的生日宴會，因為他要去做肛門（anus）手術。

小試身手UP

(　) 1. The custom of child marriage in India should be _____, or there will be many other little girls suffering from that.
(A) disposed　(B) appealed　(C) abolished　(D) abated

(　) 2. The outdoor activity has to be _____ because of the bad weather.
(A) annulled　(B) repealed　(C) abolished　(D) canceled

 Ans
1. (C) 印度童婚的陋習應該要被廢除，否則將會有其他許多小女孩受害。
2. (D) 這場戶外活動因為天氣不佳必須取消。

29 Lesson 滅除

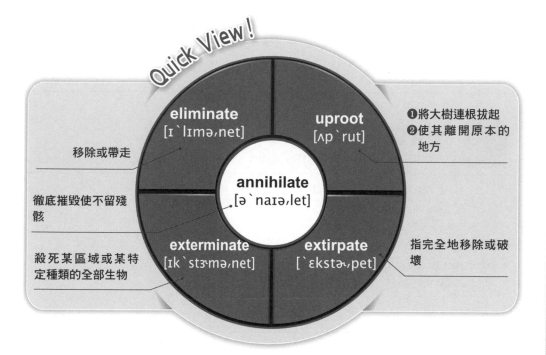
MP3 4-29

annihilate / eliminate / exterminate / extirpate / uproot

Quick View!

eliminate [ɪ`lɪmə,net]
移除或帶走

uproot [ʌp`rut]
❶ 將大樹連根拔起
❷ 使其離開原本的地方

annihilate [ə`naɪə,let]

徹底摧毀使不留殘骸

exterminate [ɪk`stɝmə,net]
殺死某區域或某特定種類的全部生物

extirpate [`ɛkstə,pet]
指完全地移除或破壞

146 annihilate
-annihilated-annihilated

vt. 殲滅、消滅、徹底擊潰、毀滅

- The fire annihilated the church.
  大火將這間教堂吞噬殆盡。
- We finally annihilated the enemy on May 18.
  我們在五月十八日終於殲滅了敵人。

衍 annihilable adj. 可消滅的；
  annihilation n. 毀滅；
  annihilator n. 消滅者
同 demolish 拆除

147 | eliminate
-eliminated-eliminated

vt. 排除、消除、消滅、淘汰

- He is trying to eliminate weeds from his garden.
  他想消滅花園裡的雜草。
- Jason was eliminated from the football game because he broke the rules.
  傑森因為違反足球比賽規則,因此被淘汰。

衍 elimination *n.* 排除;
eliminator *n.* 排除器;
eliminant *n.* 排除劑
同 remove 移開
反 add 增加
片 eliminate from 移除、淘汰

148 | exterminate
-exterminated-exterminated

vt. 根除、滅絕、消滅

- They had someone exterminate the insects in their house.
  他們派人將屋子內的昆蟲消滅。
- It's said that the eruption of volcanoes exterminated the dinosaur.
  據說是火山爆發促使恐龍滅絕。

衍 extermination *n.* 根除;
exterminator *n.* 根除者;
exterminatory *adj.* 消滅的
同 destroy 毀壞、破壞
片 exterminate from 滅絕

149 | extirpate
-extirpated-extirpated

vt. 滅絕、破除、連根拔起

- Efforts to extirpate the Ebola virus have not yet had outcomes.
  投入消滅伊波拉病毒的努力尚未獲得成果。
- Cockroaches disgust me a lot. I wish they could be extirpated some day.
  蟑螂令我厭惡。我真希望將來有一天牠們會滅絕。

衍 extirpation *n.* 根絕、滅絕

150 uproot
-uprooted-uprooted

vi. 根除、滅絕　vt. 根除

- He was forced to uproot his corn and grow vines.
  他被迫將玉米作物連根拔除，改種葡萄藤。
- The new government attempted to uproot the entire class-consciousness of the period by taking direct action.
  新政府試圖直接採取行動根除這個時期全面的階級意識。

衍 uprooting *adj.* 離鄉的、根除的
組 uproot weeds 剷除雜草
片 uproot from 從某地（故居）
　　離開

聯想學習Plus

- 她用腳（foot）把根（root）與雜草（weed）都拔除了（uproot）。
- 植物有根（root）、莖（stem）、葉（leave）、花（flower）和果實（fruit）。

小試身手UP

（　）1. The tennis player was ＿＿＿＿ from the semifinal, so he was only ranked fifth.
　　　　(A) uprooted　(B) eliminated　(C) extirpated　(D) annihilated

（　）2. The wind was so strong that the big tree was ＿＿＿＿ easily.
　　　　(A) uprooted　(B) eliminated　(C) extirpated　(D) exterminated

Ans　1. (B)　這名網球選手在準決賽遭到淘汰，所以只有排名第五。
　　　　2. (A)　風勢如此之強，大樹輕易地被連根拔起了。

擴張 (1)

🎧 MP3 4-30

amplify / broaden / dilate / enlarge / exaggerate

Quick View !

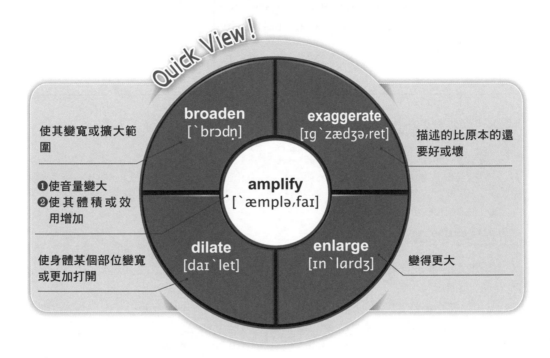

使其變寬或擴大範圍

broaden
[`brɔdn̩]

exaggerate
[ɪg`zædʒəˌret]

描述的比原本的還要好或壞

❶使音量變大
❷使其體積或效用增加

amplify
[`æmpləˌfaɪ]

使身體某個部位變寬或更加打開

dilate
[daɪ`let]

enlarge
[ɪn`lardʒ]

變得更大

151 | amplify
-amplified-amplified

vt. 放大、增強、誇大、詳述

- The megaphone amplified his voice.
  大聲公放大了他的聲音。
- Please amplify on the third point.
  請針對第三點詳細說明。

衍 amplifier *n.* 揚聲器；
amplification *n.* 擴大；
amplitude *n.* 廣大
同 increase 增強
片 amplify on 詳述

broaden
-broadened-broadened

vi. 變寬闊　*vt.* 使寬闊、使擴大

- Traveling has broadened his horizons.
  旅行擴展了他的視野。
- The local government budgeted five million dollars to broaden the road.
  當地政府編列五百萬的預算，打算拓寬這條道路。

衍 broadish *adj.* 較寬闊的；
broadloom *adj.* 寬幅的；
broadly *adv.* 寬廣地
同 widen 放寬
組 broaden horizons 擴大見識
片 broaden out 變得更寬

dilate
-dilated-dilated

vi. 擴大、膨脹、詳述　*vt.* 擴大

- She dilated her pupils with eye drops.
  她點眼藥水放大瞳孔。
- Extreme temperatures make your vessels dilate.
  溫度劇烈變化會令血管擴張。

衍 dilated *adj.* 擴張的；
dilation *n.* 擴張；
dilative *adj.* 膨脹的
同 expand 擴大
片 dilate on 詳述

enlarge
-enlarged-enlarged

vi. 擴大　*vt.* 擴大、擴展

- She enlarged her collection of dolls.
  她擴大對娃娃的收藏。
- The victim was asked to enlarge on what he had seen.
  被害者被要求詳細描述他所看到的經過。

衍 enlargement *n.* 擴大；
enlarger *n.* 放大機
同 unfold 打開
反 deflate 抽出裡面的氣
組 enlarge in size 尺寸變大；
enlargement of the EU 歐盟擴增會員
片 enlarge on 詳述

生活常用

學校工作

情緒心智

社會萬象

155 exaggerate
-exaggerated-exaggerated

vi. 誇張　vt. 誇張、誇大

- She exaggerated the size of the snake she found.
  她誇大了她看到的蛇的大小。
- She estimates over 100 copies of her novel have sold, but I think that's a bit of an exaggeration.
  她估計她的小說賣了一百多冊，但我認為有點誇大了。

衍 exaggerated *adj.* 誇張的；
exaggeration *n.* 誇張；
exaggerative *adj.* 誇張的

同 overstate 誇張

聯想學習Plus

- 與相片攝影（photography）有關的動作，包括複製（copy）、放大（enlarge）、過濾（filter）與對焦（focus）。
- 她用放大鏡（magnifying glass）來看講稿，並用大聲公（speaker）來放大（amplify）音量，好讓底下的聽眾能聽得清楚。

小試身手UP

(　) 1. The tall hat _____ his height.
　　(A) exaggerates　(B) amplifies　(C) dilates　(D) broadens
(　) 2. Cats' pupils _____ as light decreases.
　　(A) exaggerate　(B) extend　(C) dilate　(D) broaden

Ans
1. (A)　那頂高帽子誇大了他的身高。
2. (C)　貓的瞳孔會隨著光線變暗而放大。

Lesson
31

擴張 (2)

🎧 MP3 4-31

extend / inflate / magnify / swell / widen

Quick View !

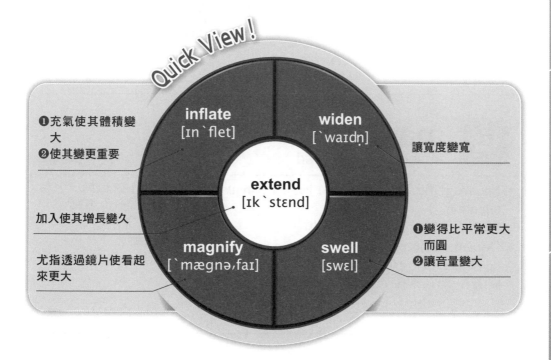

inflate [ɪn`flet]
❶充氣使其體積變大
❷使其變更重要

widen [`waɪdn̩]
讓寬度變寬

extend [ɪk`stɛnd]

加入使其增長變久

magnify [`mæɡnə,faɪ]
尤指透過鏡片使看起來更大

swell [swɛl]
❶變得比平常更大而圓
❷讓音量變大

---

156 extend
-extended-extended

> vi. 伸展　vt. 延長、延伸、擴展

- The government extended his work permit.
  政府延長他的工作許可期限。
- Applying for a Thai Tourist-Visa-Single-Entry for free has been extended to the end of August.
  免費申請泰國單次入出境觀光簽證已經延長到八月底。

衍 extendable *adj.* 可伸展的；
　extender *n.* 延長器；
　extension *n.* 分機
同 stretch 伸直
反 shrink 收縮
組 extended family 大家庭；
　extend in duration 延長期間
片 extend to 延長

157 inflate
-inflated-inflated

vi. 膨脹　*vt.* 使充氣、使膨脹

- Inflate the balloon by blowing air into the open end.
  在氣球孔吹氣，替氣球充氣。
- Some mischievous merchants will stock up to inflate prices.
  有些不良商人會藉由囤貨來抬高物價。

衍 inflated *adj.* 誇張的；
inflation *n.* 通貨膨脹；
inflatable *adj.* 膨脹的
同 expand 展開、張開
反 deflate 緊縮
組 inflate speech 誇大言詞
片 inflate with 注入……使膨脹

158 magnify
-magnified-magnified

vi. 放大　*vt.* 放大、擴大、誇張

- She magnifies her troubles to get her parents' attention.
  她誇大了問題，以引起父母的關注。
- Doraemon has one gadget which can magnify an object up to 10 times in size.
  哆啦 A 夢有一個能將物品放大十倍的道具。

衍 magnifier *n.* 擴大者；
magnificently *adv.* 壯麗地
同 exaggerate 使擴大
反 diminish 縮減
組 magnifying glass 放大鏡

159 swell
-swelled-swelled/swollen

vi. 增長、壯大　*vt.* 使膨脹

- The crowd swelled as the night went on.
  隨著夜晚來到，人潮愈來愈多。
- The population of our country will have swollen to 1.2 billion by 2024.
  本國人口到 2024 年就會增加至十二億。

衍 swollen *adj.* 脹的；
swelling *n.* 增大
同 inflate 使膨脹
反 shrink 收縮
組 swellhead 自負者；
swell can 膨罐
片 swell out 擴增；
swell up 擴大

160 | widen
-widened-widened

vi. 變寬、擴大　vt. 放寬、擴大

- They had to widen the driveway for their second car.
  因為他們買了第二部車，車道要拓寬一些才行。
- I can no longer put on this skirt I bought in my teens, so I need to widen it a bit.
  我已經穿不下這件年輕時買的裙子，所以我必須把它改寬一點。

衍 widespread *adj.* 普遍的；
　　widely *adv.* 廣泛地
組 widen horizons 擴增見識
片 widen out 加寬

 聯想學習Plus

- 他身上的腫脹（swell）已經好多（well）了。
- swollen 是 swell 的過去分詞；swallow 則是「吞下、嚥下」的意思。

小試身手UP

( ) 1. The boy _____ his arm, trying to fetch the candy jar on the cupboard.
　　(A) swelled　(B) extended　(C) widened　(D) inflated
( ) 2. A telescope _____ the stars.
　　(A) extends　(B) swells　(C) magnifies　(D) inflates

 Ans
1. (B) 男孩伸長了手臂，試圖搆著碗櫃上的糖果罐。
2. (C) 望遠鏡放大了星星。

逐出

🎧 MP3 4-32

eject / expel / exclude / oust / repel

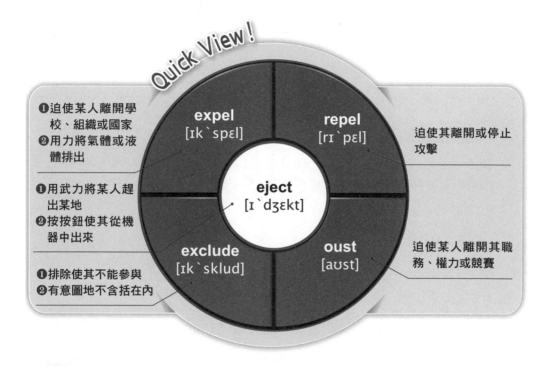

Quick View!

expel [ɪk`spɛl]
❶迫使某人離開學校、組織或國家
❷用力將氣體或液體排出

repel [rɪ`pɛl]
迫使其離開或停止攻擊

eject [ɪ`dʒɛkt]

❶用武力將某人趕出某地
❷按按鈕使其從機器中出來

oust [aʊst]
迫使某人離開其職務、權力或競賽

exclude [ɪk`sklud]
❶排除使其不能參與
❷有意圖地不含括在內

161 | eject
-ejected-ejected

vi. 彈射出來、彈出　vt. 逐出、轟出

- The CD player is broken and can't eject the disk.
  CD 播放機壞了，所以光碟片無法彈出。

- Guard, eject this rude man from the office right now.
  警衛，馬上把這個粗魯的人趕出辦公室。

衍 ejection *n.* 排斥；
ejective *adj.* 外射的；
ejectment *n.* 噴出
同 remove 移開
組 ejection capsule 彈射艙
片 eject from 彈出

162 expel
-expelled-expelled

vt. 驅逐、趕走、排出、除名

- He coughed hard to expel the dust from his lungs.
  他用力咳嗽希望將灰塵從肺咳出。
- Bodyguards expelled the rascal from the villa.
  保鑣把流氓趕出了別墅。

衍 expellant *adj.* 逐出的；
expellee *n.* 被開除者；
expeller *n.* 驅逐者
同 eliminate 排除
組 re-expel 再逐出
片 expel from 把某人驅離出

163 exclude
-excluded-excluded

vt. 拒絕接納、排除在外、不包括

- In some countries, women are excluded from taking part in politics.
  在某些國家，女性沒有參政的權利。
- The meeting excludes those to whom it may not concern from participating.
  這場會議只讓相關人士參加。

Tip exclude sb. from... 排除某人做……

衍 excluding *adj.* 除……之外；
exclusion *n.* 排除在外；
exclusive *adj.* 獨有的；
exclusionary *adj.* 排他的
同 bar 中止、禁止
反 include 包括、包含
組 exclusive right 專屬權

164 oust
-ousted-ousted

vt. 趕下台、罷免、廢黜、攆走

- The principal ousted him for starting a fight.
  因為他尋釁打架，所以校長將他開除。
- Some citizens and groups decided to oust that legislator for his arrogance and ignorance of what people needed.
  一些公民與團體決定罷免那位立委，因為他態度傲慢，又罔顧民意。

衍 ouster *n.* 罷黜
組 oust from office 撤職
片 oust from 撤職

165 repel
-repelled-repelled

vt. 擊退、驅除、抗、防、排斥

- The raincoat repels water.
  雨衣可防水。
- The navy will send a warship to repel any foreign ship that enters its territorial waters.
  海軍會派出軍艦驅逐任何闖進領海內的外國船隻。

衍 repellence *n.* 抵抗性；
repellent *adj.* 排斥的
同 rebuff 制止、抵制
反 attract 吸引
組 insect repellent 驅蟲藥
片 repel from 擊退

聯想學習Plus

- 富商不但拒絕（reject）醫生打針（inject）的要求，還把醫生給轟出（eject）家門。

小試身手UP

（　）1. He was _____ from the party because he violated its discipline. He is no longer one of its members.
  (A) diminished　(B) repelled　(C) ousted　(D) included
（　）2. The balloon _____ air and became smaller little by little.
  (A) eliminated　(B) repelled　(C) ousted　(D) expelled

Ans　1. (B)　他因為違反黨紀被黨開除，已不再是黨員了。
2. (D)　氣球洩氣後，一點一點地變小了。

窒息

asphyxiate / choke / smother / stifle / suffocate

Quick View!

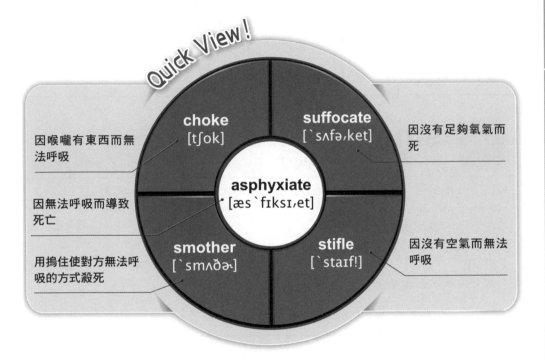

choke
[tʃok]
因喉嚨有東西而無法呼吸

因無法呼吸而導致死亡

suffocate
[`sʌfə,ket]
因沒有足夠氧氣而死

asphyxiate
[æs`fɪksɪ,et]

smother
[`smʌðɚ]
用搗住使對方無法呼吸的方式殺死

stifle
[`staɪf!]
因沒有空氣而無法呼吸

---

166 **asphyxiate**
-asphyxiated-asphyxiated

vt. 使窒息、悶死

- The boy who was locked in the car was almost asphyxiated for lack of oxygen.
  被鎖在車裡的男孩差點因為缺氧而窒息。
- Two tenants in this building were asphyxiated by the smoke.
  這棟建築的兩名房客被濃煙嗆死。

衍 asphyxia *adj.* 窒息、昏厥的；
asphyxiant *adj.* 窒息性的

組 asphyxiant toxicant 窒息性毒物

167 choke
-choked-choked

vi. 窒息、噎住　vt. 使窒息、哽住

- The kitty ate too fast to chew the food well, so it was choked by a bone.
  小貓咪吃得太快，沒有好好咀嚼，所以被一塊骨頭噎住了。
- It was said that the company would lay off 50 employees. No wonder the atmosphere in the office was quite choking.
  據說公司要資遣五十位員工。無怪乎辦公室內的氣氛相當凝重。

衍 choked adj. 惱怒的；
choking adj. 令人窒息的；
choker n. 被窒息的人
同 smother 使窒息
反 breathe 呼吸
組 choke chain 狗項圈
片 choke back 忍住；choke down 強嚥下去；choke off 阻止

168 smother
-smothered-smothered

vi. 窒息、悶死　vt. 使窒息、使悶死

- In the movie, the bad guy smothers his boss with a pillow.
  電影中，壞人用枕頭將老闆悶死。
- The police said that Patrick was smothered to death.
  警方說派翠克是窒息死的。

衍 smothery adj. 令人窒息的
同 suffocate 使窒息、把……悶死
組 smothering blanket 滅火毯
片 smother with 用……窒息

169 stifle
-stifled-stifled

vi. 窒息、受悶　vt. 使窒息、抑制

- My room was filled with the odor of her cheap perfume that stifled me.
  我房間都是她廉價香水的味道，刺鼻地令我窒息。
- I feel sleepy, so I could not help stifling a yawn.
  我很想睡，所以忍不住打哈欠。

衍 stiflingly adv. 不透氣地；
stifler n. 窒息物、絞索
組 stifle in the cradle 扼殺在搖籃裡；
stifle joint 後膝關節

170 | suffocate
-suffocated-suffocated

vi. 窒息、被悶死　vt. 使窒息

- The work environment in my office suffocated me. There was no laughter or chatting.
  辦公室的工作環境令我窒息。沒有笑聲或閒聊。
- The report said that the victim was suffocated in the water, but strangely, there was no water left at the scene.
  報告說被害者是被水溺死的，但奇怪的是，現場沒有水的跡象。

衍 suffocating *adj.* 令人窒息的；
　　suffocation *n.* 窒息狀態；
　　suffocative *adj.* 令人窒息的
同 smother 使窒息

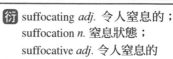

聯想學習Plus

- 他可樂（coke）喝太快，因此嗆到（choke）了。

小試身手UP

(　) 1. Loosen a bit the chain, or the dog will _____.（複選）
　　(A) choke　(B) smother　(C) suffocate　(D) asphyxiate
(　) 2. The astronaut will _____ without wearing a space suit and a helmet in outer space.
　　(A) smother　(B) choke　(C) suffocate　(D) drown
(　) 3. The school is near the factory, so the students suffer from the _____ expelled from the factory.
　　(A) choke　(B) smother　(C) suffocate　(D) asphyxiate
(　) 4. We should be encouraged to conceive new ideas, not be _____.
　　(A) choked　(B) smothered　(C) suffocated　(D) stifled

1. (A)(C) 把狗鏈子放鬆一點，否則狗狗要窒息了。
2. (C) 如果在外太空中沒有穿太空衣與頭盔，太空人會窒息死的。
3. (B) 由於學校鄰近工廠，學生們都飽受工廠排放的濃煙廢氣所苦。smother 在這裡是當名詞，作「濃煙」解釋。
4. (D) 我們應該被鼓勵發想創意，而不是被扼殺。

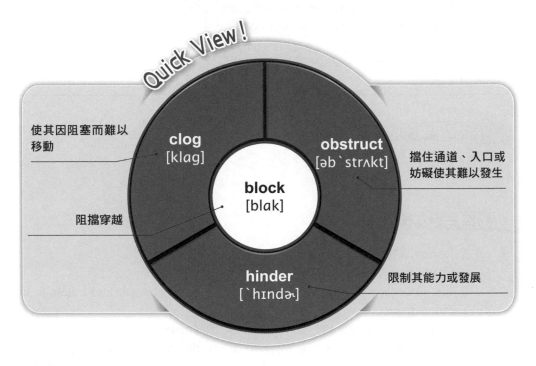

block
-blocked-blocked

vt. 阻塞、堵住、封鎖

- A car sharply cut in and blocked my way.
  一台車突然超我車，並擋住我的去路。
- The nearest convenience store is just 2 blocks away from here.
  最近的便利商店離這裡只有兩個街區。

衍 blocked *adj.* 被封鎖的；
  blocker *n.* 阻擋之物或人；
  blocking *n.* 阻礙
同 clog 堵塞
反 advance 促進
組 blocking action 阻塞作用；
  blockchain 區塊鏈
片 block up 塞住；block off 阻礙

172 clog
-clogged-clogged

vi. 阻塞、結塊 vt. 阻塞、妨礙 n. 障礙

- Don't clog up your mind with worthless information.
  不要讓你的思緒被不重要的資訊給塞住了。
- The pipe underground is easily clogged with rubbish.
  地下管線容易被垃圾塞住。

衍 clogger *n.* 木屐匠
組 clog dance 木屐舞
片 clog up 堵塞；
    clog with 用……阻礙

173 hinder
-hindered-hindered

vi. 使成為障礙 vt. 妨礙、阻礙

- Heavy rain hindered the troop's movements.
  大雨阻礙了部隊的行動。
- My gender hindered me from being promoted to a higher position.
  我的性別讓我無法晉升到更高的職位。

同 stop 止住
反 help 幫助
片 hinder from 阻礙

174 obstruct
-obstructed-obstructed

vt. 阻塞、堵塞、擋住、妨礙

- Large rocks obstruct the path.
  大石頭阻擋了小道。
- The heavy rain obstructed the driver's vision.
  大雨擋住司機的視線。

衍 obstructer *n.* 妨礙者；
    obstruction *n.* 阻塞；
    obstructive *adj.* 阻礙的；
    obstructor *n.* 阻礙者
同 block 阻塞
反 help 幫助
組 obstruct one's vision 阻擋視線

生活常用

學校工作

情緒心智

社會萬象

 **聯想學習Plus**

- 既然知道了街區（block），那就一併認識常見的巷弄街道英文是如何表示的吧：lane
（巷、弄）、street（街）、road（路）、avenue（大街）、boulevard（大道）。

小試身手UP↑

（　）1. The traffic usually ＿＿＿＿ in rush hours. So, you'd better take the MRT
rather than drive yourself.
(A) hinders　(B) clogs　(C) obstructs　(D) obstacles

（　）2. The exit was ＿＿＿＿ by a statue. No one could come in or out of the
place.
(A) clogged　(B) obstructed　(C) bothered　(D) covered

 Ans　　1. (B)　尖峰時刻交通總是大打結，所以你最好搭捷運，不要自己開車。
2. (B)　逃生出口被雕像擋住。沒有人可以從這地方出入。

學會 **7大超級記憶術**
讓大腦輕鬆為您工作！

王鼎琪《**要你好記特效術**》1分鐘速記法搶先看：

Q 你背得出台灣西部由北到南的河流名稱嗎？

A 淡水河 → 鳳山溪 → 頭前溪 → 後龍溪 →
大安溪 → 大甲溪 → 大肚溪 → 濁水溪 →
北港溪

鼎琪老師的聯想導演故事法

將相互獨立的個體，運用想像力讓它們聯結在一起。試試下面的步驟吧！

Step1：諧音轉換圖像

1 淡水河（蛋）	2 鳳山溪（鳳爪）	3 頭前溪（頭）	4 後龍溪（龍）	5 大安溪（安全帽）	6 大甲溪（盔甲）	7 大肚溪（大肚）	8 濁水溪（鐲子）	9 北港溪（香港腳）

Step2：將圖像與圖像聯結，透過聯想導演故事分享畫面

有一顆**蛋**砸到**鳳爪**後，滾到**頭前**，後面飛來一隻**龍**，帶著**安全帽**，
身穿**盔甲**，**肚子**撐的很大，正在用**鐲子**，刮起自己的**香港腳**！

透過英國牛津碩士王鼎琪老師的獨門記憶術，短時間內就能記住大量資料。
想知道更多的記憶祕訣嗎？快翻開本書，讓你的大腦革命，記憶力升級吧！

全 國 各 大 書 局 熱 力 銷 售 中　Google 鴻漸 Facebook

新絲路網路書店www.silkbook.com、華文網網路書店www.book4u.com.tw

全球最大的自資出版平台

www.book4u.com.tw/mybook

出書5大保證

創意寫作 1

寫作培訓：創作真簡單！
我們備有專業培訓課程，讓您從基礎開始學習創作，晉身斐然成章的作家之列。

2 專業諮詢

意見提供：專業好建議！
無論是寫作計畫、出版企畫等各種疑難雜症，我們都提供專業諮詢，幫您排解出書的問題。

規劃編排 3

編輯修潤：編排不苦惱！
本平台將配合您的需求，為書籍作最專業的規劃、最完善的編輯，讓您可專注創作。

4 印刷出版

成書出版：內外皆吸睛！
從交稿至出版，每個環節均精心安排、嚴格把關，讓您的書籍徹底抓住讀者目光。

通路行銷 5

品牌效益：曝光增收益！
我們擁有最具魅力的品牌、最多元的通路管道，最強大的行銷手法，讓您輕鬆坐擁收益。

打造優質書籍，為您達成夢想！

香港　吳主編　mybook@mail.book4u.com.tw
北京　王總監　jack@mail.book4u.com.tw
學參　陳社長　sharon@mail.book4u.com.tw
台北　歐總編　elsa@mail.book4u.com.tw

擎天

數學最低12級分的祕密

DVD珍藏版

擎天數學致勝祕笈首度公開，
獨門好康的互動學習光碟，
絕對物超所值！

憑DVD序號可進行線上交流

◎ 專屬的部落格交流空間，不僅有教授級名師答客問，還提供最即時的教育新知與各種讀書撇步，讓你秀才不出門，一手掌握天下事。

◎ 粉絲專頁解答國高中學子提出之各學科問題，提供最新升學、考試資訊，掌握最新出版訊息。

升大學光碟版機密題庫

◎ 考前練功房──精選考前重點摘要，詳細解析各類題型，命題精確且條理分明，為應考最佳利器。

◎ 學習診療室──包含學習紀錄和弱點分析，不但有最完整的學習歷程，還可直接連結錯誤最多的題型、章節做糾正或重新研讀，發揮最棒的學習成效。

◎ 超級題庫──高達數萬道大考中心題目與超級名師精心歸納的題型，完整掌握大考命題趨勢，運用智慧型題庫編輯系統，可依章節內容或考試題型進行模擬測驗，或是自行列印試卷練習，絕對是考試滿分的祕密武器。

◎ 考前技巧篇＆數學遊樂園──由一流名師指引，強化整體思考及組織能力，學習掌握解題要領。趣味十足的數學腦筋急轉彎及輕鬆小品，發揮數學想像力。

原價：2000元
特惠價 1380元

原價：2400元
特惠價 1656元

原價：2800元
特惠價 1932元

單點

高一篇

原價：200元
特惠價 150元

高二篇

原價：280元
特惠價 210元

學測篇

原價：300元
特惠價 225元

15141312@mail.book4u.com.tw

擎天部落格http://chintian.pixnet.net/blog

鶴立文教機構將竭誠為您服務！

獨家搶先看

畫個圓

關鍵英單
EASY K

國家圖書館出版品預行編目資料

畫個圓，關鍵英單EASY K／ 張翔、林名祐、鄭詠馨 著. -- 初版. -- 新北市：鴻漸文化出版　采舍國際有限公司發行

2019.1　面；　　公分

978-986-97039-0-1（平裝）

1.英語　2.詞彙

805.12　　　　　　　　　　　　107017528

～理想的推手～

畫個圓

關鍵英單
EASY K

編著者●張翔、林名祐、鄭詠馨　　　　總顧問●王寶玲

出版者●鴻漸文化　　　　　　　　　　出版總監●歐綾纖

發行人●Jack　　　　　　　　　　　　副總編輯●陳雅貞

美術設計●吳吉昌　　　　　　　　　　責任編輯●吳欣怡

排版●陳曉觀　　　　　　　　　　　　企劃編輯●莊瑞萌

編輯中心●新北市中和區中山路二段366巷10號10樓

電話●(02)2248-7896　　　　　　　　　傳真●(02)2248-7758

總經銷●采舍國際有限公司

發行中心●235新北市中和區中山路二段366巷10號3樓

電話●(02)8245-8786　　　　　　　　　傳真●(02)8245-8718

退貨中心●235新北市中和區中山路三段120-10號（青年廣場）B1

電話●(02)2226-7768　　　　　　　　　傳真●(02)8226-7496

郵政劃撥戶名●采舍國際有限公司

郵政劃撥帳號●50017206（劃撥請另付一成郵資）

新絲路網路書店●www.silkbook.com

華文網網路書店●www.book4u.com.tw

PChome商店街●store.pchome.com.tw/readclub

出版日期●2019年1月

本書係透過華文聯合出版平台（www.book4u.com.tw）自資出版印行，並委由
采舍國際有限公司（www.silkbook.com）總經銷。

全系列
展示中心　新北市中和區中山路二段366巷10號10樓（新絲路書店）

本書採減碳印製流程並使用優質中性紙（Acid & Alkali Free）與環保油墨印刷，
通過綠色印刷認證。